TO KILL A GOD

TO KILL A GOD

GOD

PAUL RODGERS

HEINEMANN : LONDON

William Heinemann Ltd
10 Upper Grosvenor Street, London W1X 9PA
LONDON   MELBOURNE
JOHANNESBURG   AUCKLAND

First published 1987
Copyright © Paul Rodgers 1987
ISBN 0 434 64499 4

Printed and bound in Great Britain by
Mackays of Chatham

Here's to life's rich blessings, those
marvellous shipmates who found me lonely
and quite lost upon a hostile horizon:
la belle Julie P. captaining my heart in
the turbulence and our pilot George Greenfield
inspirational through the fog.

'No man will be a sailor who has contrivance to get himself into a jail; for being in a ship is being in a jail, with the chance of being drowned. A man in jail has more room, better food, and commonly better company.'

Dr Samuel Johnson speaking of
the eighteenth-century mariner

1

*A*fter all I was very young and what other real defence is there: of course my intentions were good, of that I'm certain, but I am aware too that this alone cannot wash away the spilled blood and the stains of sin.

Sin! Where do we find such acceptable euphemisms for lies and lechery, deviation, treachery, mutiny and murder? The offences of which I am accused.

Were I born to Catholicism I could confess away my leaden soul. Yet I am almost an atheist: perhaps I heard too much of Protestant God in formative years and experienced too little of man. But I retain sufficient faith to realise I need forgiveness.

These pages might appear simply the narrative of an extraordinary adventure but among the lines is much more. For here is my life and my confession, and you the unsuspecting reader are being recruited to the role of foster priest. To simplify your task nought will be omitted, so that by the final chapter you will be properly equipped to pass judgement and decide on my conscience.

I was young. Joy, hope and sheer optimism roared like a new world river through developing veins. The turmoil of earlier years should have baffled that torrent but when those first exciting signs of manhood began, I believed that at last everything I wanted would come true, and at that time I yearned most of all to go to sea in the great war machines.

As will be gathered, the genitals had yet to make their demands. My eyes were turned towards Albion's walls of wood, as fighting sail was termed, for they staggered my imagination and overwhelmed all emotions: to feel the struggling deck beneath my feet, mountains of canvas giddily above one's head, ear-shattering cannon; this was the life I desired.

Yes, my confession begins at the beginning, before the offences began, because it is necessary for you to be utterly familiar with the scene of the crimes and to try at least to understand me.

By birth I was middle-class yet of humble roots, so two other ambitions were denied me: to study law and to be a dramatist. Coupled with sailoring, three strange bedfellows indeed! Such was my make-up. However, I was well placed for acceptance in the King's Navy, so I came to live my swashbuckling dream and dream away those performing lives.

I felt the cool ocean winds upon my smooth face and the timber groaning under adjusting sea-legs. Little chance existed to enjoy the aesthetics of my adventurous vocation as I was yet still a midshipman, at everyone's impatient call, and gale-strewn hours were spent running from one to another. However, the great guns roared soon enough and it was some time after that first powder-choking battle that I began to consider the destruction we aimed at other frightened humans.

It may encourage sympathy to say that, once the realisation was experienced, I turned from the hideous mutilation of sea engagements. But I have to admit in the cause of truth that just as my countrymen are born with brine-coursing blood vessels, so too they are born with the desire to fight.

I returned to England and sat for my commission and somehow, perhaps because the world was still revolving for me, managed to present the examiners with the right answers. I passed with my colours aflying, but the next step was unlike those of my peers. To them, and here I refer to middy shipmates, the greatest desire was to promenade the quarterdeck of the first rater, *Victory*, finally almost ready for the sea.

The great explorer's ship, *Resolution*, was returning to the South Seas for another adventure. Discoveries, natives, new lands to proclaim for good King George. This was a notion that excited me and I nervously offered my name for the expedition, little expecting Dame Fortune to treat me so exquisitely.

I was considered a good midshipman, I can say; seamanship was as natural to me as singing comes to those so gifted. I am tempted to suggest that this was the reason for my being accepted for the voyage, but I have resolved to write as the honest historian and pledge to sail this course even though it risks bringing me into discredit.

It is my belief that I was chosen for *Resolution* because of my talent as interpreter. With the tongue of Red Indians I recently learned in Nova Scotia, I could converse in five languages; for a reason I do not understand, I can easily adapt to foreign speech.

My appointment came late and I had to race uncomfortably to Plymouth in a cramped staging coach. But I took the jarring journey with excellent heart for the best news of my posting was that the century's leading explorer, Captain James Cook, was to be commander. He was my navy hero and had I known then that I would be penning this confession, I'd fear the determined veracity might err to the side of flattery. But that was then; as I have said, I was immature and the days too were very young.

The coach arrived late in Devonport (but fortunately too early for Turpin's colleagues) and, because of the hour, I was accommodated in a dark inn of low ancient beams and bugs that bit enviously at my drifting off and jovial muses in long dresses, the type of which had yet to surprise the staid Rebellious Colonies. I sat contentedly in a corner of the dining room sipping beer, humming to the rendition of Mozart by an enormous blind fiddler and admiring, if I may say so, the fair North Britons.

Looking back at my attitude to women, I do not recall the rising of concupiscence then. They were pleasing to the eye and a little mysterious. But ships were much more so and the sole cause of excitement. That women might have been available meant nothing, but I recall very clearly the disappointment in the morning when I ran down the long incline, ahead of crewmen carrying my baggage, for a first view of *Resolution*.

Here one expects to record the sleek lines, unfurling sails sun-bleached against an azure summer sky; the thrill of seeing my new ship. But she was built a collier and, sitting to her cable a little way from the shore, she looked a coal-carrying bucket and there was no gilding her any other way.

However, she was alive with activity; the crew were the size of fairground midgets from the stone steps I was instructed to report to, and they were performing all over her. I gave the earth of England a sad kiss (transferred surreptitiously by fingertip), then stepped into the pinnace with my luggage bearers; rowers with tarred pigtails and roomy whitish trousers of calico engineered the boat across dirty tidal water towards our ship. She grew and dominated my vision, then her sister ship hove into sight. No activity came from her. Her skipper was lodging at the King's expense at Fleet, an evil enforced haunt for debtors, such is the way of our money-conscious times.

I beg the reader to see the ship as I saw her that first time, to imagine himself aboard her. This is the scene of what was to follow.

The pinnace nudged the lee of the hull and I grabbed at ropes and pulled upwards, feet slipping at the cleats. Seasoned timber was before my eyes as I concentrated on that rather undignified climb; gunports were either side like the sockets of a preserved skull. The voices of the rowers came up and I was at the bulwark. A field of timber opened before me; a copse of three solid trees, an undergrowth of coiled ropes, a pasture of wood polished like leather. My shoes slithered on the caprail and an artisan hand grabbed an elbow awkwardly.

'Easy does it, sir.' A rough flat face before me spoke from an empty mouth. 'No point in 'arming yourself before we stretch the canvas.'

I jumped into the ship's waist and the luggage flew on a yard tackle like a gorged sea vulture. A stout youth came forward and his arrogance was a calling card in gothic capitals.

'The third lieutenant, is it not?'

'Aye, Master.'

'Welcome aboard His Majesty's ship, *Resolution*, sir.'

He led me aft across the deck packed with men noisily dressing the ship. A huge roll of sail waited to be hauled to a mainmast yard. A man laughed, which highlighted an odd lack of orders, for most of the good King's ships resounded to more bullying, shouts and insults than there were minutes in a jack-tar's day. Perhaps discoverers did not need impressed crews.

We climbed down a dark, finger-stained ladderway and the commotion muted as my head went below deck and became distant thumps of bare feet and industry through the heavy timbers. My eyes adjusted and we were in the gunroom; a wide, hall-like place, a gunroom in name only for no cannon these days were to be found. Boys like crabs crowding a sea-swollen sailor surrounded a long table which monopolised the centre and claws of steel emphasised their lively squabbles. I stood beside the table for a moment to study those unclear faces scavenging in the below decks dusk. My shipmates for a good three years, but none returned my friendly review; hunger defeats curiosity every time at a gunroom table.

'Over here, Mr Williamson,' the master said, and directed me to the cabin.

The gentlemen's chambers were boxes around the gunroom circumference, not unlike dressing quarters in small theatres. My tiny cubicle was glutted with narrow cot, a stand of three roughly hewn legs reluctantly supporting a matt pewter bowl, a chair vaguely reminiscent of a Queen Anne (with a droll dash of Thomas Sheraton) and an unvarnished cupboard with cantankerous hinges. It spelled 'cramped' as 'commodious' and was centuries from an Adams' architectured reception room. Thankfully God designed me a slight soul or sufficient space would not have existed within. However, these were but momentary observations; mostly I was in a state of high excitement for a private chamber in the Royal Navy is as scarce as free will in its forecastles. I turned to the master. 'Very comfortable, landlord; if you'll just have my valises . . .'

He watched the hand I extended in friendship. 'I'm Johnny, and yours?'

'Mister Bligh,' he said over a uniformed shoulder as he left the doorway.

I unpacked like a blissful bride. My Simon Harvey short-sword and telescope took their place in the rack outside the cabin and a favourite tome of Thomas Grey defied splinters on that chair of character.

I inspected the rough timber of the floor and found a copper nail which I hammered with a shoe a little way into the hull above the cot and hung there a notice purloined from the inn.

As I think back, I am surprised at how incredibly young I must have been. All memories at the beginning of the voyage are of finding a home and a place in the world. Security, I suppose. Doubts about shipmates, the captain, the voyage, enforced chastity (at least in the normal sense) found no place in that youthful brain. And of course I had no idea then of what was to happen, the way I would change and the changes I caused in others. Nor the deaths.

I recall so well climbing to the quarterdeck for the first time. The rigging stretched everywhere and so complicated, the blaze of uniforms, the smell of tar and hemp and seafaring industry. Giving that tall man my best salute. He was confronted by youth in its most enthusiastic, willing form, but was too cynical to appreciate it. He ignored me yet at the time I interpreted the snub as his being too preoccupied with our embarkation.

'Let's have the bower in, Mr Gore.' The call was no more than if we were to jolly on a river, I thought. Yet he was despatching us into space, the unknown, a void from which even in the most optimistic of terms many would not return. We were going after all where man had not been before.

The first lieutenant, a bird-like older man, passed the order, and I stood among famous men at that historic moment as our master became a demented sycophantic dog shepherding flocks of reluctant panicking sailors. Dirges came on the air with fresh sweat from the capstans and increasing families of apparelled apes hurled themselves into the living forest.

Our zealous hound barked at straining backs and the herded creatures cried, stamp and go. The cable lifted, clinking in strong clockwork echoes. Nippers were neatly nipping, and courses fell like curtains of lead, to be lightly reshaped by a geriatric breeze on the point of expiry.

'Top sails, t'gallant sails,' the old boy commanded.

'Tops'ls, t'g'nts'ls it is, sir,' first lieutenant Gore repeated in what had previously been to me an enemy accent, snapping the order louder to the indefatigable master.

'Look lively, my bullies.' Mud dripping at the manger, the crash of more falling canvas, deck crew groaning at halyards, belaying. Stamp and go! my bully boys. You up there, handsomely! The transformation was a miracle in the happening; me with the privileged of the quarterdeck surveying, with our snobbish expressions, the brutes hewing and drawing to the limit of their complaining endurance.

Now *Resolution* was no more a coal scuttle; way on, water pushing at timbers, pressure on the sails strengthening.

'We have steerage, sir,' a bass from the wheel. Mr Gore repeating it in baritone to the captain.

'Very good, quartermaster.' The captain came to the rail like a conductor. 'Now, Mr Gore, close in behind *Discovery*.'

We fell from the wind and sped astern of the smaller ship at anchor where idle men shouted abuse; staysails flapped climbing between masts; canvas hammering as percussion till the sheets were tensioned.

'Ready to go about.'

Our orderly creation lost the music; we started through the wind's eye, freed sheets flogged in pandemonium, canvas snatched angrily, bodies hauled and gangs of men ran from one gunw'le to the other and the ship found the wind, regained the cantata and advanced from the natural harbour. The tide favoured us and sounds of revelry at the anchorage fell astern as we pressed on out into the cool of the grey.

'Mind the pennants, Mr Williamson.' He had addressed me at last. Pride could not have been better rewarded.

'Aye aye, sir.' I squeezed my eyes to slits to see the ribbon below the truck revealing the wind's trickery. 'Veering west, sir.' My announcement meant depression about our world because we would not get out of the narrow sea tonight; we would tack miles offshore and back till the wind tired of this betrayal.

'Take up the watches, Mr King,' he said, which statement to the second lieutenant confirmed that the brown-green land would remain in our wake. The tide swilled into the Atlantic with a good two knots against the wind and the ship lurched in a vengeful chop; I remembered my sea-legs had yet to be unpacked. The lieutenants took over and the old boy descended the quarter ladderway; his head passed beneath us, a large hand removing the cocked hat, and he was swallowed by the darkness of the aft-cabin.

The elements were reluctant to release we hearts of oak into the unknown, for the wind persisted in the west for three days then *Resolution* found Ushant and embraced an ocean swell as if apologising for her tardy performance. Yet the wind died and the ship slowed and stopped and our sails crashed into the rigging; hemp ropes drummed spars. Oh, the cacophony of a calm! The sea shone clear blue and gradually faded in a speckling as our flotsam gathered about us until it resembled hoary Father Thames.

I was assisting with the navigation, pulling out corrected charts and filing away after the captain when the master, our Mr Bligh, entered with the defaulters' parade and three seaman stood nervously to attention before the desk.

One of the fellows had been slow, I heard from my place at the charts beside the stern window, another went to a wrong mast and I missed the misdemeanour of the third. The captain's attention was wavering too. We both had an ear towards an out-of-tune flapping from a topgallant sail.

'The fore t'gallant, Mr Williamson. Have the sail dressed immediately.'

'The main t'g'nt sail, sir,' Bligh corrected.

The captain's head clicked impatiently as it turned to Bligh. A ship's gentlemen fancy their ability to recognise sounds from different masts.

'I am addressing my lieutenant,' he said severely and added, 'It is the fore top gallant sail.'

'I'm sorry, sir,' Bligh said, and his manner showed he only wanted to help, 'but it is the main top gallant.'

'Mr Williamson. . . .'

I hurried to pass the order and the sail was tensioned.

'Sail sheeted in, sir.'

'Which, Mr Williamson?' he asked, quite certain of my answer.

'Top gallant, sir,' I said, hoping you'll take the hint, sir. But he didn't.

'Main t'g'nts'l, sir.'

He stared as if I were guilty of treason and I wondered if part of the duties of a lieutenant was to lie if necessary to save his captain's face. 'Which sail is of little concern to me; I want merely that the ship should be sailed efficiently at all times.' Bligh unwisely wore his laurels in a smile. 'Is that understood, Mr Blight?' he shouted. 'That will be all.'

'But the punishment, sir,' Bligh said, shadow moving across a clouding countenance. 'Punishment for the erring crew.'

The captain looked at the quaking offenders. 'Do you want them flogged, Mr Blight?'

The boys looked sick. The spectre of the cat was too sobering to enjoy the contempt in the old boy's voice. Anger rose like an equinoctial tide on William Bligh's immature features and as quickly ebbed and I thought, bad blood will spill before this voyage is over.

'Two extra watches for each; now leave me alone.'

2

*T*he wind relented and the ship logged distance from that nebulous hurt we call home, swaggering with canvas from deck to truck, bristling on studdingsail-booms; we had a bone in our teeth and the effect was to produce a willingness among our common people which had been absent. Soon blood would spill upon *Resolution*'s decks, but at this early part of the day we were deprived of the knowledge. As Gray says: where ignorance is bliss, 'tis folly to be wise.

A sailorman's true contentment comes not so much from the stretching of a full stomach but with the pressure of replete canvas, and the surly attitude of gunroom inhabitants who rode rusty over all duties turned to a display of *esprit de corps* the like of which I had known previously only after a successful sea battle. Japes replaced short tempers, anecdotes were swapped between youthful James King, old man Mr Gore (with blue-grey hair like a ponderous heron) and your narrator who was, of course, still finding his way. Further down the gunroom table, the midshipmen were roistering and our two sawbones were animated at the far end. To a side, almost as if he had a table to himself, sat William Bligh, still as the rest were verbose.

What a strange breed are masters! Perhaps the demands of the occupation makes them so, or are they that way in the beginning? Like facades: a poet and his melancholy expression? Did the sadness of his spirit turn him to poetry, or did the sorrow of his message shape his soul and its mirror, the countenance? The master is the muscle for the captain's will. He must work the reluctant machinery of one hundred and ten potentially seizing cogs. He threatens, beats, coaxes, inspires, pummels, whichever is required to lubricate this delicate, stubborn, human engineering. So masters are usually mature men familiar with the fallibility of our felons and are best spawned afore the masts, for who can tyrannise the working classes more fearfully than an artisan autocrat? But Bligh was a youth and, although fluent in the vulgar tongue of the jack-tar, was undisguisably middle-class. He therefore approached his task with considerable handicaps.

The barometer in the aft-cabin climbed; clouds passed over better laundered and the heavens and our highway became a deepening, exciting azure.

'Sail-ho!'

The call from the tops returned me quickly from my reveries. Because of the earth's curvature, a man high on a ship can see beyond the horizon before eyes at deck level. Our quarterdeck horizon was unhindered by sight of sail, yet incredibly from Bligh in the waist came this hail: 'Distant on the starboard beam.'

'What distance, Mr King?' the captain asked; by tradition the commander seeks answers from the crew via an officer. The sighting of this sail was no cause for alarm (or so we thought) for we could easily run if required and lose her in the night. As mariners say, a stern chase is a long chase.

'Five miles and one half,' was the reply, before James could repeat the question, and this from the master. James asked as he was bade and the reply from above confirmed the already stated estimate.

'Bound for the Gut, no doubt of it,' Bligh now added.

Such perspicacity! Not only had he observed the vessel at the limit of vision, for sail the size of a white neckerchief were rising at the horizon, but he also stated her direction and destination!

A certain strain could be heard in the old boy's voice as he asked James King if she might be enemy. Because of the international importance of our mission we were granted immunity by all sea powers; however, it was still better to show a clean transom (and a long chase) to an enemy than to humble the ship hove-to for the ignominy of a Don inspection party.

As might be guessed, the reply to the captain's enquiry came from our alert Mr Bligh. 'Not with that rig, sir,' he called, eyes remaining on the horizon, fat stained fingers providing shade in the gesture of thespians imitating sailormen.

For a moment it seemed the captain was about to run out his cannon and blast Bligh but instead large fingers pressed his temples and he retired aft to the taff-rail. The master remained at the chains and those watching this conflict of personalities relieved our breaths for it seemed the day's excitement was at an end, although it was really yet to begin. The captain was inspired with malevolence and shouted in a voice that threatened the safety of the spars, 'Hold that course steady.'

James King immediately repeated the command, in the way of the Navy, and, perhaps not yet realising the captain was dressing him down, Bligh dashed to the wheel and bellowed to the hapless helmsman, 'Hold that course steady!'

Delegation of blame, I fancied, and as in life on shore, it's the wretches who gets condemned. Peace returned. Dark petrels pecked at our quarterwaves like Dorking pullets. Then the magnificent song of the workings of timber and cordage was shattered by a discordant chorus.

'What the devil?' the captain demanded of me.

'It seems, sir, our master does not approve of goats being exercised at this hour.'

Perfectly on cue and with the sensitivity of one palsied, William Bligh shouted at a sailor promenading these diabolical butting creatures, 'I'll not have your animals defecating on my decks.'

'Get the master up here,' the captain shouted and Bligh virtually bounded onto our deck, panting joyously like an affectionate spaniel.

Captain Cook directed the master to the foot of the mizzen, the one place on the quarterdeck where a reprimanding word might be issued without everybody overhearing. 'Mr Blight, this is *my* ship, do you hear? The goats you insult are a present of the King's to the South Sea islanders. If they, the animals of worthy King George the Third, wish to stool on my decks, they shall do so. Is that understood? And I would have you look to your sails: the trim's a mess.'

Insult indeed! The matter of the goats meant little to him, his blessed sail plan was quite a different proposition. He flushed a dangerous crimson and whined, 'Sir.' But his expressed hurt was broken, for the unidentified vessel which we of the watch were neglecting re-entered our drama.

'Sail bearing this way,' came the youthful cry from the cross-trees.

The captain asked James for his opinion of her and he obligingly climbed a little way up the mizzen rigging. In the meantime, the master was snarling, 'Permission to speak, sir.'

James called from the ratlines, 'Not a high rig, sir. Two masts.'

'Speak then.'

'I beg permission to ask what is wrong with the dressing of the sails?'

'Yes, definitely two masts, sir, and coming this way with a bone in her teeth.'

'If you was referring to the fore t'g'nts'l, it may not be perfectly squared off, but that's owing to the condition of the rigging.'

'The rigging, Mr Blight? Good God, she's just out of the Navy refit. There's nothing wrong there.'

'I've got the splicing being done at the present, sir. Then we'll square off proper will we not.'

James called, 'She's trying to intercept, sir. I think she will miss us.' He was oblivious of the injured feelings down here; he had an eye to his telescope and was hanging on with the straining knuckles of the inexperienced. 'Not by much, perhaps.'

'Nobody is a better judge of sails than I, sir; I will get a greater speed than. . . .'

'Than anybody was you going to say? By God, Mr Blight . . . do you hear this, Mr Williamson? Master, your conceit knows little bounds.'

'Conceit, sir? Surely fact cannot be interpreted as. . . .'

Even James twenty feet above us could not ignore the tantrum. 'Sir, please. I think this is not a friendly visitor and she flies no colours.'

'It matters not,' muttered imprudently the angry master, 'if we are to miss her.'

Ah, passion the inciter to mutiny! Now William Bligh had gone too far. He could not speak so dismissively to a lieutenant, not before witnesses anyway, and hope to avoid trouble. But Captain Cook realised he had used too heavy a bludgeon with this canine; he diverted trouble. 'Before you return to your station, Mr Blight, please be so good as to study the vessel and venture an opinion.'

'I don't need a glass to recognise a pirate, sir; definitely privateer.'

'As to your sail plan, Mr Blight, I'll have that fore t'gallant off her.'

'But sir?'

'Now.'

James grabbed Bligh's collar and pushed him towards the ladderway. 'You'll obey orders, master.' Which returned the lad's reason, fortunately for the complexion of his back.

Bligh despatched topmen, the gallant yard grumbled and lowered and the ship slowed. We wondered what the captain had in mind, a not uncommon enquiry for officers. But even had perspicacity been our companion, we would not have believed the following orders, for now the captain had Bligh slowly strip the ship to immodest courses. The motion became clumsy and the approaching angry brig was a matter for immediate attention. A suspicion sidled upon me and sweat started down my spine. Our captain meant to fight. I had expected that a sea battle off America would be my last engagement for some years. My nerves were in a panic; layout of our magazine rushed to my mind, then became confused with my last ship's and for a second I could not even recall the size of our great guns. However, the captain looked far from worried. He said quietly, 'Call all hands, Mr King.'

A boy drummer from the marines rattled a variation which became louder and more confused when the captain called 'To quarters, clear for action' and the emotional voice of our second lieutenant repeated it, not believing, I suspect, the words of his own mouth. My face must also have been the shade of our bleached defoliated spinney. We held to our course, the brigantine came at us like a hornet and the captain leaned on the rail watching the crew at work; at the aft-cabin furniture swinging on the yard tackles and lowering to the safety of the hold; guns unlashed and prepared, the magazine opened. Mr Gore arrived and stood near the captain awaiting orders, but such reassuring utterances were not for our ears. Eventually nerves got the better of me: 'Excuse me, sir, but will there be a battle conference?'

'A what?'

'A conference when we will discuss strategy.'

'Strategy, young sir?'

'A plan of action.'

'There's no need for a conference; I have a plan.'

'With respect, sir, will you not let us know what it is so we might adapt ourselves to this method?'

He turned back to the crew busy in the waist, at Bligh staring up from the wheel, ready for direction. I waited, we all waited, but he said nothing and the visitor rapidly closed.

'What is the plan, sir?'

'Good God, man, I should have thought it obvious. To win.'

The intercepting vessel was upon us. She was lighter and smaller and her lines showed her to be fast off the wind; her coppered bottom offered a better speed all round in lesser airs. She swung to starboard a hundred yards off and dark, bearded faces stared across and seemed hardly of a friendly disposition. But, encouragingly, the turn was premature, the stance of a fighter who favours luck to skill.

'Harden on the wind. Slowly.'

A good ship-of-the-line tries constantly to guess the intentions of an adversary like dawn duellists on a common, and suffice it to suggest our quarterdeck was filled with such puzzlement. However, we were also obliged to guess our own plan. The wind came from the quarter towards the beam, and the brig altered course trying to line up for a broadside; her canvas crashed unsheeted and the speed fell quickly. Muzzles pushed prematurely through gunports resembling guard dogs at a parapet. She fired and a roar smoked frighteningly from seven cannon. She was too far off, but the scream of ball was unnerving. The first salvo is the worst; I clench my teeth wondering if it will take me; after that, there is too much noise to think again until the engagement is over and one or other sails away.

'Four-pounders,' I shouted. Which were the same size as the deadly guns we carried.

'Yes, Mr Williamson.'

We held our turn to larboard and kept sheeting in, forcing the brig to lose way. Her sails were crashing at the yards and I knew she had not guessed our tactic; but I had; to swing through the wind and crush her with our superior weight like a greyhound taking the backbone of a running hare.

'Mr Blight, as soon as we are through the wind, get everything on her again. At the double.'

The wheel swung to starboard; the wind went aft and we gybed to starboard tack. Now our frenzied youth dashed between the masts shouting, encouraging, cursing. Sails unfurled and crewmen sweated at the halyards and we were gaining speed, now doubling it. The braces, lad, lively now! Stamp and go. To the capstan. Sweat, you bully boys.

'Tell Mr Blight to station the best gun-layers there.'

'Mr Shuttleworth, liven up those topmen; they're asleep.'

The brig was alongside and we could see each of the sailors and the officers on her quarterdeck; an evil, ugly bunch. Our ensign broke out astern and the Union Jack was hoisted from the bowsprit. These were massive flags which gave us heart and confirmed to the enemy their folly of tackling the King's Navy.

'Run up, train and fire!'

The privateer raced to adjust her course like an injured fighting cock. I fancied she planned to make a run for it, but too late. Our great guns shook; a boom which seemed so much greater being our opening shots. We scored. The line of ball splintered holes along the waterline and the trucks rumbled their sensational song as the guns were run out again.

The enemy listed to starboard and the sea rushed in as if she were an inverted watering can. We closed and the sides of *Resolution* towered over the brig. Grapples scraped and caught at our sails and I knew the horde out of sight below us were now throwing themselves at the boarding ropes.

'Repel visitors, Mr Blight,' the captain called calmly over musket fire from the marines and the crew's cheers of 'Rule Britannia!' The invaders appeared at the bulwarks, came over and almost fell upon a she-goat and kid unwisely hiding by the hammock nets. Our visitors were large-nosed devils in turbans and privateer scarves. I pulled my sword from its scabbard; it held near the tip, pinged and was free and quivered in my hand like a living creature. The marines adopted a formation and several of the boarders fell back when they fired. Shots came down from men in the tops, and on the deck the redcoats struggled through a parody of reloading, for they were very inexperienced.

'Lieutenant Phillips, have your men fix bayonets. Quickly now.'

'Aye aye, sir.'

Boarders came across the deck in a small line. They slashed like farmers with scythes, and somewhat less skilfully, I thought. The larboard gun crews, redundant because we were starboard to, rushed at them with their regulation Tower cutlasses. Steel crashed against steel and, standing beside the captain, I waited, as is proper for an officer.

'Bayonets on then, lads. No, sharp side forward.'

Goats were bleating like spectators at a prize fight, and privateers grunted and swung much more after the fashion of London footpads than fighting Navy men. A dark head came up at the weather quarter near the tafferel and aimed an old-fashioned Snaphaunce musket at the captain's lively striped jacket. I shouted, but our hero's eyes were only for the battle proper. James and I rushed the would-be assassin, who aimed at me. I saw the trigger pulled and I bit hard, expecting to be hit. It misfired, flashed in the pan, and James came out of the shadow of the mizzen. His hangar-sword smashed down and carved into the boy's shoulder. Blood showered and the fighter fell back.

'Mr Blight, check the level of your starboard guns.' The brig's rigging scraped against the side of the ship.

'Elevation's good, sir.'

'Starboard guns, fire!'

The guns drowned Bligh's echo. Men torn by the cannon screamed and bloodied ball erupted through the far side. The pirates were doomed, but they had not submitted. Two broke through cutlass-swinging sailors and dashed for the helmsman. Goats stampeded heads down, clearing their way. I took the quarter-rail in one hand and swung over, falling to the waist; it seemed a twenty-foot drop. I climbed onto unsteady feet beside the wheel, facing a greasy, bearded fellow with black eyes which protruded like a scavenger fish; a taxpayer of the hated Dey of Algiers without a doubt. He seemed taller and more muscular than from above. He alerted Allah and pulled his sword back with two hands, like an axeman. I ducked the swing, *passata sotto*, bolstered my confidence in its shrill, frustated wind with the thought 'an amateur', and lunged in the vast gap in his defence; his throat waited unshielded and I took it. He dropped his sword and tried to scream, but no noise would come from that hole again. He grabbed his torn neck and ran for the brig. His heathen god beckoned at the bulwark and he plunged into the sea, a pool of soaking red his legacy on our deck and a fine hot line diagonally across my shirt.

William Bligh met the second man, who was a better swordsman than my opponent. Older and taller and he cut down, but Bligh sidestepped in a classic *in quartata*; the helmsman pulled back his hands and the blade hit the wheel, slicing into a spoke. The young helmsman stared incredulously at the embedded sword which the villain tried to pull free. The point of Bligh's heavy cutlass was touching the deck; he swung up with both hands in a stroke that was not quite textbook but most effective. It caught the attacker's groin. He screamed and pulled away and Bligh thrust for the fellow's stomach, another messy but telling tactic. The brute staggered back with Bligh holding the blade embedded up to the sheet-iron guard. Then at the bulwark he ripped the sword out with a sickening popping sound and the Arab abandoned our ship and life. *Resolution* moved for the *coup de grâce*; the falling man cushioned the crunching hulls for a second and then we jammed hard and pushed. The brig's underwater shape held her to the water. Timbers snapped in deafening booms, but the hull would not let go and the force of our crushing could only tip her to starboard.

Sailors shrieked as their world turned on to beam-ends. Breaking timbers sprayed splinters like a shower storm of African assagais.

Men leaping from the privateer were struck by toppling masts and the sea came up the bulwark, upper deck, the larboard hull and swallowed her. From the roaring, crushing and thunder of the brig being stove in, we were suddenly encompassed in the tumult of bubbles bursting from the sunclear chop in three distinct, massive, dying sighs. And then silence.

Bligh stood at the damaged wheel; cutlass, hand and arm covered in coagulating blood, his feet bright in spilled intestines. He was dirty from gunpowder and sweat shone over his smooth brow and abrupt puppet nose. He looked up at the captain with an expression of challenge, an egotist who proved his boasts. He set full sail during a gybe, carried through the captain's complicated fighting manoeuvre, oversaw lethal salvos from both gun crews, soolled our dumpy greyhound onto the fatal breaking of the enemy, and carved up a privateer twice his size. I was pleased for him as if he had been the brother I never had, yet through the pounding in my chest an unaccountable spasm of jealousy consumed me.

The captain was as silent as his jacket was outspoken. He stared down at the youth; there was no approval acknowledged for James standing nearby cleaning his blade twixt thumb and fingers; not so much as a nod for my nerve. All about us braces damaged in the collision hung like yuletide decorations and the stench of gunpowder and fear choked at my nostrils. Gun crews cheered; a rare smile broached that broad face and I felt as left out as an ordinary seaman at an admiral's dinner party.

'Resume course.'

'Permission to clear up the ship, sir?'

'Permission granted, Mr Bligh.' He had the name right this time. 'When done, stand the crew down.'

'Very good, sir.'

'And, master, I don't want to see a goat again when we go into action. Nothing bogs on my deck while we're defending the King's honour.' Bligh turned to carry through the instruction. 'And double grog rations all round. Well done, men.'

3

*T*he bow cut through rodents seeking a pelagic pied piper and burst silver on black upon a slick of scuttled cockroaches. We pushed aside puncheons, an overturned launch which breathed out and belatedly followed its mistress down, an acre of timber and a tan sail resembling a volcano erupting from the subterrane. We heaved to, tacked and beat back and were as thorough as a hungry beachcomber. Boat hooks, spare spars, a wrap of signal flags, oars lashed in pairs like Siamese-twin snakes, barrels of beef, yet for the hours we searched that ship's grave, not one body was found. It heightened our superstitions; a ravenous monster waited for human flesh wherever we voyaged.

'Hands to the braces,' the captain snapped angrily.

'Where's the mizzen petty officer? I'm wearing ship, watch the driver. Hard a-larboard.'

The chastened young gentleman of the aft-mast felt the wind go dead astern and swung the driver boom over in the lull and our ship curved downwind and came up on the breeze's other side. The yards were squared; we passed through low sunbeams and the glow silhouetted three mutilated slaves on Arabian crucifixes.

'Sir, by Jesus, won't you look!'

This call came from the marine lieutenant who was urinating into the sea; green spheres were bursting through the surface as if an undersea juggler entertained the dead. Crewmen rushed to the bulwark and shouted in horror, for this search for survivors had a nervous, disturbing air.

'It's a beast of the undersea shiting,' a sailor called and the levity this might produce in the recounting later was not present then. The balls kept popping through the surface, in three and fours until fifty or more appeared spinning and shining in the sea's movement.

'Back to your stations,' Bligh roared, bouncing in that strange gait of his to the bulwark. Fingers plucked at hair and he rested his left hand on the caprail, cunnythumbed. 'Do you hear me, you there.'

Shocked sailors drew slowly back from the bewildering scene but a young shaver threw up in fear. 'Idiots, the lot of you,' Bligh shouted, threatening. 'Even the demons of your fables don't stool apples, they do not.'

The sick Bob Cull did not recover as quickly as the others. Perhaps he wondered what freed fruit a whole hour after the dive. 'What's the matter with you lad?' Bligh pushed at the boy. 'Have you a padlock on your arse that you should shite through your teeth?'

The entertainer had finished on that submerged stage and this old sailor's saying brought the required mirth from the people. But the lad looked little better.

The sun wearied of the search and rested on the horizon, and the captain ordered our course resumed. Mr Gore took over as officer of the watch; I followed the old boy to the aft-cabin and marked our present chart with a light cross.

'And what legend to inscribe here, young sir? We cannot write North African privateer; that's too general. Spanish or French? Too political. The damned vessel didn't show any distinguishing marks from first to last. Did you see any?' he asked me without expecting a reply.

Later we officers decided she must have been an English vessel taken by the Continental Navy and snatched off them by brigands of the Dey of Algiers. God help the Americans if this were so.

Mr Gore, arms crossed like a resting marsh bird, said, 'A suggestion could be that we fired first on a vessel we did not know the nationality of, a serious matter if the admiralty. . . .'

'They won't know, sir,' Bligh said. 'There are no survivors.'

'But sailors will talk,' Mr Gore replied paternally.

'This rabble can't remember yesterday,' William Bligh snapped in hardly the right tone to address a senior officer; it was the second time today he had been out of line with lieutenants. A declaration, perhaps, that he was a one-man seadog. 'By tomorrow they'll have forgotten today.'

Mr Gore ignored the discourtesy. 'There are diarists, you know. Anderson the sawbones is keeping one, there's his assistant Samwell. . . .'

'Very well,' Captain Cook said, 'you will omit it, gentlemen, in your journals, we will not mention it in the ship's journal, and Mr Gore, I would like you to take the matter up with the surgeon and his mate.'

A vessel spiralled to unfathomable depths, taking at least eighty souls, and all that remained were a pair of fighting swords souvenired by our sailors, and stains on the deck. Such is shipboard power! Captain Cook says forget our naval engagement and we cross it from our history because a commander's kindest enemies are those engaged at sea. A ruthless, unrelenting adversary lurked on shore in the jealousy of ambitious officers who used any ruse to climb the Promotion List. Doubts about our sea battle meant questions; wisely the old boy excised it cleanly from our past.

A chest of dead men fed the bottom fish and we pursued our flight south. Among we the survivors, the drama of life continued. And so we move to the next scene, a somewhat recurring one; it may be of value to the reader to recall it occasionally and include it wherever in the saga he will for colour; it will be appreciated by the narrator who can avoid ennui risked in repetition.

The scene, obliging reader, is the aft-cabin. A wide room about the size of an Adams living room of our middle classes. We have a full width window running along one side which in nautical parlance is our stern lights. On the opposite side is a doorway in a partition wall, for when we go into battle it is removed and sent down to the hold, along with the furniture. The sides of this room are timbered, such is the fabric of our moving world, but are unadorned by contemporary Canalettos, revered Reynolds or bric-a-brac, such is the York fabric of our commander. Against the long window with its excellent prospect (landscape by Capability Brown, perhaps, in one's fashionable fancy) is a bench table of similar length on which are spread the charts. This is our tarpaulin word for maps of our watery highways. The remaining furniture is a berth to our left as we look towards the sternlights (so we say it is to starboard) and a writing desk of simple lines in smoked wood. It is at this table that our captain spends much time writing his journal, not the official diary which records starkly the vessel's business, but the books which the captain is compiling of our adventure. Heavy beams over our heads are of the type to be found in a country inn. This, then, is a roomy, airy, wholesome cabin.

Captain Cook is writing at the table; his blue naval jacket hangs from the back of the chair which looks too frail for his handsome proportions. Like the others here, it is by Chippendale, walnut and well polished with a dull red tapestry seat; the back is a cage of twined ribs. I am working at the charts and entering left is a new self-applauding member of our cast. Dear reader, may I present Omai, the like of which there will never be again. Omai (pronounced quite suitable Oh my!), the folly of good King George the Third, resting on the berth in his finery, plays a guitar. You may wonder of other sounds in this room. The captain's quill scratches nervously at thick paper, and from the timber all round comes the dull roar of the ship in progress.

Omai wears a silk shirt with ruffles at the cuffs which blur blue with the strumming of sad chords. Yes, at the berth is dazzling costumery, brown eyes, a brown pretty face with more than a suspicion of cosmetics. A perfume carries an erotic message for our South Sea sunflower.

The summer dusk of England is far behind us and the captain is hurrying to finish his day's diary while the twilight lasts. Thus my prologue is complete. The old boy is the first to speak. 'The Canaries tomorrow if the wind holds.'

I am immodestly written into the scene, but with a non-speaking part. I look up to see if the captain is addressing me, but Omai replies, 'Nearer and nearer home. . . .' As the reader will guess, Omai is – or was till a little more than a year previously – an aborigine of Tahiti.

'You'll feel different once you see your land again.'

'I like England. I like being with King George and having friends round me.'

'You'd tire of it in time.'

'What do savages know about civilities and coffee-shops, eating-houses and dressing?'

'Can you forget your past so easily?'

Omai returned to the melancholy song. 'It's about a warrior who goes over the sea and his lover becomes a tern, a sea bird, and flies after him.'

'Omai, I'm trying to write up my journal. Mr Williamson is busy with the charts; I don't know we have the time for an entertainment.' In fact I was doing no more than doodling the outline of a sinking ship; life in the services is so often a case of alluding to industry.

'This is is the saddest part. The warrior has some distance still to go, but his food is all gone and he starves. The little bird flies near. Can't you hear the wings beating above the canoe?' He was a good musician and the guitar gave more than a passable imitation of a love-lost tern. The captain put down his quill methodically, reached over his shoulders and pulled tighter the band holding his hair; it was dark brown going grey and tamed constantly in a queue.

'Now the bird flies down to the lover, who spears the beautiful creature and drinks the blood. The warrior is saved.'

'That's horrible, Omai. What do you think, Mr Williamson?' The captain said this with some amused largesse, then picked up the feather and dipped it into the ink.

Omai put the guitar down carefully, almost lovingly. 'It's beautiful because they are together as one. Death unites, don't you see?'

'Not civilised thinking,' the old boy returned, and added because he was not one for spelling, 'Two ts in astronomical?'

'How would I know?' Omai said. 'Me a common savage.'

'Perhaps it was Mr Williamson I addressed.'

But Mr Williamson knew it was not, for I might say there was a presence of friendship which had not been shared so far with others of the ship. Perhaps because Omai was a passenger the captain felt he could relax his discipline; yet Omai of the orange breeches, yellow stockings and foppish ways was scarcely more than a boy.

The captain turned to me suddenly: 'I know, make the legend, "altered away from Madeira".' He stood beside me and a wide finger, which resembled the craft of a woodcarver, pointed to an X in pencil where our brief sea battle had raged. His attention was entirely diverted to me and I thought he was going to put his scarred hand on my shoulder. Behind him, Omai decided to Exit Centre, stamping out of the cabin.

'I will say we decided on Canaria for reasons of economy. That's the way to southern hearts.' Curtain.

Now came a landfall. Island mountains peered over orographic cloud like an aged look-out; the wind changed direction, gusting off the land, but with William Bligh in the waist, and me and the captain at the quarter-rail, we held full sail and rushed for the anchorage. The bower and stream anchors roared out and heat came off desert land. Here the grandeur of rocky scenery had to be sufficient pleasure for the crew and there was no clamour to get ashore. This was a Catholic stronghold; entertainment was seldom to be found where the Pope held reign. Our stores and wine were replenished and I ticked off the lists with the purse. None too soon, we weighed.

The trades buffeted off Mount Teide and topmen struggled with the high gallant sails and the ship carved the water white. A gale blew from astern and we surged on long breakers. I shared the watch with the captain and William Bligh patrolled the waist like a hungry wolf, keeping his prey at the braces and in the rigging. Off-duty sailors slung hammocks in the foredeck and enjoyed the afternoon sun. Flying fish darted from the cutwater with dorado green flashes in pursuit; these were aesthetics that delighted my senses and had me scribbling hard and poetically in my journal off-watch. I also penned the observation that despite the empathy between captain and master sealed at the engagement, their personality swords were not yet scabbered.

'T'g'nts'ls seemed pressed, sir,' Bligh called up to the quarterdeck. I ordered them set earlier and resented the criticism especially to the captain. Bligh and I had not had words, as they say, but he held nothing sacred that could be used to elevate himself before the captain. I was realist enough, even in my youth then, to doubt that I could match the sheer force of his manner: he is, I thought, insensitive and sensitivity has been my unhappy cross.

'Fine business,' the old boy said absently, and I breathed a little freer.

'Permission to take in t'g'nts'ls, sir?' the master persisted, and I wished he'd go away. It was for we officers to decide when reefing was required and technically, at least, this discourse verged on impudence.

'This is the Navy, Mr Bligh. We're not afeared of a press of canvas.'

Our eyes took in the weather, the three masts of our coppice, the path ahead, yet wherever he looked was Bligh's questioning brow, like a carping conscience. 'What is it, master?' the captain asked irritably finally, being the possessor of a short fuse at the best of times.

'I'm concerned for the rigging, sir.'

I cannot deny William Bligh made sense; a stay snapping under pressure passed heavy loads which multiplied through the rigging and could easily fell a mast. I was piqued with his criticism, but I envied that ability to address authority so easily. In retrospect, Bligh knew he was right and nothing else mattered.

'Keep the weather on the quarter, Mr Bligh, and the strain is minimal.' And the captain was correct too until the moment a daydreaming helmsman let the wind creep towards the beam; then a ship could easily round up out of control and be liable to roll. It was a continual risk and one reason why an officer was always on the quarterdeck alternating an eye from weather to rig. The ship surged again and a hum of reverberation came from the hull. 'What do you estimate to the speed, Mr Williamson?' he asked quietly.

'About nine knots, sir,' I guessed.

'Damn, we'll have to reduce canvas,' he said, almost confidentially. 'But we'll not do it immediately; time's not quite right.' He sounded like a stubborn landowner holding back a flooding York river. He was waiting so the master could not claim credit for the sail change.

William Bligh spent his frustration on the men at the helm and the captain took up the weather-rail where the all-pervading presence might be weakest.

A boom like a nine-pounder came from the foremast and the captain raced past me and down the steps to the waist. A forestay had parted and instant action was necessary to stop the foremast from splitting. Yet even as the old boy's mouth opened to issue the appropriate commands, Bligh ordered topmen to take in the t'gallant sail. The yard squeaked querulously as it lowered and the fastest sail change we were to see was effected. Bligh had cunningly kept crew ready, anticipating just such a break. The captain could not recognise Bligh's strategy without admitting the ship was pressed, so the young master would expect congratulations for the exemplary reaction. Now he waddled awkwardly along the deck to shout the next proper order, tail wagging, but the captain was seemingly not a stranger to such conduct. He beat Bligh to the command, and couched it in such a manner that implied blame for his tardiness. 'I'll have that main t'gallants'l off her *smartly*, if you please.'

Hapless youth, outsmarted and upbraided! The voice expecting to gloat turned rapidly instead to anger and abused the watch. Then the change of duty chimed and the gusts were losing some of their edge as James King came to the quarterdeck. Perhaps he had witnessed the earlier happenings, for he immediately ordered the resetting of topgallant sails and his commands to the master's mate were of sufficient volume for even a deaf rapscallion to comprehend.

On a ship a constant war reigns between the gentlemen and the people, and the former won this round with much jubilation. But fact can be so much more protracted than fiction, for although we did not know it then, our little round was far from complete and a cast of two antagonists quickly became three when a clash of ambitions was added to the struggle.

The captain was extraordinarily gifted in the matter of navigation which, even in this century, was a science in infancy. Like him, I had been singled out for my draughtsmanship and general navigation in the Americas in the later campaigns, but my talent was less a natural blessing than a much-studied and hard-won ability. I expected to become the captain's protégé for my standard even in those tender years was far ahead of fellow officers. Yet this cherished ambition was to fall to an adversary I had not even considered. The reader will guess his identity.

Navigation is an art and the mannerisms of our Mr Bligh completely hid such a bent. Certain procedures are established by Navy tradition in chartwork. Markings are made only lightly in lead for the excellent reason that they can be erased and the chart fresh for the next time. And navigators care for their charts; they do not bend nor ill-treat them; they are vital to safe passage-making and one *never* damages them. One never, but this one, William Bligh, did. The master, permitted access to the charts through his position, was all over the navigation table, and if the reader fears exaggeration born of exasperation, allow me amplification. Bligh actually lay his bulky weight upon the charts. If the item to be studied were at the top of the sheet, no decorous bringing of the object towards him would suffice. The fat youth reclined across the table, with the disturbing habit of plucking at dark hair with a free hand. The most placid officer could hardly help but be offended at the sight on the table of a white barrel, legs the breadth of bones, mountainous twin humps thrust towards one, and in the distance the fingers imitating a barber's scissors. A fav'rite has no friend!

So now the scene is set for Act II of the winning by one at the expense of two persons.

'Are we to pass to landward of the Verdes?' This came from Bligh nearly prone on the chart. The captain was involved with his journal and doubtlessly amnesiac of severed stays.

'That is so.'

'The course I measure off, sir, differs from the one at the wheel.'

'Magnetic variation,' the old boy said, his attention remaining at that large book.

'Taking currents into account, should we not spot Bonavista before nightfall?'

'You can see my estimate; later tonight, and I doubt we will see it.' He looked at Bligh absently for an answer the youth could not give. 'Two ls in celestial?'

Bligh bounced off the chart table, rattling the hanging fiddles, and rushed out of the cabin door. The old boy raised his eyebrows and I returned a quizzical expression. The master came back and made small incoherent sounds at the table. Then he said slowly, 'We're logging six knots, occasionally seven. I'd say eight. Taking the probable distance travelled since the noon-sight. . . .' The pencil scratched heavily until the lead snapped like an artificial firework, and dividers I took pleasure in polishing for the captain measured the distance again. He cunnythumbed a fist tightly; fingers plucked at his hair nervously.

The captain was looking round from his chair, studying the habit; I expected him to show aggravation, for the old boy was no Job. But, extraordinarily, he was half-smiling at the fellow's total involvement. 'The afternoon sight is being taken by Mr Gore and Mr King,' he said encouragingly. 'We'll have a good fix then.'

Now Bligh spun from the charts and leaned on the captain's table like an angry politician, a hand either side of the journal. The pen was poised, dipping into the inkwell; the paleness of the boy's face was close to those mature features, yet seemed totally unaware of the liberty. 'Sir, we will run onto that island.'

'Have you no confidence in our navigation? Those markings there are mine, you know?'

'Sir, we are heading into the archipelago not passed.'

'My dear young sir,' the old boy said, holding onto his patience with difficulty for he had no practice of it, 'we will pass Bonavista with the greatest of ease, late tonight.' He pronounced it Bony Visitor.

'No, sir,' the youth said, closer than a fairground hypnotist. 'We'll run onto it. Soon.' His face was drawn with conviction, the shocked second look of a man who sees a ghost ship before recognising it.

'Get a grip of yourself, laddie.'

'The visibility, sir. It's all haze.' Bligh's words tripped over themselves in their rush. 'Scarcely three miles, maybe less. . . .'

'Damn your impertinence,' and the captain's barometer slumped. 'You doubt my navigation; you establish yourself as the only eyes on the ship. But where is your brain? If visibility is three miles, we can see ahead for half an hour at this speed.'

'On the surges our speed is much greater, and there's the time it takes to come on the wind. . . .' He was shaking like a bedraggled dog. 'We are really pressed with canvas and the rigging. . . .'

Ah, youth's lamentable diplomacy! Bligh abandoned all hope of victory by resurrecting the altercation of the stressed sail plan. Then to introduce the rigging!

'By God,' the captain exploded. 'I'll have you disrated, I'll . . . I'll . . . get out. Get out, for God's sake.'

Bligh stormed past the startled sentinel and the door slammed with no apology. The captain pressed his temples for a minute and returned to the journal. He muttered in growls like a wounded bear while he wrote; but the tension was too much and he stood again; he reached for the door latch, and we heard Bligh's shout: 'All hands, all hands! Furl t'g'nts'ls.'

Damn his eyes, I thought. The fool doesn't know when to stop and now the captain would have to order him publicly flogged. The captain held the latch and his knuckles and long scar were white. Then he checked himself. 'Leave it to King to sort him out.'

He might have been an off-stage prompt, for James's voice reached us. But he read from a different script and panic adjusted the tone of his voice.

'Hard a-larboard.' Feet pounded on the deck. 'Hands to the braces! Keep her coming quartermaster. Lively with your men, Mr Bligh. Full and bye, bring those yards back!'

The ship shook as she began rounding up. Timbers creaked and strained ominously and animals added to confusion by calling vociferously as the motion of running grace became a series of sickening shudders. Canvas crashed aloft. James King shouted at the mainmast midshipman.

The captain opened the door slowly and the noise of rushing feet became a stampede. Belayed lines came from the bitts; stamp and go! came in frightened chants as yards were hauled to the stays, and the jib crashed high on its boom as the weather came further forward. Beside the captain, I stared to lee across the ship, at breakers and the burnt shape of an island under a diabolical mask of low cloud. The big man gaped incredulously at surf smashing upon rocks.

We were pointing away from destruction but the sails were not yet drawing and the ship slipped rapidly downwind. The captain's teeth chattered as a tabby mesmerised by distant birds. Get those sheets in, look lively there. Watch the leeway, young sir! Ease the helm; come back with the increased speed. Leadsman over into the chainwale; a rope round him quick. . . .

He watched our destruction on the rocks crabbing closer. Muscular fingers pressed at his forehead and the sooty fluid ran back along the quill, darkening the feather. The surf roared in our ears and hurt and there was hardly time to summon God to save us, and then as if by a miracle we cleared the shore.

This evening I was invited to dine at the captain's table. Some personalities earn such an honour with lively conversation and repartee, but I was invited I believe because of my habit of being silent in his company. Certainly the day's affairs had paralysed my tongue; I saw once again in my short life how close and quickly death can claw at a sailing ship. I was in a state of shock which heightened my awe of the great man, and I saw his pig-headedness as confidence, his failures as accomplishments, his self-destructive ambition as diligence. We sipped a pleasant claret and I said nothing, yet I feasted youthful senses.

Collett brought the evening meal. Omai opened the door and suggested they drank some Madeira; a blur of colours and the captain saying he was not of the mood, the door closing rapidly. I remember well that during this brief intercourse neither acknowledged me; I wondered if I was really there. Then the captain began to speak to me, though in the cause of honesty I should say I *think* this was conversation; quiet words came over the candles and the flames flickered in his breath. I kept my eyes humbly towards beef and biscuit slowly disappearing from the plate; how could a young lieutenant look at a mighty captain? Or more precisely, a boy still fresh spots and puberty gaze upon a proven giant? But an image was beyond the candlelight through upper lashes.

'Wind dead-aft. The ship waddles like a gross woman; soon it'll be the doldrums and squalls and then the sou'-easter trades and *Resolution* straining upwind for a whole ruddy two weeks.' Then a little later: 'Three times I've taken this route through these mighty seas. The stars are the same each time, do you know that? The sun's orbit's almost identical, the moon at the same phase as last time, as if they've been like this all the time, waiting for me. A strange sameness about it all, laddie; a strange stability of regular habit, but far from making you feel stable. Do you understand?' And so my dinner companion spoke. This shepherd who would guide us, this man with the legal power to sentence us to death.

He put down his knife and fork pedantically and waited for the plate, polished empty with biscuit, to be removed. He was silent and I wanted to say, oh, sir, forget the past, talk of the voyage ahead, but I knew he would never divulge our Confidential Instructions even though on a ship there are no secrets and we knew. A fool's mission, they said, to prove a passage skirted the north of America, but find it and ships could avoid Cape Horn punishment with a shorter journey between the Pacific and Atlantic. (Discover it and fatten the purses of the plutocrats, they should have said.)

Was there such a passage? Naturally it existed because insatiable commerce needed it; would God not have provided for the wealthy? And the talk at the water butt was that these geographical romantics tricked the captain, the greatest discoverer of our times, into leading the expedition and baited a rusty blunt hook with a reward of £20,000.

Collett was at the door. 'Can I bring coffee, sir? Some port perhaps?'

'How is the mood about the ship?'

'Very happy, sir, and doubtlessly happier when we have negotiated these islands.'

'The people nervous, I expect, when we got a bit close to the rocks?'

'Not as nervous as if you wasn't in control, sir.'

'You're a ruddy romantic, Collett.'

The old boy pushed a clearing on the table for his journal. He sipped from the port and plunged the quill into an ink bottle. His writing was indecipherable to many but I knew it well and could read it upside down. I alternated between the wine and coffee. He sanded a page with the rattle of a snare-drum, turned it, and swamped the pen methodically again.

'We saw the island of Bonavista bearing south, distant a little more than a league,' he wrote, doubtlessly mispronouncing the place in his mind. 'At this time we thought ourselves much further off, but this proved a mistake. After hauling to the eastward to clear the sunken rocks that lie about a league from the SE point of the island, we found ourselves at that time close upon them and did but just weather the breakers. Our situation for a few minutes was very alarming. I did not choose to sound as that might have heightened the danger without a possibility of lessening it.'

He dipped the pen again; large masculine hands held so gently, efficiently, that frail quill of white. He stared straight at me and I looked down. 'There,' he mumbled. 'I've admitted a mistake.'

4

I circumnavigated heartily the quarterdeck for my matutinals and adjourned to the gunroom's molar-challenging breakfast on what augured as a quiet tropic day. Such was not to be.

The captain's servant Collett summoned lieutenants to the aft-cabin and the master was left as surrogate officer of the watch, flexed and fearful with self-importance, on our deck.

The old boy sat impatiently at the freshly polished table while before him stood an odd pair: a skeleton of a shaver shaking under the mask of One Terrified and tragic Dr Bill Anderson, our chief surgeon, with the philosophical, kind expression of One Dedicated. The captain suffered a frown set deep upon his brow. Dr Bill seemed all brittle jutting bones fastened temporarily by a scarcity of stringy muscles and the insufficient lot bagged in a sweaty skin like plucked chicken flesh. The lad was gaunt through hard work; his hair was an untrimmed shrub of brilliant red and his short nose was sunburned. Our sawbones was wasted by ill health which would rob his life before the voyage was over. The uniform and his grey hair were neat. He kept a steady left hand stationed in the boy's mouth while we officers filed into the cabin. We pushed the door to and the captain leaped up, removing himself from the backlighting of the windows; now we could see that the fathomless frown cravassed most of his countenance; the indications were that our commander was in a fury. It seemed prudent to dispense with morning salutations; when a storm centred on those handsome features his officers became the most cautious of mariners, reefing quickly to reduced sails of humility.

'Come in, come in, gentlemen, and shut that ruddy door properly,

Mr Williamson; I have here a matter surely sent to try me to the limit.'

The captain resumed his chair. The door catch clicked chastened and we lieutenants stood awkwardly at ease before the table. It did not do to presume an invitation to be seated. Our commander shot impatiently again from Chippendale comfort, and the dark jacket which hung from its back was unable to resist gravity and toppled it noisily to the deck. The chair lay like a drunken sailor unattended because we knew not whether to lift it into place as gentlemen or ignore it and remain attentive as worthy officers to his address; our professional role dominated.

'By God, gentlemen, I'll not have it, do you hear? I will not tolerate it.'

These lines, *non sequiturs* to this obedient audience, were delivered in a noisome style as our leader came round the table, as incensed as an insomniac chrysalis. One hand rested on the polished edge; with each signal of his temper, the fist clenched and showed four mountains of white; when it relaxed, a glacial fissure flowed between thumb and forefinger. This action was most pronounced, like a prize-fighter rhythmically flaunting muscles, and I could only return my eyes to a level of acceptable obedience by the utmost concentration.

'Dr Anderson,' he demanded, and the surgeon's hand increased its pressure in the shock of the retort, 'you will explain the matter to these gentlemen for I cannot bring myself to mention it.' The lips became a tight white line and the audience, faces creased in understandable obsequiousness, waited.

'Of course, captain,' the doctor began in his quiet educated way, fingers remaining in that seemingly pertinent aperture. 'During the routine sick parade this. . . .'

'Health parade!' the captain thundered. 'We do not have sick parades on *Resolution* – this is not a ship of distemper but one of vigour. . . .'

'. . . during the routine health parade, I inspected the symptoms of this lad. If you gentlemen would be so good as to observe.' The doctor prised wider the lad's entrance and we gazed in among blackened tombstones and a stench not dissimilar to a new grave's buffeted our way in stagnant gusts. 'You will notice the looseness of the teeth and this swelling.' The masonry, unstable and crumbling, was wiggled and the inflamed gums provoked with ragged nails. 'Notice please the colour of the tongue, and. . . .' – at last the jaw was allowed to close which it did slowly as the boy moaned – '. . . the colour of the eyes.' Dr Bill pushed back the lids and frightened eyes reviewed us through brown speckles as if we were apparitions. 'My prognosis therefore has to be. . . .'

'Scurvy, gentlemen, scurvy,' the captain shouted.

'Mild early symptoms of scurvy,' Dr Bill corrected.

The captain returned to the aft of the table, picked up the chair, and made an irritated attempt to dust the braided sleeves while his jacket clung to the walnut. 'Lieutenants, I have been proposed for the Copley gold medal for my successes in nautical medicine and now this sailing person has the audacity to develop the very disease I dread the most.'

Hear-hear politely and correctly followed the modesty of the news of the award, but the victim of the illness shook bony and terrified knees. The surgeon's hand had left the boy, but the eyes remained as unhindered as before. Woodcarver's fingers rapped on the table top and then his temper got the upper hand and the Chippendale toppled back as he returned to the front of the table. Four mountains snatched a hold of the shaver's grubby vest. 'Let me tell you something, laddie.' The captain's head was close to the beams; he placed his white breeched backside delicately upon the table edge so that he was reduced to the height of the reluctant patient. 'We all eat a diet of anti-scorbutants which I personally have prescribed. I paid out of my own purse to bring on board this vessel a goodness of food for my crew so that the wretched disease would never be known. And now you have the confounded cheek to develop it.'

'To begin the manifestations, in the very early stages.'

'What should I do with you?' The captain shook the boy until a sound of unstitching applauded this performance. The large hand fell back to the table edge. 'What gentlemen, should I do with him? I'll tell you what I am going to do,' and the hand reached out for the vest, then the old boy's commercial awareness intervened; a tear could mean compensation from the Sunday slops wardrobe. He carried the hand on upwards and rubbed the nape beneath his queue. 'You're going over the side.'

Life's playwright sympathised at this point with our lad's one appearance and silent at that, and awarded him a small speaking line. The jaw was not yet in working order so unfortunately it was lost in mispronunciation. However it emerged not completely unlike, 'Walk the plank, sir?'

The captain too missed the piratical jargon and continued, 'Or you will eat the sour krout. Is that understood?' This came at such a volume that, understood or not, it must surely have been heard.

These outbursts were known about the ship as *haka*s, a Polynesian word for war dance, and the old boy occasionally leaped into the air with anger, much as the Maoris of Zealand were said to. The captain's account of his measures to keep the men healthy was not exaggerated but, in the way of the lower classes, our men were unadventurous of diet. They consumed salt beef and biscuit at sea and were interested in nought else. This, the captain theorised, lacked certain ingredients which shortage manifested itself as scurvy and could claim a ship's compliment for Davy Jones.

The lad and the surgeon were dismissed. The captain informed us in a vocabulary that left little doubt about his feelings and we were despatched to see to his wishes.

The cause was located and fell to the name of the great vice of our age. Some will assume insobriety is meant and it is true that this social ill has much to account for, and how can it be otherwise when our leaders drink at their dinner parties till they have to be carried to their carriages by servants, when the poor will pay their last penny for diluted sulphuric acid the plutocrats call gin? But the crippling vice I refer to is gambling, which has tens of thousands of pounds changing hands in a London night. Newspapers tell of the rich wagering wives and wealth and the poor frequenting pits to bet on fighting cocks or tormented bears. But I digress and precede the anecdote.

The officers ascertained that our one-legged cook served the sour krout at the appointed time. The goodness reached the plates of the men, but why did it not make their gullets?

We studied the people at their feeding which was not the most attractive of duties. We saw heaped platters taken to the forecastle from where came the clamour of noisy eating. Crew served at the watch stations were seen to demolish the majority of the food before they discovered Mr Gore's not too subtle espionage.

The more unpleasant task fell to me as junior officer. I was made to descend to the maindeck, work through the animal pens to reach a spy hole near the crew quarters. It may seem a simple matter to enter the forecastle itself and there witness the proceedings, but tradition kept lieutenants from that unwholesome part of the ship. And, I might say, fear. Darkness and inaccessibility left it the ideal ambushing post and the grisly venue for many unsolved murders. Accordingly, I preferred to take my chances with the hoofed animals in the below-decks twilight.

It worked and I reported back triumphantly. 'Cockroaches, gentlemen. That's the enemy.'

As was to be expected, the name of this familiar shipboard creature was repeated around the gunroom table with the repetitive bark of a Puckle's Defence Gun. 'I watched from my vantage point,' I explained, 'and the men set about their favourite diet until the anti-scorbutant was reached. This sour krout was put in mounds at their feet.'

'At their feet?' James asked.

I would not be hurried; it had been an unpleasant crawl twixt the pens. 'The men were next seen taking wagers following which several containers were opened at a given mark. Cockroaches. Great longlegged athletic brutes the size of which you could scarcely comprehend. It seems these creatures have a peculiar penchant for sour krout. The said bugs stood on the deck looking about for the starter's gun and then the savoury smell tempted their nostrils, or whatever olfactory organs God gave roaches.'

'Cock-noses.'

'What?'

'They talk about cock-eyed,' Bligh said. 'Why not cock-noses?'

'God knows only too well why he didn't give cocks noses,' said David Samwell who, being a doctor, knew about such things.

'Then the creatures made a bee-line, if you'll excuse the term, for the food. A roach race, don't you see? The athletes win the scurvy food and the winner takes the purse.'

'And then?' Bligh asked.

'And then the creatures are stabled back in their containers and the leftovers thrown overboard.'

'The men are not eating it at all?' Mr Gore asked.

'Who would after cockroaches had been at it?'

'They don't seem to mind weevils.'

'Patriotism, I suppose,' I said. 'Our weevils come from England. Cockroaches were never indigenous of our fair land.'

'What did Dr Johnson say, "last refuge of a scoundrel"?' James said.

'You can see he's right.'

'Gentlemen, this is a serious matter,' Mr Gore said. 'I hope we can dissuade the men from this vice so that health will return to the ship.'

Bligh and James King shared the animal pens with me. Marines were secreted about the forecastle ladderway. We watched the meal progressing, much as it had previously. Bets were placed, the hideous beetles released, with owners crouched blowing the odour of sour krout towards the starting line. One hungry sprinter started and the race began. Bligh blasted a whistle, my ears went dead and heavy-booted marines dashed down the ladder and set about the athletes with the grace of morris dancers. So ended the vice of the people in three short crunching minutes.

It would be pleasing to begin the next scene with the revelation that the men took internally the wholesome goodness, but this is a drama of reality and your narrator will only tread the path of veracity. More men reported to the morning parades with early symptoms and the captain's well-being was imperilled by his rages. Sailors were charged and punishment varied from having food forced down their throats to being flogged at the gratings. Many relented but the mass would not be intimidated. Grog was rationed and stopped altogether, but even that extreme measure (in a sailorman's view) was not sufficient encouragement.

We passed into the doldrums and tempers flared in the absence of wind (and rum), and we officers prepared for a concert to celebrate crossing the line. I was elected producer and Midshipman Shuttleworth stage manager; with rehearsals and our duties, the task of dealing with reluctant diners was left to the old boy. Omai's guitar practised in the aft-cabin, Michael Portsmouth played his penny whistle in the forecastle and Matt Pall threw several artist's tantrums, insisting that he could not tune his violin. Then the sunsights put us on the equator and we said the concert would go well on the night. The ship rushed into the trades and water was hauled in buckets up to the deck and liberally aimed at all except officers, who wisely preferred the security of the quarterdeck.

A feast was announced. Tables came onto the waist and the cook on one of his few unhygienic excursions from the galley was ready. The captain appeared at the quarter-rail, a speaking trumpet signalling brass sunflashes from his hand. 'Enjoy your food, men; your good spirits are admired, but not your black determination. You'll have all the beef and biscuit you wish for the celebration, but I'm damned if there'll be any anti-scorbutants for you.' The captain looked unbeaten in his smart number one uniform and the men cheered this news. 'Except for the officers, of course,' he added, and climbed down the ladder to join our table. A hush greeted this as the seamen tried to gauge the captain's meaning, then the food was served and the hubbub returned. At our table the captain's best wine, esoterically signifying a victory, was being poured; our plates swam sickly with sour krout.

'Gentlemen, I've never harmed my officers,' he said with a smile that was more Garrick than correct. 'I've never believed in threatening an officer. But a warning, I think, is another matter.' His voice was low; he chose the words with care, and consequently each was muffled in thick dialect from York. 'The ruddy officer who does not shine as an actor and pronounce the sumptiousness of the anti-scorbutants will be disrated as of this evening.' He pursued last his most positive persuasion for salts of the sea. 'With remuneration cut accordingly.'

The standard of thespianism was as high at our table as will be witnessed at Drury Theatre. Much smacking of lips and congratulations hailed the chef as throats capitulated to the equally unsavoury scurvy food; in revenge a suicidal assault was launched upon the old boy's expensive wine until the last imperilled palate was licked clean. The tumult of the ratings' open-mouth table manners gradually lessened as ever-watchful sailors, wolfing dinner with their eyes to breakfast, yielded to our exhibition of performing if not exactly culinary art.

And then as the twilight began, a butt of grog was spliced and the concert began. Our stage manager was on first with a lonely melody of love that would turn the heart of the most cynical matelot. Omai followed with a moving Polynesian love song (but devoid this time of the topic of death), and tears were to be seen about the audience. Michael Portsmouth performed his musical whistle repertoire, but the audience would not let him repeat that single piece of Mozart's; he was a marine, after all, and they rated his act not up to the instrument's value. He left the stage, which was the fore part of the quarterdeck, to the accompaniment of a barrage of biscuit. Matt Pall got his violin tuned happily and David Samwell entered with a dramatic gesture of his arms and quoted a lengthy extract from Hamlet, if not quite the complete drama. The sailors were at least a little lost but they did not interrupt. Medics were not to be upset for obvious reasons and the applause was tremendous when he left the stage. Mr Gore, quietly throwing up his share of anti-scorbutants to the lee, joined James King in the limelight.

James (with pillow strapped to his stomach, in white bagwig and pompous modulation): Questioning is not the mode of conversation among gentlemen.

Mr Gore (holding large quill made from pasteboard and adopting Yorkshire patois): What did you say, laddie?

James (as Doctor Johnson again): I think the full tide of human existence is at Charing Cross.

Mr Gore (pulling on attorney Boswell-type judicial wig): They certainly dress very neaply.

James: When two Englishmen meet, their first talk is of the weather.

Mr Gore (changing rapidly into Omai's gaudiest jacket): Whether it's your place or mine, dearie.

(*Exaggerated applause from Omai.*)

James: He is no wise man who will quit a certainty for an uncertainty.

Mr Gore (as himself): But can you be sure? (Same uncomprehending visage as worn in rehearsals.) And so the sketch progressed and was generously received by the compliments. Several more of these famous aphorisms followed with Mr Gore's answers (often unintentionally much more amusing for, no matter what dialect was requested, they were all in broad New England), but the jest that drew the most mirth was James saying: 'Patriotism is the last refuge of a scoundrel.'

To which I wrote the answer thus. *Mr Gore (holding pasteboard cudgel)*: 'Then scoundrel you be, sir, for me and my gentlemen friends are from the Impressment Service.'

These thugs were the most detested part of the King's Navy, yet sailors already recruited enjoyed any jest or anecdote about this horrible practice. Perhaps like stepping into marriage (one of Dr Johnson's favourite topics), fate is more tolerable if you are not alone.

Our brother-officers exited left. And in an instant the mood of the ship changed, for we now experienced a happening that fills one with nausea and pity, shock, a demand for action and an overwhelming human desire to look the other way. Our complement was enveloped in a vapour of stench which just from its physical properties would force the most hardened nose to churn the toughest stomach. It was a fetidness that clogged nostrils and throat, a thickness of odour that clung to the surface of any bared flesh, and on this night only the gentlemen were decently attired; the people wore trousers, so mild and pleasing was the temperature.

This volume of fouled air passed to weather and the only sounds from a formerly excited deck were of the working rigging; shrouds rubbing against timber, idle braces and jigging blocks, the backbone of the vessel moving alive to the passage. Men's hands remained at their mugs of grog, some kept fists over the top as if the smell would pollute the contents. But nobody held their noses; it was as if we deserved to suffer a little for humanity's guilt, and we officers looked down at our polished cutlery and glasses, at the reflection of tallow wicks shining through the clear wine. No cry came from the watch because the slaver passed too far off to be seen in the bright night. But we had all smelt these vile carriers before; their nightmare-packed cargoes of black souls locked below with accumulating filth and multiplying corpses rotting unattended.

The fog of stinking suffering eased and was suddenly gone, and men drank again and were laughing. The captain raised his glass and, looking at each of us, said quietly, 'Liberty, gentlemen.' And we drank to that, amen, and the subject was not again mentioned.

'Come, Mr Williamson, your turn I believe,' the captain said, and I climbed the ladder and pushed away the recent misery.

'Gentlemen, people of the ship,' I began, putting down that queer disturbance of the stomach when we expose ourselves to ridicule, 'our lieutenants wished to quote their heroes, so I will follow suit. You know theirs to be Samuel Johnson, but who, men of *Resolution*, is mine?'

I had my stage props ready. I stuffed clothing under my jacket to increase my spare figure and between cocked hat and head put a papier-mâché tube to exaggerate an illusion of height. I pulled on two gigantic gloves. I began a parody of an accent of the north with several sayings familiar about the ship liberally interspersed with a certain favourite adjective. The crew loved it; the captain himself maintained a typically dour expression. Then Omai entered left in a replica of my outfit. We gave an energetic account of a war dance and jumped into the air at its conclusion, as I believe the Maoris do and know for a certainty that the object of my act does.

Now Captain Cook was laughing and when I returned to the table, he leaned across to top up my wine glass. More grog was spliced; further wine came from the aft-cabin.

The stars were enormous, as they are at sea on the equator. On a straining table a display of hornpiping progressed and increasing numbers clapped to the rhythm of Matthew Pall's fiddling. I laughed at William Bligh's jokes, David Samwell's intellectual observations, at Gore's dry anecdotes; we were a happy band.

> Wine whets the Wit, improves its Native force,
> And gives a pleasant Flavour to Discourse;
> By making all our Spirits Debonair,
> Throws off the Lees, the Sediment of Care.

Shipmates! And it seemed as if our world, remote from any land by scores of leagues, was more a heaven.

After the first watch-change in the morning, a deputation of dissipated ratings petitioned the old boy for a return to their rations of the delicious anti-scorbutants and a thoughtful, caring captain decided in the spirit of health and vigour to permit it.

I moved to a new watch and my life changed as completely as our antics were stilled when the slave trading ship passed in the night. Our home, *Resolution*, was a hundred and ten feet in length and a little more than thirty-five feet in beam, and we officers worked and lived together within twenty or thirty feet for the whole time we were at sea. Yet night watches, as occurred then, meant days without seeing the captain. On a war footing this was different and, as happened on my previous ship, we would have attended various parades and conferences. But ours was a voyage of discovery, one of the most ambitious and talked-about of the age of man. It would have meant no more to our modern world even had we harnessed the energy of the higher skies to travel to outer space. In the minds of the ordinary person, we were going where no man had been before and if we survived it would be through the ingeniousness of the Great Man, our famous navigator, and the skills of our shipbuilders of oak; of the science of our extraordinary times. The journey was being documented by our shipboard artists who would bring the new world before the people of old England. They would see what we saw.

And I was cast out of the captain's life by this change in duty, and to me then I admit it meant work and no excitement. I would hear that distinctive voice coming through the bulkheads and it soothed me like an unborn baby listening uncomprehendingly to its host's tones. I wondered if it was the absence of a father of substance that had me waking eagerly to hear the famous temper reducing some hapless soul. Days passed and I slept long and heavily as my body tried to adjust. Those nights dragged terribly, bringing the strangest longing up from the depths. And a recurring aberration came from my imagination that he might appear on my watch unexpectedly. 'Why, Johnny, what a surprise. Where have you been? I've so missed you and your help. Exemplary conduct here I notice, laddie. Do drop in afterwards.'

I was at the point of despair and then Collett knocked at my door and my time in the darkness for the present had been served. I was back in the aft-cabin and I saw it again with the eagerness and attention of a first time. My face was full with a smile which did not want to relax, and I looked at that lovely sternlights and the wake magically an unruffled path to the edge of our smooth blue dish. The scratch of the quill on the journal from the captain; his loose shirt sleeves; blue jacket hiding Chippendale, the table a small carpet. How do you spell . . .? Big hands almost hiding the feather, the top drafting hieroglyphs which inscribed my name in the air. Dipping into the ink, the stem changing colour and dripping as it came out, the shaped tip tapped on the bottle's lip. Then slowly the hand, its deep ragged scar in the sun-coloured valley, going back to the pages of the diary.

I was mesmerised by that movement and it manifested a kind of unknown madness in a mind bewildered by events and my alteration towards manhood. If that hand stretched towards my quill – and the notion raged deafeningly through my emotions like a Severn bore.

'Traversed.'

'Sorry, sir,' I stammered as if caught pushing at the swelling that increasingly demanded attention.

'Two rs?'

It broke the spell, thank God, and I returned to my workings on the chart; I had to prove my navigation was worthy of his attention. 'Sir, I make it that our average daily passage during the south-east trades was three-quarters and six knots.'

'Is that so, young sir?'

He answered, but I doubted he was listening. His back was towards me; wide of shoulder tapering to waist. I looked quickly away. 'Sir, I propose to enquire at Good Hope for other average southerly runs of ships through these headwinds.'

'Very good, laddie.'

'Sir, when you take into account the shape of the ship beneath the water, sir, I claim that on some days we have exceeded the velocity that we achieved when the wind was aft of the beam. Does this not mean that our underwater shape is better for upwind than running? Are we not learning more of the best designs for shipping from this exploration?'

'Laddie, why are you so talkative?' (Because I am so pleased to be back.) 'Can you not see I am writing up my journal? You may not care whether my daily records are finished, but I fear publishers are not so kindly.'

Music for the heart! Some words and a touch of humour. 'And my theory, sir? Would not a publisher be interested in the hypothesis of improved hull design?'

'Would it make any money? Answer me that and you have your reply.' He put down the quill and turned to me; blue warm eyes over that strong symmetrical nose. Would my features ever exhibit such manliness, I wondered? I leaned forward to appear the enthusiastic protégé. I breathed in fresh sweat. 'Our ship made such progress more likely because of the consistency of the wind, such are these trades.' I sampled every word. 'She is not every man's ship, as you know. But she is strong and sea-kindly, and I tell you this, young sir, she is simple to sail. If we lost every man-jack of our crew, you and I could sail her, just the two of us.'

He pushed past me at the chart table. He took something from his pocket and his hand touched me. I do not pretend it was the brush of attention, only an accidental knock. But for my satisfaction, it was a contact and I was the most blessed person on that ship, although I could not explain the dementia's presence. His right hand was on the chart now, tracing a line from the equator to the middle latitudes, along the path that showed our progress through flying fish and diving tropic-birds. His closeness assailed me; he explained the reason for our faster passage, but the noise of my heart was so huge and echoing that I could no longer hear individual words, only the sound of a rich, deep warmth which had reverberated through the bulkheads to my excitement in the cot. In the cause of honesty I admit to being extended, and should I receive another knock, a brush no matter how unintentioned, I would steep this cloth and . . .

Bligh stood with his hand on the open door. 'May I present my findings on the magnetic variation for this position, sir?'

'Did you take a true bearing at the meridian so you are certain?'

'Yes, sir. It is as accurate as it could be at sea.'

'Very good, William. I think we are done, Mr Williamson. Be so good as to close the door after you.'

5

*O*ur trade wind home was a platter polished blue with enforced naval efficiency; above our heads were bleached acres of tended canvas and holystoned clouds of fair weather brushing the mainmast. Our horizon did not change and you could imagine we were rushing nowhere on the same round dish in a paradise where the sun constantly shone and our nimble topmen slowed and fattened on inactivity. Summer sails, as much as the spars would carry, were spread like the span of a Southern Ocean albatross; stuns'ls stretched towards the ornate tails of tropic-birds plummeting recklessly for fish. Idle sailors amused dolphins at the cutwater with hook and harpoon and ensnared sharks which came on board snapping terrible sawteeth at the people.

With howls of savages, the sailors leaped onto the denizens and more jaws hung at the bowsprit, reminding visitors at the seats o' comfort the fate for going overboard.

Ours was a maritime heaven, the only major ocean where cyclones were forbidden by God himself. Yet the way of men in these latitudes was far from angelic; friction boiled over into pugilism before the serving of grog, after which tempers eased. This drink that turned enemies into soporific shipmates was not served to officers and gentlemen; our tipple came occasionally at the evening meal. The captain was served sherry in the late mornings, but we who shared the aft-cabin in our duties were not offered nor did we expect it. Consequently, the nerves of the gentlemen and warrant officer gained little respite. We all of us bickered; fortunately the tension did not last and soon we were friends again, except for Master Bligh and me. We argued over the navigation, over naval values, sail plans, the speeds a ship like *Victory* might attain, the state of the Continental Navy, about leadership. I believed then, as I do to this moment, that men need to be led. But William Bligh would not permit this. The admiralty provided people to work the instrument of war; each were parts of the engine; each had to do his expected share. Just as a parting stay produced loads that increased until a spar split, so a sailor who lazed upset the strength of the mighty, wind-driven machines.

'If a cog in a clock will not turn, you oil it, rather than kick it,' I argued.

'It has become the accepted practice to shake a watch the moment its ticking stops,' the master countered.

'Don't you two start again.' This remark, with an actor's inflection, came from Omai who was leaving the aft-cabin; a correcting rainbow at the door then doused in the shadow. Bligh and I were working at the charts; me attending the documents in the prescribed manner and the master dominating the table as if it were a bed shared with younger brothers.

Behind us the captain remained self-satisfied at his desk. Collett dispensed the dosage of sherry; working man's hands filling the dainty glass twice; the old boy masking it in enormous bear-paws, the firm long nose sniffing the liquor, the large head nodding in approval. Sipping like a stopped-up sink. Then he became his publishers' dutiful servant again; the scratch of the quill, mumblings, sand resonating on a sheet, the pedantic puffs to dismiss the blotting grains and a journal page turned positively and noisily like a drummer announcing an unexpected victory.

'Name me any modern leader who pushed his men rather than led them.'

'Cromwell was a driver.' But I would not allow politicians to be measured alongside militarists. ('Politics are now nothing more than a means of rising in the world,' said Dr Johnson, and I accepted it.) The dialogue of this charge and countercharge is not necessary for the reader who hopefully remembers we were both in our adolescent years, neither of us shaving yet, but cast into the world of men. Our arguments were little different than will be heard whenever youths debate; we were taken at the way matters tumbled, sometimes seeming unquestionably brilliant, from the brain to an unreliable voice-box which was occasionally surprisingly deep and to the private ear not a little sensual. This seemed as important as the point of the dispute.

'For God's sake, you two.' This exclamation came from the chronicler whose recall was disturbed by our repartee.

I felt so assured of my argument that I could see no reason why the captain himself should not declare. The pen was placed carefully beside the journal and arms came back like hairy bleached tentacles to tighten his queue. When you can lead, lead, he pronounced irritably, like a family dog tired of children pulling its ears. When you can't, push; push for all you're ruddy worth.

Our saucer began to change. Heavier clouds obeyed the summons of the barometer in its long fall. Mollymawks disputed our refuse with cape pigeons and flocks of blue-grey prions tried to smooth our wake. The sun was lower in the heavens. We left England in July heat and sailed the lazy regions. But now almost suddenly meridian shadows grew on the deck.

My expertise with a sextant improved significantly and my noon-sights were faster and more precise than those of the other lieutenants. Then the master began to join us daily and I was made to look a fumbling novice.

The captain could hardly ignore this wonder boy and more responsibilities fell his way, including access to the sacred Kendall Watch Machine, an ambition I had not even dared entertain. Now it seemed that wherever I turned in my duties with the old boy, there was Bligh. We never spoke of a competition; how could there be between a junior lieutenant and a warrant officer, for our tasks were quite different? Yet I knew I was being robbed of something unrealised and very special, and I was catching almost red-handed this insensitive half-boy, half-man; I watched him evict me with the ordained triumph of a springtime cuckoo and I ached for approbation from the captain. If only there were some route to his heart other than navigation, for in that I could not hope to match my adversary!

I tried to recover lost ground with trickery, though the devil has never favoured me. As we neared the latitude of Good Hope, I argued with Bligh in such a way that I knew he would recommend the wrong route. Ahead lay a belt of calms, as deadly at sea as treacherous quick-sands in a swamp, and I couched my argument so that pride would force him to recommend that direction. I was not wrong and before many days we were in the depth of still air. Torture for sailors. In the presence of the captain, I pressed for an entirely different route, one I knew would return us to the wind. Pride kept Bligh's eyes locked ahead.

'Fine business,' the captain said. 'Mr Williamson, bring us onto the wind and have the sails dressed.' He turned to Bligh. 'Come with me, young man, and I will show you your error; we'll leave the third lieutenant to the quarterdeck.' They vanished down the ladder, the tall distinguished man and the fawning firkin on pegs of legs. Taking sole charge during a day watch would have filled me with pride at any other moment, but now I was sick with grief. I had won, but there was no victory.

We were in the forties within two days, riding the mighty westerly swell about which I had listened to endless tales. Albatrosses hung above the counter suspended by scud racing from Tierra del Fuego, angry cloud which fumed all that unhindered distance from Cape Horn. Now he must congratulate me; here were the winds I promised in my recommended route; but no words of encouragement came, not even in the privacy of the aft-cabin.

'All hands to reef tops'ls. All hands!'

I commanded and a hundred men came up into the gale and flung themselves to the braces or halyards or climbed ratlines into the cloud. I shouted, they obeyed. In two hours I would order them back and we could set those sails again. But I could beg for attention from the one person on board who mattered and a becalming of disinterest would take away my words.

James King and I were sharing the watch. The weather was cold; my head was pulled tortoise-like into my jacket and my subconscious wondered at the oddity of the group of sailors at the foot of the mainmast, then my eyes ran over the rigging, the foremast, to the reefed main tops'l. My heart jumped.

'Mr King,' I summoned. 'Look, for God's sake.'

I pointed to the top main topgallant mast. At the truck a hundred and twenty feet above us sat a boy and the chants starting from idle sailors made me think, *By self and violent hands Took off her life.*

'Shite,' James King said and ran for the mainmast ratlines.

'No,' I said, 'we'll only frighten him if we come up the same mast.'

The foremast weather ratlines were not difficult to climb, but my shoes slipped on the cold smoothness. I climbed out over the futtock shrouds, eyes closed, for leaning away from the ship to reach the platform is unnerving. I hauled myself onto the fore top and gave James a hand. Then we began ascending the topmast ratlines. The wind seemed so much stronger and the rope 'ladder' narrower; but I pushed on and began to feel the lack of this exercise in my limbs. The gale strengthened and chilled and from my position at almost a hundred feet, the ship was a model infested with noisy ants.

I climbed onto the trestle-trees and tackled the last incline. The topgallant mast was flimsy and gave with the heavy gusts. James sat on the lowered yard; water boiled white around the rushing toy so far below. The wind shrieked in the timbers and ropes but could not disguise 'Jump! Jump!' from the sailors. The boy was balanced on the very top of the mast opposite with extraordinary seaman's skill; toes gripped a taut pennon halyard. His white face stared over and I prayed to God he was not relying on me to get him out of this. I held lungfuls of air to slow my heart.

The hopelessness of his situation kept returning favourite lines.

> You ever gentle gods, take my breath
>   from me;
> Let not my worse spirit tempt me again
> To die before you please!

My tongue has been my gift, so I have been told; somehow words are expressed that can impress and persuade and many the elder has ascribed to me the powers of a barrister. But now as I searched for encouraging remarks, a panic at the predicament hid them.

'What's the matter?'

His mouth opened and the wind took the reply. I shouted, please speak up, lad. I said we were all concerned and wished to help if we could. To which his shipmates' morbid chorus rose from the deck. Would he not climb down now, I said, so that attention could be given to his grievances?

The boy called.

James shouted from below me, 'What's he saying?'

'He wants to go home.' I called to the boy, 'Yes, I myself will see to your request; we'll all help you to get there, won't we Mr King?'

I was looking at the boy; I fancied as I clung there a few feet lower down that he had found the strength I lacked.

> Said I then to my heart 'Here's
>   a lesson for me;'
> That man's a Picture of what I
>   might be

I was wrapped well in clothes, but he wore only a shirt and trousers. His feet, small as a girl's and black from tar, were frozen. I wondered if any feeling remained in his hands, and then James called, 'Here's trouble.'

William Bligh was climbing the main topmast, and between his teeth, like a pirate of fiction, he carried a dagger. 'What the hell's he up to?' I shouted to James. I looked over at the boy, who continued to stare at me and was shivering enough to be unbalanced. He had not seen the master nor did he appear to hear the murderous chants of the crew.

James shouted at Bligh, but the commands were ignored. He was almost at the main topgallant mast. I doubted it would take the weight of two people.

'Come on, lad,' I called over. 'Let's go down now. Won't be long before it's mealtime and you can get something hot into you.'

He belched like a jammed fog klaxon. A rush came from his mouth and shot out yellow into the gale. I tried not to look, yet my eyes followed it spinning down, all that way to the frozen foam. The boy watched its descent too.

'Come on, lad.'

He now had eyes only for the sea, roaring and bursting white. A young mollyhawk joined us from the scud; it coasted on the gusts and stared with pink eyes. I was thinking, almost mesmerised by desperation, how perfect were its markings, when the boy jerked, almost fell, and regained his uncanny balance. Then I saw the reason. Bligh had reached that thin topmast spar and was beginning to shin up it. I was shaking with panic and fear and I had to force my eyes back to the boy.

If only I could get the lad to begin down the mast! They worked in the rigging in the blackest of nights, those jack-tars; this boy would easily manage the climb once started. But his eyes had turned to Bligh; they were like teal saucers with the paint still wet. Bligh was six feet from him and still climbing. Below the crew hungered for a corpse's blood and they demanded death in a clear bellow.

Bligh reached the boy's feet and I was transfixed. A boy woo'd death, a horde demanded it, two officers atop a mast were trying to dissuade him, and the burly master like an over-ripe greenbottle on that matchstick, was slashing out with the knife.

The boy screamed. The pitch and the strength of it were out of all proportion to the size of the mast-top waif. It shocked Bligh; he started. His shoes slipped, the knifehand fell away from the mast and the weapon flashed like a fisherman's lure as it plunged around and around towards the deck. The ants parted to clear its path, but the blade bounced against a caprail and sprang into the sea. The time of its fall was inordinately long and my muscles clenched in a paralysis of fear.

Bligh hung from one hand; the other fought the motion of the gale for a hold. It reached the spar as the ship jolted and the concussion came up the mast as if a sailor were untangling a rope. It tore his hand free. The boy's scream stopped and Bligh fell. He smashed into the topgallant yard, a leg either side; he yelled in pain and scratched at the canvas for a hold. Then he fell forward. The leg aft of the yard came over and nothing now could halt the fatal drop. But a foot caught in the furled topgallant sail and he dangled from a gasket like a market chicken. On the deck the crew watched, yet not one moved to help. The chants had stopped and instead turned to prayers for fate to take the nagging voice.

I looked at James; we stared hopelessly at the upended body on the other mast, at the boy on the truck, ironically Bligh's only hope, I thought.

The swarm on the wallowing anthill parted and a man in blue coat, taller than the rest, shouted in a voice far louder than Bligh's, 'Who are officers of the watch?'

As involved as was our tragedy, there could be no denying the demand. 'Up here, sir,' James shouted, unable to disobey. 'King, sir, and Mr Williamson.'

'I'll have you down this instant, if you will.'

James was retreating down the topmast; I found my muscles were suddenly free and descended with great rapidity. On the main mast, several large sailors were climbing to the ignominious upside-down figure.

'You, lad, up there at the truck,' the captain shouted again.

'Yes, sir,' the timid voice reached us on our descent.

'I'll have you down here at the double. There's work to be done.'

'Aye aye, sir,' and the boy found his way onto the side of the topgallant mast and came down like a grey squirrel escaping from winter.

We stood nervously in the waist; James King, me and a bruised master and the barefoot boy, who reached only as high as the captain's belt.

'Mr Williamson,' he said without expression, 'the place for the duty watch officer is the quarterdeck. Kindly resume it. Mr Bligh, when you are standing in for the officer do not go off making an exhibition in the rigging. As for you, lad, this is your watch period, isn't it?'

'Aye aye, captain.'

'Well, don't ruddy well fool around when you're on duty.'

6

'Deck there. Land-ho!'
'State where.'
'Fine on the port bow.'

A young buck won a silver coin for spotting Table Mountain as it climbed solid from a wave and stretched above the horizon till the anchors rang down to confound the local sou'east fury. Our four-pounders rolled out to salute the grey castle sombre at the foot of the mountain and it answered the thirteen booms.

Our sailors were as happy as hounds finding a heated bitch and bawdy dirges reached a new salacity. Then the ship was satisfactorily tethered and the men were unleashed upon the gentle Malay girls whose pretty, symmetrical features were now put energetically to work.

We officers were able to check the accuracy of our Kendal Watch Machine as the longitude at the Cape has been established to a nicety by Messrs Mason and Dixon, the noted surveyors. The timing piece, which is an imitation of the late Mr Harrison's excellent contraption, loses a fraction over two seconds per day for which we are pleased and not a little impressed.

Then we were free to explore the Cape of Good Hope, a boisterous contrast on this edge of civilisation. We saw tall natives with spears, tribal women with backsides the size of camel-humps, drunken duellists, solemn soldiers and merry Mulattos. Wrinkly bushmen perpetually stiff. Music came all day from bright cafés, for Huguenot refugees had built a small Paris here, an unexpected oasis after our stormy life. The sun held off the clouds yet devout Dutch officials remained as dour as a European winter, and everywhere were slaves: big, unbending men branded with scars of disobedience, or the docile, stamped with the despair of stolen freedom. Farmers were bulky giants under layers of clothes, talking a tongue of the past over dreaming oxen. Nomads of the veldt, I thought, navigating to a cold bible yet lost hopelessly to the coy charms of this Sodom of the Seven Seas.

Whales and seals fished around *Resolution*, so plentiful was nature's harvest. Then *Discovery*, our sister ship, pressed into the bay in full ocean plumage and Charles Clerke came aboard to disclose the notion of a cheerful captain.

Fid-fads are a weakness of sailors and pass through a ship quicker than lice. We had men wearing coloured neckcloths from Devon (mementoes from loved ones additional to those souvenirs the sawbones would treat), an outbreak of Spanish peasant hats after the Canaries and Malay wickerwork hats at the Cape. A caprice that lasted the complete voyage was for white trousers bought from the Sunday shop, which we call 'slops', and cut off at the knees. Now *Discovery* brought the latest whim and every member of the expedition, from Captain Cook to the lowest ship urchin, was involved.

Captain Clerke met us in the dusk of *Discovery*'s maindeck and led us to the arena, a piste about a sixteenth of the deck area. A wall of planks about twenty feet wide had been erected by their carpenter. Spectators, sailors and Dutch officials from the town surrounded us.

'You've not played before?' Captain Clerke asked as he handed me the weapon they call a racquet. 'The winner is the best of three games. You'll pick the rules up quickly, because there are very few of them indeed. Good luck, both of you.'

We took our places, facing the planked wall. James threw a sphere of packed cloth into the air and clubbed it with the racquet. The missile struck the wall and bounced back and I swung my racquet and returned it so that it bounced to James's side of the arena. These returns continued, then James contrived to get the spherical to strike the wall in such a way as to land distant from me. I sprinted forward, but the cloth bounced more than once on the deck which made James winner of this round. He served, as they call the opening shot, and I watched more studiously this time the flight of the object.

The racquets were made by the carpenter from two pieces of cane into the shape of a very large spoon. The centre part, the scoop in the parlance of cutlery, is tight fish-netting. Much energy is expended in dashing for the spherical and because of this and the good training for the eye, the recreation has been lauded by our senior sawbones.

Hitting such an object back and forwards may seem hardly proper conduct for officers in a fighting navy, and I admit that when the game was first described I thought it would be tedious. But in practice, it has much of the excitement of fencing, but without the risk to eyes nor the spilling of blood. It seems many were the games on *Discovery*'s passage south and, as Captain Cook attributes good health to the antiscorbutants, so Captain Clerke ascribes it to this game, invented by hapless inmates of Fleet while awaiting rescue from the Israelites.

The score reached 10 to 4 in James's favour and therefore he had won the first set or game, just as he had beaten our captain who had trounced Mr Gore.

I opened the next set. The lighting below decks was not good, but determination filled my breast. I used all my force to drive it to the proper part of the arena and, on James's return, smashed it in much the same direction. James returned it and this time I used less force and the spherical dropped short of James's position. I won the round and repeated the technique precisely for the next three, which I took, and reversed the procedure for the next four, and when James came forward for my expected gentle hits, slammed them with all my force and won the set 10 to nil.

Captain Clerke examined our racquets and declared them stretched. New racquets were produced.

James opened; he struck the ball powerfully for the first two blows and I caught each and returned them and, anticipating a short fall, ran forward to greet it. It was travelling faster than I expected and I had to leap to strike the spherical, but the extension of oneself by the racquet gives a remarkable reach. The cloth came off the wall too short for James. Our spectators were now closely involved with our game for this last set would establish the racquets champion of the officers on the superior ship. The officials, despite the sober attire, seemed the noisiest of witnesses and hissed or huzza'd with the brashness of pit patrons.

I played badly now, through exhaustion, for the exercise was very demanding.

Some insults were levelled at me in the strange patois of the Dutch settlers and I realised that wagering on anything that moves was as much an epidemic here as in old Albion. James's next serve settled the enigma of the spherical recreation for me; his eyes never left the missile. I applied this strategy; the next call was '1 to 8' and I served. I moved into the centre of the arena and would not leave till the spherical landed where my opponent was not.

Rix-dollars passed hands among the spectators but for the players there was only wounded or inflated pride to carry back to our ship.

The anchors were hauled in, muddy on the mangers, the jib-booms pointed to the ocean and our sawbones, Drs Anderson and Samwell, lined up the seamen for the French disease parade. It was a sight to swear a man to permanent celibacy.

We reached for the Southern Ocean. It was good to get back to sea, to that naval routine which is so satisfying for an officer. We encountered growing seas which threw our ship about and quickly returned to our continuing saga of shoddy rigging. On watch the first night, I just stepped down beside the helmsman when timbers and ropes groaned and crashed onto the quarterdeck. The mizzen topmast balanced itself in the cold dark and then plummeted into the decking. We spent a long, dank night hoisting a spare spar into position. *Discovery* led us through the border of the hostile environment, encouraging us with the security of her company. The sun warned a last few frightened flashes and disappeared as if this southernmost sea was too much, and the swell became staggering as unceasing depressions raged ahead in their perpetual race around the South Pole.

The ocean constantly sluiced the decks of *Resolution* and scoured riverbeds through skant caulking to our cabins; any islands left by seawater were swamped by malevolent streams of condensation running down our walls. Now we were never out of heavy weather clothing, wet within from the steam of sweat and dripping without from storm spume. Many of Farmer George's menagerie could not survive the conditions, which were worse than a northern winter. And seeking to encourage myself, I thought that at least Bligh would have his spirits scuttled too by this. Alas, the rude optimism of the melancholy!

A newly born kid died in the maindeck and was offered (after some special cooking by Collett) for the captain's table. We younger people were invited. It was a freezing, storm-riding night and James and I reached the cabin in our Admiralty-issue mageline jackets and fearnought trousers, which we kicked off noisily and left heaped like weathered corpses beside the door. We sat at the table shivering and odoriferous. Then William Bligh arrived. James and I looked the part of ocean navigators surviving the treachery of the elements. Bligh showed that mere worldly storms were of no concern. He presented himself in a uniform he had managed to keep dry. His hair was powdered, perfectly sloped upwards and back from the widow's peak; horizontal curls were rolled above the ears, in the fashion of the day, and in place of a queue, the hair was held with a ribbon matching the fresh blue of his coat. A scent snooked our heavy sweat.

The captain was in a rare good humour in the expectation of finding land reported by the Gauls, but Bligh's fashion, defying the elements as it did, established the old boy in an almost blissful state. James and I exchanged pleasantries through the meal for no other conversation came our way. Banter and repartee worthy of a coffee-house was conducted twixt fat master and cheery commander. Too soon James and I clambered into storm clothes to leave and Bligh was asked to delay a moment.

This produced a most unhappy effect, as if I were a leper too hideously ravaged to be accepted by others of the colony, and I descended to my cot with leaden heart. The noise of the Roaring Forties groaned and shuddered through the ship, yet I fancied I could hear the aft-cabin conversation as if a construction fault left my deckhead a sounding board.

'Very well, William. Till tomorrow.'

'Good night, sir.'

The latch turned, hinges creaked familiarly and the door closed awkwardly owing to its swelling by saturation. I lay still for a moment and then, unable to control myself, dashed from the bed. It was none of my business – but I must be reassured, and I pulled open my door. I stared across the gunroom. There was no Bligh. I rushed to the ladderway and balanced against a sudden jerk from the storm. I emerged into the waist.

A bedraggled wading bird was stooped in the wind as officer of the quarterdeck. Helmsman and mate were talking oblivious of me and foggy breath came from the signal gun-crew at their station. But not a sign of Bligh. I dragged sad, wet feet back to my cot and screamed to the noise of the hull and buried my ears to muffle the confirmation of my most dreaded fear from that sounding board. Youthful tears of the conquered swamped the shirt I used as a pillow.

Now there was nought to bolster my youth and our days remained a long dawn which eventually succumbed to dusk. Grey days, charcoal nights. Then out of the sameness came Land-ho! and bleak rocks appeared and grew into two silhouettes of desolation which we drove between, heads pulled down like wary terrapins into mageline jackets against the cold and damp, our unwelcome constant companions.

The depression of my spirit deepened and the captain's soared. He was among new discoveries and the fog and scud were no more than an obstinate curtain on the opening night of a new play. My feet dragged and he bounced in reborn steps; I was the soured critic seeing his performance of explorer and navigator as unmanly, and the more the audience applauded, the more my cynicism increased. The grim islands softened in our wake with the gentle shades of a Canaletto and we moved deeper into the southern gloom. We negotiated a world of greys; cloud, fog and sea vied for uniformity and only a breaking wave throwing freezing anger at the ship eased the colour. I stood within my mageline on the quarterdeck and we were hurrying through a vast cemetery and the jutting moving obstacles leaping from viscid vapour to smash against the ship were tombstones and soon I should see one marked John Williamson, December 1776. RIP.

> Here rests his head upon the lap of
> Earth
> A Youth to Fortune and to Fame unknown.
> Fair Science frown'd not on his humble
> birth,
> And Melancholy mark'd him for her own.

Our guns blasted in the thicker weather and *Discovery*'s distant thunder came back from the blindness. My grief was lasting, and youth, which usually compensates for the sharpness of developing emotions, could not answer the melancholia. I withdrew in my misery from the others and soon there was just me and that friendly, noisy creature out there; a whale in fading canvas guiding us through these mighty wastes. Fog became heavier and pressed down to the girtline and gales strengthened and lashed the watch officers with salt-laden, freezing gusts, and we had to play blind man's bluff, groping for *Discovery* with our ears.

Conversations came on that quarterdeck. The captain talking of the French discoverer Kerguelen (Cur Helen, he said), a splash of colour from Omai momentarily surfacing from his sick bed enthusing at our first calf born at sea, James moaning the old sailoring term that it was too cold to shite a seaman's turd. My only interest was in catching my friendly leviathan, as determinedly and hopelessly as if it were ambition. And I drove the men into the rigging, even if we could hold additional sail for scarcely an hour.

'Have your men ready at the braces, Mr Shuttleworth.'

'Aye aye, sir.'

Neither *Resolution* nor her men were spared. The waves grew higher and the swell from those boundless deserts was longer and sped in vast thundering trails either side of our hull.

'I'll have those t'g'nts'ls now. Lively if you please.' Topmen disappearing into the fog like Indian rope tricksters, the crashing of canvas ungasketed to the ferocity; stamp and go from the deckmen.

'Sheets, Mr Mate! Sheets, for damnation's sake, or there'll be no canvas left.'

'Fore t'g'nts'l is ripped, sir.'

'Clew it up and let's have it down for the sailmaker.'

'That's the second torn tonight, sir.'

'Don't tell me, tell your deck people. As soon as it comes free of the gaskets, they must spring to sheet or halyard, depending. I'll have each on a charge if they don't wake up. Just one more lazy sail change, mind. You tell them, Mr Mate.'

Our little world hurtled into nothingness. If there were an edge to the globe we would find it and leap into space to sail about blue Sirius and the Southern Crux illuminating the truck in the gaps of night vapour. Then penguins played in the breaking waves and long warps of seaweed worried us at the weather-rail, appearing through condensing breath.

'Deck there, land-ho!'

'All hands! Furl fore and mizzen tops'ls,' I called as a darker fuzziness came through the gloom. 'Main stays'ls off her.'

We found a small bay in this land where rocks pushed out of the turbulence like a worried swimmer's head held stiffly above waves. Our anchors screamed down and the pinnace swung over on yard tackles. I stamped my feet and clapped like a lower-order audience to restore circulation and watched men stepping ashore. They rushed yahooing about the sand of the moonscape mocking comical upright birds like clerics and martyring them for fun. Fearless fowl were thick watching the strange phenomenon of sudden death mixed with seamen's laughter. Perhaps barbarians had not been here before.

The ships rode to their anchors in an unaccustomed smooth of the lee and gentlemen attended dinner in the aft-cabin. I picked at the fresh roasted birds with their tasty crisp skin and drowned the salty meat in the old boy's wine.

The captain raised a glass of claret. 'The Frenchman may have called this point Isle of Rendez-vous.' He pronounced it Rendered-views. 'But I know nothing that can rendez-vous at it but the fowls of the air for it is certainly inaccessible to every other animal.'

Captain Clerke clinked his glass. 'But then the birds of the air have less intelligence than the animals, for no self-respecting beast would want to meet here.'

The wine in the guests laughed well at this rejoinder. Then Bligh, tumbler tentatively extended, a fist cunnythumbed, ventured, 'Except, sir, the frogs themselves.'

> So, but oft, the Grape's refreshing Juice
> Does many Mischievous Effects produce.

He had been drinking heavily, as if this were his celebration. His face was red from indulgence. I looked at the captain's heavy featured amusement; it looked something of an imitation for he was not much used to displaying it. Captain Clerke's was an honest countenance and the smile was well practised and warm, and I turned back to Bligh's physiognomy triumphing in this attempt at wit. It was a mummer's mask, I decided, put there to disguise a cunning, clever brain.

My look was critically appraising, but the old boy wore the expression of a proud father. 'Well, gentlemen, I take to being a better namer of parts than Monsieur Kerguelen.' And he mispronounced again as mon-sewer Cur Helen. 'I have named it with a fine English title. . . .'

'Rule Britannia!'

'Cheers, sir!'

'. . . and this afternoon I entered it upon the chart.'

His eyes smiled charitably enough at us, at the faces enjoying his humour round the table, at my undisguisably melancholy countenance. There was no hint of what was to come. 'Mr Williamson,' he said. 'Mr Williamson here is one of my most promising young navigators.'

This sudden, unexpected praise caused my cheeks to burn, though I wished it otherwise. I was dumbfounded, particularly as my mind was only partially involved with these proceedings. 'Do be so kind, Mr

Williamson, as to read to our assembly the new name for the promontory.'

I wished only to be silent and left alone. I did not want to attend this dinner, but the captain's requests were always our instructions. And here I was suddenly thrust into the limelight; I had forgotten my lines, I could not hear the prompter, and then the audience applauded. I pushed my chair out embarrassed and stumbled to the chart-table. An uncreased new sheet was on top; the master had begun to chart this part of the island and I had to envy the speed of his work, the precision of the outline drawn in one uninterrupted stroke. No hesitations, rubbings-out and fresh beginnings. My pride searched for just one flaw, but there was none.

'It's on the chart below,' the captain called, and I lifted the draughtsmanship and stared disbelievingly, while heads turned towards me waiting.

'The new name for the Ile de Rendez-vous,' I said, loathing the vileness of the words, 'is Bligh's Cap.'

Glasses clinked behind me. Good show, well done, sir. Super name. That'll show the frogs. Rule Britannia! I returned to the table somehow, unsteadily, like an ancient after a stroke. Collett was uncorking another bottle of port, Lieutenant Rickman offered me a brandy. 'Sir, may I offer my congrat. . . .'

But the conversation had moved on and it seemed my perjury was not required. Captain Clerke guessed at my floundering words and moved to help, but he misunderstood. 'Remember Dr Johnson, Mr Williamson. "Claret is liquor for boys; port for men; but he who aspires to be a hero must drink brandy."'

The old boy stood a little unsteadily. 'Officers, gentlemen, friends . . . let me be the first to say a very merry Christmas.'

Captain Clerke took out a large Pinchbeck pocket watch. 'I say, local time, and it is too. Happy Yuletide all.'

7

Our vessels plied a region scarcely known to civilisation and I comprehended little better the emotions that coursed through my changing body. I was suffering a low spring ebb indeed and intellect was no match for passion; what I planned was wrong, but I could not help myself. I was usurped from what should have been mine and I was plunged into a deep melancholia. What reaction is it that rises in the bosom of the simplest man, or the most intelligent, when wronged? I desired revenge and the heat of my youth was inured to the cold reason of day. Mine was a midnight repast of retaliation; warming wine for thirst, vol-au-vents of blatant flattery for appetiser and a drunk demure playmate for the angry insistent hunger; a digestive for that unpalatable rejection.

But when desire is spilled, experience remains, and I scrubbed myself in that freezing water as if I had consorted with lepers. Repentance, my carbolic, was regrettably no challenge to memory.

The rocks of this world of desolation palled with our company for it was after all a desert island in icy, stormy wastes. The island looked like an angry fist shaking at God. He hid it with a curtain of impenetrable cloud behind which the disrespect was smashed continually by the boundless, uncontrollable anger of this ocean. My work here was as draughtsman in the aft-cabin where we charted the coast, discovered and documented the substance and slope of the sea floor. My conscience was too heavy for my inexperienced heart and I wanted our wake to swallow my guilt, resentment and pain as if they were contents of the cook's misused gash bucket; for food for mocking mollymawks and the repulsive Mother Carey's geese exiled to these miserable latitudes. At the chart table I answered when spoken to and shouted within to cover exchanges between captain and warrant officer. And my conscience commanded avast there with the lead so the bottom of treacherous jagged shoal would tear open our hull and claim us along with the ghost which wrecked my happiness.

The captain announced as we worked at the charts, 'I doubted from my previous exploration that a great southern continent exists and this discovery supports my doubt entirely. Mr Williamson, a course to head us east, if you will.'

What blessed words! The pure relief to race before the unceasing westerlies, and my mind soared with the prospect of sprinting with the mountainous swells, to get away, to keep going. Gales that would clear the clogging mustiness of my personal past; jib-boom to the future, to the horizon of tomorrows. The music I longed for: stays, braces, hemp harmonising to the press of canvas, the unrelenting air and the percussion of a following sea under the keel as she thunders with a bone in her teeth; rushing forwards, always for'ards.

Yet as I took the course to the quarterdeck for the officer of the watch, I saw with frustration the slowness with which the rocks fell astern. Our sister ship was glad to be going and blossomed with sail, water shrieking white at her bows, overhauling us. I could see Captain Clerke all about his charge, encouraging the men; yet on our ship Mr Gore methodically issued instructions from the quarterdeck and the progress we could expect from our keen steed was fettered by this ponderous jockey. For God's sake, give me the reins; by the powers, we'll see progress then. But this was Royal Navy and I could not hasten a senior officer. However, an hour later, my watch began.

'All well?' I asked, as was the custom when taking over.

'Ship-shape and Bristol fashion, young sir,' Gore said and disappeared with beak chattering down the quarterladder. The navigation board showed our speed to be four knots.

'How's the course, quartermaster?'

'It's me, Ward, on the helm, sir,' and I recognised James Ward's Pompey accent. He was one of our best helmsmen; I leaned over the rail looking down on blond curls and the layers of clothing making strange shapes of the mageline jacket.

'How does the wheel feel?' I asked.

'Hardly straining, sir.'

'I've a mind to change all that, Ward.'

'Very good, sir.'

I called to Lanyon, the master's mate, standing in the waist. I ordered the mizzen tops'l set; but quietly, mind. Bare feet of yard men came hurrying past and climbed onto the ratlines. Gaskets were unknotted, muscles strained at halyards and the sudden flogging of canvas quickly quietened. *Resolution* increased her pace.

I luxuriated in the sudden release from depression, admiring the quarterdeck which was all mine for the present, the excitement of a crew waiting for my orders, and the staggering beauty of the forest of strength dominating my vision.

'Do you see *Discovery* in the lee, Lanyon? She was astern an hour ago.'

'My thoughts precisely, sir.'

'What are we going to do about it?'

'I think you know the answer, sir. And it's pretty cold for the crew just standing around doing nothing.' Not that you would have thought so; I was deep inside my mageline jacket and fearnought trousers, but Lanyon was dressed in the manner of the Cornish. Bare arms, light clothes beneath red hair and weathered complexion. His blue waistcoat was unbuttoned. Vapour came with his words, but not a movement from unkempt teeth.

Getting our driver sail raised was no silent business, with the added difficulty that the work had to be done above the captain's deckhead. But unless it could be raised quietly the old boy might have stormed out to insist on the return of a codger's sail-plan. I went down to the waist.

'How goes the wheel, Ward?'

'It wears a manly feel now, sir.'

I took it from him and the wood was hot and dry where his hands had been. The rest, like this deep scar of a swordcut, was saturated. It jolted to larboard, nearly wrenching cold muscles from my shoulders. 'There's some weather helm there, Ward,' I said, and he took the strain again. Only a man of Ward's build could hold her for long. If she rounded up, which was her tendency, the ship would be imperilled; in a heavier sea we might turn turtle.

'I could balance her with a bit more on the foremast,' I said.

Ward was smiling. 'That you could, sir, and I don't doubt our turn of speed might pick up.' The helmsman had his eye firmly on *Discovery* too. We would overtake her because hope, the new generation, took this watch and we would unfurl courage into the sail plan.

> In gallant trim the gilded Vessel goes;
> Youth on the prow, and Pleasure at the helm.

I ordered the setting of the fore t'gallant sail and watched sailors reach the foretop, lean out, climb over the futtock-shrouds and rush on upwards. Sheets were tensioned on deck. Canvas cracked like a huge bullwhip and then stretched to the gale.

'Take up on the braces!'

Ward's feet were wide and sweat stood on his forehead. The bone in our teeth now must be from some dinosaur, I fancied, for the bow-waves almost reached the quarterdeck. Our speed increased by at least two knots and *Discovery* was falling back. The officer on watch had not seen our challenge.

'Ward, come over a spoke. See if we can't mask her wind a little.'

The distance lessened. We surged again and *Resolution* found another running swell and we rushed forward, sleighing, the weighty ship flinging herself into the challenge like an older jack-tar finding youth in the hornpipe.

Eyes to weather, to the rigging, down to Ward's compass. He held the course exactly. Our speed increased and the extra canvas of the driver aft kept her to it. We came to the weather-quarter of *Discovery*, and we were flying.

The wind was snatched from *Discovery*'s sail. The ship seemed to collapse and mizzen, main and foremast sails crashed as we stole the gale. A young officer swung to stare to weather, shocked; our jib-boom was tearing past him, fifteen feet off. Skuas flapped in dark brown anger from our ploughing cutwater and *Discovery*'s masts rocked with the release of pressure; she fell into the calm as our three pressed banks came along her length.

'Frig!' came over from the startled lieutenant and then Captain Clerke was beside him, staring in disbelief.

The ship had all but stopped, but the sea was still going. A wave crashing through our wake rammed the stern and poured white and green over the tafferel and along the poop-deck. 'My God, I hope those sternlights hold,' I prayed aloud. It didn't pay to stove in a captain's cabin windows.

We were past and going. A cheer came from the watch which startled a gliding royal albatross. Our bow-waves ploughed high, struck at her larboard, built the quarterwaves and cascaded over the caprail and into the waist.

'Good day, Charles.' Our captain stood in the waist, waving his cocked hat at *Discovery*, with the calm of a Sunday jolly. But I waited for the *haka*, fearing the worst. 'How goes it, Mr Williamson?'

'Making progress, sir.'

'Perhaps a fraction too much?'

There was little to be said in mitigation; whether a ship in the open ocean is overpressed is often a matter of opinion. 'Well, sir,' I tried, 'we are Royal Navy.'

'Absolutely, young sir; a word at the weather-rail, if you please.'

I expected the war dance now and could only be grateful I was to be dressed down in the relative privacy of the mizzen.

'It's a good idea to double up on helmsmen when you are, well, progressing like this. And change them on the half hour.'

He disappeared into his cabin and I breathed again. *Discovery* was well astern. Fog returned and cleared and the sun allowed us to dry out the ship, then came more Southern Ocean storms, with three men fighting to hold the wheel, running under bare poles, as moving mountains roared about us. The problem of poor refitting struck during Mr Gore's watch, even though we were carrying precious little of canvas to my way of thinking. An almighty cracking came from for'ard and I ran from my cabin fearing we had rammed *Discovery*. The main-topmast was waving only just in position and the split of where she had sprung was growing. A wandering albatross passed above the swinging truck, examining the damage with Celtic eyes. It banked away and the mast broke loose and went by the board, taking the main topgallant with it.

'All hands, all hands!'

The mainmast itself sat as secure as a sawn tree trunk, stumpy and ugly in our ravaged forest. Forestays hung like cut vines dragging from amidships.

'Axes. Bring axes,' Bligh was calling.

I dashed along the waist determined to stop him. 'Avast,' I shouted. 'You're not going to cut the whole of that timber adrift?'

'It's hammering against the hull, sir. It'll hole us to be sure.'

'For God's sake, man, get a rope around it and we can hoist it from the sea.'

Damaged shrouds were carving splinters out of the caprail; the situation was serious, but there was time to try to save the mast. Then he asked permission to address the captain and I agreed; in the quarterdeck, he argued that the masts could not be brought on board. I told the captain, 'If we can hold the thing clear of the water, we can get a tackle round it.'

'I'm reluctant to risk a man's life in doing that, sir,' Bligh said mendaciously, even though he knew I was aware no risk existed in retrieving the timber.

'I saw the mast going, sir,' I said. 'The main-top was wrecked, but there was nothing wrong with the main topgallant.'

'Cut it away.'

'But, sir,' I tried. 'There is no spare mast.'

He looked at me for a moment and then, as he turned away, he said, 'Spars are not so hard to replace. Life is impossible.'

You misunderstand me, but there was no misunderstanding the gloating smile the master wore.

Rocks jutted from mounded surf. High mountains of Van Diemen's Land came pale blue in the dawn, and turned to deep jade as we approached an extraordinary land. The ocean became a green I had not seen at sea previously. And with the sighting of the Mewstone about six leagues from the shore, anger, aggravations, hate and envy were put aside and a unity we had long forgotten returned to the ship. We were involved in a common purpose. Discovery. And as strange as it is to record, Bligh and I named some of the promontories like shipmates and navigated our vessel to the eastern coast searching for Adventure Bay.

Squalls raced from the south, across our path and followed a bight inland. We sailed through flocks of silvery prions which resembled fairies protecting paradise from worldly man and I believe most wept at the majesty of this kingdom suddenly rising on our saucer of travels, reminding us that our voyaging was unnatural for man; despite our adventurous facades, we were of the earth and it was on land that God meant us to be. Very few people had seen this new world and few would venture this way again, I believed. The beauty was too heady for civilised man who needs the rounded stability of mature England, the streets of modern London.

Within a short while I was to see my first native women. They were of my own height and one had large paps which were firm and undisguised. She was black and attractively formed but her face was sleepy in the middle of the day. Her tribe preferred to lie in till the sun was high.

8

Night is little different from day in the illumination of the cabins, but I knew it was dawn and I dashed from my berth, through the gunroom and up the ladderway into a steely blueness ballasted with the odour of forested land. I could taste its freshness. The blue star Sirius hung above our ship like a vast fat gem and the still water was polished smoked glass; the trees were wakening and perhaps returning a respectful look at their distant cousins put to excellent use, and behind this picture were sharp mountains clear and fascinating. And, reader, oh, the sound of the dawn chorus!

> Innumerous songsters, in the freshening Shade
> Of new-sprung Leaves, their Modulations mix
> Mellifluous.

Not altogether perhaps as James Thompson would have it, for these New World creatures are not the singers of Europe. It was almost a cacophony, but who could deny such enthusiasm for life and to ears hungry for the reassurance of earth, it was a symphony the like of which even fashionable Amadeus has not matched.

> And each harsh Pipe discordant heard alone,
> Aid the full concert.

I was transfixed. It was marvellous and the blood soared and I realised I had dwelt in a coma, but thank you God for getting me here. Such magic, I thought; such an extraordinary promise of fulfilling life!

Then I turned back and down the ladder and drummed heartily on the cabin doors of James King and David Samwell; how they would appreciate this! A white diaphanous apparition like a castle ghost passed me, grumbling, 'God, but you're noisy'; and Omai night-uniformed in silk was off to admire the dawn, the *mal-de-mer* that chained him to his berth unshackled.

The other side of the world! Take a common or garden pumpkin for this experiment and call it the world. Choose the latitudes where humans have survived somehow (despite themselves) since Adam, plunge in a spike and where the point protrudes is the region of this strange, beautiful haven. Van Diemen's Land. We, so Captain Cook concludes, are at its very southernest point. In a previous voyage he visited its northern coast; a huge continent without a doubt. In my pleasure and excitement at being here, I dressed with extra care and around the gunroom came the sounds of people rising early. Awnings were being erected above the waist, and Bligh's shouts interrupted momentarily the feathered chorus. I could hear Collett polishing the captain's shoes in a rapid rhythm at the gunroom table, pewter plates rattled as they were set for breakfast. The view of dawn and land had entranced our Omai, who now was possessed of an extravagant mood, distributing affectionate terms to those about him as he fussed and dressed and tantrummed over clothes that would not do, and what King George confided to him about agriculture and which newspapers said what about what at such-and-such a parade. Poor, misguided Omai, I thought; a forgetful chameleon in a to-do about what to change back to.

Morning duties were delegated, the pinnace swung over the side and I delivered a message to *Discovery*; compliments to Captain Clerke, and Captain Cook wishes that her marines will act as guard this day.

Smoke rising inland last night had not produced natives so far. The shore breathed innocence, powerful and rich like a Bach concerto, and I sat in the sternsheets waiting, the crew with oars raised. Beneath us the fathoms were clear to the seabed. We watched the scarlet reflections of *Discovery*'s marines as they set out inelegantly for the shore. The noise of splashing oars was broken by distinct shots of the captain's shoes stepping across the deck to the gun'ale. The stockings came over and the polished leather found the hull-cleats as he descended. The pinnace lowered and stretched to take the sudden weight. Crew held the boat close to the hull. He came unsteadily towards the sternsheets and summoned Omai, and whistled wolf calls announced the appearance of our passenger. His giggles and tender terms preceded him to the gunwale over which he negotiated tastefully, as cleverly as a maiden mounting a carriage modestly keeping ankles covered. Such was Omai.

Purple half-boots glided down, white silk stockings, sky-blue breeches with tassels and gold buttons, the last word in fashion of course. Orange silk shirt, double-breasted coat in navy blue and a brimmed hat to set it all off, as doubtless to some purple does.

'Make way for Omai,' I said smartly to our rowers who pouted and teased him with, beside me dearie, and here's your pretty little seat my duckie-o.

Omai found his way through the boat like a nervous debutante on her first outing, a long kerchief trailing perfume among the baser scent of our crew. As he wondered where to sit an expression of panic came over those made-up features; for a second he resembled an aristocratic butterfly trapped in the web of a plebeian spider.

'Let go the hull.'

We pushed off from the ship's side, from this woven timbered creation that had taken us so far, and rowed on the untouchable blue, leaving the two creatures tethered at their cables, cold fingers of empty masts warming to the rising sun.

Captain and passengers were despatched at the shore, their shoes avoiding the water (and so me avoiding a rough word from Collett for damaging his handiwork). The marines would guard us, so now began the routine work at a landfall before the compliments relaxed. Wooding and watering, cutting grasses for the animals, enough to see us to the next land, collecting anti-scurvy plants, carpenter Cleveley and his mates building a new topmast and felling spares.

I was in charge of the pinnace and we ferried workers from both ships to the shore. We picked up the astronomer, cadaverous Bayley and his paraphernalia, and I watched the tight nervous expression ease as his delicate foot touched the land. And then our task was to carry fodder to the ships; the lengths of timber, messages passed back; it was work that allowed for idle minds and we stood down mentally. I was developing a notion about the purity of this continent, of the good effect it must have on our rough people whose experience of land was confined to dirt, destitution and debauchery.

'What are you grinning at, Watman?'

'I'm not grinning, sir.'

'What *were* you grinning at?'

'The marines, sir.'

I spun our boat about and we raced for the scarlet reptiles. The disorderly bunch was falling about as if they had been drugged by poisoned arrows. I ran from the pinnace as we touched the beach; the men were drunk, like grinning corpses, and we heaved them into their boat with the dead bottle of grog. I established a new guard with some sailors and wondered at such a contrast. As an officer I was concerned with the risk to the captain while these delinquents drank, yet I was bothered by their desire to discard consciousness in a setting as perfect as this.

Yard tackles were necessary to get them on board and then we resumed our duties and the peace of the surroundings filed away the unhappy episode.

'Mr Williamson, sir.' I looked down from the waist as we loaded fodder from the pinnace. 'It's natives, sir; they're friendly like and the captain wants your interpretations.'

Dear reader, what a scene unfurled as I splashed through the wavelets and ran across the short undergrowth. A group of naked natives stood yawning, half asleep, looking at our officers, who offered smiles and polite nods. The natives, who I discerned to number eight men and a boy and to be of moderate height, were unarmed. One or two carried staffs, and I wondered that these aborigines did not appear surprised, as if to come upon English folk during their matutinals was a normal daily happening. There was no disguising, however, that discovering brown men with fuzzy hair and beards dressed in ochre balls was unusual for us.

Our people were the none of them very close to the natives, but not because of the ripe odoriferous cloud which hung about. (After all, our jack-tars could present as confounded a hogo as any beast of the field.) We were taken with the historical importance of finding these people and the emotional significance of discovering distant descendants who journeyed all this way – God knows how – from Mount Ararat those centuries ago. But here they were, as bare as the day they were born, prepuces uncut, their language unlike anything I had heard. And they were much scarred, I noticed, with wounds that healed badly.

The captain was involved in a lively conversation with James King and at the same time, nodding, smiling and directing at them, 'We are here in peace; peace, my friends.'

The natives giggled behind their hands.

'What do you make to their language, Mr Williamson?'

'Not from Africa, sir, and it doesn't sound like Polynesian.'

'Definitely not Polynesian,' Omai said petulantly and surrendered his nostrils to a perfumed handkerchief.

'Try some different dialects,' the captain said impatiently.

'We come from afar.' Not a world-trembling statement, but I offered it in Maori, Xhosa, Gaelic, and macro-Algonkian; I pointed to the captain's breeches and used the words of various countries. Captain Clerke arrived and I indicated his cocked hat and gave the varieties for that too, but our hosts laughed and hid their teeth.

The sun toasted us from a cloudless sky, the undergrowth was soft beneath feet used to timber and the scenery gentled eyes accustomed to grey. The exchanged smiles continued and an anthropological argument gathered way between the captains.

'You cannot call the hair woolly,' Captain Cook said.

'It gives this impression . . .' – and here he smiled at the inhabitants to imply we are admiring you – '. . . because of the grease attached to the ends.'

'If that's not woolly hair,' Captain Clerke said, 'I don't know what is.' And he took hold of a native boy and began inspecting the scalp. The shaver grinned, happy to help with the argument. 'Well,' Captain Clerke said thoughtfully, 'it's generally free of dirt.'

'And lice?' our captain asked.

The boy laughed. Captain Clerke said, 'Not many. In fact there's a lot more on the body than in the hair.'

'So you can see it's straight hair, at least.'

He let the boy go. 'Sorry, James, it is woolly.'

The natives, not feeling in the least afraid of us, moved among our number inspecting clothes. Omai received the greatest attention, as befitted the owner of a courting butterfly's wardrobe.

At Omai's insistence, I enquired in sign language for the purpose of their staffs. The message was not easy to convey, especially as at that moment the old boy decided to present our hosts with some knives. Eventually I got through; they gabbled in their queer tongue and set up a branch about twenty feet off.

'Look out, sir,' James King called.

A man was urinating close to the old boy. He jumped to avoid the stream and the native turned in surprise and was hosing again like a damaged park fountain towards the captain.

David Samwell had been watching at a safe distance but now came to us enthusiastically. 'They have much less idea about decency than an English dog,' he said and the natives shared our humour. 'At least the dog will lift his leg, by which you may guess what he is going to do. But these gentlemen, whether sitting, walking or talking will pour forth their stream without any preparatory action or guidance, or even appearing sensible of what they are doing. And not in the least interested whether it trickles down their own thighs or sprinkles the person next to them.'

A native threw the stake like a spear and it pierced the earth beneath the target. His smile was incredibly similar to ours when we take pride in a good shot.

'James, do let me show the savages how our muskets work?'

'Thank you, Omai, but we don't wish to die in your demonstration.' Omai's accuracy was worse perhaps than the marines'. 'Mr Williamson, take the musket and fire at the target.'

The shot cracked in the stillness. The natives stared, paralysed for a moment, and then ran madly for the trees. Black backsides disappeared through the undergrowth towards the watering place where, unbeknown to them, our men were filling the casks. In a moment sailors dashed from the bush. This was their first sighting of the natives, and from the shouts they believed they were destined for the cooking-pot.

There was, of course, much mirth among our group at this and the terrified sailors did not stop till they reached their boat, further round the bay. They were trying to launch it when the natives came from the trees in pursuit. But they appeared even at our distance much more children at play than savages shopping.

The captain called, 'Mr Bligh, fire a musket if you will.' The gun sounded and the natives stopped, looked back the half-mile to us, and ran off into the trees. The master was despatched to return some courage to those hearts of oak and the men to the watering.

We were to have left the following morning but such a perfect calm hung over the bay that there was not even a zephyr to work the ship. We had no choice but to stay another day.

Poetry and worship of the scenery were notions that took me, not the demands of recreation in below-decks dusk. The roughness of the ocean had stopped the recreation even among *Discovery*'s hardy determined players, but with smooth water, the play-off was under way, and from our ship, James Millett was the winner of the crew and Phillips from our marine detachment. They were both giants so which won meant little to me. We three were rowed to *Discovery* and had I been more optimistic of the outcome I would have studied closely their play. But while spectators betted and bellowed I watched with eyes of defeat. Phillips was announced the winner and after a play-off between *Discovery*'s marines champion, a slight lad called George Moody, and a hulking crewman, our match was held to choose the racquets champion of *Resolution*.

Marine Lieutenant Phillips served and, putting his great weight to advantage, rushed the cloth so that it thundered against the wall and spun at me with enormous velocity. I could do no more than block the spheroid and let it fall to the front of the arena. This was not really sufficient to match Phillips's because his size enabled him to control an incredible arc and he took the first game.

The second set proceeded much as the first for there was little variety to the fellow. He fought as a bull and each swing carried a similar strength; I felt I would be happy when the competition was through and was tempted to act like Omai and parade back and forward in lurid costume and not hit the ball once. His match against the slight Michael Portsmouth had been the shortest of the whole competition. But I knew I could not just give it away to a marine. The second set came to a close, 10 to 9; my game. This upset Phillips. He knew he should have won and this time the cloth was smashed at me with unbelievable strength. I clubbed back, guessing where was the object. My racquet found it, the missile crashed against the wall and caught Phillips accidentally on his forehead. He looked as startled and accusing as if I had struck him with the racquet. I countered the ball in two-handed swings and he struck out as if it were the most loathsome of vermin and our score climbed 3 to 4 and then 5 to 4, in a pendulum for neither of us deserved any point. The further into the game, the more violent and angry did my opponent become. With me, the opposite happened, for the continual blasphemies were farcical. At that stage of my life, I was not practised at keeping from what the fairer sex refers to as giggles, and soon a titter came from me, then more. This was as a red cape to my snorting adversary and the remarks came the more plentiful; soon the total was in my favour and we closed the set at 10 to 7. I returned to my solitude a wiser youth, having seen how anger can rob a man of victory.

At the captain's conference in the aft-cabin we dispensed with the tally of the animals, the amount of fodder shipped and the health of the men. We were about to leave for duties ashore when Bligh said, 'And the punishment for the marines?'

'I told Captain Clerke that if we decided against leaving today we would carry it out here in the senior ship.'

'What punishment?' I asked surprised. Who could think of punishment in this setting?

James King replied, 'The marines who were drunk.'

'I knew nothing of this,' I said, a little out of line, but it was a subject I had thought much about last night when sleep was slow to take me.

'Well, it's settled,' Bligh said impatiently. 'The men were drunk; the guilt was there for all to see.'

'But why were they drunk, that's the point?'

The captain had taken little interest in my comments until this; he snapped, 'The point, Mr Williamson, is that they were on guard and risked the lives of all.'

'Sir, may I speak to this?'

'If you must, but my mind is made up.'

This brought my temper close to the surface; the insensitive attitude took no account of the lot of the marines. But I held firmly to emotion and addressed them quietly and I hoped with persuasion. 'Sir, if we are looking for a guilty party let us take their senior officer who did not bother to be present on shore; let us look to the poor shipboard security that allowed a bottle of grog to find its way into the hands of a post of guards.'

'Poppycock, Mr Williamson,' Bligh interrupted. 'You know nothing of what goes on in that ship. Officers, security? Red herrings, sir. They failed in their duty, that's all.'

The captain opened his mouth to condemn Bligh's discourtesy, but more was at risk than my pride. I pushed on. 'I quite see your point, master, but please. . . . We don't send men into the rigging without an officer or a midshipman in charge and our men could not be more familiar there. Yet those boys were cast into a role they had no experience of; after being cooped up, surrounded by people for months, they were suddenly dumped on the shore of a vast open land with nobody in control. If our Mr Bligh wants to flog someone, I say choose the marine officer too disinterested to command them and the watch warrant officer who allowed them into the boat carrying a bottle.'

'That will do, Mr Williamson,' the captain said impatiently. 'The matter's settled and I'll not listen to more. Now, is there anything else for the conference?' As we left the room, he said to James, 'If I'm guilty of some misdemeanour, for God's sake make sure our Mr Williamson is my ruddy counsel.'

The coats of the marine guard glowed on the mirror surface. The reflected hull looked faultless and *Discovery* was as breathtaking above and in the image as a thoroughbred stallion drinking at a pond. I saw her as the extraordinary blend of aesthetics and the science of our age, and our anchorage was a haven, an establishment of Dame Nature's herself, designed, I fancied in my musings, as a place where peace and joy might be the delights of man.

We officers stood in uniform, swords at our sides, on the quarterdeck of our machine of war; civilised people in the warmth of this unspoilt spot. About one hundred and eighty souls faced us. Men, I believed, refreshed by these waters, washed, scrubbed clean; brains purified by overwhelming scenery and perhaps influenced a little by our meeting with humans who lived in great innocence. Private Michael Portsmouth's drum-roll brought our minds back to ship's business.

'There is a time for taking grog,' the captain said. 'It is not, I repeat not, while any man is guarding his officers and people from a possible adversary.'

The marines were in a line like a varicose vein before Collett, in his role now as master-at-arms. Gratings rested beside the wheel in good view of the complements of both vessels crammed like pit patrons in the waist and foredeck.

'Do the men have anything to say, Mr Bligh?'

'No, sir.'

'Carry on with the punishment.'

'Aye aye, sir.' He turned to the offenders. 'Strip.' They replaced bright jackets with spotted pink bodies. 'Seize him up.'

Pintado petrels came over the poop-deck, reviewed our formal lines, and flew lazily towards the shore. Racquet champion George Moody was grabbed and his wrists fastened above his head to the gratings.

'He's tied up, sir.'

We tucked our cocked hats under our arms and the captain read angrily from the Articles of War. A cry came from the boy's lips for he knew what followed. 'Do your duty, master-at-arms.'

Collett brought the whip down. The familiar sound of cord on flesh rose into the rigging and seemed to carry to the shore. The pale skin disregarded the stroke at first, and then after a distinct pause violent red lines surfaced. The boy screamed. The cat scratched again and the cry came quicker. Moody's background, I thought, would differ little from another marine; seconded to the ship, a shaver still some way from his twenties. His duties were to act as policeman to sailors as ignorant and harassed as marines; to protect the officers and their lot was miserable. Because they aided authority they were despised.

The back was arched, as if it might gain pity by exposing fully the wounds of pulped flesh. Moody was a skinny youth and the only muscles were two that crossed the shoulder blades and resembled gash bolt-ropes. The stroke came again, followed by a longer scream. Our training as officers put us beyond caring about popularity with the men, but these lads had no preparation. Marines were the minority who suffered the strength of the majority; they were always in the wrong because they could hardly please their superiors and equals at the same time. The former would flog them for misdemeanours and the men threaten reprisals or the taff-rail. A marine disappeared at night on *Discovery* on the voyage here. There were no witnesses of course.

The lash cut again and blood flowed to his buttocks. Then the penalty was paid and the lashings were cut. He fell onto the minced wounds and the next trembling figure was pinned in place murmuring the Lord's Prayer and the cat raked her nine claws. A different flogger, a fresh executioner this time, and the boy discovered that God cannot intervene in a matter of the King's Navy. Twelve lashes for each of the five boys was the penalty and the cuts echoed from the bare yards into the peaceful bay, screams and groans mingling with the still trees and the song of the native birds; actions of the autistic, I thought, in this ambience of angels. Omai, standing to one side, pushed passed me to the rail and threw up.

Our native visitors returned in the afternoon. They showed no fear and the captain gave them more presents. About twenty stood watching us and some admired a bright jacket the captain wore. The colours were stripes that would have pleased a biblical Joseph and the natives made signs to show a great archway in the heavens. He took off the coat which he wore during the sea battle a long time back and gave it to the admirers whose gratitude could have been no greater had he actually presented them with a rainbow. The natives watched Cleveley and his men felling trees and took a hand with the cross-saw, pulling when it was their turn. They laughed with the sailors, and the scene now was a strong contrast to earlier matters.

The captains returned to the ships and the women arrived. They were escorted by a black gnome with a hunchback, much given to giggling and urination. Some came to me while I stood with James Ward and a few midshipmen. They wanted to converse, but I could not translate; they touched our hair and chests and giggled and made sounds which I took to be praise. We youths could hardly keep our eyes from their bosoms which were most pronounced. They were quite naked and we could have so easily touched them. My heart almost leaped from my chest at the presence of these talked about objects. Their hair was shorter than the men's and some had a side of the head shaved, and others the crown, resembling a friar. A soft downy hair covered their bodies, and had they been more attractive of face, I believe we would have overcome our shyness and sought favours.

Several of our people came over to see if any entertainment was available. They made gestures with their hips and offered trinkets and shirts. The native women did not appear to understand till one man took out his extended person and pointed it towards their quarters. The native men came to us hurriedly and ushered their women back to the forest. They were only just in time for one had taken an interest in this flesh, though possibly more for the offered reward of a shirt and waistcoat.

The ships were made ready for sea and the old boy invited officers and gentlemen to dinner. The chart-table was covered with a cloth and extra chairs were brought from the gunroom and *Discovery*. The captain sat at one end and Captain Clerke dominated the other.

The conversation over port turned to the women of this paradise, and it was obvious that *Discovery*'s captain was particularly grieved not to have been present when they appeared. William Bayley, the astronomer, scraped mould from a lump of cheese and announced, 'They mistook several of our young lads for women.'

'There was much touching of the hair,' I said. 'But I don't know that they could have mistaken us for girls. I might say, sir, our Mr Bayley was very watchful of the occasion.'

'Stars are not the only heavenly bodies our fine astronomer has an eye for,' Captain Clerke said.

The thin farmer-turned-scientist flushed. 'Their bodies smell very disagreeable and they have many lice sticking about their necks and other parts of the body,' he said.

'I wonder what other parts you was looking at,' Lieutenant Rickman said. As a non-Navy scientist, Bayley was available for everyone's humour.

'I don't doubt we can all guess,' Bligh said from his corner of the table. His face grimacing in lechery resembled a deformed swede. His fingers clipped at the vegetation.

'I expect fair hair fascinated them, particularly if James Ward was with you,' the old boy pronounced.

Captain Clerke smiled, sipped the port, and said, 'Most likely. As they are the possessors quite clearly of woolly hair, our type must appear very strange.'

A little later, the captain said, 'This conduct to Indian women is highly blamable.'

Bligh and Bayley had both fallen forward at the table, sleeping off excesses, and some others looked not far from it. Such is the manner of carousing in our century. 'It creates a jealousy in the men that may be attended with fatal consequences, without answering any one purpose whatever, not even that of the lover obtaining the object of his wishes. I believe it has been generally found amongst uncivilised people that where the women are of easy access . . .'

'Easy of access. I like it, sir. Cheers to the accesses!' Captain Clerke raised his glass enthusiastically, but the old boy was not to be interrupted.

'. . . the men are the first to offer them to strangers and where this is not the case they are not easily come at. Neither large presents nor privacy will induce them to violate the laws of chastity or custom. The observation will hold good, gentlemen, throughout all parts of the South Seas where I have been. Why then should men risk their own safety when nothing is to be obtained?'

'That desperate appetite for hog-eye, sir,' Clerke responded. Dr Bill, now much the worse for a malady, slowly fell forward and joined the increasing number of slumped heads, like mangel-wurzels on market day.

'A toast, sir. Here's to the Polynesian islands where the women beat the men to offer up that glorious honour.'

The old boy looked at him with a distant smile and sipped the port silently. But from those still awake, often and enthusiastic came the echoes of amen to that, dear God.

9

*O*ur coal-scuttle ships reached the other side of the world with a mixture of daring and science, the like of which had scarcely been dreamed of before. We journeyed twelve thousand sea miles to where civilised humans, as we know our mysterious species, were a stranger. People live on one side of the globe as is proper for convenience and satisfactory intercourse in trade. Dame Nature cleverly balanced our healthful spinning top by filling this side with boundless ocean. And here in the water hemisphere we were not turning back but preparing to push deeper still into the unknown. Not only would we seek Zealand, but we would pluck other coral islands from the mighty Pacific with no more than sextant and Kendall Watch Machines. And not satisfied with exercising the necessary courage to do this, we would push onwards to the very top of the world, seeking the elusive passage around the north of the Americas.

We raised anchor in Van Diemen's Land and ran straight into a white storm, another of the terrifying unknowns of this weird and inhospitable hemisphere. The rigging troubles we had experienced this far were to multiply and our chances of survival were to be reduced from bad to worse; unhappy navigation, misjudgements and tantrums were to risk the lives of every one of our expedition. And these human frailties, when added to the brutality of the elements along our route, made a miracle of any recovery for us at all. However, my advertisement is getting ahead of the narrative.

Upon leaving Adventure Bay, talk about the ship was of our proposed meeting with cannibals who had eaten some of Captain Cook's men on the second voyage. The inferior people of the ship welcomed the opportunity for some Old Testament philosophy; in the absence of culture and social discipline they were becoming little more than animals, fighting over their food like dogs, and sinking ever further into the mind's abyss for excitements for unfulfilled lusts, such as the black pit.

The narrator digresses further in the urge to whet the appetite for excitement to follow. Yet for me and my adolescence these were frightening, disorienting times and I record them in the name of honesty. Let me promptly return to our anchorage in the region of the Tired Tim natives who were unable to get up in the morning. As we weighed, the sun had still to reach the t'gallant masts and consequently the natives were not on the shore to bid us adieu.

'Steerage way, sir,' came the cry from the quartermaster, and some cheered for we had beaten *Discovery* to be under way.

The waters of the bay were levelled flat but our bank of canvas found a breeze. We looked on a prospect of perfect peace which was to be heightened in memory, for hell was about to burst upon us.

We officers were on the quarterdeck. The old boy rested those large hands on the rail as he studied the rigging; an older blue naval jacket was worn for the departure; first lieutenant John Gore stood beside him, dignified with grey hair and gaunt frame; James King and I were either side. The waist and foredeck were a swarm of industrious sailors.

'Fore t'gallant sail, if you please, Mr Williamson,' and I relayed the message to Bligh in the waist.

'Main t'gallant sail, Mr King,' the captain said quietly and the order was passed on.

A third of our swarm ascended our private forest; men covered the yards, unknotting gaskets, unfurling, shouting. The hull quietly pushed through the still water and our stuns'l booms virtually brushed trees, surprising into flight some indigenous birds. We left the land and a gentle swell took the ship and light airs found still more of the canvas. The Southern Ocean sky was a deep blue and deceivingly not broken by any white. Stamp and go! the men chanted and sails opened on the mizzen and were squared to the breeze. The woods of the land fell behind and now the trunks were not distinguishable and water seemed to stretch into the undergrowth.

I was overseeing the storing of the cable and again I heard reference from two idle lads to the black pit; I hurried them about their business and put the thought from my mind. With the cable descending into storage in a satisfactory manner, I returned to my place. The captain said, 'You might like to look to preparing the staysails, seeing's as your preference is for an urgent pace. And the sprits'l too, if you've a fancy.'

'Thank you, sir.'

The captain called over the rail, 'Stand down the off-duty watches as soon as you're clear.' Half of our cast vanished as if the captain had waved a wand and I had the quarterdeck to myself. The land was a blue mountain in the distance and staysails climbed lazily between the masts. I took up a part of the weather-rail the sun had found and relaxed in the warmth, like some domestic tabby so far away in England. Rubbing braces and sheets began a nocturne and an accompaniment was provided by shrouds creaking. Calls came from men on the jib-boom when a sheet caught and as the sprits'l was shaped beneath its yard, whistles echoed from a school of dolphins playful at the cutwater. Marvellous treatment for the ego; my ship, my man at the wheel, my watch to do my bidding and that mighty sunbathed jungle beautifully employed above. I was gentling my mind with some recitation of Gray when a look-out called 'Deck there!' in our abrupt fashion.

'What is it?' I was too comfortable to look up.

'A bit of a line squall, sir; very light though, far to weather.'

'Very good,' I said. I looked in that direction but the rich blue of the heavens stretched over the horizon. I returned to my reverie.

'Mr Williamson, sir?' Collett was climbing the quarterladder. 'Captain's compliments; he says to keep a good weather-eye as the barometer is dropping.'

I looked at the green sea, the azure above and a rusty Mother Carey's goose flapping unpoetically as is the way of these ugly sea vultures. 'Thank you, Collett,' I replied unworried.

A little later, the lookout called again. 'Squall about four miles, sir.'

A thin line of wispy cloud was all that I could see towards the weather horizon. It was good to know these boys were being attentive for squalls have spelt the end to many a sailing ship, but the strength of the gusts in our hemisphere is indicated by the blackness; the darker the more dangerous. This would be hardly a cough.

It transpired to be a white squall and as it rushed towards us, the barometer fell quickly and the temperature suddenly rose. We were all of us only beginning to feel some disquiet when the first blast struck. It tore a jib and the ominous whip-cracking of the canvas was the only harbinger for a huge rush of air.

'Helm a lee,' I shouted, perhaps even before the danger had properly reached the activity centre of my brain. 'Call all hands, master. Now. . . .'

The second gust hit our acres of canvas from the beam; it was as if a Brobdingnag giant in the sea lifted the starboard till our hull cleared the water. Men were appearing slowly, but this quake through the ship hastened their step.

'Dead down-wind,' I shouted. 'You there, put some beef into that helm.'

Three men now held the wheel and directed us off wind. The gale arrived and assaulted the ship with a scream that threatened the eardrums and our very existence. Our only hope was to put our stern to the storm while we fought to get the sail off her; the safest course in an ocean is always away from the wind.

A prolonged ripping came from the foremast and its topsail exploded into a hundred strips and smashed and cracked in the rushing air.

'All hands, all hands! Reef to forecourse.' It was a rare call on a ship which moments before had been wearing all sail. Bligh was present now and took command of the hands. Midshipmen climbed the masts with the men as sail was slowly taken in. The squall was fully storm force; to look upwind meant to risk one's eyes being drawn from their sockets. With our yards squared off to the fury, we raced across new rising waves and it seemed the helmsmen would not be able to hold her. Halyards were eased and men on the yards snatched at sagging sails.

The noise was bewildering. The captain was bellowing to be heard. I helped men at the helm; waves that crashed against the rudder jolted through the system like cannonball ricocheting to us on the wheel; burly, sweating sailors grunted with each of the blows and swore in a manner that distinguishes a seafarer. The mizzen topsail blew out with the boom of a *Victory* broadside; floggings of the loose sail were like thunder. Bligh's voice came over us and below the animals were crying in panic; a horse freed itself and galloped on the timbered 'tween-decks. Noisy confusion came from the galley where the cook was being forced to put the fire over the side. It was followed by pots of hot liquid and the offended screech of the one-legged gentleman.

'Mr Williamson!' I looked up. The captain was leaning over the quarter-rail. His face was red from shouting. 'To the mizzen, do you hear. The driver's jammed.'

A helmsman replaced me and I raced up the quarter-ladder and pushed head-down into the storm until I made the mizzenmast. This crew had brought in the torn tops'l, but the peak was jammed into the rigging and the powerful driver sail was fully set; it was giving us enormous weather-helm, trying to force the ship round.

The sheet hung from the driver-boom and flicked angrily through the waves as we roared on downwind. I had the men haul on the rope, to try to centre the boom, but the wooden peak on this triangular sail was well caught. There was only one answer; I slid across the rocking deck to the weather ratlines and my shoes slipped as I went up. Sweat sprung from my body; muscles ached as they were forced to climb and to hold on. I edged onto the yard. Now the joltings of the ship were exaggerated and to move was to invite death. At my feet the peak slammed at the yard; it chipped wood and tore canvas, and threatened to topple me into the sea. I wrapped my arms round the mizzen and kicked at it; but that did not work. I held tighter to the mast and threw both feet onto the mizzen, jumping like a child springing on its parents' bed, but it would not budge. I was exhausted; and I had to rest a moment against the timber. Then I saw the trouble; the halyard was trapped on the yard, by the flogging peak. I shouted the necessary orders to the crew below, but they could not hear me. I looked for'ard in exasperation; most of the sails were in now; five men fought at the wheel to hold the ship against this driver-sail. Jesus, I thought, and reached for a brace; I closed my eyes and forced away the fear in my stomach. I slid down the brace, hands on fire, and only stopped praying when my feet hammered onto the deck.

I gave the order, the mizzenmen heaved and the peak came clear and we hauled down the sail. A dozen men leaped onto it, overpowering the crashing canvas with gaskets, as if this were a living demon bent on our destruction.

The forecourse and only one jib remained and we drove downwind at more than ten knots. Now only two helmsmen were necessary. Exhausted crewmen stood in the lee of the forecastle and under the quarter-rail while the storm blew its vicious self out.

'Permission to set main-course and tops'ls, sir?'

The wind was down to near-gale; it was still my watch and I wanted the captain to know that my enthusiasm was not beaten by one extraordinary blow.

'Very well, young sir.' The captain looked unnerved; we had had a close brush with fate from conditions we had not previously experienced. I passed the order on to Bligh, who resembled a caveman for the wind had blown his hair from the queue and it hung greasily about his face.

The captain summoned me with a nod. 'Bedlam. Was that your home, Mr Williamson?'

'Sorry, sir?'

'Are you a lunatic, young sir? I wanted that driver off her, not a nonsense of heroics.'

'We got that sail in as quickly as possible. . . .'

'You *played* with getting that driver down. Could you not cut it off the boom and sheets and reef it on the peak?'

'It's always better to have the gaff down, sir.'

'It isn't better. You wasted time, risked my ship and lives.'

'But, sir. . . .'

'Think. That's what I expect of my officers. When I want a sail down, I want it down. Down! Do you hear? And don't let me see you running along a ruddy yard again. Nor coming down a brace, in or out of a storm.'

In the cause of honesty. A phrase I have mentioned before. When accusations are made what else can we counter with but honesty? At the end of the trial of life when the jury of the heavens is about to consider the depositions, only honesty will save us.

In the last reported incident I retrieved the damaged sail as well as I could; to tell my story honestly is to show these happenings through my eyes so that if I am judged, I can be judged fairly. Now is the time chronologically to disclose another matter which I do in the cause of honesty. I admit it does me no credit, yet I hardly ask for approbation. I seek only 'understandable in the circumstances'. I survived but, remember, so did my reason; age will make a man's psyche grow quieter, but it will not still the conscience.

So extraordinary is a voyage through the darkness of the water hemisphere that normal behaviour is not to be the yardmeasure. And in mitigation, I was very young and when I returned to my series of night watches, my little hold of stability was whisked from under my cold and continually damp feet.

The wind stayed in the south and we came back to the easterly heading. Topmen cleared the torn sail and new canvas spread like leaves in a Wiltshire spring. Capstan men sweated at their coarse and occasionally sad songs. Then the westerlies returned and blew hard and kept us at courses and occasionally main and fore topsails. We were at a new phase of the moon and none of its comforting light reached my watches.

An unearthly darkness filled those Southern Ocean nights which was too disorientating for my sensitive mind, as the cold of the gales was too sharp for my mageline coat. I came to be haunted by the shadow of the nights, particularly by the period between the watch end and when sleep came so reluctantly. The further our voyage raced in those desolate wastes the more loneliness took an unnatural hold of me. I began to prowl about the ship at night on either side of my watch. I could do so without hindrance because duty men huddled in the lee of the forecastle cold and unseeing. Where did I go on these jaunts? I would stare over the waist weather-rail at the explosions of frightening, hypnotic light beneath the ship. Sailors claimed the sight changed the mind, but I could not avoid it. My eyes desired the waterborne lightning and I would come from the blackness of my watch to feast on this kaleidoscope of unreality. Cannibals formed and dissolved in polyp pyrotechnics, ghostly shapes in a pitch pit; paps came to life and keloid scars ripped; native phalluses throbbed in black outline. And I resolved to find the black pit.

I trailed the men who spoke of it, to the heads, to the forecastle; they were inseparable and covered their spoor well. But the next evening I espied my quarry going down the companionway. Night, blackness, my hated companion, would protect me below decks for it was very dark there. I left off the clothes that would distinguish me as an officer and wore slops trousers; I did not replace my shoes in the manner of the common sailor and the deck was unbearably cold.

I went down the ladder and my men were beyond some barrels. The ship sounded a stranger to me here and the smells of mariners and sweat and ratdung were strong. Quietly, quietly and an animal sighed close upon me and I jumped, and nearly revealed my presence. I stood beside a pillar and now I could hear the men at their fun among the enclosures. One groaned in pleasure and the other pressed for a turn.

Portsmouth's repetitive Mozart whistled sadly through the bulkhead and broke the spell. I turned quickly for the companionway.

'All quiet,' James King said when I relieved his watch.

I looked at the board which was kept of our progress. It gave our course and speed; six and a half knots. I took up the weather-rail and scanned rigging and sails dutifully but little was to be seen. The moon was swallowed by our wake. Above the course-sails was only darkness. Bells chimed marking the passing of time, the passing of our little world over the great globe. The sound of the ocean roared in my ears, shapes like ghosts were beside the ship as sea fowl fished in the night. I was almost asleep inside the collar of my mageline coat when a movement startled me. A midshipman was beside me on the quarter-deck.

'Sir, it's lights, sir.'

He was consumed by a great coat. Fair curls came from a woollen hat and he looked like an eccentric blond bear cub.

'Lights?' I was returning from my inner world.

'Aye, sir, to leeward.'

I crossed the deck quickly and the *aurora australis* played beams across the sky.

'What are they, sir?'

'Southern lights, lad. The sun's shining on the ice of the South Pole. That's the reflection up there.'

It was an extraordinary picture which instead of inspiring me only magnified my instability. I thought of cosmic searchlights playing the skies of Venus for our flying ship. Lighted shafts to a black pit of space, where men from foreign planets groaned in disgusting content at a moistness promising release and I held tightly to the hand. For security, for . . . I came back as it were to earth; this young middy had taken my hand for reassurance. My body was swamped with gratitude for this little act, then I was the duty officer, irritated that the boy had let slip naval discipline; but my conscience calmed it. He was alone and lost and I knew the feeling. I let the hand go. 'How is it at your station?'

'All quiet, sir.'

I had to dismiss him from the quiet of the officers' deck back to his watch, to the premature responsibility of his rank. The blackness hinted at older hands mistreating him without a thought for his innocence. But I was a Navy officer and this was my watch; the safety of all my responsibility. 'Back to your post, lad. And make sure the fore look-out keeps his eyes skinned.'

'Aye aye, sir.'

The bells rang for the change of watch. Mr Gore crossed the foredeck. 'All quiet, Mr Williamson?' His breath was musty from sleep.

'Aye aye, sir. The ship handles well in this gale under our present canvas. There was an aurora . . .' but I did not want to say more.

'Fine, fine. Stand your watch down, young sir.'

I did not look at the fire in the sea. I took off my fearnought trousers, breeches underneath and stockings and changed into thick clothes I saved for bed; the warmer I was the better the chance of sleep. I pulled damp blankets over my head and prayed for peace. The hull returned the noise of an angry sea, but the sounds which reached me were pure masculine lust; delivering oneself to a masturbatory machine with unquestioning cogs of concupiscence.

I could not stay away. The deck was cold and wet with night. I flattened against the side of the bulwark when Gore's feet sounded; then I heard him at the weather-rail; I hurried to the companionway. I descended into the warm, stale air of sleeping men and animals and a rat ran from under my bare foot. I held back a cry. The dull light from the companionway helped me get bearings, and I moved swiftly to the direction of what I could not hold myself from. My hand found the pillar I leaned against earlier and warmth reached out from the King's animals. I went towards the pen as sure-footed as if lanthorns were lighted here. I feel what I know will respond to my touch. Whiskered wetness and I am eager to work this instrument, but the picture of an ambitious officer is before my eyes and I see him shamed, disrated and flogged before the people. I want to do this; the sounds of suckling come from my fingers which the vacuum has taken up.

A noise, a footfall; my heart leaps and I pull back. At the pillar, in the pitch, I make out a form going to the pen. Then a creature stirs and quickly comes a half-broken stifled cry. Which I recognise. I dash forward and grab and the boy is terrified. I drag and push him up to the deck where we appear to weather, away from the duty watch. I am torn by conflicts. I want to hurl him over the side; the deceit of that countenance of innocence! The shock to my heart that one so scarcely formed should know and practise such degradation. And the torment of my own hunger. We stand together at the cathead; he is holding my hand warmly, reassuringly again and we stare like two lost souls at the blackness of our future. Then a torment throbs, pushing for attention. I am unbuttoned and overwhelmed by the excruciating pain of anticipated pleasure. My heart booms at enormous speed, deafeningly, and I can't breathe. These words come through my head and are repeated like a martyr's prayer to a pyre:

> Far from the madding crowd's ignoble strife,
> Their sober wishes never learned to stray;
> Along the cool sequester'd vale of life
> They kept the noiseless tenor of their way.

I know what I am doing is wrong, but I cannot resist. A sudden heat of his attention and I cry tears of remorse mixed with my metre of Gray and conduct the vital cadence with hands round the woollen hat of my pretty fatted calf.

10

*T*he darkest time, they say, is about an hour before twilight, the herald for that vast deceiving promise orbiting these watery undrinkable wastes. I shivered in slops trousers, shirt and jersey waiting for the cot blankets to lose their dead man's touch while half-dreaming of bluebells in an English dell.

My attention rushed suddenly back to the cabin; the door was opening. My heart leaped and I cursed that my sword should be on the rack outside. I strained over the drumming of the pulse for another sound and told myself I had to be mistaken. Then a restrained breathing came from the doorway; a new cold current opened onto my freezing feet. Jesus! What a place to be trapped. I panicked for a plan; I thought I would leap from the bed with fists clenched as a battering ram, smash at the intruder, then try to reach Simon Harvey's razor-sharp workmanship with its engraving of a hunting wolf. A perfume came on the draught.

'Omai, what on earth?'
'Ssh; you'll wake the others.'
'What do you want?'
'Can I come in?'
'I'll light a candle.'
'No, no, I don't want you to see me like this.'
'Like what?'
'I've come to say goodbye.'
'Start again, you've lost me.'
'Ssh, can I come in?'

The door closed quietly; my cot sagged as he sat and my heart still beat rapidly. At least fear had despatched the cold.

'Where are you going?'
'It's no good; I can't go on. I'm afraid to.'
'Oh.'
'Don't you want to know why?'
'Yes, I'd very much like to know. What about over lunch?'
'But Johnny. . . .'
'I've just come off watch and I'm tired and. . . .' I tried to sound callous, as much as one can when whispering, for a suspicion groped with a clammy claw. I regretted my own recent indiscretions; I was determined they would not happen again. I was a man, and I was not interested that way in my gender, scented or sweaty.

'It doesn't take long to say goodbye.'
'Omai, save it for the morning.'
'Goodbye.'
'*Haere ra*,' I said in Maori and the bed moved; I heard the door close.

Damn, damn, damn, I cursed to the shirt I use for a pillow. Damn and blast conscience, and I leaped out of bed and flung open my door. The gunroom was equally as dark and I walked into Omai, I collided with his face; he had been crying; the wetness of his cheeks smudged against me. His arms came round my neck and he hugged me; his body was extraordinarily hot. He shuddered with silent sobs, and his tears must have been waterfalls for they soaked through my jersey and shirt. I thought, Jesus, if someone comes along now with a candle, we're going to look a fine sight. 'Come into the cabin, for God's sake.'

He obeyed like a child, sniffing back sufficient tears to drown: he tried to climb into bed, but I said no. I took my rightful place and left him sitting on the side. The room was without any light; I thought I could distinguish his silhouette. On deck night watch-mates assume a completely distorted outline; Omai, I imagined, was a huge, sweet-smelling gorilla.

'Now what's up?'
'Please hold me, John.'
'Omai,' I tried, but it was easier to oblige this indulgence than explain in whispers diplomatically that I was not of the persuasion. I put my arms around him; the back was wide and muscular; the gorilla head was enormous on my shoulder; I was sitting up in bed, feeling again hot tears soaking through clothes I went to enormous trouble to keep dry.

'They hate me, John.'
'Who do?'

'Everyone.'
'Not everyone.'
'Yes they do.'
'Poor old Omai,' I said, and the body shuddered again and heavier showers fell.
'I don't want to go to Tahiti.'
'You're a case for Bedlam, my friend. It's your home; you'll love it when we get there.'
'They'll kill me.'
'Would the captain let someone kill you? Would any of us, for that matter?'
'Let me go home, John.'
'We're taking you there.'

He pulled away abruptly. His breath burned my face. 'No, my home is England,' he corrected. 'To London. I'm not a savage any more. I'm . . .', and his sobs took away his speech for a moment, '. . . I'm a gentleman; the king said so. He said, Omai, you are a real gentleman, and he said, you're more of a gentleman than many who have been about me all their lives. He said that to me, John.'

Omai spoke with naive passion and small hot spits, like the arrows of Lilliput fired with each word; he must be trying to stare into my eyes in this pitch. His arms came back to my shoulders: the gorilla became coquettish and I imagined the head at an angle, eyes wide, imploring. The king gave him a suit of armour: a suit of armour, can you believe it, Johnny? Boy, what will the natives say when they see that. Oh, Johnny, my clothes; such a wardrobe; what colour and style I will bring to my people. Aaah, it makes you think; they'll never be the same again. The envy I will generate among those ignorant peasants. You'll see, Johnny. And so Omai went on and sleep nearly took me. Then his arms tightened, his whisper was loud.

'Guns, Johnny, I've got some guns; the savages won't be able to take my things. I'll shoot the buggers first, I promise you.' There was a pause and the arms were gentle again. 'And what do you think of the steed King George gave me, eh? How will gentleman Omai look on that prancing around his island domain?'

His head was heavy on my shoulder; he was giggling quietly and as quickly the tears returned. 'But I can't stay on the frigging horse. I keep slipping off.'

'There there,' I said and patted that huge hairy mantle.

Omai cried and my back gradually gave way to the tiredness; slowly we fell and soon this unhappy being pressed down on my chest, heavy dampened perfume at my nostrils, rain soaking through unchecked.

'That's why I'm going, Johnny,' he was whispering. 'The tafferel-rail; it's so easy.'

'Poor old Omai,' I whispered.

'I'm scared, Johnny.'

'We all are.'

When I woke Omai was gone, but the puddles remained. Hell, I thought, and ran to his cabin. No reply came to my knock and I rushed out through the empty gunroom for the deck. Omai was beside the wheel, in the lee of the quarterdeck, eyes downcast in a suit of rusty velvet, manicuring elegant nails. An enormous floppy-brimmed hat kept the Tasman sun from his creamed complexion: a picture of crazy incongruity on this man of war, and I returned to my cabin, to dress with a happy heart.

Every ten days I would pay my respects to the wretched captain of the galley, and in return for lending a sympathetic ear to his health I was allowed a corner of his fire to make muffins. I brought the ingredients from London, replenished them at Good Hope and now had only sufficient flour for one last batch. Usually I would gorge myself in the galley and retire below to undergo the painful, worthwhile ordeal of digestion.

'How's our fine chef this day?'

'You is it, Mr Williamson?'

'There's a rosy colour to the cheeks, my good man.' As may be observed, I would stoop to any embellishment to be allowed my pleasure.

'Not feeling up, at all. But there'd be no letting you in here for even a moment; I'm too busy.'

I sought the cause of his unwell-being; he leaned against the lee bulkhead, hands resting against the equally filthy apron, attacking the lack of professionalism of Doctors Anderson and Samwell, and I mixed the dough and toasted muffins to near perfection.

'No butter left, I suppose?'

'Not even to grease the smallest pan,' he said, a chipped wooden leg crossed over the gout-distorted good one, like a relaxing shire and not smelling so dissimilar. 'Carpenter used the last on the sheets and the like. Went completely ranc-kid before Van Diemen's Land.'

'A new landfall tomorrow, chef.'

'That so, young sir? Zealand and the cannibals it must be then.'

'I wanted to butter the muffins; you see, they're for a friend who's down today.'

'Not like you to give 'em away: there's a bit of dripping in a tin o'er there.'

I scraped where the cockroach tracks were thinnest: I presented the two toasted treats to Omai on the waist, bowing in a grand flourish. 'My lord,' I mimicked our chef's gravelly Cornish, 'a little treat with the third lieutenant's compl-y-ments.'

Zealand came over the horizon like a young lizard, hiding occasionally beneath its white sleeping cover of long cloud. We passed from the deep blue of the ocean over the continental shelf and the water sparkled like the gems they call greenstone. The land and this coastal water contained a magic that had my heart racing. It even returned enthusiasm to the sailors, an energy they are normally strangers to.

Strain etching the captain's face eased as his eyes welcomed the greenness of this glowing land; he hummed the bass to the sailors' songs that fell heavily from the rigging. We entered the wide channel between the two major islands of the group, close to Te Waka a Maui; the verdant sisterland was a display of sharp mountains and thick woods carved from polished jade.

'Well,' he said with an unusually reluctant tone, 'here we go.'

The helmsman pulled the wheel to starboard and we pushed into a long fiord. A young fresh land jutted Irish shades on either hand; the mountains were as sharp as sea over shallows; none of the roundedness of the hills of old England was to be found here. Michael Portsmouth signalled the men to quarters and gangs of crewmen stripped the aft-cabin, sending the furniture, the wall and the door down deep into the guts of the ship. Hammocks were handed up from below, tightly rolled in the traditional way and packed into the re-erected hammock-nets and marines took up positions behind them. Boys now employed as powder monkeys carried fresh charges onto the waist and the equipment for battle was made ready behind the four-pounders; cutlasses and muskets were counted off and rested in barrels for the gunners; sailors working capstan and the running rigging put swords into their belts.

The marines lieutenant and sergeant climbed into the tops and the cook swore loudly as his galley fire was put over the side, sizzling as the coals sank. The great guns were loaded and run out in what sounded like a legion marching through Scaean Gate.

We were entering the land of the cannibals and the gruesome thought of these English flesh-eaters brought an anxious silence upon the ship. We eased deeper into the fiord and the entrance fell in the distance.

'Stand by with the bower, Mr Bligh.'

'Cleared away and standing by, sir.'

The trees of the forest were dark green and trunks stood tall and firm like the legs of a Zulu army. Ferns shone silver from the forest floor; grass grew high in clearings and our animals, disregarding the nervous disposition of the men, smelt it and called. But there was not a sign of the natives, of the tribes under the warring Kahura who had wiped out and consumed ten sailors of the second voyage.

The leadsman called the fathoms from the main-chains and the bottom of the sounds came up.

'Helm a-lee, quartermaster,' the old boy called. 'The canvas off her, if you please, Mr Bligh.'

Resolution came slowly round on her length, the wind catching us on the beam and going forward. The breeze pushed before the sails which topmen were taking in. Halyards eased, the strain taken up, and yards were lowered.

'Avast there with the lead.'

'Boats cleared away, ready to launch.'

'Stand by gun-crews.'

'Mr Bligh, launch the boats. But be ready to retrieve them if necessary.'

'Let's have the pinnace first, Mr Mate.'

The captain leaned over the quarter-rail. 'Omai, I would recommend alternative attire if you wish to go ashore. Should you happen to come out of the boat, it'd be difficult to raise you from the seabed.'

'Boats launched and ready, sir.'

The sun glinted on the smooth visor as armour-clad Omai clunked back to his cabin.

'Lieutenant Phillips? What do you see?'

'Not so much as the hair of a child, sir,' the marine commander answered from the main-top.

'Have half your detachment come to shore with us.'

'Aye, aye, sir.'

The marines chosen to go ashore looked pale and those of us to remain on board needed no reminder to stay alert; we expected a multitude to come screaming from the bush at any moment.

The oars cut the surface and the party headed quickly for a clearing used on the last voyage. They almost reached the shore when Lieutenant Phillips called, 'Native canoes sir. Larboard quarter.'

Eyes strained across the fiord; the dug-outs resembled three fat caterpillars coming swiftly for us. Our launches heard the cry and were quickly turned about and *Discovery*'s cutter headed back to her. The men came over the caprail in an orderly enough fashion, but faces did not disguise their fear.

'Resume quarters, Mr Bligh. Lieutenant Phillips, have your men on deck fix bayonets.'

Bligh was shouting forward, 'Midshipman there, stand by with those boarding nets.'

'Mr Gore, signal *Discovery* to hold fire.'

The old boy turned his attention to the ship. 'Mr Bligh, I'll have quiet from the men.'

Bligh shouted and the ship became silent. 'They lost another marine overboard from *Discovery*, sir,' James said quietly.

'How so?'

'It happened not far from Van Diemen's Land; he just disappeared in the night.'

'Did we know him?'

'George Moody. He was a marine private, one of those who got drunk on shore. A good racquets player, too.'

The captain was silent as he studied the canoes, now a hundred yards off and approaching much more slowly. 'Hmm, sad business, Mr King.'

Oh, that I had the gift of an artist for this is the precise moment I would choose to paint my portrait of Captain Cook. It was I think the last moment of his exalted ascendancy. The sun has to fall after its noon height and so no less does a man. I looked at him straight from the fury of the Southern Ocean at this peaceful anchorage, with enemy hoving into sight. This, I fancied, was what the old boy was really about. The explorer, discoverer, circumnavigator; friend of humanity and fighting captain. An olive branch in the scarred hand, a batch of four-pounders primed in case. He was in his element. Our Father relaxed and we his charges were tense, frightened even, at quarters, yet confident he would bring us through.

The newspapers report Dr Johnson, the monarch, Gray and Voltaire. Our captain was too often at sea to dominate the columns; for me, here was the most remarkable man of the century. Splendid in second-best uniform; erect, big hands behind him, huge coat of blue with gold edging, passably clean white breeches hanging loosely from a stomach exceptionally trim for a man near fifty in our corpulent age. Hair still thick and taken back to a grey queue. The nose dominating manly features, wide eyes, a fresh shaving cut; a hint of the unsmiling southern snob as he studied the canoes, and I wondered if he was thinking exclusively of the Maoris or was there room in there for poor Moody who screamed when his back was skinned, who abandoned the loneliness of an impossible role?

The change we were to see in the captain was beginning; he had been slapped in the face too often by a world he was increasingly disappointed by: were he a Gaul or Don, he would have been an admiral after the first voyage; this was his third marathon peregrination and petty jealousies kept his rank at post-captain. Even the savages treated his openness and good intentions with treachery. He had given these Zealand people presents, his heart and his trust, but when his back was turned they ate his children. I think that even as he looked down on the brown men coming alongside, his mind was undergoing a change. Here they were at last, cannibals who could chew and swallow the flesh of humans, his sailors. Was there anything more vile and incomprehensible to an explorer? Perhaps another cog turned towards distress as he looked at friends turned fiends.

'Mr Williamson,' he said. 'Wish them a good day from us and the King of England.'

Brown countenances stared up sullenly as the boat slowly passed along the length of *Resolution*. They were young men and spiral face tattoos helped disguise expression. I called, but they did not respond. A second and the third canoe followed the same course and remained silent. Few weapons were to be seen in the dug-outs, so we could feel confident that their intentions were not entirely warlike.

'This is very strange,' the captain said. 'I recognise many of the natives, and I'm sure they must recognise me.'

'They must, sir,' James said. 'That older fellow in the third canoe. You showered him with presents on the last visit. What's his name?' He turned to Omai, standing in the shadow of the mizzen, and then to me, but neither of us had been in these beautiful sounds before.

The captain asked Omai to address them. 'Conversing with primitives is not really me,' he said in a most affected, piqued air. 'I mean, look at them; half-naked, dirty, tattooed.'

Omai's blue waistcoat, snow-white shirt and yellow breeches established him firmly on the side of civilisation, yet we had let him taste only enough to catch the colour of the leisured dandies, but not sufficient time to acquire judgement, to learn the briefest outline of our new agriculture nor the sciences. Yet this blaze of little-learning was going back to dirt floors and ignorant ways and the idea appalled him. Here he was, one-to-one with fate; he had stumbled unawares upon an honest looking-glass and was suffering a shocked double-take: a Polynesian looked back, the savage he had been and would be again.

'Obviously, James, they want no part of an official chat and I can't say I'm sorry,' Omai said, searching a sleeve for a perfumed handkerchief at which he took an exaggerated inhalation. 'I suppose I could try a private parley.' The rainbow walked to the taff-rail and let an English expletive drop from the transom; he waved for the canoes to come closer and reluctantly spoke in his own tongue.

He told them that we were not here to harm them, but came only in friendship. A voice from a canoe called back that they believed the captain came to avenge the cannibalised sailors. But they, these people of the canoes, were not responsible and if desired would gladly assist in the hunting down of the tyrant Kahura. Omai reported back to the captain.

The old boy snapped his telescope closed. 'Tell them I will think over the matter of their help, but in the meantime I would like to renew friendships. Ask them to come on board.'

A silence came from the canoes while this message was digested and then they were as children summoned for a scolding but given sweets.

The natives came up the side-cleats in such haste that the canoes were left hitting the ship untethered. They stood on the upper deck and a welcome *haka* was performed with the men leaping into the air. It was my first view of an authentic war dance and I knew why certain tantrums were so named. The leader of the party pressed his fat nose against the captain's and several of us had to undergo the odoriferous experience. The natives giggled, touched our uniforms, admired fittings around the mizzen and gave many assurances of assistance should we need it. We were at peace.

Grass was cut for the animals and brought back to the ships and great industry began on shore; wooding, watering, brewing spruce beer and melting oil from Kerguelen seal blubber. We were at quarters through that first night, but no attack occurred and the following day the ships returned to normal. Mr Bayley's observatory was set up on shore and a garrison established. Carpenter Cleveley was set to work with his mates on repairs and gathering new spars and the evocative odour of sawn timber hung deliciously on the air.

Word passed among the savages of the fiord that Captain Cook was not here for revenge, *utu* in their tongue, and hordes came out of the bush like army ants on the march. Whole families appeared on shore, jabbering among themselves for places on dug-outs. They wanted to inspect the great canoes which sailed from an unknown part of an unknown world, directed here by the good King George, the pakehas' paramount chief.

A settlement grew like Middlesex mushrooms on shore as natives erected makeshift huts so they could be present for the length of our visit. But friendship was not their only object; they were here to make money, or for what to them was currency. In all of Polynesia, a hunger for iron was more urgent than our desire for gold. They remembered that Captain Cook's men were a lusty lot and they brought forward their courtesans, gawdily painted and noisomely scented. When the act was finished were the girls female spiders who supped on their mates? So our men feared and, not having the natural enquiry of scientists, they were robbed of desire.

In our gay London it is a courageous soul who looks askance at the wares parading Poland Street, and so here the refusal to buy the women caused distress among the traders and prices quickly tumbled, even if the sailors would not. However, tempers were restored when natives discovered a market existed for another easy commodity, food, particularly fresh fish. Courtesans wiped off the greasepaint and took up rod and line with the pimps for a hooking of a different sort.

The old boy planned to show the cannibals mercy which is a characteristic of our thinking age. He would pardon the murderers, but he wanted an enquiry into the affair and the matter recorded. Five boats left the ships and we rowed the leagues along the fiord till we arrived at Grass Cove.

I could prate on the sinister darkness of the inlet, the twitching of hair at the back of our necks, at the odour of wickedness that clung to the vegetation of this dreaded location. Yet I fear such a narration cannot be made, as honesty is the first aim of our disturbing history. No, the scene would have been a perfect luncheon spot for the middle class of our capital who set off in post-chaise for repastment taken among idyllic surroundings. Native bush pressed down to a wide bank of lush pastures; a beach of golden sand fell gradually, lazily, to the clear still azure. Birds sang with the chimes of bells and our people came out of the boats and took seats on the lawn, their rich colours adding much to the brilliance of the setting. Two old men were summoned from a local tribe to give evidence; yet as they unfurled their tale, it was almost impossible to believe that scenes of such loathing to the civilised mind could have taken place here.

Our main witness was one Pedro, an old fellow of sagging brown skin and legs of protruding bone. He was known to the captain from his previous voyage, but when the old boy ran from the pinnace to *hongi*, the said witness and his equally elderly friend pulled back; they believed they had been called for execution. I was required to use my most persuasive Polynesian to have them understand we wished no harm. But it was the presents that Captain Cook gave that turned the look of fear to an expression of cunning friendship. As was to be seen, and more often than just in Zealand, charity inspired by conscience was interpreted in a very different way.

'Old friend, Pedro,' I translated when the hearing began. 'King George of England is most desirous of knowing the truth of the unhappy circumstances of this cove. He has said to me, ask our trusty friend Pedro for the truth of the matter, as I know him to be an honest gentleman who would not himself have been involved in the wicked proceedings.'

The captain's words had little regard for my elementary Maori and the translation, one ought to admit, did not emerge in quite the way the ears received them. However, I have noticed that their orators, when struggling for words, use the term *mea*, thingummy, to get them by. Suffice to say that *mea* was offered several times that afternoon.

Omai occasionally challenged a word of mine, for his Tahitian was very close to this dialect. But our colourful translator had retired among the spectators; the odour of our unwashed witnesses had the better of him, he confessed.

'Ra was in this position when the tragic circumstances of which we speak occurred,' I relayed. Pedro's arm pointed to the sky well to the west so we realised the time was late afternoon. The victims were members of the sister ship *Adventure*: it is sufficient for this anecdote to say that *Adventure* became parted from *Resolution* in thick fog and came to this prearranged rendezvous. 'The ship's people arrived at this cove by boat to collect grass. At this time, they had stopped to take victuals while around them sat the people of the chief Kahura.' The old fellow's voice lowered and he looked not unlike a starving ferret about to attack. 'Now one of the watchers stole some bread and fish. The thief was punched by a sailor and this upset Kahura who immediately began to argue.'

His voice was raised now and an arm held up, fist clenched. 'You know, captain, and through you King George, that the tempers of men are not harbours of reason and soon a musket was fired and then a second.' He used the term bangstick. 'One of Kahura's people fell and he was dead before he reached the ground we now repose upon. Hands reached out for another musket, men struggled to hurriedly insert death into the sticks.'

His account proceeded apace and the men sat forward, eyes wide as their ears, as if we expected to witness the fatal folly of such rashness by a hopelessly outnumbered group. 'The fighting men of the murderous Kahura did not give the visitors a chance. They jumped upon the sailors and brought down their cudgels on the heads of men trying desperately to reload muskets. One screamed, his head split wide and the fleshy matter therein pummelled to nothingness. Then another was killed and the screaming of the assaulted and dying men became fainter as increasing numbers succumbed.'

Pedro strutted with the gait of a victorious chief, little different from the winner of a cockfight, flax sandals shining in the place of silver razor-sharp spurs. 'Here was where lay the crew, their lives expired. And over there,' and he pointed to a place perhaps two hundred yards away, 'was where their small vessel was pulled up on the beach. Guarding it, his eyes wide with terror, stood the servant of the captain, a very-black.' This term was for a Jamaican and there were many in the Royal Navy. The servant's chances of escape would have been minimal, for the Maoris feared darker people. Their aristocrats, who doubtlessly instilled this prejudice in their subjects, were light-skinned. Pedro stopped. Silence followed, save for the gentleness of the water touching the sand, the birds of the trees and a distant chorus of cicadas. Pedro's companion now climbed uncertainly onto scarecrow legs and took this proscenium.

His voice came in a wild accusation and it was a moment before my ear could tune to the toothless pronunciation and begin translating. 'He was the cause of it!' The mouth was a virulent vulgar pit and an accusative finger pointed at the place where the ship's boat had rested. 'He, the very-black, for they come from darkness.' His hand came down and he moved painfully a few steps; then began his dialogue. 'You see, one of the natives stole something from the boat.' He stopped abruptly and it appeared he was trying to remember what item, but the aged mind would not oblige; he shook his head impatiently; *mea* would do. 'Upon being discovered by the very-black, the native struck at the servant with a stick he carried and knocked him down.' This statement he quoth in dramatic strength and while he restored his breath, I looked towards the seated Pedro, expecting a correction. But it seemed their histories are recalled not so much in the cause of honesty, but with a view to the orators' arts, thus making the work of the chronicler most enervating.

'Now the servant called in a terrible voice. Hoy! Hoy! I am struck to death by this thief and the pale ones rushed to the aid of the very-black. But at this Kahura's men pounced on the sailors and struck them down before they could arm themselves or flee in the canoe-of-the-ship. They fell a sacrifice to savage fury.'

The speaker was done; he looked spent and a stillness hung upon the people of the hearing.

Captain Cook pushed himself up onto his feet and addressed the men. 'This is not the first variation we have heard of the tragic events that unfurled here. There is however one distinct point which arises each time.' He illustrated this singularity with a large carved finger which wagged several times in agreement and then smartly hid in a pocket. 'The quarrel first took its rise from some thefts which the natives committed. All agree also that the thing was not premeditated, and if the thefts had not unfortunately been too hastily resented, no ill consequence would have attended.'

(With the power of hindsight, oh! but how prophetic were to be these words which I precisely recorded of the captain then.)

The pleasant Dr Anderson stood now, a gaunt man, dressed in a terminal mask of age despite his years. 'My understanding of the affair was that Kahura called a considerable number of his fellows to the spot after the trouble began. Two muskets were discharged but it seems that the other arms were in the launch. The natives rushed in among the sailors and killed some on the spot. But I believe the others not immediately. However, the man in the boat, the negro servant, was the last victim of their rage.'

We sat quietly on the edge of our nerves, listening to the crisp, educated voice. He said slowly, 'He must have felt the most horrid sensations on seeing his companions murdered without the least hopes of giving them assistance or delaying his own fate.'

The denouement: early the following morning, a boat from *Adventure* searched for the missing people: Kahura and his tribe were discovered in this cove picnicking on the fallen shipmates.

The final of the racquets competition was played in the Sounds and I discovered that Captain Clerke, the originator of the sport in the ships, was indeed undeniable champion. I found too that our simple rules had multiplied greatly during the play-offs, so indefatigable is man in writing laws with which to fetter himself.

'Out!' called Lieutenant Rickman, one of two umpires now required by the regulations.

'Sorry, sir,' I said. 'But I've returned it as required. Surely Captain Clerke should have hit it.'

'Change in the rules,' Captain Clerke said. 'When served, the spherical must cross the tarred line.'

'Why didn't you strike it over?' Captain Cook accused from the sideline.

'I didn't know about it, sir.'

'Didn't you tell him, Charles? Look, I'll not have underhand tricks played against *Resolution*. The rule's dismissed. I declare in favour of Mr Williamson.'

'Of course, sir,' Lieutenant Rickman hurriedly conceded.

But I was no competition for Captain Clerke, who took the championship as he had at Fleet Prison. Two sets were sufficient, Captain Cook ruled, for he would not have *Resolution* sullied by obvious skulduggery. Afterwards, as we stood beside the arena to get our breathing back to normal, I said Captain Clerke deserved to win.

'I have had a good deal more practice.' He turned to Captain Cook. 'You left Plymouth and I was still in debtors' prison and I was beginning to think they had swallowed the key.'

'Your brother's debts, I know,' I said politely. 'Well, it's common knowledge about the ships that you were guarantor for your brother and when he sailed with the fleet, commerce pounced most unfairly upon you, upon an officer of the Royal Navy. I suppose this sport in prison eased your fury and frustration.'

'You see, gentlemen, the gaoler himself was racquets champion, a very proud cuss despite his trade; he could not abide being beaten. I could hardly afford to bribe my way out so I practised night and day until I beat him easily. He was livid; he'd never lost in three years. On the following days, I trounced him time and again and he just couldn't take it. He let me appear to escape.'

'I don't believe a word of it,' our commander said. 'But you could try to persuade my officer and me, perhaps with some refreshment in your aft cabin.'

When the cutter returned us to *Resolution*, Captain Cook said, 'Avoid debt, young Williamson; you can see it does strange things to a man.'

11

The fate of the butchered crew at the Cove underscored our problems with Polynesians: misunderstanding could cost us very dear. The English (your Roman-Saxon-Danish-Norman-English, as Defoe would have us) have always been a people for pigeon-holing personalities and these South Seas fellows did not fit conveniently into our slots. We needed an archetype of the region, but they were all so damnably different. On the one hand we had Omai who with a short exposure to civilisation changed character and in his manners was indistinguishable from many Britons. We had orators like Pedro who, on recounting the tale of the loathsome affair, strutted proudly like the beast Kahura even though he knew that we, the audience, held the subject to be detestable. We had the canoe people who came bravely close although they expected us to open fire in revenge and when saved offered to help us track down the cannibal chief. We had . . . we had problems.

We puzzled the Maoris and later the others of Polynesia with our strange conduct; our intelligence barred us from turning superior weaponry onto them. But they took this to be a lack of desire for revenge. And this 'failing' of ours was as despicable to them as were many of their customs tc us. We were hell-bent on a course of disaster, but as Captain Cook's prophetic words showed, we did not realise it. Where ignorance is folly, 'twould be bliss to be wise!

The riddle of the massacre and the enigma of the Maoris themselves exercised the minds of the officers and was well aired when we next met, which was at the captain's table. The subject of the slaying was introduced by the old boy in conversation with Dr Bill: 'You know, the unhappy victims could have had no comprehension of their impending fate, otherwise they would never have sat down to a repast so far from their boat among people who the next moment were to be their butchers.'

'Absolutely, captain.'

'Kahura's greatest enemies, those who solicited his destruction the most – and there were many of these – owned that he had no intention to quarrel and much less to kill till the argument actually commenced.'

The dinner fare was exceptional. A cultivation left by the previous voyagers remained unharmed and our pig was complemented with onions, parsley, cabbage and, to David Samwell's great and expressed joy, leeks. This night greater discipline was required for our practice of politely keeping forks poised and waiting while the captain talked.

'While I was writing up the report of the evidence, sir,' I said, 'I was struck by the thought that we must ever be on our guard with these people.'

William Bligh snorted. 'Take that philosophy to its conclusion, sir, and we would find ourselves fearing our own shadows, would we not.'

'You're both correct,' Dr Bill said in his encouraging tones, 'but only because, Mr Bligh, you agree with Mr Williamson. You see, the Polynesians consider the bodies of their chiefs as sacred. An accidental brush from a commoner can have the most serious consequences. So we must be on our guard from these people and from our own shadows of ignorance. The more I dwell on the affairs of Grass Cove, you know, the more I feel it likely that when the argument occurred, the first assault was upon Kahura. It may have been no more than a push, but were that the case, gentlemen, the fate of the whole party would have been sealed.' He stopped to blow a cool breath on some cabbage. 'We must tread warily with these natives, no matter how friendly they appear disposed to us. They may haggle with us, Dr Samwell, over the price of their young nymphs, but their customs are completely unbending.'

The old boy's jaws clicked as he ate, a certain sign that he was digesting the conversation as well, particularly the opinions of the senior surgeon, for Dr Bill was possibly the best thinker of our complement. The captain did not agree entirely with the assessment and this, I think, was a significant clue to his change. Despite the provincial prejudices often to be found from those of the north, the captain had not been one previously for self-delusions, but now he would see only that the natives' friendship was genuine. Those with the slightest grasp of the language knew they were laughing at us: we were weak with them; we would not argue much over market prices for fear of giving offence, we would not take revenge because of our civilised thinking; if they begged us for a gift, we could not refuse them. These opposed their own attitudes. I explained this to the captain but received only a *haka* in return. I went further and told him that they charged us with the most unmanly behaviour for not avenging the deaths of our eaten comrades. He refused to accept it and when *Discovery*'s neural first lieutenant suddenly raised this similar topic, his appetite lessened while his temperature increased.

Mr Burney was talking to David Samwell and the preceding remarks were lost in the noise of unrestrained dining. 'They often appear to have a great deal of friendship, speaking sometimes in the most tender, compassionate tone of voice imaginable.'

The large nose to the left of my vision turned to this conversation, expecting to hear more of a view that coincided with his own. 'But it not a little disgusted one,' the lieutenant continued, 'to find all this show of fondness constantly ended in begging.'

Collett moved among us collecting plates with the solemnity of a parson taking in prayer books and Mr Burney fell silent. I watched the captain. He tried to withdraw from his eavesdropping; his displeasure with the conversation's about-turn showed clearly, but he could not help himself. 'If gratified with their first demand,' Mr Burney said, condemnation sounding firmly around the wine, 'they would immediately fancy something else, their expectations and importunities increasing in proportion as they were indulged.' Hirsute nostrils added their support and the edges raised slowly in a sneer.

William Bligh pushed into the conversation. 'That is far from my experience with natives, Mr Burney. It always seems to me that firmness in dealing with. . . .'

'Firmness, for frig's sake, Bligh. I'm talking of supposed friendships. We have instances of them quarrelling after having begged three things because a fourth was denied them.'

Bligh smiled condescendingly with his gift of winning enemies. 'Perhaps their attitude is different towards the escorting vessel.'

The patronising jest pushed Mr Burney into a temper. 'It seems evident that many hold us in great contempt and I believe chiefly on account of our not avenging the affair of Grass Cove, so different would have been their own response.'

'Mr Burney,' prompted Captain Clerke quietly across the table, for he could see our commander was looking increasingly unhappy with these sentiments.

Mr Burney's nose resembled a firing double-barrel musket and he aimed it across the table at his captain. But he either had not heard him or chose not to, for he could guess that the famous Clerkean oil for troubled water was about to flow; Mr Burney was a young man and scathe now, soothe later seemed a better philosophy. 'Another cause could be that they get from us so many valuable things for which we are regarded as dupes to their superior cunning. And as example of how little they respect us, one man did not scruple to acknowledge his being present and eating *Adventure*'s people.' His eyes were brown dishes as they came round the table, staring into the minds of each diner to see if we understood the evil crime of these natives only a few hundred yards off; whether we realised that they mocked us for not striking back *as gentlemen*.

Captain Cook would not accept the enquiry; instead he was on the point of offering an unwelcome entertainment, the quarterdeck *haka*. But Captain Clerke came to the rescue, as perhaps only he could. 'Mr Burney, you should say this is how you feel *at times*. You, me, Mr Williamson, Mr Gore; we are all men first and officers second and when men's passions are roused we do not always think positively. We forget two vital factors which make us different from the Indians.'

He was speaking so softly we had almost to strain to hear over the noises of the night; the watch moving about, an argument among some Maoris on shore, Portsmouth's penny-whistling. 'Our education has us carrying a word in our hearts – conscience. And this amorphous presence stops us from cutting down these ignorant brown men. From our education comes intelligence from which springs the word, responsibility. We have to be responsible and act with our conscience and not slaughter these natives as ignorance or unenlightenment demands.' We remained quiet while Captain Clerke took the bottle of port, slowly filled his glass and handed it on. 'We, the gentlemen of the Royal Navy, set the standards and follow them through. We are never guided – and should try very hard not be be affected – by the ideals of savages.'

This was the eighteenth century; people of breeding do not applaud at the theatre and similarly we could not here. But the hush that followed was packed with silent approval.

A little later Captain Cook said, 'We must, you know, live by our civilised principles no matter how much pressure there is to let them go by the board.'

12

*T*he day the waterspout bore down in fury on our tethered ships, we were resetting topmasts and gallants after a vicious storm. Our anchorage in that fiord looked idyllic, but treacherous tempests roaring along the narrow strait between the islands confounded us with demonic windshifts. Captain Cook took great care in choosing the best of moorings but the weather here challenged his skill.

To keep the ships from being driven ashore and wrecked we struck the yards and gradually all hamper above until we were stripped to the girtline. It was dangerous work for the weight of the wind threatened to hurl men from the rigging; the tempest screamed through the night and all hands were kept on watch. Then in the morning, the gale suddenly diminished to calm and I supervised the setting up of masts and rigging.

The men began the chore with a willingness and chants came lively from the capstan crew, yet as the morning progressed the voices oddly quietened. Soon the only sound was of a light zephyr that wafted in from the north. The notion struck me that we were tip-toeing for fear of waking some unknown monster. I looked at the men working about the mainmast and there was no disguising that a certain reluctance pervaded their efforts, almost like men robbed of their spirit. I once had the misfortune to observe this when a slaver disgorged its cargo of reeking misery after a long and storm-filled voyage. Our sailors too wore this look of dread, not as strongly as those shackled natives, of course, for here we were free and well fed and living in a place of extravagant scenery which seemed to symbolise hope.

'You there, Portsmouth,' I said to the young marine drummer. 'Call Mr King, if you please.'

The youth was on duty at the foot of the quarterladder, scarcely a body-length from me, yet he seemed not to hear. 'Portsmouth,' I repeated louder. His head took an age to respond: the eyes came upon me in a dream and then focused over my shoulder as if a ghost stood beyond. At that very moment the orchestra of cicadas and birds abruptly ended their music; it was a frightening silence.

'By the devil,' Portsmouth said and I swung to see what his eyes beheld. He was staring at the shore and, before those disturbingly quiet trees, natives were on their knees as if begging to some deity; I turned swiftly in the direction of their supplication. For a second terror dominated my Navy training. Coming slowly towards us in a wavering dance of destruction was a massive whirlwind. Its base was the length of a ship and the white spiralling funnel reached up to low cloud. A soft, almost pretty rushing sound came from it not far removed from the poets' babbling of brooks; I stopped paralysed. The thought flooded my brain: I am mesmerised by this image of death as surely as a rabbit in a ferret's stare; our lot was impossible, hopeless.

'All hands! Portsmouth, call all hands.'

But the youth had turned his attention to the vortex and could not see nor hear anything else. I grabbed the lad, shaking him, but he would not look away.

'All hands, all hands!' I shouted as hard as my lungs would allow, but the men in my watch were standing as if thunderstruck, their faces staring at certain fate waddling towards us. I ran to the mainmast and pushed one and then another and all the time shouted 'All hands!' but none would move, let alone take up the call and summon shipmates. I could hear myself ordering 'Strike yards, topmasts!' but with the closeness of tragedy, it would be as futile a gesture as my words were hopeless. But we must do something. I drew my sword and came down on Portsmouth again, but my threats were ignored. I ran across the waist and hammered on the aft-cabin door with the silver hilt.

'You there,' I repeated to the men in the waist, 'strike yards. . . .'

Bligh emerged from the cabin in a trance. His face was blanched and damp like a new corpse and he stepped slowly to the weather-rail, towards the vast convolution which was either side and above him, and I thought, you'll be the first to be sucked out of the ship.

> Regardless of the sweeping Whirlwind's sway,
> That, hush'd in grim repose, expects his evening-prey.

The light was failing: in the middle of the day night was closing in and the sound of disturbed air came much louder; the music was replaced by a noise like water rushing across rapids. Over the din I was shouting at Bligh, but he seemed deaf. I pushed at a shoulder, but he was far heavier than I imagined and he remained adhered to the deck like marble awaiting a sculptor; I pushed at a corner of the stone, I heaved with both hands, the Harvey sword raised unintentionally defiant as the white mass came closer in the new dusk, but the fear-ridden bulk would not be moved. I turned back to the transfixed crew, their faces whitewashed as this weird darkness painted everything, and above the unnerving shriek came the cries of terrified natives ashore. Kahura, Kahura, Kahura! they cried and the captain appeared at the door.

'Jesus, sir, permission to strike the yards,' I began and my words were interrupted by my breathing which had jolted out of its natural rhythm, and in the mixture of emotions that swamped me a mad laughter burst. I saw the captain as unmoving as an alabaster statuette on a mantelpiece; perhaps all of us in the waist were really displayed on some sideboard in a middle-class home, merely examples of the miniaturists' art, and for a moment I feared we were all dead, but my faculties were more or less still present; I could move about, I was not entranced like the rest; perhaps this meant I would be the survivor: me and the natives who believed it the incarnation of a tyrant. Yet still the thing advanced hissing to a roar, tacking across the fiord as powerful yet slow as a first-rater. Water was being sucked into the circle, bubbling as if it boiled in a cauldron and then disappearing with great rapidity; beyond the fringe of the white leviathan was a hollow and I wondered if I were actually looking down into fathoms of vacuum. The darkness was upon us as pitch: the noise was that of a hurricane yet our rigging had not moved and it was hardly further off than the length of the pinnace. White faces stared from the weather-rail of *Discovery*; we must both be destroyed.

Through the fear, the memory flashed before me of prisoners from the Continental Navy who talked of tornadoes which sucked men and masts up into the heavens, and I realised the waterspout was stopped. I laughed hysterically again: I could reach out past Bligh's shoulders and touch the thing. Then a blinding light burned into my eyes and I put up my hands to protect them.

I remember so vividly the sound of the sword falling bouncing, twanging with the ring of expertly forged steel through the cascading of crashing water, like the cataract of Niagara and a dozen others all moulded into one enormous thunder, and the brilliance remained pink through my fingers and when I took down my hands the vortex was gone.

The water about the ship heaved with driftwood and pushed at us on our snatching anchors, but the wind and tumult had disappeared along with that mighty fist of uncontrolled energy. The cicadas and birds took over from the silence. Life had been breathed into the alabaster which turned away to the cabin door.

'Sir, I. . . .' Shock, fear, enormous relief were waiting to be expressed but they muddled and throttled themselves like a retreating army in my throat.

'There are stronger powers than ours, Mr Williamson.'

'I thought, I mean, God and. . . .'

'Thought you had seen your maker? One sees him in a lee shore, an uncharted sandbank in a North Sea gale, why not a tornado?'

'But. . . .'

'In God we trust, young sir, and don't leave that lying around.' I picked up my sword and he returned to the shadow of the cabin; his face was still very white.

Fair weather returned for our last days in Zealand. I was in my cabin writing up my history, in the process of sharpening a quill at the time. It was a little while after dawn. Country church bell-ringer birds were busy and the orchestra of cicadas was tuning up. Not too loud today, lads, I thought; the captain held a dinner last night and in the relief of being alive I drank too deeply. A hammering on my door was not appreciated by my suffering head where port-wine lingered malevolently. It was Collett summoning me to the quarterdeck.

I tucked my shirt into my breeches, slipped on my hanger-sword (in second nature) and emerged into the sunlight. I blinked and it took a few moments to adjust to the bright morning. The captain was at the caprail with James King and Mr Gore and the marines were discharged onto the deck from the companionway, lugging muskets in their distinctly unmilitary way.

It could not be as early as I imagined for Omai, a perpetual late sleeper, was standing by the wheel; a gaudy summit with a coiffeured peak pushing through orographic clouds of scent. A sword with an intricately, almost lethally carved hilt was at his waist. The swashbuckling mountain was fuming.

'We have visitors, Mr Williamson,' the captain said as I came up to him. 'I want you to translate if you will.' I looked over at the helm and he guessed my question. 'I would ask Omai,' he said, 'but he wants to act as some sort of judge and jury with this visitor. I require only a translator.'

I looked over the rail into the crisp new day. A small fleet of canoes encircled us; these vessels were quite the smartest we had seen here. They were light and looked fast and at the stern of each a tall, ostrich-like neck extended and I thought of a walking bird they talk of called a moa. The necks as with the strakes were delicately carved. One had a bow-piece of shaped ornamentation, most likely for ramming enemy canoes. The visitors appeared to be armed with only a few spears; they wore a variety of flax cloaks and dog skins and squatted in the boats in the queer manner of these people. At a little distance, they resemble a collection of rocks.

A canoe came beneath me and an extensively tattooed man commanded our attention. I guessed him to be the demon Kahura. Dark eyes looked out from black eyelashes. I wondered if he really had eaten our men, for he showed no fear of our likely anger; I felt more than a little unnerved by his presence.

His hair was the shade of coal and pulled back to a queue, only higher on the head than our style. Two feathers stood up like an impolite gesture: jade earrings rubbed firm powerful shoulders; his moustache was of the fashion of the Dons and the brows had been as perfectly manicured as the whirls of the face tattoos were painstakingly symmetrical. He was of handsome proportion, I thought, but the expression he displayed of mild curiosity did not conceal cruelty.

'They told me you were here,' he called quite matter-of-factly from the canoe and I translated. 'And they told me you were leaving soon, without, I understand, a thought of visiting me at my pa.'

'Tell him we are indeed going soon,' the captain said quietly, his eyes holding the look of the savage, 'but would be happy to receive him here on King George's ship.'

The chief looked round at a splash from *Discovery* which was launching two boats; people were climbing down into them. 'Kindly suggest he should make up his mind whether to call on us with some haste for there may be those who would not receive him so courteously.'

Kahura smiled and reached for the side ropes.

'A piping, Mr Bligh, with due ceremony,' the captain ordered. Bligh was quick for the whistle sounded as the murderer's head reached our level. Bligh stood to attention.

'Mr Kahura and retinue,' he announced and thirty warriors young and old came onto the deck. One took the cloak of feathers from the chief's shoulders.

'Welcome to His Majesty's Ship *Resolution*, Chief Kahura,' I translated, though my attention was more on the white teeth of this butcher than on the formal words of the captain. 'King George, through me, assures you of your personal safety while aboard this vessel.'

It was obvious from his manner that the savage held little regard for us; the sailors about the deck made it plain he was fortunate to be alive. The old boy stopped and now it was the time for reply, some rhapsodising rhetoric by local custom.

But with indifference to the temper of our captain, the fellow declined to respond. He strutted about, flexing the muscles of his legs and pretending to observe this part of a shroud, a planed knot in the deck planking, the craftsmanship involved in the caprail.

The captain's face flushed and later some hapless sailor would be set about scrubbing the places where the villain touched with his vile hands. We expected our own *haka* to burst out on the deck, but he turned slightly away from the group and pressed fingers against his temples.

'We shall dispense with the formalities usual for a person of chieftain rank,' he began and then pulled himself back from the temper and instructed me to say instead, 'Would you care to take tea with me in the aft-cabin?'

He looked at the captain with an unchanging expression and said he would care to do that, yes. Members of his retinue had no reluctance whatsoever to be entertained on the great ship of the King of England, and they pressed forward; but the chief would have all the honour himself. He held a hand to stop them being admitted and displayed both selfishness and foolhardiness in entering a room packed with armed gentlemen who despised him.

Collett put a chair in the centre of the deck and cleverly placed over it a colourful blanket, a present from Mrs Cook, I believe, and this gave it a throne-like look. I followed the broad brown back into the cabin. Kahura took the chair and Captain Cook pushed behind his desk.

Suddenly the fellow leaped forward and all around hands reached for their swords. But Kahura was beside the captain; the head of the cannibal went forward and the captain accepted a *hongi*, a nose-press.

This pleased Kahura, but it brought a low hiss from the officers. We could not forget that the moustache which brushed the mouth of our commander must have dripped with the cooked fat of English sailors. As he stepped from the captain, he saw a recent Webber sketch of a local chief. In the picture the man stood beside Captain Clerke. 'Who is he whose likeness hangs here?' he asked, but I did not answer because I was sure they were not strangers. Kahura took up his throne. 'I would be willing to give such a likeness,' he said.

The captain smiled at him. 'It might be worthwhile to have the rogue's picture so other visitors will know who to watch out for.'

'What is he saying?' Kahura asked.

'You will be pleased with the likeness our artist will portray.'

'Am I not finely made?'

The door opened for Mr Webber, but Omai pushed past into the room, his eyes swathing angrily like the slice of a sabre until they reached Kahura. They were now wild and threatening as if they would stab that cold heart, but face to face Omai was no match and he had to look away.

But where the eyes failed, the tongue would try. 'He is a killer!' Omai shouted in our confined space, but the voice too was weakening, now a little too high. 'He has killed and eaten pakehas; he must die.' He wavered, the eyes took in the sight he dreaded, the courage failed and poor, well-meaning Omai rushed from the room. Bravo, Omai! I called inwardly; at least he had the courage to shout what we all felt. I sympathised too with what he had been unable to overlook. Brown chalk and cheese they may be in facade: Kahura's simple garment of flax, pronounced brown muscles, unquestionably masculine; Omai's foppery the blaze of wild flowers in a gale, hair curled, perfume, make-up and the exaggerated poses. Yet there was no disguising that Omai could pass for the cannibal's younger brother.

Kahura asked, the interruption already forgotten, 'Where will you go in your large canoe?'

Webber the artist filled the Chippendale, crossed his legs and pencilled an outline with the speed of Bligh as draughtsman. His chubby face remained expressionless, despite the dramas that continued. The eyes hardly left the drawing paper as if ever conscious of their wide spacing; nostrils were fixed in offended indifference.

'We pursue the matters of his Britannic Majesty, stocking the islands of Polynesia with animals King George himself is presenting to the people. Our guest, the chief Omai, will be returned to his home and then we will seek discoveries to the very top of the world.'

'I hope you will win many wars.' He sat fiercely upright like an army general, aloof and firmly in control.

'We do not go in war, but with peace which is the way of wise men.'

'Wise men will be dead men.'

'War is coming to an end, Mr Kahura. Men are learning there is more to be gained by working together and building a proper world.'

'You speak of weak men.' His voice tended towards belligerence and it was clear he held little regard for philosophies of the ships.

'On the contrary,' the captain was replying. 'These men I speak of are the strong men. It takes strength to resist a challenge.' The old boy said this slowly while he came to the side of the desk, resting the hand with its long scar upon the varnish. 'If I were to interpret your tone of voice as challenging, Mr Kahura, would I not be strong to refuse you?' Our people were leaning forward in the tension of the words. 'After all, I am armed with a sword with which I am most handy.'

The native sat through my translation maintaining defiance, his face not changing for an instant. The reply was equally cool. 'A coward would not accept a challenge.' There was something in the look in his eyes that caused me to reach the sudden conclusion: the man is acting and really is terrified of the script his mouth speaks. It was a dangerous performance, because at any moment tempers could break and he could be slain by one of us.

The captain's hand was at his sword and the tip was over the heart of this killer-cum-actor in the most surprising speed. His face remained as still as the native's and his voice equally as calm. But around these two, breaths were being quickly drawn and minds begged the captain to destroy the brute.

'So you see, Mr Kahura, the easiest would be for me to accept your challenge and run you through. Then I could avenge your insulting thoughts and my own pride would be salved.' The blade hovered for a moment longer, a shine of the steel reflected on the cannibal's face, and then came the metallic rasp as it returned unstained to its sheath. 'To resist your challenge is to go against the primitive urge. I have the greater power and therefore can so easily destroy you, and consequently will not. That takes the strength.'

Around the room, hands remained on hilts with knuckles white in fury. It was difficult for us to hold down the urge the captain described as primitive. Yet the butcher sat quietly, proudly, unaffected beneath the weight of hate. And I thought, unless this man really is a greater thespian than legendary David Garrick, nothing will ever bow his head and there is no method to implant intelligent ideas into that cruel brain.

But possibly Mr Garrick relaxes when the audience goes home, and so with our Mr Kahura. Webber announced he was finished, placed the sketch of proud savagery on the desk, and left.

A transition came over the fellow that was extraordinary. As directed, I repeated the question: 'We would like to hear what happened on that fateful day, what led you to kill and later eat my people?'

Kahura actually hung his head and if his vocabulary included shame, that was the feeling he tried to exhibit in his demeanour. He expected a punishment, submitted to it, and I imagined him quaking as so many of our leaders in history had on the scaffold.

'Come now,' I repeated, 'the details of this slaying.'

The head bent further as humility increased. He was as he might have been from the start; a prisoner of people whose loathing of him was only matched by their detestation of his practices.

'My God, captain,' I suddenly said, in a most un-Navy-like way, so staggered was I by the realisation. 'This savage, this cannibal has his eyes to posterity with the determination of a politician. While his picture is being sketched he holds the image he wishes the future to know him by. But now he has no audience – for he despises us for our principles and does not care what we think – he quakes like a cowering dog.'

As may be interpreted, I was in a state of high dudgeon; it is far from easy to remain patient with an offensive creature that has the audacity to return one's own revulsion. And so it was, for our actor-politician-cannibal was as a simpleton child to the questions which anger caused me to put caustically and censoriously. I have mentioned this matter of my lawyer tongue, and it came to icy life.

I admit that little new was discovered. He claimed the sailors took an axe from the natives and so caused the argument that brought such dreadful repercussions. But Captain Cook would not accept this; he believed it was no more than a red herring and he did not request that I reduce the cutting strength of my interrogation.

'Very well,' the captain said when our quarry was much reduced. 'We have heard it from the man's lips and let this be the end to the melancholy affair. We will stand by our conscience and hope that a lesson has been learned.'

I offered the portrait of the proud cannibal chief to cowering Kahura. 'No, that for King George and the people of your land,' he said. He was already regaining his poise as he went through the door to rejoin the retinue.

For all the fury of the elements at our anchorage, when our forests grew their bleached foliage and we reached for the ocean, the winds were light and fitful and as leaving England had been slow, so now was our departure from Zealand.

Some families followed us a little way in their canoes, but they soon fell back; we worked our way along the inter-island straits and emerged into the Pacific. Within sight of the incredibly green coast, the wind left us and soon our flotsam grew on that jade ocean. We had two new people aboard the ship; two boys were recruited by Omai as his servants. At this time they were wailing, homesick lads, but they soon acclimatised to shipboard life and became very popular with our people, which was odd for no race had been more scandalised than the cannibals of this fiord.

We carried with us too an impetuosity that was to be the undoing of the entire expedition. The admiralty expected us to reach the high north latitudes this coming season and we would need every favourable wind to oblige. Yet the charity of the wind god was not with us and failure and frustration came to dog us.

The sea was flat. The coast lay on the horizon and a launch brought the officers of *Discovery* over for dinner in the aft-cabin. Wild pork was on our menu, plus a native cabbage called *puha*, and *kumara*, the sweet potato that grew wherever Polynesians settled.

'The people were not pleased at the men's unwillingness to trade in their women,' the captain said when the dinner-table discussion returned to a favourite topic. 'The seamen had taken a dislike to these people and were unwilling or afraid to associate with them. It had such a good effect that I never knew a man to quit his station to go to their habitations.'

Dr David Samwell was making quick work of a tibia of pork. 'But, sir, did you actually look at the women,' he said excitedly. 'They like other courtesans were so lavish of red paint in daubing their faces and so fragrant of noisome smells that they did not meet with many admirers. And this, gentlemen, even among the ship's company who upon these occasions are never known to be particularly nice in the choice of their paramours.'

Dr Bill leaned suddenly, enthusiastically forward. 'The noise about the woods, a perpetual and universal chirping, took my attention and I resolved to enquire into the cause. Upon investigation, I found it to be occasioned by a large kind of fly that rests on the trees in great numbers and goes with much velocity from one to the other.'

The senior doctor saw a look of disappointment at that, for many of his findings were to do much more with the mating habits of natives: he discovered that some boys had their prepuces tied to a belt about their middle; somehow he also found that young high-born girls kept *in situ* a plug of leaves as an additional protection for their chastity, and also that among the low classes, coition was indulged in from early childhood.

This was a practice much discouraged in our world for scientists believed that early experience before a man was properly formed could cause lasting damage.

'They call them *muta*, doctor,' I said of the cicadas. 'The natives pound them up and consider them a delicacy.'

'Someone's been doing his homework,' James King commented and Dr Bill cleared his throat.

'While I was investigating this matter,' he continued, and silence fell around the table again, 'I perceived of another sound and not from one of the birds that tolerably stock the woods. Quantities of underwood and climbing plants render travelling for pleasure through these places of vegetation uncommonly fatiguing, but I discovered soon the cause of the music.'

'Music?' said David Samwell. 'My dear sir, you didn't mention a song in the air.'

Several jocular remarks were tumbled in the way of Dr Anderson's anecdote, but he kept pushing on, as if he were back on that probe in the Zealand bush. 'It was a young man and I signified I would like to see the pipe upon which he played.'

'Um, tell me more,' Omai interrupted in an exaggerated manner.

Dr Anderson was smiling. 'Exactly, Omai, for the pipe, you see, was a penis.'

'A penis?' This chorus came from many diners.

'A dried penis from one of their cannibal functions and he operated it as a musical instrument.'

'A whistle actually,' I said keenly. 'I've heard about them from the natives, but I doubted the truth. They call the whistle a *nguru*.' We thought on this and through the drink savoured the knowledge with amusement and not a little horror.

'What do you think, Omai?' David Samwell said, his face resembling a shining pomegranate in the candlelight. 'Have you ever made them whistle?'

'David!' Omai feigned shock yet managed to contrive a certain knowing expression.

James King's knife fell noisily to the plate. 'You know why he can't get music out of them,' he said, his expression bright with wine and good humour. 'You're supposed to blow, you native clot.'

'The way our Tahitian plays,' David added, 'the music comes from the owner's lips, if not from the instrument itself.'

'You brute,' Omai pouted, 'you promised not to tell.'

David and James leaped up and strutted about the cabin like idle beaus of London and, far from looking disturbed, Omai luxuriated in his chair beside the captain. But our commander, noisily reducing some roasted fat, hardly seemed to notice. 'You know, Charles,' he said to Captain Clerke, 'a connection with the women I allow because I cannot prevent it, but I never encourage it. Many men are of the opinion it is one of the greatest securities among Indians, and it may hold good if you intend to settle among them.'

We listened, our forks waiting in the air politely till he returned to his eating. 'But with travellers and strangers, it is generally otherwise and more men are betrayed than saved by having connection with the women. And how could it be otherwise since all their views are selfish without the least mixture of regard or attachment whatsoever?'

I repeated a proverb of the fiord people. '*He wahine, he whenua, a ngaro ai te tangata.*'

'Meaning?' asked Mr Gore.

James King tried, 'By land and men . . . no.'

'By women and land are men destroyed.'

'Well spoken, Mr Williamson,' Captain Cook said.

'They've got their own Dr Johnson here then,' Dr Bill said.

Later David Samwell said, 'You know, if I may sir, I'd like to say something that I've thought a lot about since the matters of Grass Cove.' His voice was heavily brushed now with the colour of Wales; it was incongruous to have so many different accents in that cabin on the other side of the world. Yet it was oddly reassuring. 'It's a serious note, gentlemen, and one you should keep with you. When natives are warring, on no account turn away; they will not strike a European while his face is towards them; I think it's to do with the superiority they assume a white face to have. A simple matter but so important in the saving of life. And that I believe is a vital clue to the matter of the massacred sailors.'

'I agree absolutely,' the captain said. 'Gentlemen, please take note.'

Collett was replacing a bottle of port. Captain Clerke stood and raised his glass. 'Here's to being back at sea again; the only place for a sailor.'

We cheered heartily to that, but then we had no idea of what lay ahead.

13

A weak current claimed the land on our horizon but the wind stubbornly remained reclusive and disobliging. Rowing parties were made up, the pinnace swung over the side, and we bodily hauled our ungainly ark onwards. The rowers were changed every two hours, but the men wearied from the unfamiliar activity as their spirit slumped. As is usual with the sea, tempers match progress and our progress was very short. Men usually obedient on watch snarled back at orders; the sun scorched our decks from an unclouded heaven and ocean birds became too despondent to struggle into the air. At first the grog allowance was increased to swill away discontent; when this failed punishment became the enticer. The sound of the lash on skin and of screaming men echoed on our decks.

The wind moved the sails and returned and could have averted the trouble threatening, but instead lay directly in our path so that the ship began the clumsy gait characteristic of sailing full and bye.

Frustration was shared evenly about the decks and perhaps the captain's conscience got the better of him over the floggings for now he struck out bitterly at officers and we who are as filled with humanity's weaknesses as any landsman retaliated blindly. Our animals caught the discontent and called in distress, whether penned below or brought up for their daily promenades. As the ship's government kicked our brutes of burden, so the governed maltreated the beasts. The animals' only revenge was to demand more food.

We had thousands of miles to journey, yet we could manage scarcely fifty a day. If we could continue non-stop we might succeed: there would be treasure for all if the passage above America were discovered; where there's booty, men will survive on the poorest rations, but not so the property of our rustic regent. We had to find an island to feed them.

'Mr Bligh, these animals now; we're going to have to cull some,' the captain announced at one sweltering conference in his cabin.

'The majority of fodder is taken by the cattle, sir,' I prompted from the chart table.

'That is so,' Bligh agreed.

'Good God, have you both gone mad? The cattle are the King's presents to the islanders.'

'They'll die anyway if we don't get them there soon, sir,' Bligh said, a little recklessly.

'They will die of natural causes, Mr Bligh, *before* we'll take a knife to them. What about the sheep?'

'The sheep and lambs make up the bulk of the stock, sir.'

'Very well,' the captain said. 'Serve fresh mutton to the ship's company.'

'But, sir,' I protested, 'we officers and people of the gunroom bought many of them.' We clubbed funds for occasional treats of fresh meat and these animals had travelled with us from Good Hope.

'Not just you; I bought a number too out of my own pocket,' he said. 'Carry on, Mr Bligh.'

The foredeck was washed red, sheep was boiled for three meals a day and the crew fished in their relaxations for the army of trailing sharks.

The Southern Ocean was a cold memory in our wake and we roasted instead in a floating oven. Condensation, which curled the corners of the souvenired sign on my cabin wall, was replaced by freckles of dried mildew. The uncertain breeze stayed ahead and we shouldered on grudgingly through the blue. Mention has been made in the narrative of the health parade, as the old boy called this daily gathering of the infirm. It was my duty today to maintain discipline among the assemblage in the forepart of the gunroom where was situated the sickbay. Victims of headaches, knife wounds, burns and rat bites came forward when called; I checked their details on a midshipman's report and delivered them to David Samwell. They removed their garments, though these days they wore only trousers, and after a physical examination would explain their problem. The sickbay was two cabins without the joining partition, and as the reader will appreciate, the space was restricted, the lighting poor. There was a canvas-covered bed on which Dr Anderson lay and an aged desk of indeterminate lineage where David Samwell made his notes.

Once this surgery was finished, the doctors continued with the daily plotting of the course of the consumptive Dr Bill Anderson. This malady, an evil killer of our age, robbed him of his breath and energy and soon would take his life too. He was confined to bed these days, but rather than wait for death, he contributed to our world by giving prognosis and advice from the sickbay berth. This marvellous display of courage gave David Samwell rare training for when he would take over as surgeon and it encouraged others who suffered the same malady, which regrettably included convivial Captain Clerke.

The dying doctor was weighed, measured, prodded and questioned as the consumption's progress was logged in the comprehensive file. One day it may help man to eradicate this disease, and all who watched these medics at work would say amen to that.

'Next.' A gunner came forward. His rotting tooth gave him extreme pain, sirs, and it was to be removed today and here, gentlemen, was his friend from the forecastle who would be donor. Both patient and mate were quickly sedated, which became an increasingly noisy procedure as the grog took effect. Although this was the first time the extraordinary operation was tried on our ships, I had witnessed it once before. Fairs were particularly popular in England and tooth pulling and mending a regular attraction. The great medic stood on a stage with the hapless victim seated. The anaesthetics at the time I refer to were volunteers from the audience, two muscly fellows and me; our task was simply to hang on. The offending molar was wrenched out amid blood and screams. The victim's father climbed onto the stage and his one remaining tooth at the front was hauled out, without so much as a whimper from the old fellow. Now the amazing tooth-doctor thrust it into the son's mouth and the audience applauded with the enthusiasm of the artisan class. (For people of breeding to demonstrate in this way was definitely *infra dignitatem*.) Our gunner slouched in a chair, close to the head of Dr Anderson's bed. I stood behind holding wide the gaping mouth, looking down on the fellow's eyes which rolled about like a drugged bay's, not from pain but from the painkiller, one of two methods favoured by these humane surgeons.

'Steady there, my beauty,' David encouraged in his immaculate Welsh, but our patient's ears attended only to Morpheus.

The surgeon pushed a pair of evil-looking pincers between my hands while I held tightly to the head. I admit I closed my eyes. I felt a heaving, followed by a grating which travelled through the fellow's skull like a shock of electrification.

'There!' David announced with pride and an object not unlike burning coal dripped from the surgical implement.

'Now the donor, if you please?' The victim staggered out and the shipmate entered looking close to death for the grog had not completely despatched his faculties.

Dr Anderson's skeletal arm held a candle for additional light. 'The actual trick of the technique as I see it,' he said, 'is to try to match tooth for tooth.'

The lad sat and I took up my position. 'As you'll see, John, the grinder our Dr Samwell has extracted is very similar in size to this boy's; surprising, too, because he is of much slighter build.'

David produced the offending molar and held it close to the jaw to illustrate the truth of the statement. The boy's green eyes crossed as they followed the path of the bleeding pliers. He looked even paler.

'I think I'm a-going to throw up,' he said.

'Not yet, lad,' David replied. 'This will only take a moment and then you can be sick all you like.'

Dr Bill continued as lecturer-assistant. 'Now see how the pincers go round the tooth, which we are calling lower seven – we always count from the left – and Dr Samwell will grasp and with a flick like this remove it.'

The boy screamed, I held grimly to the head, and despite my interest in science, declined the kind invitation to witness the complete miracle.

'No?' said Dr Anderson quietly when the boy's interruption calmed. 'I think if it's damaged, Dr Samwell, we should try its corresponding number on the other side.'

'I won't say there wasn't a great deal of pressure upon the molar,' David Samwell said, 'but I think – if you could hold the candle a little closer – yes; thank you. No, the tooth is fine. If you'll just hold tightly again, John, I'll do it now. Are you all right, my boy?'

But before the lad could reply the muscles on the sweaty arm flexed, a concussion came through the jaws and the doctors were exclaiming over the perfectness of the operation. The lad was pushed promptly from the room and the patient proper returned. He looked soberer as pain elbowed the unconsciousness. I held the mouth wide and David Samwell took up the tooth from its safe position in Dr Anderson's hand, clotting beside the candle. In a lurching ship, it wouldn't do to put the tooth on the table because it might be dashed to the floor with the attendant risk of not finding it in time.

'We're working on the theory,' Dr Bill said as the rusty tooth disappeared into the unhappy gap, 'of minimum heartbeats to pass while the donation is outside the body. This way we believe it will pick up the blood vessels and imagine perhaps it's never been anywhere else.'

'I'm through here, Dr Anderson,' David said. 'What do you think?'

The older man could not quite see, so the patient who had abandoned our waking world was hoisted closer to the bed. White elbows strained as eyes hiding in their deep sockets admired the handiwork. 'By George, that's excellent. Well done, David.'

'Thank you, sir, but without your. . . .'

'Perhaps we're making medical history, here in the wastes of the Pacific.'

The patient fell back onto the chair. I said, 'I hope our man doesn't swallow it after all that trouble.'

'Well, there are always risks,' David said thoughtfully. Dr Bill was about to add to this remark, but the consumption struck; David took the candle away while the coughing increased.

The most serious charge in the Royal Navy is mutiny, necessarily so, for the people outnumber officers so heavily. Guards keep murderous crew from a captain's throat, but on our ship the company of these protectors, the marines, was slight indeed. The complement had power through their numbers and it was for a wise commander to use it to his advantage. The word mutiny as an insult is a two-edged sword which can cut deeply on both sides, and when the accusation surfaced it took me quite aback. There was discontent in the ship; we had been beating upwind for an age, progress was mortifying and such conditions do not make for happy seafarers. But mutiny?

I had the afternoon watch. The captain was below me in the waist, standing at the wide base of the mainmast; he glared at the acres of canvas trying to draw progress from the fickle breeze. Extreme irritation showed in his demeanour not uncommon at times like these, and wise men kept a distance.

Bligh and mate Lanyon appeared from the companionway, and insensitive to the wisdom of angels, immediately approached the angry figure. Bligh's cough was ignored, which should have been warning enough. Perhaps the heat evaporated any stealth the master may have possessed, for it was a scorching day and sweat poured from the mate's wide forehead.

'Permission to speak?' Bligh said.

'Go ahead then. Speak.'

'In your cabin, sir?'

'I'm out here for the present; speak now, or wait till I'm ready to go inside.'

They stood obediently beside the weather-rail where the captain left them for exactly an hour. The cabin door had not long closed when word was passed for me. I put the duty mate in charge.

'Are you, or are you not officer of the watch?' the captain asked me as I entered the stifling room. The old boy sat behind the desk like a Buddha on fire. His uniform coat was off and sleeves of the shirt were pushed up to the elbows. Perspiration stains like maps of the North American continent stretched from armpits to waist.

'What do you know of this business?'

'Business, sir?'

'Mr Bligh, this is the officer of the watch. Please be so good as to acquaint him with your discovery, as you should have done in the first place.'

Bligh and Lanyon stood before the desk. I was behind them and though the master was addressing me, I suppose he felt obliged to face the hostile commander.

'Mr Williamson, the mate and me have discovered that pilfering is going on.'

'Pilfering?'

'Pilfering of victuals, sir, both individuals' and ship's.'

The captain snapped, 'Don't look so offhand, Mr Williamson, this is a serious business. The master and his mate have had a number of thefts reported to them by the cook and from certain of our complement. Thieving, Mr Williamson, is a cancer that can become malignant. What are you going to do about it, young sir?'

I had no reply. 'Very well, pass the word for Mr Gore and Mr King.'

The other lieutenants hurried into the cabin, both looking sleepy; it appeared they had been following the hot afternoon practice of the Dons.

'Gentlemen, have you lost anything?' Bligh and Lanyon remained at attention. I was to one side not daring to move and James and Mr Gore stood beside me, so now two formal lines were before the desk. 'There is no point in my asking, because like Mr Williamson you will not know. However, thieves are loose and victuals belonging to the ship and to the people are being taken. Gentlemen, I will not tolerate it.' He moved his seat till he had eyed us all. 'There is an idleness about that I do not like. It proves ill-discipline is settling on us and it will stop; perhaps my officers cannot halt it, but I certainly will. Gentlemen, I want the culprits caught and by God I'll thrash them as I've not. . . .' He was standing now and shouting in that hot summer cabin. 'We must be in the high northern latitudes within a few months and I cannot get you people to move the ship at all. Now I find that the discipline has gone. From this moment there will be no fresh meat until the thieves are handed over.'

I wondered if he really expected the crew to give up the thieves whose identity they could not know. And what a strange penalty; they were happiest with salt meat and treated every other food with suspicion. So when officers and master were next summoned to the aft-cabin, our news was obvious, but the outcome disturbing. 'You haven't got the thiefs then, Mr Bligh? Very well. Mr Gore, have the people brought to the rail.'

'The people, sir?'

'The crew. I will address them.'

The marines stood with bayonets fixed between us on the quarter-deck, and the people crammed onto the waist.

'Thieves are at work on this ship,' the captain stormed. 'And I mean to have them. Deliver them up and no more will be said.' The captain waited, the ship sailed silently. 'Very well, you will be on two-thirds salt ration till you turn them over.'

James Millett, who resembled an awkward rectangle, spoke for the men he beat easily at racquets. 'Sir, we don't know who they are. . . .'

'Shut your mouth, you impudent dog,' Bligh roared from the quarterladder, and not just the men cringed from that acid blast.

'No, master, let our man speak.'

'Thank you, sir. With the greatest respect. . . .'

'Get on with it, Millett,' the captain interrupted. 'If you knew respect you wouldn't be speaking at all.'

A few men tried a laugh in case this was humour, but most knew him better. Even in distraught moments he would not forget naval discipline and captains did not joke with crew.

Millett said, 'The men feel it is unfair to blame and punish us all for what one or two are doing.'

'Is that all?'

'Aye, sir.'

The captain's sunbrowned hands gripped the rail and the long scar stood out like a waterfall on black rock. 'I look upon this refusal to hand up the guilty parties as a very mutinous proceeding. If you was honest men you would assist me as is your duty, so the number which is involved must be great. You are all on two-thirds today, tomorrow and every day till the culprits are handed up.'

'But sir,' Millett began.

'Take that man's name, Mr Mate,' Bligh roared. 'We'll see if he'll talk back to the cat.'

Lieutenant Phillips and the marines surrounded the captain at the bottom of the ladderway and escorted him to the cabin door.

I drank tea from the mug. I looked at Samwell sipping from his cup quietly while he read and mused at the strange world. Seamen were murdered and eaten in Zealand and the captain himself made a particular statement and here we were at sea with the crew stirred up and all over some petty thefts.

'Discipline's an odd thing, David,' I said at last. We were alone at the gunroom table.

'You can't sail without it.'

'You could sail, but you'd not have any crew.'

'I know the old boy takes the thefts seriously, but I think he has to,' Samwell said. 'Thieving is a problem of this age of development.'

I replied, 'If the newspapers are to be believed, we have one hundred and fifty charges which can result in a man being hanged. One's of course for murder, but the majority are for taking someone else's property.'

'Cynics blame the church, the plutocrats, the government,' he said. 'But I believe we can be proud of our century.'

'Some things are easier to be proud of.'

'Man is becoming educated and sophisticated, but we need firm laws. Look, John, not everyone can benefit from the changes – not overnight. Success is rewarded by a measure of riches. A man uses this to pass on education and advantages of our scientific times to our children.' He sounded sincere but I could only stare into my cup. 'You see, if those yet to experience the advantages of the age could just snatch the next man's purse, they would not pursue education. I mean, why bother? They can stay idle and ignorant and yet live well by stealing from people who have the discipline to apply themselves.'

I said, 'Laws seem not to be having much effect on the Dick Turpins of our age.'

'There are fewer highwaymen these days. John, our laws are improving. Taking a sack of potatoes from a farmer earns the rope. But if you can prove you picked up those vegetables from the ground and put them into the sack, your guilt is one of trespass and is free from corporal punishment.'

'We back our society with hanging *and* drawing and quartering. Not very enlightened.'

'Obviously the notion of dying and being castrated into the bargain is not attractive. But that's the philosophy of punishment, to frighten the potentially guilty. Don't you agree?' We sipped our tea quietly.

'I think this might interest you more than politics,' Samwell said, waving at me a slim volume he had been perusing.

'Good grief, David, you've not bought that dreadful manual?'

'Do you mind?' he said, swiftly pulling the book from my outstretched hand. '*Harris's List of Covent Garden Ladies* is a work of merit. It's the result of exhaustive investigating journalism.'

'I'll wager to that.'

'You're against art, that's what.'

'Look.' I took the book from him and turned some pages. 'Take this, for instance. "A fine bouncing, crummy wench". And this one, "scarce a tooth in her head but incomparable fine legs". Art! You say.'

'What would you call it?'

'Libel.'

'I take it you've never been to Covent Garden.'

Cattle bellowed for food and men became more belligerent, but the thieves were not found. Then the look-out called Land-ho! We found an island called Mangaia surrounded by reefs we could not cross. But we had a visitor, a brown sack of bones, who clambered up a side ladder and stared unbelievingly at our pale countenances and our colourful clothes. The people were hypnotised by this little man who looked more like a naked pixie than a Polynesian chief.

He smiled at the captain and that strained face bent to a slight grin, like an obstinate sprits'l being unfurled. The visitor came out of the aft-cabin and stumbled over a goat chewing a sailor's shirt. 'What sort of bird is that?' he asked matter-of-factly and I translated without thinking.

This was a break the men needed; they laughed as if this were the joke of the century. 'Huzzahs for the nigger king,' James Millett called and the little man was given a fine farewell. We found another island and we were able to get our boats to the shore and collect food for King George's animals.

We were in the latitudes of the light-fingered. These simple people, uncomplicated by church doctrines, stole for pleasure and our captain set about teaching them our Christian attitudes. But perhaps it was the visitors who learned a lesson in the end, though we had to part with our fondest asset in the acquiring of it.

14

'Do you mind me saying something?'
'Something like what?'
'Serious and personal.'
'Why should I mind?'
'You suck up to the captain. All bloody day and night long.'

The forecastle is out of bounds to officers, as much for our own health as because of ship's rules, yet we officers and gentlemen were in the midst of frenzied scenes in the crew's quarters; what started with a pint of black strap over a gunroom dinner became a late party with the men in the forbidden portion of the ship. Grog flowed, the fiddler played, men clapped and stamped on the timbers in dances: hornpipes, jigs, reels. We sat on cabin trunks, leaning against pillars when weariness became too demanding. And the rum was dispensed. The men threw it back, their eyes hardly so much as blinking, but the liquor burned my throat; I could only sip it which I did secretively turned from the brilliance of the overloaded candle holder. We danced a folk movement with these rough ignorant hands and we were all friends in drink, the grand leveller. The music stopped and I fell from the group and collapsed upon a solitary William Bligh staring into his pewter mug; my old shipmate.

'To the captain?' he replied, slowly seeking words from a deluged brain.

'Yes, the bloody captain, that's who,' I said and felt unafraid.

'I've never sucked up to anyone. Listen, Johnny boyo, I'm a Navy fellow, am I not?'

'You're a bloody warrant officer, that's what you are; not even a gentleman.'

'That is where you are wrong. I'm only a warrant officer because that's the quickest way to being a captain, is it not?' A fat arm came around my shoulder, like a slow-worm with five eyes.

His strange lips moved in a pink, freshly scraped dish upon which a clump of fair mould grew where his razor had missed. 'Lieutenants become captains, warrant officers become older warrant officers.'

'Listen, I'll have a command within three years, I'll wager to it.'

David Samwell turned quickly past like a child's top among the group of dancers and a soprano whoopee followed; then his shoes faded among bare feet and a drunken sailor stumbled along dispensing a jug of rum. A group of revellers blocked the candlelight like a shower cloud passing a gibbous moon, and the beams returned and our mugs had been filled.

'All Cook's boys get promotion; to sail with the old boy is to ensure a quick climb up the ladder. You know that.'

'Warrant officer to captain is a bit more than a quick climb, old bean,' I said and my arm encircled the wide middle. Good chums, and the grog tasted better.

'The captain has promised to recommend me for a command. Honestly, Johnny, I kid you not; and our captain's pretty influential in the admiralty.'

'So you admit it. You suck up to him.' I pulled my arm away at the nagging from a long time ago of competition. Another drink, another yell from Samwell. His shoes were tapping a rhythm and his body came down beside us. 'You look like a cooked pomegranate,' I said, watching sweat rolling down that cheery face.

'A man could perish for want of a drink hereabouts,' he said and took my mug so that I might be parched first.

'And what are you two hatching; another mutiny?'

'William Bligh here,' I announced, struggling with words which were becoming most elusive, 'is about to be made a bleeding admiral.'

'That, my dear John, is because he sucks up to the captain.'

'This is a conspiracy,' Bligh said, trying to stand. 'Between you two. I'll tell you Dr Taffy Samwell I've not sucked up to anyone and I've no need to. You know why?'

'No, and I've no wish to know and I wouldn't be at all surprised if the same went for my gentleman friend here.'

Bligh, a blurred egg on matchsticks, was standing. 'Talent, that's why. Natural talent.'

I pointed an unsteady arm at prominent kneecaps and mimicked Dr Anderson's voice. 'A most interesting case, my dear doctor; dislocated saucers.'

Dancers dimmed; legs and white cut-off trousers stretched for unfocusing miles. Matt Pall began 'Rule Britannia!' and Bligh sank slowly down onto his stockings; he was singing to me; lips moved and I was staring into a checkerboard mouth. Once his voice came through the choristers and I felt sad for he who sang so lustily; I took a long draught in pity. When my eyes opened again Samwell and I were wrapped in our arms and his falsetto harmony came down from the beams.

'Tone deaf.'

'Pardon?' David shouted.

'Poor old Bligh is; he's not got a lot going for him.'

'He's got his talent,' David shouted back very close and the inside of an ear was wet from his words. 'And slipped saucers.'

'I'll miss him when he goes.'

'Goes?'

'To be an admiral.'

My eyes opened and bodies lay like litter after the races; a few diehards were performing an energetic hornpipe. Samwell and Bligh argued about the captain.

'But dammit, Bligh, the fellow is a dictator.'

'He has to be. He gives the orders, John and his lieutenants pass them on; me and my mates ensure they are carried out. And the bidding is done by our complement of nigh on one hundred and ten souls. Someone has to have complete charge of our fates and this makes the captain the loneliest man in the world; does it not?'

'It's time for a change.'

'It can't be otherwise. What do you say, John?'

'I could do with some water.'

Bligh shouted through the drinkers and the jug boy appeared out of the shadows.

'Leave it there, my man,' Samwell said; we were the crew's guests here, but orders were still orders.

'I'll tell you this,' Bligh said, 'he's the finest man in the Navy, he is.'

'Bless him, that's what I say,' David said, and we clunked mugs to the old boy.

I confessed, 'You know, I loved him.'

'We all love him,' said Samwell.

'He's a splendid captain,' said Bligh.

I sipped from the pewter which I held tightly to, but my grip of reality was not so firm. My eyelids came down slowly. There was a different sound to the voices. My eyes focused on the ankles of a woman; I saw widening nostrils above a urethral mouth; the pomegranate was painted white. A sabre glinted ominously as candlelight danced along it; a woman shouted with a man's voice. I could not catch the words. I rested my head on David's shoulder.

Bligh was on his saucers; an argument raged and the blade hung waiting from the tart's hand. The sailors had abandoned the dancing; it seemed some bother was in the air and a circle grew round us. I thought silly Bligh, bullying with that tongue of his; it'll be his undoing. I sipped my grog and my ears popped. Bligh was demanding a cutlass; David Samwell was trying to medicate tempers. All I could say was, oh God! If anyone got injured here . . . and the image of a dressing-down from the old boy cleared my mind a little. The girl with the sabre fell back from Bligh and started to disrobe; an overskirt of dark green velveteen, a striped underskirt fell to the deck. She kept an eye firmly on Bligh and a hand tight on the sabre's hilt. A light green bodice came away and a man stood with the painted face of a harlot. He (or she) stood over six feet in grubby linen, and black shoes. Hair stiff from the twist of a pigtail hung about his shoulders like a Swift Yahoo.

I looked round for my worried pomegranate when the slash of the blade brought me back to the sailor-tart. Bligh stood unsteadily before this creature and parried with a cutlass. The sabre rushed through the air again in a two-handed swing, the grog swayed inside Bligh and he fell clear of the arc.

Sailors were cheering. The tart fought like a big man, using extra reach and muscles to drive the blade as an axe. Bligh ducked and the sword went above him. He stabbed with his cutlass, but it was a poor aim which went wide. But I could see Bligh was too drunk to match the axeman; our young master would not be walking up the fo'c's'le ladder or anywhere else again.

The man-tart was quickly getting the better of Bligh and forcing him to retreat. The spectators leaped back and re-formed so that as the fight progressed across the forecastle, a moving circle of audience ringed them. The blades cracked but the steel held; Bligh fought silently, trying to concentrate; the bigger man grunted and snarled with each swing.

'We'd better do something, John; I don't think Bligh will be able to hold out much longer.'

'Bligh's a good man with a blade,' I tried.

'He's too far into his cups to fight.'

We heard a twang, the noise of springing metal, and then the clatter of a cutlass hitting the deck. I could see a head of untidy red hair but no sign of Bligh; he had fallen below the level of the crowd. The sailors chanted, 'Kill! Kill!' They were never ones for fair play when foul would do as well.

'Come on,' I shouted to David who held closely to the grog jug; we pushed through the people pressing round the victor and emerged like a cork from a bottle into the ring. The man stood over Bligh. The people chanted and the brute, who seemed a giant as I stood beside him-her, raised the sabre. I kicked at a bare, hairy leg and pain burst from my bruised toes. The creature turned and Bligh was safe. I would engage him in some discussion; the master could pull the sabre away and we would overpower him until the temper subsided.

The audience was silent. 'Listen,' I began, 'you've had your fun and you've won. To go further is only to invite real trouble for yourself. Why not shake on it, like proper Englishmen, and. . . .'

My oratory was overpowered by drink and any convincing argument was slow in coming; the response from this maddened male-tart was the scream of the sabre cutting through the air. I jumped back from the attack.

'Look, really . . . ,' I started, but hate burned from that face. Bligh was still on the floor and I searched a desperate eye for David Samwell, my only hope. He came beside me and pushed a cutlass in my hand. 'For Christ's sake,' I began, but I was deeply involved involuntarily and I prayed that the alcohol might go away: or better that I might be dreaming.

The fellow slashed again and the razor's edge sung its melody of destruction as it came for me. I pushed towards him, ducking, *passata sotto*, as we say, and missed the scythe. My body feint surprised him, and he pulled back a little. He quickly returned the blade from left to right as if he were swatting a wasp. Riposte, and I stood and brought the blade up in my attack, reaching for an arm; a surface wound may well take away the courage of the grog. But his reach was so much greater; I stood only as high as his chest and was possibly half his weight. But the unfairness of our inequal match had little tempering of his intentions.

The bright lips were wide as he slashed again. I wondered if by ducking about I could hold out till he tired, but I quickly dismissed that idea. If just one of those swings connected, it would continue through flesh and bone.

A painful death if a rapid one. I swung the cutlass to parry the sting from the next attack. The steel rang loudly and the concussion was like a hammer blow to my wrist. I daren't do that again or bones would break.

The Tower cutlass was much heavier than my hanger, and far from as well balanced. But it was exactly four inches longer, which would help. I was in need of a strategy

I decided to use my greater agility. I pulled back from the swings and lunged, bringing the blade now within a dash of those painted cheeks. He fell off with a cry and then attacked. The air screeched above my head as I doubled in another *passata sotto*. I lunged the cutlass up again scarcely an inch from his eyes and he screamed. I had to frighten him into submitting to superior swordsmanship for he knew I dare not kill him, because I was an officer. He returned to his lethal wasp arcs in a burst of about half a dozen swings and pressed forward. I gave ground and begged God that a bulkhead may not be behind me. Silver flashed a code as individual candles in the candelabra tray were reflected on the sword.

Sweat was pouring down his face, mixing ghoulishly with the cosmetics; if only it would go into his eyes. He grunted with the strokes, and spat sweat, hot and salty. He hesitated and I pushed forward. He parried and I lunged in small stabs, as if I were jabbing for his face. He fell back. We returned along our unhappy piste. David Samwell was standing inside our moving ring, grog jug in one hand, refreshing his mug in the other; at least he looked worried. Bligh was unconscious still and several people fell over him.

'David!' I called. 'The anaesthetic.'

We reached the end of the man's attack and I came back with short stabbing movements which he had to strain to see and avoid. I shouted, 'The second method.' With heavy emphasis on what is not said, if you follow me, doctor. I pressed the riposte and tried to lead the lumbering parrier towards Bligh, so that he might trip. The sabre-swinger retreated, and David was behind him. Then the swordsman spun and we turned. I grabbed David's mug of grog. We twisted again while I continued my thrusts and David brought the heavy pewter down on that large untidy head. This stunned him and I threw the mug of rum. It missed the opponent and hit the audience. They pulled back in shock. My adversary was regaining his composure; I could still run him through, but my conscience was in the way. Then first one and then several spectators tripped on Bligh and jolted into the bank of candles. The tray catapulted on its chains and the momentum doused the light. Blackness closed over the scene of pandemonium. I grabbed David's arm, we found the prostrate body of Bligh through the shouting, disorientated drunks and pushed for the fo'c's'le ladder.

Somehow fear gave us strength to retreat with the near *corpus delicti* and we recovered in the sickbay with a glass of anaesthetic (number one) and water.

'I've never known a sailor who could fight like that,' I said as we toasted Dame Fortune. 'And I kept thinking he was a bloody tart.' Bligh was slumped on a chair; Samwell sat on the berth often occupied by his senior.

'It was that marine, didn't you know?'

'What marine?' I said.

'Bloody Lieutenant Phillips, I kid you not,' the angry accusation came from Bligh stirred by the memory of the conversation with blades. 'I'll skin the bastard alive tomorrow,' he said, but we knew we dared not air the matter tomorrow or again.

'What was he doing in that costume anyway?'

'He often does it,' David said, crossing his legs contentedly. 'It makes the crew laugh and then they're pals with him. It's not easy being a marine.'

'Perhaps, William Bligh, master of this here ship, you'd be so kind as to tell me what the fight was about.' The grog's magic was returning. 'After all, you nearly had me killed.'

'The captain's honour. He called the old boy a prick.'

'No he didn't,' Samwell said, dispensing more medical spirits.

'That's how it started.'

'My dear William, he said you shouldn't treat the captain like one. He said you made your own orders when the captain was out of sight.'

'But I thought . . . I mean you're kidding. . . .'

'We were all fighting for the captain's honour?' I asked.

'I can't think of a better cause,' David said. 'Here's a toast to the old boy.'

'It's all right for you,' I said. 'You didn't have to fight.'

But we stood as best we could for the toast just the same.

The fodder bays were filled; we had replenished our stocks and were packed with fresh food. Now we could push for the ice with an easy conscience. True, Omai would remain with us longer, but he would hardly complain. We could carry out the exploration of the north and then return our Tahitian prince to his home and complete the King's wishes by stocking the South Seas islands. The major mission after all was seeking the North-West Passage which was where lay the £20,000 reward. The captain would share some with the complements and that would be good booty for us.

But it was not to be. Procrastination dragged her irritating heels upon the exploration. Captain Cook hesitated and then we were far too late and the blame he might have reserved for himself dispensed about the ship in black rages. But it was not only the people who were to suffer.

I do not pretend to a gift for augury, but when we took up station off a Tongan island I could see us locked on a course for trouble. In Zealand our ship's people did not hide their contempt for the natives, and without the captain's protection Mr Kahura would have been dancing from a yard tackle. But I quickly discovered that among the South Seas islanders there was not a fragmentation of loyalties. Here a chief was everyone's chief and was treated with extraordinary respect and devotion.

The captain had been ashore when I first witnessed this. I took the pinnace to bring him back and explained, 'One of the minor chiefs was on board, sir, and I was showing him about. Wherever we went, so stood the islanders, perhaps three hundred of them. The chief was amused at first at my polite requests for them to let us pass so I could show something else to him. Then he lost his temper and ordered them all ashore.'

'Did they go?' he asked. We were sitting in the stern sheets, the rowers facing us. I guided us through some Indian canoes resembling shaped driftwood; curious paddlers waved.

'Without a question asked. Straight off the ship and paddled quickly for home. But so inquisitive were our visitors, they came back. They followed their instructions, and there had not been a word against returning. However, sir, this chief took exception. He picked up a large stick and beat them unmercifully. They did not raise a finger to protect themselves or to stop him. One man, sir, was struck over the side of the face, and blood gushed from both his mouth and nostrils. He lay motionless for some time and was at last carried off in convulsions.'

'Is that it, Mr Williamson?'

'This chief was told he had killed the man, sir, and his reaction was to laugh. He actually laughed about it.'

'Is there a moral?' There was a fierceness in his voice that ought to have warned me. 'Only that they are unlike the Maori chiefs. We could have struck down Kahura without trouble, but I fear the men ought to be warned against laying a finger on these people.'

'Would that advice not go for the captains, too?'

'For anyone who cares for the welfare of the people.'

'It sounds like an unhappy threat.'

'No, sir, it is not meant as that; the people would have killed Kahura without your interference, but here the effect would be. . . .'

The pinnace hit against *Resolution*. 'Poppycock, young sir. You've been here five minutes and you want to advise me on how to treat these people. I've been among the islands before and the man who tampers with the chiefs is higher than any chief in the eyes of the natives.'

I should have let well enough alone, but I feared for him; for us all. 'A deity? He would need the help of the real God, sir, should his guard be down for a moment.'

'Avast with this talk. I'll teach you a little of what I know soon enough.' He grabbed the side ropes and swung to the cleats. His breeches went past me, the stockings, polished shoes, and he had made the deck.

The thefts started and the captain saw each incident as a personal challenge, as if our philosophies had been marooned in Zealand. The first stolen item was a junk axe and then any small souvenir that could be lifted. James King, Mr Gore, and I were with the captain entertaining a minor chief when Bligh hurried into the cabin to report a yarn-winch handle missing.

The captain stiffened. We feared a European *haka* might be performed for our guest, so upset had the old boy become over the thefts. Mr Gore said, 'Come now, Mr Bligh, how do you know it is missing?'

Bligh loathed explaining anything to anybody but the captain. 'Because, sir, I have had men spinning yarn. They put the handle down only for a moment and then. . . .'

'Get someone to search around for it....,' James King said in a tone which hinted that this was no time for such a petty matter.

But the captain was upset. 'Is this a conspiracy? I have asked the master to keep a weather-eye to the thefts. Our passage is hardly over and the chattels of this ship are required till the end.'

'But sir,' I tried, 'a winch handle, a piece of hollow metal?'

'And where will it end, Mr Williamson?' He turned back to Bligh. 'You are quite right to report it to me. Examine the natives on the deck. Do not let one go till you are sure their person is innocent of the object.'

Bligh the zealot rushed from the cabin as if he were embarking on a favourite game. No wonder we jibed him over subservience to the aft-cabin.

'Explain to the chief what is happening.'

I said diplomatically, 'Chief, an item from the ship has gone missing and the captain is concerned about thefts and wishes to have the natives searched to make sure they have not inadvertently picked it up.' I daresay I sounded apologetic; I wanted to.

'What did you say?' The captain was trembling with rage and I would rather face an 84-gun than see that expression turned on me.

I repeated at once my translation and began to explain why. 'Damn your impertinence. Who is captain of this vessel, me or this trumped-up little nigger? You will tell him that I am searching the natives and I *will* punish the thief severely. *Will*, not *wishes*. And you will say that I do not ask his permission. I am the paramount chief of this piece of the world, if you don't mind.'

An unhappy interpreter set about relating this change of mood. However, he must know from the outburst and admonition that it wasn't me nor the other lieutenants who offered such discourtesy.

'Tell your captain there is no bother,' he replied. 'We live in a community where each object belongs to everyone and sometimes we unintentionally, well, collect things that do not necessarily belong to us.'

And the chief smiled, unconcerned. The captain paced about, stepping to the door and back; he was like a child visiting relations, forced to be with the adults when youngsters are at play.

The chief said, 'I think I will now take my leave as I hope to see my friend chief Finau on shore soon.'

The fellow moved towards the door and the winch handle fell from his robe.

'Mr Bligh,' the captain shouted, and the call seemed to come before the metal announced a challenge upon the wooden floor. We lieutenants stood open-mouthed; the chief had been proven guilty right before the captain whose face was red with a personal gale. Bligh came into the room and the *haka* began.

'Take this rogue off, Mr Bligh. Strip him. Strip him, do you hear? We will show these niggers that they will not make light of His Britannic Majesty's equipment. You, sir, you . . .', and he pointed a large finger at the fellow's chest, '. . . are a thief and a rogue and by God, sir, I'll teach you that no chief or peasant comes into my ship. . . .' He was in the eye of his storm and collapsed, canvas emptied, on the chair at the desk. 'A dozen lashes, Mr Bligh. Twelve of the best, and I'll ask you to have Collett lay them on thick.'

'But sir. . . .' Even Bligh looked incredulous. Flogging sailors was a routine. Punishing native chiefs was another matter.

The captain's temper reached the other side of the tempest's centre. 'Now, Mr Bligh. Now. It does not mean in ten minutes. Call all hands, and we'll have the other niggers present as witnesses.'

Bligh grabbed the arm of the chief and pushed him out. We all knew that commoners touching chiefs was a cause of great trouble. What flogging them would do we could only guess. We could hear the marines summoned, a call for Collett, the drum-roll for all hands.

The colour of James King's face contrasted vividly with his pale shirt. 'Sir, please, a petition from your lieutenants.'

'What is it?'

We heard the gratings being removed and falling heavily upright against the quarterdeck, ready for the victim.

Mr Gore spoke quietly. 'Sir, you've given the fellow a fright. Let's leave it at that, sir, eh? Come on, we have the handle retrieved and we've already roughed the fellow. . . .'

'Roughed, Mr Gore? I see no blood. Ask Mr Williamson what their interpretation is of rough.'

'Let's push the scoundrel off the ship and have his people rescue him,' Mr Gore continued. 'That ought to be a sufficient loss of face for him, and satisfaction for us. What do you say, captain?'

He walked slowly for the door. 'Come along, gentlemen, or we'll be late for the punishment.'

'Sir, I implore you to change your mind. . . .' But I was wasting my words.

The crew filled the deck; most were at their relaxations, so they were in their finest clothes. But holiday expressions were tightly furled for they realised the captain was sailing full canvassed into a hurricane's most dangerous quadrant.

'Collett, lay it on now. Proceed.'

The cat bit and Bligh counted off the strokes. Blood did not appear till the fourth cut. On the eighth, it was flowing freely. The back was pulped. The chief was in his middle years and a collar of fat hung at his waist; his buttocks were like empty bags. Only strings of muscles showed when the body flexed to receive the next blow. He fainted on the tenth swing and Collett was breathing heavily before he delivered the last.

The drummer stopped his roll. Bligh untied the man's hands from above his head and, perhaps because I was the closest of the officers, I moved to catch him.

'Stay where you are, Mr Williamson,' the captain snapped. The chief fell to the deck.

'Lieutenant Phillips, throw the rogue onto his belly and tie his hands behind his back.'

The captain climbed to the quarterdeck and stood to the landward rail. 'Have two of your men haul him up here,' he called. Marines supported the fainted chief. 'Do not steal from His Majesty King George and you will have nothing to fear. Translate that for me, Mr Williamson. Louder.'

I related our meanness. 'Tell the natives that the chief has been lashed and is now being fined,' I interpreted. 'He is being fined a hog. And when the hog is delivered, he will be released and all will be forgiven as far as King George is concerned.'

I followed the orders which was my duty as a Royal Navy officer. But my offended youth cried that the native might be forgiven, but the show of madness would not be forgotten, never.

15

*T*ime became a greater enemy than the disaffection within the ship or the anger of assaulted and insulted natives without, and yet we now idled away six months in these sunny isles. This extraordinary circumstance may well give rise to a set of questions from the publick. At which stage were the officers informed that the voyage was postponed? Did the officers accept the change in plans without comment; were there no petitions? If the captain displayed such disregard for admiralty orders, was not each and every commissioned officer obliged by duty to question him and to attempt to alter the decision?

Yet as the reader has been informed, the commander played his cards so close to his chest, as it were, that officially the officers did not even know the purpose of the voyage. I dare say Captain Clerke was informed, being second-in-command, but certainly nobody else. Of course, on a ship there cannot be secrets, and we expected to leave at any moment for the wastes of the north until such time passed that we knew we could not hope to reach the boreal summer.

And so for the majority, life settled into a happy rut of seeking islands, feasting with chiefs, drinking potent spruce beer and distributing our farmer King's menagerie through the archipelagos. Most natives were seeing white faces for the first time and any natural reserve they may have possessed was abandoned. From the first island to the last we carried a far greater complement than our victualling list showed; whole families settled on the ships, travelling to visit distant relations. They brought vast quantities of food, their own tipple and music. Every night now violin and the penny whistle were supplemented by the most romantic of songs. I was pleased we would not experience rough weather in this part of the world for as hosts the crew could be as changeable as a barometer. Among the anfractuosities of the sailorman's mind is the superstition of blaming women for a tempest. Many were the tales in the old days of innocents being turned into stormy seas; lovelorn girls hiding on a ship to be with their men have been murdered for no more than a prolonged gale of wind.

I relate that the natives as a race were fascinated by our different features, but the effect upon the womenfolk was the more remarkable. Blond hair and blue eyes won the ugliest brute a fair damsel the like of which he would never expect to find in old Albion. Girls moved in like ships' harlots of the victualling ports of England, only these were not gin-disfigured heavy women of indeterminate age. These were young lasses of infinite grace, and the only charms lacking were occasioned by a paucity of years. Officers were restrained in these matters by education and because it was not done to take to a coloured woman, although of course some did transgress. However it was our jack-tars who could not see beyond their priapism.

It would defame the inhabitants of balmy Polynesia to suggest that all girls were liberal with affection. Damsels of their working class were often entirely promiscuous and not in the least hindered by marriage. However, a higher class of natives were chaste and then faithful to their chosen husbands. It tells something of the avarice of the human heart and our ultimate damnation that this custom was a constant irritant to our common sailor; many considered the chosen virgins as a challenge to pride and unhappily there were times when packs of our animals fresh from a licentious feasting freely given would seek out the high-born girls and souvenir without conscience nor pity this membrane.

The sun warmed our browning features and light airs filled the canvas. We ate almost constantly of fresh food and, upon reaching a new island, accepted the local custom of gorging ourselves. Older shipmates grew excessively corpulent. The people enjoyed themselves as few sailors had before or since, but our commander retreated to the aft-cabin and introversion. The dinners were discontinued and the only time we broke bread with our most senior officer was ashore for a chief's feast. Then he was friendly yet oddly only with the dignatories. I was a vehicle for his conversations, being the most fluent of our translators, yet he seldom had asides even for me. He must have known I harboured resentment for the cruelty to the chief far back in our wake, but he was not relaxed with the other officers either. We were shamed by that unwarranted display and, as the reader will presume, it was not to be the last of such acts, which became retrogressively worse. Yet my history is of our voyage, not of disgrace brought upon England, and therefore I would beg the reader's indulgence in being permitted to embrace and relate other matters more consonant with our values of justice and fair play.

The further we voyaged the closer we were to Tahiti and the youthful leader became increasingly irrational. He ignored Polynesians who lived aboard and would only converse in our language. His wardrobe became more extravagant, without the least regard for the temperature. We would hear rusty squeaks pervading the ship as he dressed and then the noisy negotiation of the ladderway, one servant pulling mailed hands and the other pushing a metallic rump, and he would appear suited in armour. Omai posed against the weather-rail as if there were nothing out of the ordinary in his appearance; tinny legs crossed, a hand supporting that great weight against the caprail. A defect kept the visor from remaining open. Each of his theatrical remarks had to be accompanied by a spare hand clearing his vision and this procluded mannerisms with a kerchief held in the tips of his fingers. A favourite of his. Soon he would hurry below, as best as he was able in restrictive metal, in a frustrated fury to change.

'John, you've got to help me, old bean.'
'Of course, Omai.'
'You must speak to the old boy.'
'What about?'

It was not a new conversation these days; Omai on this particular occasion in a costume of burnt orange. Some fop-tailor sewed it in hessian and it looked as uncomfortable as it was distorted. Avanteguard, the native beau would have said. The breeches did not end till the ankles, which – according to the tailor as related by Omai – would be the new trend. He wore blue shoes of leather with enormous silver buckles. Our native prince leaned against the mizzen mast, hands deep in sackcloth pockets.

'Please John, don't let them leave me here.'
'Where else can you go?'
'England.'
'This is your home.'
'England's my home. London, aah, London and the theatre and. . . .'

'Omai, you know I'd help you if I could.'

'Aren't we friends, old bean? Don't English friends help each other?'

'You're not English and you know I can't.'

'King George wants me back as a friend. He said so. He's going to knight me, you know.'

'I can't do it, Omai.'

Then the tears threatened the perfect make-up and in the aft-cabin the quill was busy over the journal. The master was at the long table, putting finishes to a chart of a coral reef which almost completely circumferenced our last island.

'No, no, no, Mr Williamson. I've had petitions from Mr Gore and Mr King on Omai's behalf and now you. God knows how many times the ruddy subject comes up from the fellow himself. No, I have my orders; Omai stays in Tahiti.'

'But sir, he says King George wants him back in London.'

'The King has told the lords of the admiralty that on no account must Omai return; he must settle back with the natives and teach them what he has learned.'

'How to outdo a peacock, I suppose? Sir, I like Omai; I wish we could. . . .'

'That will do, young sir. Our duty is to return Omai to his land. . . .'

'But, sir, if. . . .'

'By God, don't try my patience. I'm going to do everything I can for him. We aren't going to maroon him. We'll find the most suitable, hospitable island. Whatever he needs from the ship he can have. . . .'

'He'll choose a four-pounder.'

'Except the great guns. We're going to build a house for him, a decent one that will give him prestige.'

'The natives will prise the nails from the walls.'

'I'll thank you not to remind me of the thefts. Mr Williamson, I have long thought of that problem and the carpenter is at this moment designing a habitation which can be constructed with wooden pegs. Now, if you don't mind. . . .'

And despite Omai's prayers, sharp mountains came up over the horizon; we had found Tahiti. Chiefs rowed out to the ship and natives swarmed on board. They remembered lusty English boys from the previous voyage and the women were fragrant with desire. They brought flowers and the ship was resplendent of blooms; only Omai felt sad in this island paradise, even when he heard that the jealous hierarchy on his home island would not take him back at any price.

If a high-ranking native could be encouraged to take an interest in Omai, he would have a safe home, but the hapless young man refused to speak to chiefs and instead made enemies of his people. We travelled among the archipelago and eventually an island was found which would tolerate the youth and his servants. The local chief, an elderly and gout-stricken fellow, was bribed into accepting this new settler with presents from the captain and a considerable purse from Omai for the hire of a large, two-hulled war-canoe plus crew.

Carpenter Cleveley built a house without nails and lockable cupboards and chests were installed for Omai's muskets, suit of iron and clothes. On our last night, Omai entertained us in the new timbered villa. Local natives dressed in a rough parody of English waiters served suckling pigs and island produce. We officers sat at a table with our host who sparkled in the most lavish foppery. A chain like a lord mayor's hung at his neck and reflected the light from the elegant candelabrum. People from both ships sat about the grounds with women friends. Natives performed sensual dances and the ships' crews went turn about with presentations. Bagpiping, violining, then our marines gave a marching display and an exhibition of shooting, but the standard was such that our commander, sharing all of our embarrassment, ordered some fireworks to be ignited. It certainly had the natives forget our ill-practised soldiers for this pyrotechnia terrified them, at which unhappy consequence Omai and the captain expressed much mirth.

Then the dancing resumed and the wine was poured. Omai made Collett take a place at the table and poured wine for old times' sake, old chap.

A little later, I clinked glasses with our host who gazed sadly at the faces round the table.

'You're feeding almost all of the island, but I don't see the chief.'
'I didn't invite him.'
'Why not?'
'I don't think he likes me.'
'There's not going to be much love if he's the one inhabitant not invited to your functions.'
'I'm not worried about that.'
'Omai, you are such a crazy person; he's a chief; you know how great are their powers.'

'Let him come, I've got guns.'
'You and your two boys can hold the island at bay?'
'I'll be the chief here one day, you'll see.'
'You know what King George would say to you?'
'Come home to England.'
'He'd say, Omai, give the chief many presents, make him your friend, then at least you can live in peace. What do you say to that?'
'Oh, I might, old bean.'
'But you won't, will you?'
'I think I might build a ship and sail to England.'
'With those soft mitts, Omai?'

The people of the ships stood in formal lines in the waist and Omai, in a near imitation of an admiral's rig, moved among them. He shook each man's hand and said Cheers, old bean, frightfully, more than a hundred times. And then he moved among the officers and there were only two farewells to go. Now tears fell freely, flowing canyons through greasepaint. I saluted him and put out my hand. He held it in both of those perfumed manicured paws with the desperation of a drowning sailor. Cheers, Lieutenant Johnny, see you in England. Then he shook the captain's hand.

'Frightfully nice passage out here, old bean,' he said in the worst accent we had yet heard. 'Take care of my old shipmates, don't you know.'

He turned to the caprail and Portsmouth began a drum-roll. A piping commenced and Omai sprang back to the captain and then disappeared over the side. He went down onto the *Royal George* as he had named the war-canoe rafted beside us. We saluted him with thirteen guns and our bower came in. We followed *Discovery* through the coral channel and the *Royal George* kept us company for several days. We called at our last island before leaving for the north, but the war-ravaged people had little reason to bless our visit. Then Omai, still in the admiral's uniform, set sail for his new home and we spread our widest bleached wings for the equator and the far north. The expensive perfumes of Omai lingered on the ship, but we were not to see him again.

A landsman may anticipate our narrative recording refreshed, happy mariners rushing towards new discoveries, but the ways of old Albion's hearts of oak are quite different. Our minds did not embrace the excitement of land to come, only the paradise in our wake. We could count many enemies along that disturbed seapath, but there were friends too and for our sailors, feminine experiences which they could never expect to repeat; in fact, after such heavy indulgence they could have been content with a future of chastity.

Accidents, pugilism, damaged sails and angry scenes were the lot from our men until feet and hands hardened under rope and timber, stomachs adjusted to beef and biscuit, weevil and maggot, and wills surrendered to discipline. We crossed the line, but no merriment rang through the ships. We found a low flat island, but it offered only turtles and sharks, and we climbed through the latitudes expecting no excitement till we found New Albion, the west coast of America, which was a long way off. Beyond lay hardship, gales and bitter cold. So our bodies were grateful for the warmth of the sun while it may last and minds coasted under a leisurely spread of nostalgia. We saw to our duties, without actually seeing, as it were; we had been drugged and we were not in any haste to greet normalcy. The unorthodox cry that came from the mast-top was therefore not perhaps to be such a surprise.

'Deck there! Jesus Christ, but it is. It's land. Yes, it's land.' And then in a panic, 'By the frig it's an island, huge.'

And so our ship discovered a land mass where none was expected and not as it came over the horizon, but within five miles. The look-out had not believed his eyes until the blue peaks and dazzling green base would not go away. Shock and excitement went about the ship more dramatically than St Elmo's fire. Men stumbled from their relaxations to the lee rail to stare at hope suddenly so close. Our serious work was at least postponed and a cheering took the men. As was to be expected, our captain, with the master in tow, was on the quarterdeck displaying an enthusiasm the like of which I had not heard since Kerguelen. Each man was consumed by a mad optimism that the island might be inhabited, perhaps by women with favours to offer. We thought of fresh food, suckling pigs, fruit and a new batch of heady spruce beer. Such was our notion of a paradise that this island might become after weeks at sea with expectations only of unpleasantries.

But in the matter of honesty, I can report that nobody in their wildest imaginings anticipated the welcome awaiting us. If the food was delicious before, here it was more so; if the maidens of the past were emotionally warmed to us, here they were a stoked furnace; if some of the people in our wake revered us, here they fell to the ground in the worship of a god and his children.

The land became a group of islands that swung before our eyes like the shining pendulum of the hypnotist and we were beguiled while the wind came against us and we had to beat the ships uncomfortably, jarringly, towards our uncertain haven. A day, two days passed and the land was out of reach but so close that we pressed on with the patience of a wind-driven spinning spider. Then a strand was easily discernible and we could see settlements and clusters of people, and a canoe came through a low surf, and another, and the frail swift vessels reached the ships and natives called up and I strained to catch the language.

'My God, captain, it's. . . .'

'I can't believe it, Mr Williamson. Speak to them, see if they understand your Polynesian.'

I called to the handsome figures, '*He wahine, he whenua. . . .*'

And back came, '*A ngaro ai te tangata.*' As if it were a passphrase.

'Captain, how could Polynesians have travelled this far?' I asked incredulously.

But anthropology was far from the minds of the ships' people. They shouted to the natives alongside who threw into the sea the boulders they carried as weapons, and pulled themselves up the side-ropes.

'Their eyes are like saucers,' James King said as we received them in the waist. 'They can't believe we are real.'

And it was obvious at the joyous way the natives gazed and touched and laughed in disbelief that they had never seen a ship o' sail before. Their faces were wide eyes and shining teeth as they stared up into our forest and cautiously descended ladders. They came into the aft-cabin hackles raised, claws out nervously, like cats in strange territory. They touched the Chippendale chairs, the desk, the captain's open journal, the chart-table and the draughtsmanship of Bligh, the open sternlights letting in a cool breeze, staring through the glass and each making small cries of surprise and pleasure. Then one gripped the smoothness of the metal arm; it fell and the window crashed closed with the noise of a carronade shot. The group leaped in shock and rushed for safety; unfortunately they chose other windows and as they pushed through, these crashed closed like explosions, and glass splintered. The cabin emptied in seconds and canoes outside recovered surprised swimmers.

'We would wish to trade with you for fresh food,' I translated to a boy who had charge of a canoe.

'We would happily trade for this,' the lad said. He was holding a metal shroud fitting.

'Iron,' Captain Cook said. 'How could they know about it?'

I interpreted the question. 'It comes with driftwood from the sea, but very rare.'

'From shipwrecks, I would think,' the captain said. 'Tell him we would be pleased to trade for this metal.' The boy shouted the news to others, and the decks cleared and canoes paddled for the shore as natives-turned-traders rushed for their wares.

'These Polynesians have such a desire for iron,' the captain addressed to Bligh as we returned to the quarterdeck.

'It makes a cheap barter for us, sir,' the master said. 'Who would ever expect the common nail to command such a price?'

'It is a very happy occurrence,' the captain said.

Many islanders came out with fresh meat and fruit; bargaining was fast and carpenter's supplies quickly obtained more than a day's victuals for the complete complements. The people's bellies would be full, but their appetites went further and a spokesman came forward to ask if the natives would bring out women. The captain looked shocked: it seemed that the freshness of the land and these curious children of nature had kept his thoughts on a higher plane.

'By God, Collett, you and your men are the essence of coarseness itself,' he war-danced to the surprise of the natives. 'I'll not have you infecting their girls with your foul sickness.'

'But sir. . . .' Collett began, but did not complete the sentence; he saw Bligh coming from the mizzen to the quarter-rail.

'Collett, you can tell the people that there will be no women because I will not have the venereals spread to these folk too. You have done your damnedest in Tahiti and it'll not be repeated here; these natives have never seen a vessel before and we can presume they are free from the vile disorder.'

The natives, of course, were unable to understand the words, but they nevertheless enjoyed the impromptu, red-faced shouting performance.

'*E koro* of-the-white-foreheads,' their chief bargainer said. He was a well-muscled fellow of middle years with a look to his eye that established him as a stranger to innocence. 'The hunger of men is not only appeased from above the stomach. Our women are attractive and strong, would you not wish. . . .'

I looked quickly towards the captain hoping he could not guess the ill-timed words, but he was still coming down from the temper to whoever would listen, in this case to Dr David Samwell. The conversation was overly spiced with ruddy venereals and ruddy disgust.

'No,' I hastily trimmed the suggestion. 'We do not wish to be involved with your women. You must tell them that our chief will not permit them on board.'

He was not offended; perhaps from my worried look at the captain he had guessed the meaning of the previous outburst. 'There is no point in that,' he said. 'Deafness ails women when a reply is not as they wish.'

I smiled at the internationalism of fair damsels and in this happy frame of mind was directed to launch the pinnace, to visit a watering place ashore. The boat swung out clumsily on the yard tackles and rowers and butts were lowered. We carried a small band of marines for protection. The distance to the shore was covered quickly and the vibrant warm land stretched out for us. Our journey was watched by people from a village who hurried to the strand. Such was their enthusiasm that I felt it better to go further on, but they raced along the shore in pursuit, like happy children. There was much shouting and laughing and this latter sound caused me to decide that caution was unnecessary. I pushed over the tiller and we ran in.

A flock of fairy terns flew above us, the sun was hot and a languidness enveloped the white sand. Then the villagers arrived. They ran through the waves and grabbed for the gunwales to guide us in. I was smiling and begging them to take care; yet none replied. Perhaps the dialect among the common people was a little different. In a trice our boat was surrounded by natives who smiled and pushed at the uniforms of the men; they had seen nothing like us and were lavish of attention and quite like affectionate spaniels. However, these beings were much larger and far from easily dissuaded. They bodily hauled a sailor from the boat and were trying to help out others. One had the anchor over his head and spun round with it. The group was growing all the time and what had begun amusingly became rapidly frightening. The marines looked terrified; the NCO asked for orders, but what could I say? We could hardly fix bayonets, for these simple villagers would run onto them in their welcoming madness. I tried to stand in the sternsheets, but hands reaching for us like tentacles from a cave of octopus pushed and I fell onto some rowers. I recovered to a position of dignity. The faces of our people were bewildered; soon they would take the law into their own hands.

I gave the order to pull back into the surf so that we might be free of the natives and ready for a new strategy. But to issue orders is one thing; for the men to try to see them through was another. The crowd was so thick about us, we could not put so much as a foot over the side.

'You four,' I pointed to the marines. 'Go to the bow and push us off.'

The water still lifted our stern, so refloating would not be difficult if only we could get the men out of the pinnace. We shouted at the natives, the marines pushed and punched, but those suffering close to the gunwale could not stop the pressure of eager souls on the perimeter. I grabbed my brown bess lying in the bottom of the boat; I would fire into the air praying the noise might startle them. A hand grabbed the barrel and then another. Perhaps this was a stick and they would help me out with it. The faces pressed on us, brown hands groping, the shouts of a multitude, and we were suddenly at the mercy of a mob. How could life so filled with bliss one moment offer such imminent tragedy the next? I pulled back the flintlock and squeezed the trigger.

The bang from the old musket was enormous even in that clamour. For a moment I thought it had been simply a flash in the pan. Then the crowd unfolded from the pinnace as if they were thrown apart by the impact of a bomb exploding. Pink nails and dark oily fingers were on the gunwale one moment and above their close-cropped heads the next.

The gun had indeed fired; a tall youth, his genitalia modestly held by a loin cloth, smiled as a patch of red spread across his stomach. He put his finger in the hole and pulled it out for inspection and I needed to vomit. He picked at the burnt lint wadding round its circumference and turned to his comrades and laughed, a good-humoured, friendly sound. It was loud and his teeth shone before blood suddenly stained them. I think the pain burst at the same moment for the laugh fell and the features became absolutely smooth. He pitched forward in the sand, and the crowd stood in their circle also absolutely still.

'Jesus,' a voice said from the boat. 'We'd best scarper.'

The familiar cockney patois brought me back to reality and I returned the marines to the order. The anchor and stolen items were collected from around the body; we rowed away. The silent people picked up the poor fellow and returned slowly to the village.

'Damn your eyes, Mr Williamson. Can I not send you on an errand without a likely war being triggered?'

'Sir, I am truly sorry.'

'By God, you'd better be.' The *haka* was being performed as I expected, but not at the intensity it might have. 'I detest having natives killed, do you hear me?'

'I know you do, sir.'

'We had to shoot some on my first voyage. By God, I can see their poor ignorant faces even now. All they were doing was protecting themselves from foreigners, a practice we are no strangers to in old Albion. It was a mistake to shoot them; I regret it to this day.'

'Sir, I did not want to shoot the fellow. We had to do something. . . .'

'You could do anything, but not murder them.'

'I'm sorry, sir, I. . . .'

'I'm not going to argue with you; remain on board for our time here. Mr Bligh,' he shouted through the door, and when it opened said, 'Prepare the launch, I'm going ashore myself.'

'I'll come with you sir,' Bligh said.

'Of course, but I'll have your musket uncocked. Tell Lieutenant Phillips to provide a detachment of marines.'

The launch and pinnace reached the shore. A few villagers watched but they kept away. Sailors lifted out barrels and the party set off for the watering.

At the end of the evening meal. David Samwell sat alone further down the gunroom table. 'I want you to help me,' I said, moving along the bench opposite him. We were slow eaters; he was gazing sorrowfully at a solitary vegetable on the pewter plate.

'Not you with the venereals, too,' he said.

'You know me better than that. David, I want you to come ashore with me. Tonight.'

'Haven't you had enough of the island?'

'That's the thing. I want to apologise.'

'Who to?'

'The people, or whatever.'

'I heard you weren't allowed ashore.'

'I don't intend to seek permission. I want to make my apologies, try to explain how it happened and give them some presents.'

'You feel that badly?'

'I feel much worse, but what else can I do to make up for it?'

'From what I hear the fellow had hold of your musket. He was running a great risk and lost. Perhaps there's no need to do anything.'

'What could he have known about guns? It's that the whole thing got properly disorientated and now some innocent is dead.'

'Why me to go with you?'

'We're friends aren't we, shipmates? Some of the people have agreed to row me there and wait. But I don't want them to accompany me; the first thing they'd do is stir up trouble.'

'They'll do just that if you leave them on the beach.'

'There's no other way.'

'And you want me to come with you? You must think I'm crazy or something.'

'Well, you volunteered for this voyage, didn't you?'

We took the launch because it was smaller and needed fewer oarsmen. We left the ship undetected and nobody was to be seen in the light of a waxing moon. Four rowed us smartly to the beach and the waves had almost gone. The men would wait, they said, and I led David across the beach to the low scrub, rather than go directly to the village. If there were guards, a track down to the sea was their most likely location. We passed under coconut palms and across open ground. We came over a slight incline and ahead were village houses, in strange letter A shapes. I stopped to look at the layout.

'What now?' David whispered behind me.

'I don't know.'

'Don't know? By the powers, we're risking being impaled at any moment by some guard. . . .'

'There may not be guards.'

'I'm going back.'

'Hang on. This is Polynesia, there are bound to be signs of a wake in progress.'

The houses made of matting and branches were widely spaced and we soon heard voices. We walked round the side of a sharp-roofed habitation and an open fire burned brightly. About twenty people sat on their haunches around the body of the slain villager. He lay on a bed of woven flax and a garment was wrapped from his arms to his knees.

I coughed and surprised looks challenged us, but none of the people stood; they simply looked and I fancied that neither pleasure nor unfriendliness was shown. I said slowly, 'We come to express our condolences.' A man seated near the head of the corpse pointed to a house perhaps fifteen feet away. It resembled a small barn, with one low door; we could not see any windows. I repeated my words at this entrance and we were bade to enter. We had to crouch to do so like a goose under a gate, and came into a tall square room. Flax mats were spread over a dirt floor. The room was the dimension of the house for there were no floors or divisions as in our homes. A large elderly man sat on his haunches, with a woven garment about him. Bare feet retreated through a door in the opposite wall and now he was alone.

I said I wished to express my sympathy to the family of the deceased. The light from tapers was good. The old chap did not seem surprised at my grasp of their language; he bade us sit which we did. His hair was white and pulled into a topknot, very much after the style of Kahura so far back in our travels.

'You may pass these condolences on to me.'

'You, *e koro*, are his father?'

'His father was killed in battles a long time hence, as was his mother. He was betrothed to my child.'

'We wish to say that we are sorry for the affair. I personally regret the accident.'

'An accident?' The man's eyes held mine for some moments and I feared my well-meaning visit may have been a tragic error. 'The ways of the gods are no accident.'

'But in the haste of the moment. . . .'

'When we are no longer of value to this world, we are not to know. When the time comes for one to be despatched, it happens.'

I explained to the philosopher that my companion was not with the tongue and translated the proceedings to David Samwell. 'How frightfully English,' he said, 'to see the event as an act of God.'

'So it seems.'

'Well, they've had no previous experience of muskets.'

I turned to the old man. 'Whatever is the cause, I regret his passing, *e koro*, and would like these humble gifts to be accepted as an indication of my remorse.' I put before him the parcel I had been carrying.

He unwrapped it and studied the knee breeches, several stockings and a sailoring jersey. I would miss them on the voyage north, but these were the only items I had that may be of use to natives. 'Your gift is appreciated.' He found a hole I had neglected to darn in a stocking. He pulled the material about and seemed impressed that it did not tear. 'The deceased was of a high family, but he was troubled by the moon as a child and did not recover his senses. Perhaps he will be more useful where he has gone.' He moved on his haunches which I thought might be an indication of an end to the audience. 'You should not have bothered with the gifts,' he said, but kept a firm grip of them. 'What is your name.'

'Lieutenant Williamson, *e koro*.'

'That is what your friends call you?'

'Johnny.'

At that moment a head of dark hair pushed through the door of the disappearing feet and a young woman of extraordinary looks entered. Her eyes were dark and wide; the brightness of their whites and the length of the lashes burst through my guard like a sword thrust. *The bloom of young desire and purple light of love.*

'This is my daughter, Mahia,' the old fellow said, and her eyes were on my eyes; my heart boomed and David Samwell and I were outside and walking past the body and the mourners towards the beach. We came along the undergrowth on the route we had taken before, yet I could feel nothing beneath my feet except warm air. The moon reddening low to the west was the most beautiful planet I had ever seen. From the beach came the sounds of women giggling and as we approached a group of village girls stood admiring our sailors and the courtesans they immodestly dallied with. Three men pushed the launch into the waves and the fourth joined us just in time.

'Cor, they's a lot better'n a-stooling,' he said clambering over the side.

'That's enough of that talk; take a hand to the oars.'

As they rowed the men were not shy in recounting their most recent adventures, yet not one gave so much as a look or a wave to their hosts.

David accepted the mood. 'I must say, our John, I would have liked to dally on the beach a while. Oh, those Polynesian girls. In Tonga one night – I don't know if I told you – we were being entertained to fish and yams by some of the servants of a chief. Our Dulcineas were fine girls and we laid together in one room upon mats and were covered with a large quantity of Indian cloth. One girl, upon hearing a rustling of the bedclothes, cried out, "What's going on?" The other, who was the occasion of it, said *misi-misi*. Well, John, the meaning is of course to suck. What hospitality.'

'It can also mean coition,' I added matter-of-factly.

'Well, what do you think to it?' David persisted in an enthusiastic whisper as we neared the anchored ships.

'I'm sorry, I was really thinking of something else.'

'Well, you weren't there at the time.'

'Actually, I've never even so much as touched a native girl.'

David Samwell cleared his throat in the manner one uses after revealing an anecdote of indelicacy to the wrong audience. 'This would not have been worth mentioning but it shows in a striking light the great simplicity of their manners.'

We came quietly alongside and David was looking up for the side-ropes. But my eyes were seeing again that strange building with the child-woman of the mesmerising eyes.

16

I slept poorly. The vision of an angel hovered in my dreams; her wings were of the purest snow and she was faultless, bronzed by the sun with an aureole of vitality and innocence and I knew I could not survive, nor desire to, lest I saw her again. At three of the clock I lighted the candle and wove four lines of verse with words that I scarce thought of before. I knew now what it was like to want to sacrifice one's life to a woman; I resolved to jump from the taff-rail clutching my ode to Mahia the night we sailed from this heaven.

I had no appetite for breakfast and reported to the aft-cabin to work on the new charts of this land, but the clear mathematical brain required for the task eluded me.

'Mr Williamson,' the captain stormed from an end of the chart-table, 'I'm speaking to you.'

'Sorry, sir.'

'I want the sounding off the beach properly annotated before we move on.'

'Move on, sir?'

'Move on to the north. What is the matter with you today?'

Bligh was beside me. 'Dame Palm and her five daughters I wouldn't be surprised, sir.'

'I won't have you so address my officers, Mr Bligh,' he snapped at the master, and I thought of this mixture of coarseness and bullying and realised that I was not for His Britannic Majesty's Service any longer.

After an interminable time I went off watch; I packed my case neatly and thoroughly and put in last the damaged sign from the Devon inn. I closed the lid and left it on my cot. I folded my officer's jacket in approved style and placed it on top of the hold-all. There, all ready for the ceremony of the 'dead man's clothes' at the mainmast on the first Sunday following my disappearance. I removed my shoes and put them on the deck, admiring for the last time their fresh polish and shining buckles. This nearly caused a tear, but I held back.

I came out of my cabin into the noise of the gunroom devouring the evening repast. I pulled the door to, taking a final proud look at the Simon Harvey hanger and brass telescope neatly ready on the rack. Cheers, old friends. You've served me well. The diners did not glance up as I glided past to the companionway: I went up the rungs and beyond the odour of cooked meat and tobacco and David Samwell's high-pitched thespianism followed me on the ladderway. 'Ha, Ha! What a fool Honesty is! and. . . .' And I turned my back on the voices of my messmates too forever.

A light breeze was wooing the rigging. I went quietly to the mainchains in my stockings, slipped a foot over the side and clambered into the chainwale. I took a breath, slipped past the dead-eyes, plopping like a tropic-bird into the warmth of the Pacific. The water came up and bubbles were silver; I seemed to go down forever and I heard an old man whispering Mahia and it sounded like a Zealand zephyr among manuka and I thought of Samwell's quotation and added the part I missed: 'And Trust, his sworn brother, a very simple gentleman!' I'll miss David. Then I was rising and I overtook the bubbles and saw the gibbous moon before I broke the surface of the water. Ahead was a flat squat lizard, the land and hope and meaning. Behind was . . . I would not look behind because that was boyhood and the future was something else. I swam breast stroke in gentle movements so that I would not tire quickly. I did not know if I could swim so far, but there was no other method of one-way transport. The swell was enormous from this level and blocked my lovely reptile for moments at a time. Thumps against my legs could have been sharks which frequent these waters, yet at the time fear did not enter my head. There was a more dominating thought, a driving insistent demand, and I was out of the Navy; there was no going back. Such retirement they called by another name, for our language is rich in nouns of unsavoury sound for whatever a man will do. If ever detained I would swing from a yard: no, there was only forward for me, if I could keep these arms and legs going. I said Mahia with each of the strokes and in the broken water about my hands I saw her eyes, her firm dazzling features.

I seemed to have been swimming an eternity and the lizard would not come closer. My feet sank and I swam in an upright position, slowly, while I restored energy. To seaward were the outlines of the ships. Lights were set on the deck and in the rigging and this extraordinary sight was becoming very distant but I could not tell whether the tiny ships or the lizard were the closer. I resumed my stretch for the shore. Mahia, Mahia, Mahia, I said and tried not to think of the fate that waited if my energy expired. A line of breakers lay ahead lighted by Hine the moon, and I feared it indicated a freshened wind. A chop now would cover my head and take me down. My feet were getting lower in the water. Soon I had insufficient strength to maintain a picture of virgin loveliness. I fought against the weight of my legs which seemed as substantial rocks. The feet were going deeper; my end was near. Will it hurt to breathe water, I wondered and my toes hit an obstacle. Sunken driftwood, perhaps a sandbank, and a wave came over my head and I was swallowing brine. I slipped beneath the sea and banged my knees against that solid something. I pushed my head up. I was on hands and knees in scarcely a foot of water. I crawled onto the beach and collapsed.

The moon had gone. I said Mahia and dashed for the undergrowth. I preferred the stubble under stockinged feet than to be surprised by some zealous guard. I kept the romantic sound of the water to my left as I ran and stumbled towards the village. I made the incline and there were the letter As. I tried to count dwellings as I went, but I could not concentrate. I found the open ground but there was no fire at this hour. The flax mat and the permanent sleeper lay as before and I staggered towards it and fell with my head at the still feet of the moon-brained corpse. I could not move. Mahia, I whispered and fell into unconsciousness.

I have never been on the run from authority, though I have too often watched deserters struggling for an age from the yard tackles. I had only a little pity then for they knew the risks when they jumped ship. Now I sympathised with every one I could recall, so young and unbending when their shipmates shouted stamp and go and hauled them choking to the heavens, so stiff and distorted when they came down. Each sought freedom not to escape intolerable discipline but because men sometimes hear calls stronger than fear. The Maoris knew . . . by women and land are men destroyed.

I woke cold and cramped and choking in a dream that I was on the third descent. Aged toes stood at my feet and I looked up at the old man's priest-like silhouette in the rising sun. A number of natives were about me with countless dark eyes staring down. I was being questioned, but I could not discern the words. 'Mahia,' I whispered.

The voices debated and I shouted again, 'Mahia! Mahia!' And the sun went away. Daylight arrived and faded and I was being jolted on a litter surrounded by dark heads, coconut palms cast passing shadows and then I was in a hut far from the sound of the sea. Mahia was here and she blew cool breath on my temples; she was whispering a song that reminded me of Omai.

I could hear musical birds, the scent at my nostrils was a tune also. My recent actions were reckless beyond measure yet so worthwhile now, and I felt at peace with this stranger kneeling beside me. This must be heaven and paradise is everlasting, I thought, even though it lasted for scarcely three hours.

I would not speak in Polynesian. I did not have the courage to so address this rare creature for she might contradict me. I told her I loved her from the moment I first saw the top of her head, the power of her eyes. I pursed my lips and she brought that smooth plateau of forehead down to be kissed. Her eyes were lowered, the long lashes hypnotic. Occasionally she would say *Hone*, the Polynesian pronunciation of Johnny, and it had the sweetest sound and then those vast orbs were upon me and I knew I would die a hundred times if necessary to experience this.

Our affection was of the purest, most sacred order, I imagined, and we would consummate it with innocence.

'You are my first love. I have never felt this way before. I thought I was married to the Navy and that was satisfaction enough for me; until I saw you. Oh, Mahia.'

And she responded *Hone* and back came the eyes and my heart raced in youthful marvellous torture. Her full breasts were hardly hidden by the fresh cloth of yellow, and yet my eyes did not seek the physical side; I was nervous, excited and totally satisfied that she should be near, that she could call my name.

'Well, you're a fine one, John.'

'Oh, God, no. . . .'

James King stood at the entrance of the hut and my heart was torn out and I wanted to throw up and die, to smash James's face, to pluck his eyes from their sockets, and to fall against his chest with tears of hopelessness.

'Can I come in then? It's been a fair climb up the hill.'

I could not reply; in a sudden I saw the loss of Mahia, the spectre of that slipknot, the smirks of lasciviousness of the duty party holding certain fate in the grip of the rope.

James pushed the sword to a side and sat on the floor, his back resting against a support, his cocked hat on the end of the bed. 'My God, you, of all people,' he said, and he chuckled in a not particularly amused manner. 'Who'd have thought you had it in you?'

I eyed the pistols in his belt. An idea rose like a type of phoenix from my one love's smouldering ruins. I did not know if I could do it, yet to die here, where I had known this brief happiness, made a sort of sense. 'Couldn't I, couldn't you let me have a pistol. By mistake, you know.' The voice was distant; I wondered if it was really mine, yet there were only the three of us. Me on the bed with the second lieutenant's hat at my feet, James against the door, Mahia watching the inevitable drama from a little beyond my sight.

'You, my fine young man, can be thankful you have the commander you do. He wants you back alive.'

'I deserve to die,' I said in self-pity.

'I expect you do, you lucky blighter, but not today. If I can get you back, he'll accept that you fell over the side and some natives rescued you. No words will be passed about any other matters.'

Events were passing too quickly. I was free for a new life in Eden with an Eve who completely involved me, then I was caught and would die as my throat slowly crushed; now I was to be spared. I cried a lot and I laughed a little; hysteria James would think. 'I can't go, I'm sorry. I couldn't live without her.'

'And you can't live with her, old mate. You're in the King's service and you don't quit when you've a mind to. And I'm in His Majesty's service too and I won't be leaving this hut without you.'

'Please give me a chance,' I pleaded.

'You've got it; your life is spared.'

My Polynesian returned before we left the hillside village.

'Wait for me, Mahia. I will be back.'

We heaved in the anchors and the capstan men intoned a chant of melancholy. With canvas shining in the morning sun we left for the north with reluctant *Discovery* dragging at our heels. We worked like automatons; we were Royal Navy with a duty to perform as regulations required. But the King's Regs. did not insist on a smile and we sailed full and bye and fully by the rules.

We could not expect the good fortune of another island group like the Hawaiis. But before the reader questions the narrator on the unfulfilled expectation of abundant pleasures, let me counsel patience; all will be disclosed, but in chronological order as is proper to a historical discourse. The advertisement was to tempt the reader to dig deeper into this prose. An addendum can be written to it; although we did not expect it, we were to fall in with a new people soon enough. Ahead on our voyage lay the ingredients of such an extraordinary and lavish nature that they could be made the sole subject of a tome of weight. Suffice for the present for the publick to know the narrator left these blissful isles with heavy mind and a heart filled with the vision of his new love, the princess Mahia. And although feminine wiles would soon be frequenting again the decks of *Resolution*, the narrator had only eyes for the lady of his affection.

The further we progressed, the lower fell the mercury and no longer did our forest present the same foliage. As the wind increased, the canvas was withdrawn until in the heaviest of airs we would be down to courses and mizzen staysail, and then jerkily the leaves would return in stages till our sails stretched as high as the liquid metal of the barometer.

The dramas of meeting barbaric people were replaced by the incidents of our small wooden world; a sailor falling from the rigging and breaking a collarbone, friendships quietly made and falling noisily apart, often to the accompaniment of fists. Our heavy sails were retrieved from the breadroom to be hauled up on the waist and distributed among the masts. But as the third large bag was produced, muscly jack-tars rushed for the deck complaining they were attacked by an army of giant roaches. The marines were despatched to work their grape-treader cure, but the fate of athletic cousins on the other side of the world seemed common knowledge in the insect community and they eluded the crunching leather boots. We burned sulphur before the last of the sails were brought up. Soon buckets of dying roaches were put over the side, along with one hundred and seventy-three substantial rats unable to avoid the poisonous vapour. We climbed the latitudes and mageline jackets and fearnoughts were distributed. Tanned features gave way to gooseflesh, chilblains and coldsores and the crew petitioned the captain to be served again with the delicious anti-scorbutant food of sour krout.

My duties were as officer of the watch and I would order the setting and taking down of our copse's covering and dream upon the sight of the whales we encountered. They were going south and I requested more than one to recruit me as navigator, that I might return all the more quickly to Mahia.

And our hands and feet hardened to the shipboard life and taking celestial sights became second nature again. Yet the more our people acclimatised to the life, the more the substance of our world, *Resolution* herself, showed her lines of age; a slower pace, an elderly reluctance to keep going. We manned pumps in gales and shipped a disturbing amount of the sea. When New Albion came over the horizon as a long blue line, we were impatiently seeking an anchorage for repairs; but we were not to make land without a fight for fate tempted us as sirens and then pounded us with such onshore might that we were forced to haul the tacks on board and stretch off with all sail the ships could bear, and the land disappeared.

The pumps were constantly manned and the rigging twanged and rubbed in rheumatic complaints even in lighter airs. No satisfactory amounts of rain could be trapped in frequent squalls. So our fresh water began to run short. Hope – land – was just over the horizon, we knew, but it seemed Dame Fortune was neglecting us; then one morning mountains were in our path and the cold wind brought us towards tall green conifers. Telescopes followed the coast and we found an inlet into which we nervously crept, our eyes searching for rocks and ears fastened to the lament of the leadsman.

'The bower, Mr Bligh. The canvas off her, Mr King. Take bearings of the shore, Mr Williamson. A launch over the side, if you will, Mr Gore.'

And the cable ran out and our ship rounded up on the smooth water. Sharp mountains ran inland; to our stern were monstrous large boulders and firs stood to our starboard higher than our own masts.

'Welcome to America,' the old boy said, walking the length of the quarterdeck, gazing into the trees.

'America,' I repeated quietly. The name was familiar and pleasing. 'And much warmer here, sir, than in this latitude on the other coast.'

'Aye, young Williamson,' Mr Gore said, and that grey face was smiling. 'But east or west, it's home. Just smell those pines, captain.'

James King's shoes sounded over the noise of our activity. 'Visitors, sir, port beam,' he called up to us at the rail. 'They're not armed, sir.'

And we rushed like children to see, for suddenly our safe landfall needed the confirmation of human contact; colonists perhaps, with temperaments and intelligence similar to our own. Or maybe the amused gaze of the Micmac Indians I knew in the America war. But the visages that our eyes lighted upon were different from anything we had heretofore seen. No cousins of Omai these, nor were they as dark and fine-boned as the Van Diemen's Land people. But it was difficult to see exactly what they looked like for they covered their faces and hair in thick grease and were of a fragrance that disinclined the nose to further investigation.

'My God, what is it they coat themselves in?' James King asked as we leaned on the rail staring into the boat.

'Lard, I think, but so thick.'

'And ochre,' Mr Gore said. 'They paint their faces in some sort of design with it. Red, black and a dirty off-white.'

'What say you to the tongue, Mr Williamson?' Captain Cook asked.

'I've never heard anything like it, sir.'

In the centre of the large canoe a man stood shouting and haranguing like a London street merchant. At his feet was a solitary oarsman, his paddle dipped idle in the water; the rest of the occupants, perhaps fourteen, sat looking interestedly at us or chatting among themselves, yet ignoring the orator. His hands were held high and emotion filled the grunts and coughs and indecipherable words. His dark hair was greased thickly to his shoulders and he wore a wrap of some dull material. This only went to a little below his waist with his arms down, so in his passionate rhetoric modesty went by the board. None of his companions, men and women, showed the least curiosity about this either. Then the fellow sat down and another leaped to his feet, suddenly animated, almost overwhelming the dug-out as his temper grew and the words, like the former orator's, became lost in the development of aggression until he raged and struck his arms at the heavens. All this punctuated by animal-like barks. A heavily greased part of him shook at the water like a bored adder. His glow was suddenly spent, as if he had been a live coal doused, and he sat down. His friends in the canoe may not have been impressed but the people of the ships were and huzzas rang among the trees. This stopped the next orator in mid-cough, as the inner fire was being stoked, and instead the queer mounds of canoe-bound humanity began a strange song, beating the rhythm with deer hooves on cloth, with rattles and by drumming the boat's sides. The sound from this chorus was unlike any mankind music, not so different from the cry of a beluga whale; it was uncannily attractive and brought tumultuous applause from our people.

Savages or not, we were gratified to find other people alive and breathing and the performance was more memorable and appreciated than any theatre evening. The exhibition went on; another orator, singers, the beat of an unusual rhythm, struggling to catch their words garbled in bursts of excitement, and while the actors pursued their craft, we busied ourselves getting the ship snug for our stay; running out warps and anchors so that we would be safe in whatever the elements' moods. The next day the canoe occupants ended their concert and decided to inspect the ships.

And once again on our extraordinary voyage of discovery, civilised Englishmen stood face to face with stone-age savages; our blue eyes smiled encouragingly and dull black eyes returned the gaze, yet without warmth and with little enough recognition. The Hawaiians believed we were gods in our floating temples and that made our existence simple to understand. But these people puzzled over us. Their deities did not have a place for Europeans, their history had no record of us and their geographical world lacked room for strangers. Perhaps we did not exist, perhaps we were figments, and so in these early days their faces did not know which way to move and expressions remained suspicious, poised and incomplete beneath the grease and dirt.

The women were well covered in a material not unlike the New Zealanders', but the men cared little for their clothes. Many wore pointed straw hats, almost glued in place by liberal grease. More canoes and increasing numbers arrived to stare; my eyes searched for Mahia but of course we were latitudes and a whole world away. Mahia dazzled with vitality. These were a small race and the cheekbones of the women too high; they had small orifices for mouths. They did not please my eyes and nor did they those of the men of the ships who were, as David Samwell reported, not the most discriminating of Romeos. Yet it was the young doctor himself who was to reach out for this strange apple tree in our American Eden.

Our early days were filled with labour for as long as the light lasted. Bibs and trestle-trees were found to be wanting and the masts had to be struck and the slow repairs begun. The sounds of sawing timber came all day from the forests as trees were felled for spars and timber for the galley, and the odour of sawn wood on the air was magnificent. Water barrels were filled for the exacting time ahead; decks needed caulking again and additional rudder chains were attached for extra strength in the ice. When the majority of the tasks were completed, idle time fell to us and now we could learn more of the inhabitants of this region, people who after an initial rush of trading developed a light-fingered trait in the style of their southern neighbours. The Polynesians would steal anything they could; here the natives would take only what they particularly wanted.

Sailors who lost items were roundly lashed by the captain's tongue, an experience many considered worse than the cat, and accordingly they watched the natives with great vigilance. We were swinging the new mizzen mast onto the poop when the captain called, 'Get down to the waist, Mr Williamson, to the larboard. Roberts is going to lay out a native with that stretcher.'

I ran to the quarterladder. Roberts, an old North Briton of irascible disposition, was shouting to a greased Indian in a canoe. Beside him and completely ignoring the noise was Lieutenant Phillips, bargaining for a bow and arrow. I made the bottom rung as Roberts threw the large boat-stretcher. He looked weak, but there was power in the despatch. The timber spun through the air, just missed the native and tore open a side of the canoe.

'Roberts!' I shouted, but the damage was done.

'Not my bloody fault, sir. This bugger were a-stealing from the launch.'

A cry of anger came from the native, that characteristic of theirs to get quickly steamed up, in daily life as well as oratory.

'Look out, Roberts.'

The native picked up a bow from the hull and was pulling back an arrow, aiming for our quartermaster. My call warned Phillips. He fed an arrow into the new purchase, pulled back the string and fired. The shaft screamed but somehow missed the native, who dropped his weapon and felt for his ears, certain at least one had been carved off.

'Lieutenant Phillips. God, man, you'd have killed the fellow if that struck,' I shouted, shocked by his extreme action. 'The captain would have torn you apart if you'd been a better shot.'

Phillips sneered and walked off without a word, but perhaps he knew more than I did. The next day the captain caught a native taking some small item; he snatched a musket from a marine sentinel and fired at the escaping boy. The brown bess was fortunately loaded with birdshot and the lad and nearby natives were not permanently wounded.

The ships sat gently sleeping in that quiet cove and I was busy catching up with the writing of my journal. In rough weather I kept fulsome notes because the bucking of our fine steed when spurred by a tempest made writing in the confines of the cabin impossible. Many of the notes were marked with Mahia's name and the enquiry of what she might be doing. As I pick one up at random now, it says, 'Oh, Mahia, a wave drove down at our stern and clearly like a great Canaletto was your features attractive and perfect in every detail as indeed you are.' I cannot write letters as I would like to; Hawaii has no delivery facilities. My journal instead has to be the depository of the heart's sentiments.

'John, come on, my man!' This call plus the heavy pounding of my door came with an excited Welsh accent. I quickly returned the current journal to its accommodation in the cupboard for I would loathe my true feelings be held to ridicule. I opened the door.

An odd smile was spread on Samwell's wide face. His shirt was undone to the chest; a pair of carefully maintained white knee-breeches reminded one of his good breeding. 'To the sickbay, my friend. I have news and excitements for you.'

He turned and vanished into the gunroom twilight and I followed. The door was opened to the accompaniment of giggles of a ribald nature. I was about to turn away as I would rather read the worst poetry in my relaxations than suffer bawdy humour, but David drew me into the candlelit atmosphere of a gagging, almost impenetrable perfume.

Two young women the size of our smallest chits stood in the centre of that tiny infirmary. They were dressed in the native manner, a fine cloth from neck to ankles and a more than liberal coating of fat and dirt. The brown cloths were uninviting enough, but the depth of the make-up! 'David what the. . .?'

'My dear John, your relaxations are spent entirely in your cabin quill-driving away at God knows what. I have decided to break this unhappy spell which weighs upon you, and what better method than through the pretty feminine gentleness of young nymphs.'

I stared in disbelief, I confess. That red face alive with the joy of lusting, a lewd eagerness which was not unbecoming if only for the power of youth. His tongue was exposed shining in a smile, his eyes almost closed with his contemplations. And yet beside him, dear reader, were two creatures with the like of which no civilised man could imagine relations.

'Jesus, David, they're. . . .' I hesitated for fear of giving offence, though what could be more offensive than the reek of their persons, the odour of which appeared to be rising in vapours.

'Do they speak English?'

'Good gracious, no,' he said impatiently. 'I cannot imagine anything more obscene than a courtesan with whom one could converse.'

'I can at this moment. Two, in fact. Look, I don't want to seem critical but they are loathsome and despicable-looking and dirtier than anything I've seen before. Their hair's full of filth and it's hanging over their faces in clots. For God's sake man, you're not seriously thinking of . . . of. . . .'

He laughed in a pitch that was too high to be real, but in singing he attains notes beyond the reach of most mortals. 'This is what the tub is for.' Behind the girls, who took not the slightest interest in us, was a wooden bowl of hot water. Perhaps it was this that gave the stench an appearance of mist. 'You see, there is a purse for courage and perseverance; in attempting to refine this ore we have sometimes found jewels that rewarded our trouble.'

'Jewels? I shudder to think of things beyond the range of vision.'

'Two sparkling black eyes accompanied with a beautiful face . . .'

'You've the morals of a stoat!'

'. . . and when such was our fortune we never regretted the time and trouble it cost us in digging through loads of red ochre, soot and other dirt to get at them.'

'Samwell, for God's sake, even the crew won't touch them.'

'All the more for the gentlemen. And it's had an amazing effect on the market price. Both of these fair virgins for three tin buttons.'

'Virgins?'

'Comparatively.'

'I believe you've been there before.'

'A man's a man and one day North American women will be in great demand.'

The girls could have been twins; their faces and hair were limp of grease and dirt and the design thickly laid upon their countenances was identical – a triangle shaped in black on red on a nose that was all nostrils and whirls of white on black around their eyes and cheeks.

'And now what we call the Ceremony of Purification.'

He smiled encouragingly at the first girl and started to undress her; she came to life and began clearing garments from the area most likely to be of interest with the grace of a street-sweeper.

'Who's the we?'

'Well, me and the young gentlemen.'

'You mean you and the others have been bulling these natives, ones that not the ugliest sailor on board would touch.'

'Sailors have no eye to the aesthetics.' The girl had her thighs bared and pushed this part of the anatomy forward as coyly as a cat on heat. David said sweetly, quite musically through the lard adjoining her ears, 'Purification first, my little nymph. Purification.'

The girl stood naked before him; fat paps bounced in the speed of the disrobing, and he did the same to the other. Suffice it is to relate that the remainder of their anatomy was no more attended to than the hair, yet David was not in the least perturbed.

He pulled the tub between the two naked odoriferous women and a leg of each was dunked. The doctor's shirt, breeches and linen came off and he was as pink and scrubbed as they were dark, pungent and infested. The girls appeared to take no interest in this glowing hygienist whose seductive voice rose higher and more lascivious; I thought of him as a starving mongoose wooing a rattlesnake, though in this a voyeur serpent was not without immodest pangs too. He now applied the ingredients of soap and water to which the girls were clearly strangers. And I stood not an arm's distance from the bosoms, suds and rampant stoat (or mongoose) not knowing whether to laugh or run, while the following was recounted in the queerest, oddest tone.

'I am the officiator at this ceremony, performing with much piety and devotion, and taking as much pleasure in cleansing naked young muses from all impurities as a young confessor would absolve a beautiful virgin who was about to sacrifice that name.'

The sponge performed its service at head, body and thighs and David encouraged, aah beautiful, my dears, beautiful, perfect.

'When this ceremony was first performed, my dear Johnny, our fair Americans found it very strange for they had gone to particular pains to daub their hair and faces well with red ochre to render themselves agreeable to us, and to their great astonishment we took as much pains to wash it off.'

The sponge splashed back into the tub. 'Finished. What say you to that? By the heavens, what do you think now? Such beauty, such delights, such charm.' The examination of his handiwork was thorough. 'Now, Johnny-oh, you can have this one or this one or this one. . . .'

I quoted, 'For who wou'd so much satisfaction lose, As Witty nymphs, in conversation, give.'

And he went from one girl to the other with the mono-eyed slow-worm twitching in spasms while the three-buttons' worth held black eyes, jutting cheekbones and tiny mouth-holes in a flat stare.

David's retentive memory carried him through his rejoinder, for concentration on Steele's words seemed most unlikely.

> 'Me Cupid made a Happy Slave,
> A merry wretched Man,
> I slight the Nymphs I cannot have,
> Nor Doat on those I can.
>
> This constant Maxim still I hold,
> To baffle all despair;
> The Absent Ugly are and Old,
> The Present Young and Fair.'

The girls were lovingly lifted into the berth which had held Dr Bill and there they sat, legs wide, while a lusty serpent writhed hungrily and noisily at the orchard sailors had found too sour in our peaceful paradise.

17

I looked up from my chartwork to watch Vancouver Island slowly sinking beyond the sternlights; soon those sharp mountains would be beneath the sea as we pressed on for the frozen regions.

'I propose to follow the land north, as well as the weather will allow,' the captain said, and I plotted a course accordingly and studied the mercury, hoping it would stay steady long enough for my sea-legs to return; but it was too low and a familiar disturbing decline had begun. Captain Cook seemed to make a habit of departing when conditions were far from propitious; from England all that time ago when a westerly trapped us in the channel, the white squall from Van Diemen's Land, calms on leaving New Zealand. Why not wait for favourable weather, I wondered, as I had on many of our departures, yet it was his constant practice not to delay for the right wind but to look for one at sea. It is an English seafaring characteristic; a Dutchman, for example, never stirs from port till the wind is settled. The Hollander acts upon a safe plan, the Englishman on a bold one, and the consequence is that the latter may sometimes be lost by his rashness, but in general he makes three voyages to the other's two. Bligh was beside me, adding some soundings to his chart of our cove.

'And are we to find this passage and all be rich, sir?'

His question brought into the open our questions and this secret of the captain's could be all our property, and officially.

'As to riches, I wouldn't know,' the old boy said, standing between us looking out at the wake.

'And as to the passage?' Bligh pressed.

'Good God, Mr Bligh, if I knew that I would not be here. Is that not so, Mr Williamson?'

'You would not be here now,' Bligh said eagerly, 'because you would have been here earlier, so keen would you be to put your name to the discovering of it.'

I saw the captain giving Bligh one of his admonishing looks that began with a wrinkling of the brow and descended to half-closed eyes, flared nostrils, whitened lips. I knew it well. Bligh's pale hurt expression followed quickly.

'Is that correct, Mr Williamson?'

'I suspect, sir, you would not be here for what is there for a discoverer if the discovery is no longer in doubt?'

'Absolutely. Quite so, quite so, young sir. You see, William,' and he turned to his desk, to the inevitable scratching of the insatiable quill, 'the whole magic of searching is because we do not know. Surely much time and exasperation could be saved if one were to happen upon high road milestones saying North-West Passage this way. But when we found it, what satisfaction then? No, I'll deal with the unknowns if you please, young master.'

'But the reward of £20,000?' Bligh said.

'The reward could be eight farthings or a King's ransom. It makes no difference, until we find the passage. Then let's think of the reward.'

'Until?' Bligh asked.

'Unless. Unless we find it.'

I remained quiet. I enjoyed my work of navigating and it was a happy alternative to unceasing duties as officer of the watch these days, but my attitudes were not lessened any by the passing of time. Never for a sober moment could I forgive Bligh for taking the role of protégé.

'So what do you say, Mr Williamson?' Bligh asked, and my lawyer-brain recognised it for its inverted meaning; to get me to solicit his opinion, in the absence of anyone else seeking it. But I did not mind; it was not my conversation.

'Perhaps your expectations would be the more valued,' I offered.

'What do I think about its existence, you mean?' he asked without waiting. The quill behind us was not engaged yet in that difficult sloping style; it amused me that the captain might be interested in our opinions. 'If you look at the globe as we know it today, you can see that a passage exists; unquestionably.'

'If it exists will we find it?'

'My dear third lieutenant,' he said in an expansive mood, 'that goes without saying, surely. This is a voyage of discovery undertaken by none other than Captain Cook.'

'I'm sure you don't mean that quite as sycophantically as it might sound,' I replied. 'The worth of our discoverer is unquestioned; the likelihood of our discovering it was my point.'

Bligh looked along the chart-table, to see if my expression revealed what my voice disguised. But debating, like a conversation of blades, is best conducted with a bland visage. 'I can only say I believe we shall. What is it you philosophers say about these matters: where there's a will there's a way.'

I wondered if I dared the remarks that were surfacing and I concentrated on the jutting rocks I was inscribing upon the chart as if they might guide me. 'Oh,' I feigned. 'You see a will in this expedition?'

I felt the captain's eyes on my stooped back. 'For God's sake,' Bligh said, 'I'm not referring to the jack-tars whose will is no more than his orders. I speak of the ship's government, do I not?'

'In the government there's a will, you say?'

My question upset Bligh for he feared as he always did when we argued that footpads may be hidden among the words and waiting.

'Certainly. There's a will among the officers. . . .'

'And warrant officer?'

'Of course; I mean, should I not presume that you have a will here?'

'My will in this adventure is as the captain's.'

A silence fell on our cabin. Bligh was scanning sentences in case an ambusher may have head or buttocks imprudently raised and give away my intentions. He could feel danger; he knew instinctively his only safe course was to retreat along the path whence he was being led, but he was too impetuous and curious.

'Are you suggesting the captain lacks a will, sir?'

It was an impudent question to ask out of the old boy's hearing, but within inches of him was foolhardy. The gentleman himself I suspect was ready to angrily interrupt, but perhaps like Bligh he could not guess what lay round the next bend of this treacherous avenue. 'It is not for me to suggest anything. But as a normal intelligent being, I might myself question why we are in these latitudes a year late. And I think we might assume this question was asked a year ago by Lieutenant Richard Pickersgill who was due to lead an expedition up the other coast expecting to meet us. . . .'

The Captain could not hold back. His hand came down on the desk like a nine-pound shot. Our prattle had continued long enough, he said; he had need to recourse to concentration. And an eternity of silence later, my watch came to an end and I excused myself. The captain said, 'Come to dinner tomorrow night, if you will, Mr Williamson. Good day.'

The mercury did not lie. The ocean was truly named in the south, but here it erupted with an anger that seemed certain to sweep the ships back to the Indians and wreck us ashore. Waves grew and cascaded over themselves in brackish fury and our canvas was reduced to courses with a staysail on the mizzen to keep bow to weather. We clawed into the tempest; there was no other way to travel without going ashore and if our nautical term sounds like an injured bird trying to escape the jaws of a predator, that is an exact description of our unhappy lot. Huge foaming breakers thundered into our bow and threw the ship about. A catapulting effect shocked down the spars; but for the repairs just effected we would have been a dismasted hulk to be played with and destroyed by the elements.

The mercury eased, I dressed with care in my second-best uniform, belted on my hanger, and appeared tired but hungry at the aft-cabin door. The table had been laid by Collett. A cloth a good deal cleaner than our gunroom fabric was spread and a candelabrum of teak, presumably the handiwork of a jack, held three flames in place. It was a warm, pleasant room and, after the exhaustion and fears of the storms, reassuringly homely.

The captain stood beside the table, a hand resting on its edge, solid legs crossed casually to suggest an appearance of ease.

'Of course you'll have some claret.' He took the crystal decanter, wide-based and the colour of blood, in his hand and as large as was the container it hid in that fist, and when he poured a glass I remembered a fairground magician with asses' milk flowing from a palm. I put out a hand for the glass; at that moment he leaned down to take it from the table and our gestures crossed. The wine was where I had been standing and my hand was where the glass was filled. He coughed and I blushed and we met clumsily in the air. I muttered 'Rule Britannia', sipped it and silence followed.

'That storm, eh; ruddy rough, didn't you think?'

'One of our nastiest, sir.'

Conversation faltered and the ship lurched on the storm litter; we both leaned to the starboard and followed the strain to larboard as if we were a comic act.

'Collett will bring dinner in a minute.'

'Thank you, sir.'

Another silence, another seventh wave, a long draught of the wine, feeling its warming passage down inside. 'I suppose, sir, the others'll be here shortly.'

'Others?'

'To dinner, sir.'

'Good heavens, no. No others, Mr Williamson.'

'No others, sir.' I repeated this and thought of a long meal of silence. We had done that together in the past, thousands of miles ago, and I had been gaga in his austere presence. But an immense volume of water had passed beneath the keelson. I was a growing man, I was in love; experience had straightened some of the question marks.

'John, if a captain cannot treat his third lieutenant to dinner occasionally, there's something wrong.' He pondered on this for a moment; I thought on the Christian name. Bligh and the senior lieutenants received this familiar treatment, but it was a first time for me. I was not certain I could altogether approve; perhaps if it had not stuttered on his tongue like a steed unsure of a fence. 'Don't you think?'

'Oh, yes, sir.' And then to fill that following space, 'I'm most grateful, sir.'

'You've been here to dinner before as my guest, of course.' I wondered if it were a statement or a question, then Collett came in with a tray and announced dinner and the captain took his place. I was opposite and I could see him through the candlelight, and it seemed for a second that the years fell away.

'No corned pork left, sorry, sir. But I think you'll like the way the pig is prepared, sir.'

'Don't fuss, Collett.'

'No bother, captain. Now this is cabbage.'

'I can see what it is.'

'And a little of the potatoes would be good for you.' The faithful servant served his master and the dainty gestures seemed incongruous for this big man who had flayed so many backs since the voyage began.

'Now, Lieutenant Williamson, are you for the sour krout?'

Collett left us. The captain carved some meat and shovelled a large piece into his mouth with the style of a stoker; his cutlery lay on either side of the plate. He chewed methodically open-furnaced till the fuel was reduced to a paste.

'You're smiling, sir.'

'The natives there. Lovely people really; quite charming in their own way.' He was eating again and I thought of him peppering a youthful kleptomaniac. 'You'll recall our Indian friends attended us until we were almost out of the sounds, some on board the ships and others in canoes. Anyway, one chief named, what's-his-name – do have some more wine, John – attached himself to me and was the last to leave. Insisted on it. Before he went I made him up a small present and in return he presented me with a fur skin of greater value. This of course occasioned me to make some addition to my present, upon which he gave me the beaver skin cloak he was wearing and this garment I knew he treasured. I was desirous that he should not suffer by his friendship and generosity, so I made him a present of a new broadsword with a brass hilt which made him as happy as a prince.'

I laughed, politely, and also because the anecdote charmed me; he was never a story-teller and I was being especially flattered to be so entertained.

'It's as well he wore little else of value,' I offered.

'How so?'

'Or he might have offered that and you would then have felt obliged. . . .'

'I don't think I'm with you, Mr Williamson. Do you not think the broadsword a particularly fine present?'

My tongue saved me before I had an inkling of how to answer this deafness to humour. 'I think it is a marvellously generous offering and I venture, sir, that future visitors will profit greatly in the hospitality which will arrive from the splendidness of your gift.'

'Yes,' the captain said, staring through the flames now. 'Yes, indeed.'

Collett came in and the dishes were removed and abandoned among the charts, while debris was swept from the cloth and plates set for cheese. He produced a bottle of port and the cork came out with a loud sucking sound; I thought of the moon-turned man pulling his finger from a perfectly round wound.

'Englishmen,' Collett said in a manner some might reserve for the word millionaires. 'Only cheese and port will do for Englishmen.'

'You're a ruddy romantic, Collett,' he said, and the master-at-arms disappeared beyond the door. Silence returned.

'Ruddy candles,' the captain suddenly declared and a large hand snaked to the middle of the table and took the flickering lives of two. Shadows leaped from the stern window and the perimeter of the room; we were marooned in a small island of light. He looked at me now; our solitary candle made his left eye flash like a distant warning beacon and I thought what a remarkably lifeless orb. He was about to speak; words were examined in his brain, then tasted on his lips before he was ready to serve.

'You know, John, I was looking at your papers today.'

'No, sir.'

'You know you're likely to be seconded to admiralty after this voyage.'

'Not really, sir.'

'Please don't interrupt me, lad. It's, you see, your ease with your tongue, if I may put it like that. You will work in courts-martial; I don't doubt you will get extra training. Anyway, this is the recommendation of your last commander. He seemed impressed.'

'Thank you, sir.'

'That's as may be. I'm not sure what to recommend myself as to your future.' He stopped and I wondered if this were a jest and so I compromised and smiled behind a hand; if a visible appreciation of mirth were necessary I could pull it away and expose the expression. 'I would like some advice.'

'Sir?'

'Private, mind.'

'Of course, sir,' I said without thinking.

'You were fond of Hawaii?'

'Aye, sir.' The reply caught in my throat and I wondered if this were the point of the evening. Was I to be questioned about the debunking, for not one word had been said since? It was so widely accepted that I had fallen overboard and been rescued by natives, I would have doubted the happenings myself had not the packed case waited on the cot in my cabin. 'I would like to settle there, sir,' I said, so that he would understand my intentions were of the most honourable.

Anger moved like a line squall across the ageing features and showed bright at the base of the newly greyed hair. Then as quickly, the weather cleared. 'So you know about this god business, Lono?'

'A little, sir.'

'Tell me of it.'

'They took you to be the god Lono, sir.'

'Poppycock. I won't hear of it. But tell me the legend.'

'He is an important god to Hawaii and is intensely worshipped. I gather he lived in the archipelago and is expected to return one day. Legend goes that he travels in a moving temple and will circle Hawaii when he goes back.'

'And what of his appearance?'

'He's a supernatural, sir. He could be like the grotesque outlines of their carvings or have the features of a dolphin. It matters not to their way of thinking because carvings and the like are always allegorical. They think you are . . . I mean, they could easily take you, sir, as just such a reincarnation. When all's said, sir, the god may well use the body of a man. Any man he chooses.' As I spoke these last words, his hand came across the table to the candelabrum and rode up its spirals and turns, creeping for the last light like a mantis after a cicada. The fingers suddenly darted like a predator's tongue; the flame sizzled and choked. The finger tip glowed blood red in the sudden dark and then the hand withdrew and the dying wick mesmerised me as it quietly faded.

'Rule Britannia,' the man opposite said and sipped his port.

'Rule Britannia, sir,' I repeated, found my port and drank.

Now he spoke quickly as if the candle could light suddenly of its own accord and the secrecy that belonged to our darkness might be lost forever. 'Suppose you were a lawyer, John.'

'Aye, sir.'

'Suppose you was defending a captain who was delayed from carrying out the wishes of my lords of the admiralty, from conducting his mission immediately. Do you follow me?'

'I think so, sir.'

'Do you follow me, Mr Williamson?'

'Yes, sir.'

'So upon his return to Albion, he finds he is to be prosecuted for this delay. It is possible, is it not, that he could be so court-martialled?'

'I suppose so, sir.'

'So there you are. What would you say?'

'Say, sir? I'd be very surprised.'

'God damn it, Mr Williamson, surprise I don't look for. What would you say in his defence?'

'I would think about the matter seriously.'

'Is it a subject that needs to be thought about?'

'Of course, sir.'

'My God, you try my patience, young sir. You *have* thought about it and I'll wager you know the answers.' His hoarse whisper was on the point of shouting; he breathed noisily and it returned to an even keel. 'Of course I know some answers too, but I would be pleased to hear yours.'

I was disturbed. How could I try to outline a defence without conceding that the captain might well be guilty. We were too late for the expedition which pushed up past Canada in the hopes of meeting us and it would not be unprecedented for jealous factions to press charges so the cost of mounting Richard Pickersgill's expedition might be recovered from Captain Cook, or at the very least to taint his record and so frustrate his progress in the Promotions List. And if I played this pretend courtroom game, I might find him my dearest enemy at the end of it for agreeing to a possible guilt. Impasse, I thought, and pushed noisily back on my chair and made to exit left.

'You don't leave this table till I say so, young sir.' A match struck, and a candle returned to life. 'I'm asking you for matters I would like an answer to; I'll not hold any of this against you afterwards.'

'But, sir. . . .'

The wick lighted and a second and a third and now the room was bright. A glow of eerie sea lightning from the stern windows quickly receded. I blinked in the comparative blaze; his face was worried, angry and very old. He stood, pulled the Chippendale from under him and brought it round beside me. He put it down, methodically; two large hands on the embroidered seat, planting it carefully, precisely, on four legs. His body was so much bigger than mine. My head ended where his shoulders began. He leaned confidentially towards me and we were so close that I could see the havoc from gales upon his complexion, as you see with Scots shepherds. It seemed all flakes; to rub a hand over his face must produce a snow shower of dead skin. His nose, so penile and firm, was reddening as a frieze of capillaries succumbed to weather and wine. His breath was heavy with port which stained his tongue and teeth. His brows were perfectly symmetrical with none of Mr Gore's jutting thick hairs of age. A feeling of affection that I had long forgotten came back; it sounds romantic to say he put me under his spell, yet that sensation flowed through my body and flashed images from a memory I had long trampled down.

'Here,' he said in a quiet voice, clinking glasses with me. 'Here's to you.'

There had been so little sleep with the storm, the risk of being shipwrecked and the fear always is heightened when fighting off a shore in the dark. Suddenly I relaxed for the first time since whenever; I was filled with compassion, and not far away, tears. Tears for every thing that had gone wrong; Mahia, the murdered aristocrat orphan, infatuation during the hermaphrodite period of my adolescence, for Omai, for jealousy over Bligh, the black pit and the boy, my carelessness with the driver-sail in a white storm.

'I'm a sea captain. Giving orders requires little oratory, little thinking of that devious way, if you'll excuse me, of the quill-drivers and court persons. Give me an inkling of what I might well plead.'

'Sir, you keep a journal,' I began quietly. 'In it, in your normal way, introduce the subject of whether blame might be attached to you. Then answer it too in your own hand. If you've raised the subject yourself, no one can really beat you to it.'

'Raised by a guilty conscience,' he said moodily.

'Raised by a diligent conscience that is ever eager to please the lords of the admiralty.'

'Oh,' he thought for a moment. 'You say to answer the subject too.'

'Yes, sir, and the answer is the weather. It beat us at every turn in our quest to continue with the voyage. A simple thing like that is your answer.'

He pushed the chair back thoughtfully and turned to the sternlights. He looked at the reflection which must have been mocking him for he suddenly dismissed the suggestion and spun back angrily. 'Weather, be damned. You can't talk about weather to landsmen, they won't begin to understand.'

'Admiralty's not landsmen, sir.'

'They've not been at sea for so long they've forgotten. Damn it, young sir, is that the best you can do?'

'It's the truth, sir.'

'Who wants a lawyer to mouth the ruddy truth. I want the answer, or I would not have troubled you. You think I want to spend my night babbling to a third lieutenant when I could be. . . .' He stopped and I added in my mind, 'when you could be entertained by bloody Bligh.'

'The answer then is you, sir.' I didn't care what he thought any more.

I had offered my friendship to him again and again he turned from me. I was a mere sailor to be used to get him to his mission, or for whatever whim. He and Bligh thought the inhuman same, they were welcome to each other.

He was sitting on his side of the table now. I was leaning towards him and I thought I give not a jot for your feelings, sir, nor these interminable sirs with which we are forced to punctuate our sentences.

'Tell me about Mrs Cook?'

'I don't understand you.'

'Does she have a lover?'

'By the. . . .' He rose from the chair, his face a growing blood blister. 'How dare you, you. . . .'

'Why should such a statement surprise you? When did you start on your first voyage?'

He stopped on the rise and his mind pushed through the port wine to my new question to the answer for the previous question, to the audacity of someone speaking like this.

'Your first voyage. On *Endeavour*, when you discovered New Zealand?'

'August 26, 1768.'

'But you were involved in the fitting out, were you not?'

'Yes, I was at Deptford for each of the fittings, except for this voyage.'

'So that's six months before departure.'

'Yes.'

'According to my reckonings, you've been at home only two years since then.'

'I wouldn't know.'

'I would. You returned from that voyage on July 13, 1771. You left next on July 13 the following year and you returned on July 30, 1775. We left on July 12, 1776. So you have lived on board a ship for more than eight years. The two years' leave is actually two periods of a year each between the first and second voyage.'

'Yes.'

'And on the second leave, you were rewriting your journals for publication, planning for this third voyage and attending to the demands of the admiralty.'

'Yes.'

'My God, you were a tired, exhausted man when you began this voyage. How could the admiralty or your supposed friend Lord Sandwich send you. . . .'

'What has Sandwich. . .?'

'You know what Thomas Gray said of him?'

'The opinion of a poet is of no. . . .'

'It is an opinion shared by many.'

'Leave Sandwich out of this. . . .'

'I don't think you should. However . . . if you were tired, what about *Resolution*? She covered all those miles – three years and eighteen days is a lot for a ship, too. She was strained and exhausted. Then the naval yard got her, supposedly to overhaul her, yet instead she was hamstrung by those get-rich-quick merchants. And another of your friends. . . .'

'Do not bring Palliser into this. The requipping was not so. . . .'

'It was worse. They raped *Resolution* and even stole some rigging and tackles that were much superior to theirs.'

'I cannot write of this in my journal.'

'Then you don't want to save yourself.'

'I . . . I . . .'

'How old is Mrs Cook?'

'I'm not sure.'

'You have six children; the last two coincide with your leaves. What are their names?'

He smiled, then the warmth turned to a frown as he failed in the attempt to switch his mind from the sea.

'Does Mrs Cook have her own teeth, on what side does she part her hair, could you ever describe your wife as a friend, or is she not really a stranger? Have you not in effect been married to the admiralty? These are matters for disclosure in your journals and then who could question you?'

'I see what. . . .'

'So I ask you – as you must ask yourself in your journal – does Mrs Cook have a real lover? And where does cuckolding Sandwich fit into all this?'

'By God, sir!' He jumped from his reverie and stood before me as an angry gorilla, his arms flapping, uncertain of whether to hit me or charge me. His anger was still building and rushing to be expressed. 'These things have nothing to do with the question I sought an answer for.'

'They have everything to do with the possibility for a court-martial. Underline the weather problems in your journal, and raise these myriad dreadful questions and thereby let them and the publick see the tremendous sacrifice you have made. No one will throw accusations then, sir.'

A banging at the door interrupted us. It flung open and James King, wrapped in mageline jacket, shouted, 'Sir, a hole's opening up in the starboard cheek. Water's pouring in at a terrible rate, sir. The carpenter's measuring now, but he says the hold is half filled already.'

The call sounded for all hands and I stared at the captain.

18

The door slammed. The captain shook like an enraged bear pinioned equidistant twixt matching demands. The tear in the hull needed his attention; the questions weakened the blind stability which permitted his marathons and this breach quickly needed plugging too. I sat at the table staring at the port; a darker line halfway down advertised the quantity we had consumed. Next to the bottle was the shining wood of the carved candle-holder, three flames countermanding the ship's movement and beyond, that large mass of angry indecision. I was waiting for him to make some move, to say on guard in our duel of words, but he remained transfixed and I reached for the bottle and began to pour a glass.

'What the hell are you doing?' He rushed from the doorway and leaned across the table. His hands pressed on the cloth in a temper, making the scar stand out like knotted rope. I thought he might set fire to his hair above the candles.

I put the bottle down slowly, lifted the port and tossed it back. An arrogant gesture; but he offered me freedom to outline a defence which I did. Now he found it was not to his taste; it burned his palate as the port-wine did my throat. I took the glass from my lips; there was a sudden draught and a hand swept within a trimmed fingernail of my mouth. It caught the glass. I followed its trail, picked out by a glinting reflection of the candles; it seemed a shooting comet. The glass exploded to the larboard and I heaved back instinctively on the chair; the scrape of wood pushed rapidly on planking roared as in thunder and added to my confusion. In second nature my hand was at the silver hilt of the hanger. The chair was falling backwards, Chippendale walnut bouncing, and the deckhead was drummed by feet rushing in the panic of an aperture that threatened our survival.

Through this cacophony, I heard every fraction of the withdrawal from the scabbard of the Simon Harvey blade. The metallic song was alerting adrenalin to the activity and at the same moment unsettling my teeth. A conscience screamed from afar and was muffled by the heaviness of the thick red liqueur and the running wolf kept baring itself. The tip made a distinct pinging sound as it broke free; the muscles in my arm, now swollen tight, hauled the razor edge towards the adversary. An antler of the candelabrum leaped into the air, the blade took out the second light and it continued its deadly swoop. The captain's head pulled back from the riposte, *in quartata* in swordsmanship language, he ducked (*passata sotto*), and the shining steel had completed its first swing. At that second I came into control. In the blue of that solitary flame I saw the image of a familiar figure hanging from the mainyard, shoes swinging shining, silver buckles reflecting the first of Aurora's smile.

I turned my back on the captain and exposed myself for an easy killing if he so wished; I held firmly to the slot of the scabbard and ran with all my might the sword back into place. The metal screamed, the blade carved into my hand and the hilt smashed down on the loose skin. I turned back to the captain, blood pouring from the trapped hand onto white breeches. His sword was untouched. He stared across the table and I tried to return defiance in the want of any logic. Then the pain exploded with the illumination of a fork of lightning. I could hold his gaze no longer and my eyes sank into submission.

A quiet, nervous voice said, 'The call has gone for all hands, Mr Williamson. Kindly follow the order.'

I rushed past the table and the captain; I grabbed for the door and hauled it open in the roar of confusion that addled my senses. Blood followed me in a stream. The marine sentinel was not there. I closed the door slowly with sudden politeness, then eased the sword's hilt from my crushed flesh.

I hungered for sleep. I wanted no more than to retreat to my tiny cabin and disappear into blackness reassured by fug accumulating in damp blankets which I would pull familiarly over my humiliated head. But personal demands seldom are satiated in a ship, especially one reaching the high latitudes. The press of officers and men stumbling; the crowd hurrying to climb the quarterladder and pushing down it urgently, business-like, trapped me until my sailor instincts got the better of youthful desires; I was compelled to assemble with the worried mob on the starboard quarter.

I pushed through the men and joined Mr Gore and James King at the bulwark, staring over the caprail. *Resolution* was halted by reversed topsails, and we lurched in the manner of a ship hove-to in a rough sea. I leaned over in the hope of seeing the damage; a splash of brine found my hand and the pain doubled. I held back the tears.

'Sir, sir!' A panicking cry came over my shoulder and carpenter Cleveley was pushing through the sailors. 'Water's up to the orlop, far as I can tell, sir,' he addressed Mr Gore. 'I can't get a candle to stay lighted and. . . .'

'And the pumps,' I interrupted, 'are they holding the level?'

'Can't be sure, sir,' he said.

'Are all the pumps manned?'

'Manned and pumping like the clappers, sir. Except the spare'ns.'

'Why not the spare pumps?' I asked, exasperation in my voice. When a ship's taking water, getting every pump working is the first consideration.

'Nobody mentioned them.'

I stared around me and found the plump outline. 'Master, set those spare. . . ,' I began for there is little likelihood of surviving an hour in open boats in the cold North Pacific. But at that moment I saw the captain standing beside Bligh and I adjusted the tone of voice. 'The spare pumps, Mr Bligh; kindly have them set up and in action.'

A white nightgown showed from Mr Gore's mageline jacket. 'We need someone to look at the damage, Mr King. If there's no seeing it from the inside, we'll have to go over and inspect.'

'Aye, Mr Gore,' James said. Water dripped from his clothing and he resembled an exhausted water spaniel.

'How did you get so wet?'

'I was diving in the hold to try to see the damage.'

'It was that full?'

'I think we're sinking.'

James's expressed fear brought the captain through to us. 'Who's to inspect the damage then, Mr Gore?'

'Dunno, sir. But it had best be quick.'

I looked at the waves hitting the quarter. 'Nobody would survive in there, sir,' I said. 'They'd be hammered against the hull or dragged underneath by the surge.' The ship disturbed the water sufficiently as she made leeway to stop larger waves breaking onto the hull, but occasional monsters swept with fury beneath us. 'We could turn her about, and put the damage to the leeward. It ought to be safer then.'

'What are you saying, Mr Williamson?' the captain shouted. 'If we put a hole the size we believe it is deeper in the water we'd go down even faster.'

'Sir, what would you have us do?' Mr Gore asked gently, being the only officer who really knew how to handle the captain.

'I'd have a few ruddy seaman-like suggestions made for a start,' he snapped. 'Get a volunteer over the side immediately.'

'It's possibly too risky, sir,' James King said.

'Too risky!' The captain turned on the shivering figure of the second lieutenant. 'Everybody's lives are at risk at this moment.'

'Very well,' Mr Gore said slowly. 'Mr Williamson, call for volunteers. Preferably a good swimmer.'

'Swimming won't do him much good,' I said and turned for the quarterdeck to follow the order through.

'Where the devil are you going?' the captain stormed.

'To call for a volunteer, sir, as Mr Gore. . . .'

'A volunteer? Mr Williamson, all we need is a swimmer of note with the courage of a swordsman and a clear-thinking brain. I think we have that in you, do we not?'

'But sir. . . .'

'Come now, where's the spirit we have recently seen?'

I stared imploring at those faces about me but the word had come from the captain and no one could help. I could climb over the rail like some theatrical hero, or delay until he forced the order ignominiously at the point of a pistol. I might as well go in style.

'I'll take the driver sheet, sir,' I addressed Mr Gore, perhaps too optimistically. 'Using the blocks on the boom, you'll be able to get me back easier.'

I tied a bowline round my waist and added a doubled bight for extra protection. I climbed over the caprail and slid onto the hull; I grabbed the rope with my left hand, but it bit to my bones. I let go and cried out with the pain, but the noise of the sea on this weather hull was so great that even I did not hear it. I would manage the rope with my left hand and negotiate obstacles with the right, trying to keep the thumb pressed into my palm to reduce the stinging and the blood. My left foot found the ledge beneath the sternlights on the corner of the ship. My other shoe scraped at the wood like a mountaineer searching for a crevice. This drop was sheer, dripping from the continual dousing and it shook as if in the grip of an earthquake. Seamen above eased the rope as I made my descent. I was in a hurry to try to save the ship, but not in such haste that I might be left hanging from the bowline with the noose cutting under my arms. My head was level with the upper deck, then the main deck, and now the orlop. The freezing sea rose up to my knees, thighs; a bitter feeling of hopelessness chilled me as it soaked through to groin and waist. The surges pushed up to my shoulders and searched and stung at the wound. The swell pushed me up and I feared being dashed against the hull; then the ship raised too and we climbed and fell on the flowing hills; I clutched to that huge vessel like a barnacle, my head level with the hold. The water was at my neck and I held my breath and it was above and it pressed into my ears; it went down and my eyelashes were stuck and the salt hurt and blinded me. A current set under the hull, drawing my legs underneath trying to trap and drown me on the keelson. I held to the edge of the ship as best as my nails would allow, and ran my hands along the buttocks. They were as smooth as a larded native's and there was no rip; I did the same with my legs, pressing in to the hull with the surges, searching for a stove-in plank. Nothing. I held my breath. I went further down and felt desperately with hands and legs as before, but I could not find any damage. I came to the surface spitting salt and blowing stinging water from my nose. I was frozen and the sea was making me sick. I pulled the rope three times. It was jerked with great rapidity and I had the utmost difficulty in holding it from tearing my skin as I was hauled up.

I grabbed the caprail with dead fingers and looked into the face of the captain.

'Can't find it, sir.'

'Can't find it! Speak to him, Mr Gore. Find out what you can.'

Mr Gore was at the side, 'Sir, there's nothing stove in where the damage is supposed to be, nor within several feet.'

'You searched with your hands, did you lad?'

'Jesus, Mr Gore, with fingers, toes, you name it. But if a plank's broken, it wouldn't be hard to find.'

'You're right, lad. What do you think, Mr King?'

James was shivering in the wind; I realised it was warmer in the sea. 'This is where the damage is, I've no doubt of it.'

'It's not there and I'm bloody cold. Bring me aboard for God's sake.'

The captain appeared again in a bear's silhouette. 'Mr Williamson, there is a serious leak in the ship. There is no point in your coming back aboard for it seems we are all to go to the bottom because of a sudden myopism on your part.'

'But, sir. . . .' It was a waste of energy. The rope lowered and at such celerity that no allowance was made for me to catch the join of the stern. I swung and hammered into the hull. I eased two of the swings with a hand between me and the ship, but on the next my face crashed into the side; pain burst from my nose, and icy water rose rapidly up my legs, seemed to linger maliciously, then snatched at my thighs, waist and chest and I choked as my head went under. A surge caught the ship and a volume of water rushed under the quarter. It took me and the rope continued to run out, the hull pushing past with eerie flashes of undersea lightning; the growing fouling was shaggy and matted like Samwell's recent muses. I held at my chest to stop breathing. My nails scratched through the pubic growth to halt the descent and my head smashed into the keelson and we stopped. The torrents continued their dash under the ship so the pressure was great and I began to spin like a fishing lure in a trout stream. My head knocked continually against the jutting keelson and rudder. Mahia was beside me. I cried, my hand is killing me, Mahia; my head is bruised, the cold numbs every part of my body. I cannot stand this agony in my chest too.

Then breathe you stubborn man; you'll be all right.

I was deceived. I breathed a solid mass into my chest; I choked and vomited; the pain was of a level I would never have believed possible; my lungs burned and were frozen and I screamed. The fires dazzled in the green about me; I threw up blood or port and a laughing mad desire took me to sniff in the love hairs of my courtesan ship. The rope tightened. It came from my waist and pulled up my shirt and the hemp found my chest and ripped along the skin till it found my arms, in the vicinity of a thumping speeding rhythm, and the bones of my breast opened like fingers in a fist of hate altering to a beckoning of forgiveness. The rope caught in the gap between rudder and keelson and rode up to the first pintle. I knew I would die. Mahia! I cried. And the rope slackened and a surge took it clear of the hazard. My head found the hull and ploughed a track back to the sides and the air. I surfaced. Fingers clawed crazily and my shoes scraped at the timber for a foothold. The rope slipped and I went under again, away from the ship, and the pain returning under my arms proved we were ascending. I came from the surface and struggled for a hold like a stricken cat. The toes of my shoes found a gap in the timbers and I was just able to support myself and cough and choke and, dear God, to breathe fresh air.

The gulps of oxygen came in a purgatorial bellow and my vision was of the oddest nature. I could see so clearly every contour of the quarter, the path my nose rubbed in the hull as the rope pulled me; beyond, everything was black and terror-filled, yet I understood.

The burning stopped at my armpits. Hands held me. Eyes, wide and frightened, stared. The pain was a raging furnace in my lungs. 'Second plank down,' I tried and lost the battle with my chest; and then the coughing stopped again.

'Second plank below the waterline, sir. It's stripped of oakum and there's a gap; a foothold, that's all.'

I heard Cleveley shouting that the pumps were holding and I returned to life years later with David Samwell looking into my eyes as he removed a bandage. It hurt.

'Go away, and practise on someone else.'

I recovered slowly; the pumps were noisy whenever I woke and when I next stepped onto the deck, we were passing snow-covered lands and the sky had been changed into that strange soft azure which comes with very high latitudes. The temperature was frosty crisp. We were searching for a place to repair the damaged hull which was fothered with canvas. Fortunately this coast of America was not short of likely coves and when the weather favoured us, we sailed carefully across shoaling water. At last we could let go the bowers and haul the ship over onto her larboard and expose the starboard which had left my head and body a mass of lacerations. We found that many of the planks had lost their oakum and a band of caulkers got quickly to work.

The reader may recall a previous reference to the captain's philosophy of departures, and when we left this sounding we were almost cast to our destruction. The wind was light and uncertain, yet the tide strong, and soon we were set onto a collection of rocks that would have quickly undone the good deeds of the caulkers and the builders as well. Fortune saved us without a moment to spare. The ill-fated cutter from *Discovery*, later to herald the worst tragedy of the voyage, was in the water and quickly took us in tow and clear of the hazard. The inhabitants of this lonely region canoed around us to wave goodbye in their grotesque fashion; the men had a slit like a second mouth cut below their lips and through this they waggled their tongues disturbingly.

By the law of mathematics the further we pushed north, the more likely we were to find the elusive North-West Passage, and now a host of amateur discoverers was found among the officers who each knew that this or that inlet would lead to the Atlantic.

Mr Gore suddenly became impatient with a hunch that a large bay we were crossing was definitely the way to the east, and we pushed into an inlet that continually narrowed. We sailed for two hundred miles and brine gave way to fresh water and the bottom came up and we turned about and sailed back to the sea and Mr Gore said he was very surprised by the turn of events; he had been so certain, so absolutely sure, he said.

As students of the science of geography will realise, we now had to find a passage through the Aleutians. We pushed along the coast and our old adversary from the Southern Ocean struck again. Fog came down and blocked our view of even the forecastle. Dr Samwell was the first to give the alarm. He had been standing in the waist staring into the vapour when he called to the quarterdeck that he could hear breakers. The leadsman had been shivering in the chainw'le. Twenty-two fathoms, he chanted. Captain Cook dismissed this as deep ground, but the doctor insisted we were closing with danger and persisted with his remonstrations till the old boy hailed *Discovery* and we both dropped the anchors. The fog lifted about three hours later and revealed an island right in our path.

The people looked upon this near-catastrophe with surprise and terror.

My wounds began to weep and I was ordered back to bed. I could hear the sounds of the ship, but relied on David Samwell to bring me news when he changed the dressings. I did not eat for I had no appetite. I heard the cable rattling out and we came to rest in Unalaska, and my body was grateful for the calm after being continually rocked upon large scabs which hurt and suppurated. I slept in a fever and the dreams were frightening.

David was changing bandages and with each unwrapping found a new pain. He talked rapidly and loud to cover my groans.

'In the forenoon an Eskimo came on board who was no stranger to the customs and manners of Europeans for the first thing he asked us for was a quid of tobacco of which he was very fond.' The bandage was off and he rolled it ready to be returned.

'Soon after he begged a pinch of snuff – hold steady a moment; fine, that's better – and he showed by motions he knew how to take it. Finding him so well acquainted with these luxuries we concluded that our gentleman would have no objection to that general concomitant of snuff and tobacco, a dram.'

'Jesus, easy, David. God, you're rough at times.'

'He showed great aversion to this idea, you know, giving us to understand by reeling and staggering the effect it would have upon him and he refused to touch it.'

'I'd be happy to have the dram the visitor declined, if you could arrange it.'

'No alcohol, doctor's orders.'

'What? You're the doctor around here; you can see I need something to cheer me up.'

'Sorry, no, and that's an end on it.'

We spent another day at the anchorage. I felt a definite improvement, but not well enough to eat nor to venture on deck. The day passed slowly for David did not visit me until the early evening. Some of the wounds hurt still, but the majority had begun to itch as if crusty coverings were as anxious to be gone as I was to be up and about.

'Where have you been, David?'

'Ashore,' he said in an amused way.

'I'm dying and you've been away excursioning. You should have been here with your patient.'

'I think not. Especially when I tell you the interesting pleasures your friends have been about.'

'Please warm your hands before you start on those bandages.'

'You see, we were returning from a visit to the island when we espied an Indian friend from yesterday who said he would be our guide. He took us to an Eskimo village and the great quantity of fish hanging to dry made it appear at a distance like a glover's yard.'

'Easy, please, doctor.'

'We were much surprised at finding small hillocks of earth and dirt scattered about here and there with a hole in the top, through which we descended down a ladder made of a thick piece of wood with steps cut into it. We entered a dark and dirty cave seemingly underground where our noses were instantly saluted with a potent stink of putrid fish which was scattered about the house. This one's not healing well at all.'

'How can it? My caring doctor is out visiting natives instead of looking after the wounded.'

A sharp tugging of the chest dressing silenced me. 'We were welcomed into these murky caves by the master of the house and his wife and other females sitting together in one part of the hut.'

'Damn your eyes, David; if this turns out to be another promiscuous adventure, I'm going to run you through.'

'We visitors were well used to seeing strange scenes since we left England, so we spent no time staring about us with vacant astonishment but immediately made love to the handsomest woman in the company . . .'

'No, I won't listen to you. . . .'

'. . . who in order to make us welcome refused us no favour, even though her husband and father stood by.'

'I don't believe it; even an audience doesn't inhibit you.'

'Steady now, this might hurt a little.' It did. 'Having thus paid proper attention to the women we had time to look about us and admire the structure and furniture of these strange habitations.'

'David, I can guess what you're going to say. Please don't, let me imagine it was a little bit nice and pleasant.'

'You mustn't deny yourself a knowledge of reality. Now, we went into a passage and there was a large bowl of stale urine just lying there and much stinking fish scattered about.'

'This is making me feel much worse.'

'I have to tell you, John, that the habitations are excessively nasty; they appear on the outside like a round dunghill and the whole town stinks worse than a tanner's yard occasioned by the fish and whale blubber suffered to lie about in a state of putrefaction. The Eskimos we have seen in the canoes alongside the ship appeared very cleanly but now we have seen their houses we cannot but look upon them as a filthy set of people.'

'You are a stoat.'

'The sea gives a man an appetite. Now, one more dressing and I'm done.'

'I hope you washed your hands before you started on me.'

He turned to the door and a look of victory clung to a foolish grin. He seemed to be stepping at least an inch above the deck in a sort of dancing prance; he was like an imbiber enjoying the euphoria after a heavy night of port. David the muse-conqueror, I thought.

'Has the captain asked after me?'

'Yes, every day; perhaps more than once.'

'You know, I think I've burned my bridges with him. I'm sorry.'

'On the contrary, young sir. I think he cares for you a very great deal.'

I woke impatient for breakfast. It was an indication that I was almost mended; the beef left my teeth sore but happy after unaccustomed exercise. I hardly tasted the biscuit as it went down and even begged one from Mr Gore. I tapped it on the table to evict lingering weevils; unlike many of the ship I do not find the taste pleasing. I wiped my fork on the tablecloth and carefully climbed the companion-ladder to the deck. My eyes were met by a sight the like of which I had never imagined. Instead of the blue I was accustomed to, a massive wall of white stood before the ship. Ice; a tall castle-like barricade that stretched as far as we could see. The temperature nipped at the tips of ears, but I hobbled to the rail to stare in wonder at the incredible view. I could not imagine anything so perfectly, aesthetically designed; it seemed an end to our progress had been arranged in a theatrically overdressed spectacle. It would have been impenetrable to the largest army and it was obvious we had come as far north as man could hope to venture.

I watched mainmast crew dressing the yards. I asked the midshipman, Shuttleworth, for our direction. 'Why south, of course, sir. We cannot press further now.'

'South? But south to where, to England?'

'To Hawaii, sir.'

I turned my back on the grandeur of the ice towering over our masts; I had seen enough. I only wanted now the vision of a sunbrowned creation of my own height whispering 'Hone'.

19

*H*onour seals the lips of gentlemen and denies the publick knowledge of much which may be in their interest to be informed upon; but honesty is so vital to me that I am prepared to sacrifice all to it, no less this variation of honour. And accordingly I will now disclose the surroundings of the murder of courageous learned Dr Bill.

The crime was suggested in the greatest of innocence, of that I am certain. It manifested itself at the gunroom table after our fellow pigs swilled and were gone one evening and David and I remained chatting over a pint of strong black strap. The plates were cleared and the table cloth given a feeble shake, but such industry did not interrupt us. We talked politics and prosody, the monarch and medicine, copulation versus chastity, Gray and Garrick, doctor and death. It was on this last subject that the conversation turned to our absent friend and thus established his fate. In fairness one could argue that death was firmly stamped on his countenance; it was merely a question of when. Alternatively, each mortal will die some time and one is not to know that a victim of a murder who may appear perfectly healthy before the fatal blow is wielded would not have succumbed quite naturally minutes after the violent death. Had it not occurred, that is. I fear your narrator is guilty of an excursus.

We remained at the table for an hour and I was ready to return to my cabin for I had begun another verse of an ode to Mahia and a creative mood took me. Yet I knew that David did not wish to leave and I quickly discovered why; we were drinking and no preoccupation is better designed to loosen the tongue, although veracity may sometimes suffocate along the way.

'You see, it's my colleague and I really can take no more. The fellow cannot sleep and as determined a scientist as he is during the day, he is surely the most complaining sufferer by night. The groans and agony; I'm sorry, our John, but I cannot. . . .'

And so David disclosed that our senior surgeon was at the latter end of the malady and approaching death for already he suffered deprivation of self-dependence and dignity, fate's pitiless price for removal to a better place. I suggested that we ought to take some wine to Dr Bill's cabin to cheer him up.

David said, 'Absolutely not. It'd overload the heart; it would be the end of him for sure.'

'Painlessly, though.'

'Without a doubt.'

'And he does like his tipple.'

'Well, the man's a doctor.'

'It seems to me, David, that we never get to choose our own end. It's always wretchedly demoralising, as though fate is determined we'll be glad and our comforters relieved when death takes us.'

'Of all the wonders God accorded man, his brain, his superiority over the beasts, the intensity of an encounter with the fairer sex, he somehow got death all wrong.'

'No wonder the dead are not allowed to speak.'

'What a mountain of complaints there'd be.'

'And we could take some of your anaesthetic with us.'

'It would seem more suitable.'

The word was not put to our intention and neither one nor the other could appear more guilty. A clever attorney might point at me, arguing that I was warned of serious consequences yet still tried to persuade my accomplice towards this folly. A better counsellor of course would argue that David Samwell's reply was not indicative of innocence nor shock, for obviously the modulation had to be rent with irony. No wonder the legal profession alone wins in what we call British justice. (Dr Johnson said he did not care to speak ill of a certain man behind his back, but he believed the gentleman was an attorney.)

We took the remainder of our wine and collected some anaesthetic Number One. The stench of his illness and the groans of pain assailed us before we reached Dr Bill's quarters. However, we were determined upon our course which we felt was correct and humane and opened wide the door to allow a circulation of air and put outside the cabin his pewter wash-bowl so that there might be room for both of us.

Dr Bill's face was far whiter than his nightgown and his mouth was a grey milky abyss; despite the coolness of these high latitudes, bedclothes were pushed down from his sweating body and the gown raised to a basket-like chest, so that we witnessed that face of sinking life, the skeleton with a covering of loose puckered skin, a dirty shallow navel and a buttock gangrenous from the pressure of his lying upon it; not surprisingly, larvae of flies were present. A contradiction struck me forcibly on this bed of misery and despair; his member which lay against a scarcely covered thigh bone displayed the health and vigour of youth. However, these observations were made fleetingly (though the memory was to last forever) for we wished to ease some of the dread of our dear friend; we wanted to renew our covenant of cordiality on this last night, and his with the blessing that comes from a bottle with the boys.

David took the wooden chair and I sat on bedclothes saturated with suppuration and filth. We spoke heartily, ignored entirely the terrible moans and quickly decanted a draught of the wine into that wide orifice. The anaesthetic was held in abeyance, for surely a shock of overproof rum would despatch him too quickly; first he must experience friendship and humour.

The effect upon the patient was remarkable. That swollen tongue rose like a charmed snake, the eyes which stared into the forehead flickered, the brown pupils appeared and focused and I swear a hint of colour returned to those sunken pasteboard cheeks. Suffice it is to say that we administered more sips of black strap and watched his virtual return from the grave. The body bent forward and we hastily removed costumes from the cupboard to use as pillows to support his back. The pain increasing on those terrible buttocks must have been insufferable, I thought, but it soon transpired that our hapless companion was mercifully without sensation in his lower region.

David Samwell, clutching the wine to his chest, now gave us the benefit of his beautiful voice. He sang David Garrick's 'Hearts of Oak' and quickly followed it with a popular melody, 'Where the bee sucks'.

To add to the jollity, David joined me in unseemly applause and Dr Bill tried his best to move his arms. I sang 'Blow, blow thou winter wind' which seemed appropriate in these latitudes, but it was a poor voice after David's and only determination to entertain the gallery let me see the number through. David recounted some particularly risqué jokes that he said were favourites of Dr Bill and it seemed the muscles of that hopeless face moved. We applied more of our warming medicine and our patient's jaw returned to life and the black strap was finished and the good company moved onto the anaesthetic. More songs followed and gave way to parlour quizzes; one I recall of all innocent matters was for guessing derivations of day names.

'Tuesday?' I shouted.

'From Tiu,' David replied equally as noisily. 'Old English word for Mars. And Wednesday?'

'Woden's Day,' I rejoined. 'Old English for Mercury.'

'Thursday for Thor's Day,' David Samwell returned. 'Our old term for Jupiter. And Friday?'

David and I were dragging a little with the pace of our medicating, but Bill, like a disciplined patient, kept up measure for measure. At about this time, some of the famed Samwell anecdotes were aired. The last we heard that night was:

'And the landlady replied: " 'pon my word Dr Samwell you've only paid half the lodgings" and I knew I was being tricked, but what to do when her voice was so noisily pitched to attract neighbours? I rushed her back into the room and pushed high those hoops and horse-hair and entered in a trice and fucked her from apron to robe à l'anglaise till she shrieked in joy unequalled; I gave her a thundering scalade such that the very marrow of her bones was electrified.'

'And the rent she demanded?'

'She returned the amount I'd paid and offered me a week's free accommodation. You can see, Dr Anderson, John, what a peacemaker is the gristle of love, the magic wand of wonder, the mediator. . . .'

'The umpire,' I offered.

'The bond of union,' David continued, his face animation and licence. 'The rod that's never spared, the knob of nourishment. . . .'

'The plenipotentiary.'

'The sword of success, the quill that never empties. . . .'

'The bone of contentment.'

'The horn of plenty,' Dr Bill added hoarsely. And we cheered and dispensed further anaesthesia and huzza'd life and love and Hail Noble Albion!

The audience accorded our guest of honour a standing ovation as once rang about auditoriums and he stared in appreciation and friendship and stared no more and we sat him against the bulkhead and took a place either side on that reeking cot with a comforting arm each round him. We drank more and sang 'Rule Britannia!' again and who could say that poor brave corpse did not join in. The next morning Dr Bill was committed to the deep in a canvas wrapping that was well weighted owing to the lightness of the decimated remains.

I watched this funeral of a scholarly friend and thought of a line of Gray's, 'The paths of glory lead but to the grave'. And I wondered what in life didn't.

Fate was a whirlpool which began to influence us the moment the jib-boom turned from the ice towards the sunny latitudes. We were returning to warmth of climate and of affection and we had every reason to be in good spirits, yet a disquiet affected us tentatively at first but then with a grip that tightened increasingly until we were in the very eye of the descending torrent out of which looked death in the guise of bloodlusting hordes.

The captain ordered some sea horses we saw on iceflows shot to improve the diet, but the crew stubbornly, bluntly told the captain they would not eat the blubbery meat. The old boy picked up the gauntlet and stopped all rations except walrus. The unrest developed quickly into a confrontation, but the offending food ran out and the normal diet and peace had to return. A further cause for concern: the captain 'discovered' an island we found on the voyage north and refused to accept the mistake.

The mercury improved and our storm canvas was replaced with lighter sails and we found our Polynesian satellite. I dreamed of Mahia, but the wind kept us from that island and we began to run along the archipelago, seeking a fair anchorage. Each mile from that beautiful island seemed a hundred to me and no dazzling sky and high mountains could lift the weight from my heart. The captain traded for sugar cane from the canoes that came out, the people were employed brewing cane beer and I kept up a constant vigil for Mahia.

The beer was usually made from spruce leaves, but sugar cane seemed a happy substitute. There was no reason to expect that such a pleasant tipple should bring resentment. Last year the captain asked the men if they would drink beer in the warm climes and save the rum for the colder regions and they agreed. Yet for no account, this time he ordered the supply stopped and only beer to be consumed. The sailors rebelled at the thought of grogless days and the old boy danced his quarterdeck *haka* and called the men his turbulent mutinous crew and it seemed leaders would hornpipe from yard tackles. Fortunately several canoe loads of handsome women came out from an island we were passing and a new mutiny died. They tasted the beer and loved it. And so it was in these strange pinpricks that fate swooped threateningly on our well-being.

The weather ought to have been blissful. We were about five leagues off an island, sailing pleasantly, when shortly after midnight a calm set the rigging complaining and an inexplainable swell came in from the north-east and hove us fast towards the land. Thunderstorms raged with contradictory gusts and we tacked and stood off an island; in the dawn our course was proved to be wrong and we were closing a lee-shore. It was a mistake that we navigators could not explain. A furious surf broke upon the beach which now was half a league off. We had been in the most imminent danger during the night and to claw away from destruction would require tremendous fortune and skill. The wind slowly began to veer and for a little while we could do no more than follow the soundings along; at any moment we expected the terrible shudder of the keelson taking the ground. Our nerves were raw; the only words were orders from the captain on the quarterdeck. Then a crashing to shatter eardrums exploded over our heads.

> How the poor Sailors stand amaz'd and tremble!
> While the hoarse Thunder like a bloody Trumpet
> Roars a loud Onset to the gaping Waters
> Quick to devour them.

The leach rope of the mainsail gave way and the material rent in two and at that very moment when every inch of remaining canvas was vital to our survival, two topgallant sails split and exploded into fragments. There was no chance to alter the sailplan; for a full half-hour we struggled for our lives and the destroyed sails boomed and cracked above more tumultuous than a sea battle. We prayed and gradually the bearings twixt us and shore took a favourable turn. Yard by yard the sounding improved till we cleared the island. So close was the mishap that no man shouted huzzas, but all thanked the good admiral upstairs for saving us.

Officers were summoned to the aft-cabin and our remonstrations about the shabby state of the equipment supplied to *Resolution* were now incontestable and the captain paraded before us shouting and furious as if we were the crooked Pallisers and his ilk of Deptford who lined their pockets with the evil misery they foisted on us.

White-crowned peaks called out in an ethereal beckoning we could not resist and the ships drove down on this last island and in a light breeze our boats discovered a satisfactory anchorage and we turned a corner in the approach.

And now the reader, who has long indulged the narrator with great patience, can be at last confronted with the heaven promised from the promotion in an earlier chapter. We entered a land of plenty and such scenes to pass could not have been witnessed before and I am certain are unlikely to be repeated. How often is it that a god is reincarnated?

Hawaiian savages believed our captain was their god Lono when we brushed against the lesser isles; this time we had all but circumnavigated the archipelago as is foretold of Lono in the fables. As soon as our sails were seen again natives rushed for this island, the place where Lono would walk again upon Hawaii, and when we came in sight of Kealakekua Bay, a roar of approbation rose from a multitude and overwhelmed the senses.

The jade ocean between *Resolution* and the shore was thick with double-hulled craft and still canoes came from the beach and pressed closer in foaming wakes and our people were transfixed at the rails, unable to believe the incredible vista. We eased into the bay under full sail and wondered where we could steer, for all about were the vessels, and the chanting and cries so affectionate, that we would not forbear to so much as brush close. The backdrop to the extraordinary vision was the rising ground of browns and greys extending to high snow-capped peaks. At the foot twin villages were irradiating green splashes above bleached surf. Two months it had taken us from sighting the archipelago to finding this happy anchorage; eight weeks of fighting the unexpected treachery of the elements. I will not pretend that the feeling of foreboding was gone, but for the present we who had climbed so high on our globe were returning to warmth and admiration that seemed as fabulous balms to our many ordeals. We carried their god to their world; to us it seemed we were the mortals arriving in their heaven.

And now, patient reader, comes the reward for our hearts of oak, for the canoes began to disgorge their cargoes of curious beauty. Young women handsome of face and comely of body came up the sides of the ship and sought out our sailors. They embraced our people without introduction, with neither of the parties able to comprehend the other's language, and the scene was of a hunger that would never be assuaged;

we were constantly short of manpower to reduce sail and lower the bowers and our seaman-like activities could continue only as Dame Nature would permit. All the while, the numbers increased. Those who use planks for riding white horses paddled out in the hundreds. Uncountable numbers of dark heads covered the bay as the people swam to us; James King estimated nine thousand borne in the canoes and a goodly ten thousand lined the shore, a slice of packed brown over the white of the surf.

On the quarterdeck we were considered priests and spared the lust of our admirers. Priapus had never been so honoured and our hosts mated in their hundreds with our men until the decks shook with the queer rhythm and the air was filled with cries like cats screeching into the night. I translated for the captain, and we managed to locate a man of influence so that the ship could be worked. Our ordinary people were in such demand that they could not finish with one girl before another would demand her share, and so the nymphs of Hawaii welcomed god's children. Eventually brown bodies had to be heaved into the sea and as the last of three hundred people were so removed from the upper decks, we completed our anchoring. Sails were clewed up and furled, yards struck and our temple was at last still on the sea and a chant rose about us, slowly at first and then increasing in power as a mass cried,

'Lono! Lono! Long live Lono!'

I searched each of the canoes for Mahia, even though this was so far from her island, and the people prepared for the arrival ashore of the reborn god. And yet, even now, Captain Cook would not accept that this was so. He was, he said, considered an important chief and this can only be ascribed to a surprising modesty or a European turn of a blind eye. We were guided by Kao, the high priest; he resembled laundered bones with a face in need of ironing; but the washday illusion could not disguise wickedness from anyone but our captain. We went ashore and the people prostrated themselves. The priest took him to a *tapu* place where, in our commander's words, we witnessed a religious ceremony; he would not accept it as a deification ritual. Then an enormous pageant was held in which we received the King of the island group and the high priest. An abundance of gifts and mountains of food were heaped upon us; the people were determined to give all they had and no treat was withheld.

Repairs began at leisure; we expected to be here some months before searching again for the elusive ice passage. Sails and masts for repair were taken ashore and the sailors relaxed in the substantial generosity of the attractive women. But I, who wanted no other company of the heart but my Mahia, could not so easily ignore the evil that hung about us.

'If you want my opinion,' David Samwell said, leaning against the open door of my cabin, 'you're doing the wrong thing. This girl you are so taken with is high-born and you know as well as I do that a state of intactness must remain till marriage. Now then, our John, if you were to form an attachment to one of the gorgeous gells of the ships, you would sample the delights of the low-born. Aristocracy is not theirs, but nothing else is denied them and by the graces of generous cupid, nothing of their splendid wholesome forms is denied us either.'

'David, I'm in love and she who has taken my heart is the one I want.'

'Then don't let our visitors take your heart, let them be enriched by Albion meat, the like of which their glorious parts must have ached for for generations. Don't be selfish, give them some enjoyment.'

'I don't notice any going without.'

'One is.'

'Oh.'

'John, I have the pleasure of three of the fairest muses and not one is beyond fifteen summers. I would only admit it to you, but as glorious as the challenge is, I am weakening. I will not manage the third; come along and help.'

'You've aged ten years in the few days we've been here, David. You should give it a rest; take the night off; send them home.'

'But it's the quantity. It's quite unbelievable; I mean, do you realise that so far I have had the pleasure of no less than. . . .'

'No, and I don't want to know. David, I'm only interested in quality if you like and that, for me, is Mahia. Do help me talk the captain into sailing to her island.'

He ignored my entreaty. 'I don't want you to misunderstand why I'm doing this. It's for investigation, for medicine. I am going to donate my body to science, you know.'

'Do you think there'll be any of it left?'

The next night I was called to a visiting canoe and I hurried to the deck, not believing my own optimism; Mahia was standing in the waist. Beside her was a young native man; he spoke and it took a moment to change my ear to the dialect. Our concourse was busy with island visitors; they recognised this couple and stepped about them with reverence.

'My sister wishes to visit you,' he said in an easy manner. 'Our father has allowed that this may be so; he feels as does the family that she can be trusted in your care, for you are of intelligence and not of the low-born. I will return at this time in three days.' He did not wait for a reply and I stood staring at this gorgeous woman while people moved about us and my heart hammered.

She walked a little along the waist. I followed. 'You smile, you say nothing,' she ventured. A light garment was wrapped about her, but not in the European fashion, for this began below her breasts which were firm and smooth, and I concentrated on her face which was unmarked and perfectly symmetrical about a slim nose. The breasts belied a certain boyishness; a number of hieroglyphics were tattooed on her upper arm and wrists and these seemed far removed from aesthetics of savages, but as a variation of bangles that English women are proud to wear. Her hair was dark and long and new blooms issued a perfume that caused my blood to race stronger. And so the holder of my love was with me after months of agony; and she was amusing and assured and wildly alluring; I thought she was yet to see the year of seventeen, yet the confidence of her rightful place in life made me awkward and nervous and very English. We promenaded the decks as a Sussex couple on esplanading Sundays and traded the names of stars. On the poop-deck, under the mighty Plough constellation, I at last summoned the courage to kiss briefly her lips. I knew then as my senses went mad why I had been prepared to throw away my career and life; I could not leave this ocean without her. While the noises of excesses of drink and coition filled the ship, I told her of my plans to stay after the next search for the North-West Passage. She did not comprehend what I meant by our discoveries, but she understood that I would return for her and remain in this place. We were happy. She slept in the cot and I made myself comfortable on the deck of the cabin.

I introduced Mahia to the captain who was nice to her and saluted when we left and called her m'am. Mahia did not speak in his presence and I do not know if she regarded him as a god. She did not bow to him, but as she was of aristocracy no conclusion could be drawn from this. I did not think to ask her about it; a sailor has subjects other than the captain when he is with his true love.

As her visit was to be of such short duration, he stood me down so that we were able to visit the villages and walk the steep foothills. I learned about the way of life, the gods, the heavens, the class structure and idiosyncrasies like the courageous island men who would face any adversary no matter how powerful by day, but turn from the weakest at night. They believed their spirit would be lost in the darkness and never find heaven. I watched her lips move, the brightness of her teeth, the laugh as proud as any English aristocrat's and the way it ended with eyelids lowering. My heart swelled and I loved and adored her; Britain would never do for me and the more I gazed into those brown deep eyes, the less I cared for the drab Navy life charted ahead. I would, as they say, go native; my emotions were not addled by concupiscence but with a pure love that had no need of the lust and intoxication which powered the affairs of the people of the ship.

Mahia was the only person to see my journals, but she had no notion of writing. Many islanders believed the main business of the ship was painting cloth, which is what they understood our journal-keeping to be. She thought our quills inferior to the brushes they made to fill a similar role.

I wondered how to explain, then I asked Mahia to sing something I had not previously heard. She did so in her full earthy voice and I noted the words. Now I sang to her, reading the recorded verses. What wonder and astonishment passed over her features at this magic.

We travelled between the land and shore by boats and the sailors assumed our sexual attachment; I longed to correct them, but Mahia was very beautiful and I let pride get in the way. I was proud of our innocence yet I was happy for the people to believe I was one of the few chosen to consort with a higher-born. This custom was a matter of anguish to our jack-tars who wanted everything, not dissimilar to punch-mad pugilists.

We spoke of the flowers, the birds and the fish and we dived about the ship while the watch looked out for sharks. The sea was pellucid and as she swam ahead of me I could not help but observe her completely and I was more in awe and deeper in love. Once when we surfaced, holding to the side of a moored launch, we giggled and I kissed her lips and studied with fascination the sheen of her dark hair, the perfectness of the line where smooth gentle skin joined it. Her smile faded at the approach of a canoe.

'The high priest,' I said.

'I know,' she said quietly. I thought I noticed a shiver. 'Kao is powerful throughout the islands.'

'He's only skin and bones; an empty calabash almost in its grave.'

'You mustn't underestimate him. He will use your people if it suits him.'

'I don't think so. The old boy's a bit cleverer than any. . . .' I was about to say savage, but hastily added 'priest'.

'He is not a good man, Hone.'

'I think there is something evil about him; but there's something evil hanging over us all, all the time, as if. . . .'

'Sh,' she whispered and slid under the water so that he would not see her, and I filled my lungs to follow her down.

'What's this?'

'It's a mirror. You look into it. See?'

'Who? Who is this?'

'It's you.'

'Me?'

'Have you not seen your reflection before?'

'Only in a pond.'

'Well, Mahia, let me introduce you to Mahia.'

'Oh, Hone. She is beautiful. Is she not beautiful?'

'Aye aye, *e hine*. She is indeed the most beautiful creation of God.'

'I cannot believe how fortunate I am.'

'Nor can I.'

We remained on deck late at night and stared at Cassiopeia chasing the Plough around Polaris, at the outline of the island, the shining peaks. She talked. I gazed upon her until I was hypnotised and sometimes my brain was too intoxicated by happiness and could not translate and I could only hear that voice. There was no simile for it; it was just the most beautiful sound I had ever heard and on the last night I presented her with shy Phecda in Ursa Major and she used another name and promised to leave the star in place till I returned when we would both share it. As we would share everything. We said farewell. Mahia was at the waist and climbing onto the ladder and our parting did not seem possible; then her head lowered out of sight and I had to look over the bulwark to see her. Mahia climbing into her canoe with her brother and another rower and suddenly they were mixed with the others; then the canoe was slicing through the water seaward, and away from me with the marines in their launch following to give protection to the edge of the bay, and the dusk fell rapidly on Mahia waving. Her tears spilled into the Pacific fifty yards off, and the night took her. I stood at the waist staring after her; but for natives and sailors pushing past, I could have been up there in the heavens. As the dark pressed firmly down, I saw Mahia had been true. Phecda kept its place in the Plough until we would be together again. My heart was filled with joy at that prospect and in the next second I was swamped by the tenderest grief; how could I survive these months till we were together again? And I longed, begged God, to rush the time past until I could return to Mahia and marry her. First in her own faith and then with an English bible. Mahia was out there on the long voyage to her home. They would stop at islands along the way and proceed as conditions were right, taking each step in a proper seafaring way. I was not concerned for her safety; these people were every bit as confident voyagers as ourselves.

Perhaps I stood at the waist for an hour. A commotion was going on out of sight; screaming women were nothing new in our world of lust now and I accepted the invitation to drink with David and James King in the gunroom. The wine flowed.

In my loneliness I imbibed deeply, laughed politely as required and listened only a little to their stories of conquests and sailoring until the maudlin stage was near. I went to my cabin and they to indulge refreshed appetites.

I closed the door gently and took off my clothes and lay quite naked on the cot. The smell of her was all about and I took it down into my lungs in excited happy draughts. I stared at the fading inn sign, remembering how I tried to explain its meaning to my lovely fiancée. I fell into the most delicious of dreams and the portent of evil was a world away. I wore a beatific expression and I was blessedly sad in the way of first lovers. How long this euphoria lasted I do not know; the smile was present in my sleep and her vision was strong. Then for no reason that I could account, I heard her scream. It was the long-drawn-out scream of a mortally wounded woman. I heard it once in the American war and I *knew* it was Mahia. I sat up in bed with the utmost dread. I strained to hear as if she might repeat it. But about the ship the noises of this anchorage continued. Bawdy humour, a sailor shouting, native girls giggling. A nightmare, I thought, and yet I could not recall one dream in which happiness did not reign. Then came the noise of coition from the main-deck; a number of lovers at a lusty girl, a group activity. I forced a smile and stood up; it was a popular sport among the people, but its attraction was lost on me. I thus tried to reassure myself. But a cold hand remained clamped to my heart and I did not want to sleep naked now. I dressed in my nightgown and brought the blankets up over my head as if we had returned to the ice.

I returned to duties with a government conference in the aft-cabin. The captain wanted reports on the progress of the many repairs needed, which because of the hospitality were proceeding slowly. Bligh reported of salted stores, including thirty-nine puncheons of pork. But both James and Mr Gore spoke of the unprecedented respect the captain was receiving. There was much flattery along this path for the old boy and though I still experienced the queerest weight upon my spirit, I was happy in my recent nostalgia and keen to encourage our commander.

'I think, sir,' I said when a space in the conversation allowed my observation, 'that the dreadful high priest better look to his laurels, so high a regard has his congregation for you.' As may be realised from the choice of words, it was meant in humour.

'I would be most pleased, Mr Williamson, if you would refrain from this determination that I am seen other than as a senior officer in His Britannic. . . .'

And thus spake the captain in his dour manner when the door opened and who other than the unpleasant topic of conversation should enter. He went before the desk and looked up at Captain Cook, who was now standing and seemed a giant before this apparition.

'I hope I am not disturbing. . . .' he began.

'Your translations if you will, Mr Williamson.'

I got to work, something that I had not done often here as the priest preferred to guide the captain with sign language; he was determined his people would not see his need of an interpreter when speaking with the great Lono.

'I wish to make some enquiries which are as you will realise most important for our King's attention,' the old fellow said. He was a hopeless politician, I thought, watching him, for he could not disguise his feelings. Some craftsman had done his best in this regard; the right half of his face was tattooed in a succession of zig-zagging lines, a contrast to the New Zealanders' spirals and circles. The line between marked and unmarked skin went right up the centre of a cruel nose to his low hairline. This part of his anatomy was cut in the style of the islands, short sides and a long centre strip rather like a rooster. But this aged fighting cockerel's comb was permanently limp.

'Yes, of course, Mr Kao. You know we are eager to help. . . .'

'The King has asked me to enquire, *e Lono*, when you and your children will be departing.' There was a space while I translated and a shock followed from our side, as was to be expected. 'Of course,' the priest hastened, 'this is only because we need the time to get together a suitable present to sustain you on your way.'

I interpreted this and added, 'Sir, he has left a long enough silence for you to realise his politeness may not be entirely sincere.'

'By God, young sir, I'll thank you for your translations alone. I will interpret meanings.'

The silence returned and the priest continued to stare at the commander. He would not demean himself with a look at the others in the room.

'We will have to think this matter over, Mr Kao. There are numerous repairs to be done which we are proceeding with apace and many are our thanks to the King for his great help and to you Mr Kao, too, for your considerable. . . .'

'Yes, I said to the King that our busy Lono would hardly be able to stay long. Very well then, I will say *haere ra* for the moment for there are matters to be seen to in the preparation of the farewell. I am personally very sorry you will have to leave in haste, and so will be the people. And so yes indeed will be the people who fancied themselves greatly elevated with the visit of such a deity.' And he was gone.

'Mr Williamson, perhaps some of these Hawaiian words are different. God, if only Omai were here. You will persist with this deity business.'

'There's one thing we can be sure of,' Mr Gore said. He was sitting against the chart-table, studying his folded hands. 'We are being told to go.'

'That can't be so,' the captain said. 'Take the welcome, an extraordinary affair by any standards, and we've always been hospitably received in Polynesia for months or more.'

'Nothing makes sense with savages, sir,' Mr Gore said.

'I think our Mr Williamson may have been right,' James said. 'I think the old bugger's jealous of you.'

'I can't accept that at all.'

'Did this princess friend of yours say anything about the priest, John?' James asked.

'Only what we knew; he's an evil devil and powerful. I suppose like all priests, his *mana*, his reputation, depends on his rating in the eyes of the people. He must come a poor second at the moment.'

'Mr Gore, kindly inform the young lieutenants who quite suddenly know more about these islands than I do that I will not tolerate their libel of this generous host. And what is more, I perfectly accept his explanation. They expect us to be about our business and want to prepare a fine farewell.'

The Polynesian weakness for thefts was rekindled and we began the guard duties again. Respect for the god continued wherever the captain walked, but good relations were deteriorating. Sailors could no longer take just any lower-class girl they fancied and stones would rain down on parties ashore. The number of our visitors dropped sharply. A cold shoulder was being extended and even the captain could not deny the chill of it. He announced a day of departure.

Men paraded the streets of the villagers like our bellmen of England, crying that we were to leave and all natives must contribute to a farewell present.

We came ashore to bid our adieus; we were confronted by huge mounds of cloths, feathers, metal which the people had purchased from the ships and food. We took this to be the present for Lono, but Kao claimed a large portion of it as his tribute to the monarch. The King seemed much impressed by this fidelity. We were given the food which came not so much from generous hearts as from the island despotism, and so we returned quite the bigger majority of the vegetables, fruit and pigs to the people.

Natives lined the bay to farewell us and some canoes followed a little way, but the difference in feelings in the short fortnight did nothing to lessen the dread which hung over the beautiful island as it fell quietly into our wake. We prayed, each soul of the ships I would wager, that we should never suffer this anchorage again.

20

The acceptance of matters supernatural is difficult, I know. A life of pleasant country walks, the reassurance of Adams architecture and the spectacle of the English arts makes us just too civilised. But the narrator wishes to inform the reader that the events related here occurred in a foreign place where veneration of heathen gods was widely practised. And it was the only worship.

I beg the reader to accept the possibility that these gods of Polynesia can wield an influence. I watched the deification of our commander and the performance was closely connected with witchcraft I have read of, and the old devil Kao was as close a resemblance to a wizard as one is likely to find.

It is the acceptance of your narrator from the matters he witnessed that dark forces were at work. It is likely that much of our predicament rested with the jealousy of an unpleasant, power-mad high priest. Yet certain questions come to an enquiring mind: what if Kao sincerely believed Captain Cook were a god? What if he put the captain through the ceremony and made the people pay homage in the genuine belief that our commander was the reincarnation of Lono? A little after we had been among them, he could see that the ways of Lono's children were more those of horny pigs than disciples. One of our number, William Watman, died while we were at Kealakekua Bay and the priest officiated at the funeral. Kao must have asked himself how Lono's children could die as mortals. And Kao was as much a politician as religious fanatic; his mind would never be very far from jealousy, doubt, cynicism and suspicion.

Darkness brushed against our lives and was to descend and crush us and I was forced towards this question: if there are gods as the

Polynesians believe, what would be their reaction to an impostor? Remember, they are quite free of Christendom's charity. And so with this idea mooted, our narrative continues. A presence hung about the ship that was as obvious as the massive long swell of an approaching hurricane.

The men applied themselves to the duties of the ship with a will that was remarkable considering we were leaving an island of incredible pleasures. We were sailing for the far north so they had no reason to hasten the ship. No reason we could see. Yet they spread our canvas from deck to truck and out to the stuns'l booms. Our spritsail was set and staysails climbed between the masts and a makeshift watersail hung beneath the driver boom. We were ready to jam any puff of the fickle wind which might come our way. The mercury remained high and the offduty watch stayed on deck in case anything further could be done to take us more quickly from the foreboding of that island.

Gradually the mountains of Hawaii island went down and our defences lowered a little too. We had a fresher breeze and the counting of knots revealed a better speed. We felt less on edge. I dreamed of Mahia and woke to hear myself laughing as my unconscious relived the splendour of our hours together. Fresh meat was served with the meals and fruit was for the asking. We pressed on through the archipelago which stretched before and behind us, and bright turquoise seas and verdant islands on the horizon mocked our fears. A whale swam beside *Resolution* and we lined the rail, and the creature blew and the water and vapour drenched the quarterdeck. The people laughed. A huge school of dolphins overtook us and the splashings of their progress sounded like a mighty waterfall. We were very interested even though they were a daily sight; their presence gave us something else to think about. The sun felt hot again and first one and then more jack-tars took to lying on the foredeck, obviously relaxed. We began to think we were safe. Then that nebulous whirlpool called for our ship and this time there was to be no avoiding fate.

The mercury was the harbinger of the tragedy that would change our lives. It dropped a little, steadied, and then it showed in a panic how the air pressure was lessening. The sky stayed clear, but the barometer continued its worrying progress. Eyes scanned the deceiving azure to weather and furtively beyond our wake to an island over the horizon.

Then clouds came in like dirty hammockrolls and lowered and the wind rapidly increased. High sails came down, topsails were reefed and taken off her and the barometer plummeted. We began sending the heavy guns down to the hold as the wind rose above a gale, and when the storm arrived we feared for our lives. It was night, unlit land was about us and the changing wind direction had to be watched out for when the disturbance line arrived. Waves heaped into sharp foaming edges and hammered the ship; we were pooped and Mr Gore was swept into the scuppers. He was taken below, shaken but unhurt, to change.

'My God, what's that?' James King shouted on the quarterdeck.

I strained my hearing into the centre of the ship from where a muffled roar sounded while trying to avoid the spume that filled my mouth and nose, collected in my ears then worked down my neck.

I thought it might be a topgallant mast splitting, but I was loathe to suggest this in case I might prompt fate. 'It's from the hold,' I shouted when the rumble came again.

'Oh, shite,' James said. 'Better get Bligh to take some men down.'

'I'll go if you like. The topgallants have to be struck, anyway. His lot could do that and I'll take some men below.'

I turned to the quarterladder and we both saw a body in the water. I gripped the rail in shock.

'For Christ's sake,' he shouted into my ear, 'what the hell?' and a second girl swept past in the leeward waves. We called to Bligh and rushed to the poop, but there was no sign in the overtaking waves astern.

'It's a native,' I said.

'They both were.'

'Should we try to recover them?' But the answer was written in the spume-driven waves; there was no going back for our square rigger.

'My God,' James said and was sick down his mageline jacket. 'They wouldn't have a chance.'

'What is it, sir?' Bligh came up the ladder like an unsheeted jib.

I pointed to the wake. 'Girls overboard, Mr Bligh. Two of them. But I don't think we'll be getting them back.'

'No,' he said. 'Jonahs and bloody superstitious sailors.'

'What?' James shouted.

'Native stowaways, are they not. The sailors blame them for the weather so over they went.'

'You let them?'

'I did not. I didn't know till a moment ago. My mate tried to stop them; it was too late.'

'How many?'

'I don't know.'

'I've heard of this before. But I can't believe it of our age,' I said.

'There's nothing new to it,' Bligh retorted.

'By God,' James shouted. 'Have the lot on a charge.'

'Aye, Mr King, but we've got to survive this weather first.'

The thought of the fate of the native women made me ill, but I pushed it from my mind; whatever had broken loose below needed to be bowsed down. I took three men from the watch and we pushed into the foredeck companionway. The shriek of the wind was snatched from our ears as we passed through the maindeck, and at the orlop, the noise was of orchestral percussion as the ship moved uneasily in the heaped seaway. In the hold, the rumble of casks crashing about was like huge drumrolls; it would be too dangerous to move among them till our eyes had adjusted. Then we made out six barrels that raced to the centre of the ship and roared like charging cavalry for the hull they seemed determined to breach.

'You two, grab the first two barrels and we'll take the third. Swing them up onto their ends and then we'll stow them proper.'

'Aye, aye, sir.'

We were hindered by the dismal light and the wild motion of the ship, but we got three under control and then after some near misses the last three.

'What is this stuff?' I asked.

'Seal blubber we rendered down from the Ker Goolans, sir.'

'Lasted a long time,' another of the men said.

'Let's put it to use,' I said and ordered them to heave two barrels up to the deck. We got them out through the companionway into the storm and the men began moving them carefully to the waist. I decided to make an inspection of the remainder of the lower ship before the sea got any worse. I worked my way through part of the hold, came to the orlop and found everything ship-shape. I entered the maindeck; the noise had been strong through those cramped levels, but here where animals had lived was queerly still. A goose walked over my grave and I hurried across to the mainway, to get back to the battle on deck.

The pens were empty and quiet now, but a movement of the ship sounded like a cow rattling her throat. I remembered my first night here when I discovered a midshipman, but conscience intervened and pushed away the memory. I recalled the sour krout and the racing vermin and a half-smile came to me. I turned to the ladder and heard a murmur that was not of the sea. I stopped and stared in its direction but only darkness came back. It must be my imagination; I wanted it to be my imagination. To a youthful mind many unlikely fears lurk in the night. Then came the flicker of a light; the beam danced along the timbers of the hull and flashed white on my hands clenched on the ladder. It was dark again and then I heard a voice.

I opened my mouth to issue a challenge and to this day I do not know what changed my mind. Instead I walked forward with great stealth. A sound like the shifting of an animal came again and soon I was beside a pillar, the self-same I imagined from a previous time. The light blinked; blackness returned. Then it shone like the deceiving beacon from Cornish wreckers. I stared and the lighthouse flashed and now I could see the reason for the intermittent wink. A group of people were engaged beyond the animal pens and one or more stood between me and a lanthorn. A storm threatened outside and something weird was happening here and a desire clutched at my breast to turn about and go. I felt instinctively evil about me, yet I was compelled to see. I waited a moment and moved quickly forward, hoping that no impediments to the progress might trip me in the darkness. I kept a hand outstretched and touched the timber enclosure. Now the murmurs were much stronger and I could make out the silhouettes. I was no more than four yards off.

The light remained dimmed by a man; a stream of sweat crept cautiously through the hair of an armpit and tumbled down the side of my stomach with the cold touch of a high priest. Then the figure stood to a side; I saw four sailors, perhaps five. Someone lay struggling at their feet. I stared and the light must have reflected on my startled features like a hallowe'en mask. One of the figures brought a dagger down on a young girl tied and gagged. In that instant a muffled scream came despite the sailor's tight neckerchief and it filled my brain and I saw the dark shining hair, the aquiline nose that reflected so well in the looking-glass; the firmness of her suddenly broken flesh, breasts of brown warmth turning a borrowed shirt crimson. I recognised the scream tearing inside my head. It woke me after she left in the canoe under the protection of the marines. I shouted; it was a howl of rage. I recalled sailors' games with native beauties too proud for them; the hunger of these animals for pack violence despite or because of the easy gentleness available. The silhouettes turned and I pulled at the Harvey hanger at my waist. It came singing free in my fury and I paxed it the heart of each. I screamed at the scum who were not content with their violations; at the superstitions of Jonahs. I swung into them; my muscles were as iron and my eyes bulged with madness. Nothing connected with the steel. The lanthorn light had belied the distance. I slashed quickly back to rip. . . .

From the corner of my sight a cudgel emerged from the darkness; it came down and swamped the pain of my vision, of my dying love, and spiralling lights of a half-tattooed face echoed in a long scream.

My return to the world took perhaps a minute and lasted a lifetime and I was sitting on the streaming deck against the companionway. James King's anxious face was close. I mumbled about a body and people pushed past me down the ladder. Pain throbbed and clouded my head and eased and returned. David Samwell applied a bandage. James went back on his haunches and the noise of the storm rushed into the emptied space and I slowly became aware of spume in the air and bare spars above collecting rain and dropping it upon us in spasmodic aggravating bucketfuls. The running rigging fought against the elements and vines of our jungle swung about and slapped trunks in echoing shudders. Apes appeared out of the shadow and became sailors in David's lanthorn.

'Not a body there, sir,' a voice said a long way off. The lie came in a Warwickshire accent and another patois more familiar accused them of blindness and the sailors became apes as they disappeared back down to the void. That voice now screamed in pain.

'Listen, for God's sake, John.' James's face was close again and I put my arms round the thick collar. 'Some natives have gone over the side. I don't know how many; I couldn't recognise any. That's the way things are; you know how these tars act in a tempest. Now forget it for the moment, my friend; pull yourself together, please.'

A long cry came from my lips as I saw the knife strike again and I forced my body up from the cold wet deck and rushed forward. James's arms reached for me and fell away and David's hands held my wrist for a moment, but I broke free and charged in the sway of the ship. A sentry stood soaking at the aft-cabin door and I pushed him off balance and burst into the room.

'They've got Mahia,' I shouted, and a heavy bitter smell swept out into the night from the warmth of the light. The captain appeared from the private heads, pulling his breeches into position; the mouth was wide and demanding but I could not hear the words.

'What's wrong with your frigging ship?' my voice charged but I was not responsible. I was on the inside with the throbbing from a concussion and a bleeding from my heart and my nerves were scratched with nails of burning iron.

James and David ran over and I was pushed into the room and the door closed some of the storm noise. The ship shuddered on the edge of a wave and we toppled to leeward. David and James were in their storm clothes and water pouring from them turned red with the blood splashing from my shoulder. The bandage fell onto my eyes and I could not see. I clutched at the wall as the ship came up and David pulled the dressing free. The captain was steadying himself in his white clothes, but his face was the shade of rage and his mouth kept forming words which did not reach me.

Then I heard James. 'He's badly concussed, sir; he thinks he witnessed the men killing someone.'

'He thinks it was his Mahia,' David said, 'but I don't know how that's possible.'

'The thing is, sir, there's been some stowaways gone over – girls we think – and there was nothing we could do. You know how superstitious crews behave in a bad storm, sir.'

It seemed we were hornpiping as the ship struggled to survive. We were pushed from one beam to the other, from for'ard to aft; each taking steps to counter the pressure.

'Is there any ruddy proof of this?' the captain shouted.

'Well, no sir, just. . . .'

'Get him down to the sickbay. Now. Dr Samwell, he's your patient and he's badly injured.'

'Yes, sir; I think he's a fracture of the skull. . . .'

'Keep him in the sickbay and tie him down if necessary.'

We turned and goddamned Phillips stood in our way. I almost walked into his chest and I felt positively his outline was in the lanthorn light.

'Nothing there, sir. No sign of nothing at all.'

I turned to the captain. 'This is the bastard, sir. I saw him.' The pain and emotion made my words pitch too high, too confused. 'Mahia, sir. By God, have the courage to ask him.'

'Mahia?' the marine lieutenant looked at us, that broad face feigned into a look of innocence.

'You know who I mean. She was going to another island and your launch escorted them from the ship.'

'I couldn't say who this is he refers to, captain.'

I heard the false sound, the naive expression on the wide, wind-whipped face. 'Mahia. It means nothing to me and anyway we escorted so many canoes from the ship and. . . .'

Lieutenant Phillips left the room and I was exhausted and sick of life. David took my arm and we hurried through the night to our companionway, and I let him help me down to the gunroom, to the sickbay. My clothes came away and I climbed shivering between sheets and blankets and begged the pain to go. But he began dressing the wound again. 'You're going to have to recover very rapidly, our John, you know. The ship is in a great deal of trouble and I'd not be surprised to find us taking to the boats.'

I remembered the casks. I said he had to tell James about them, to spill the oil to weather slowly so that the sea would leave us be, at least for as long as the blubber lasted.

'But it's only seal oil,' he said.

'We used this type in the Americas and it works. Tell James. Please, David, it may be our only chance.' He took little notice of my pleadings at first, for those who had not seen the miraculous effect of oil on stormy seas seldom believe the change that even the smallest spillage can do. But I convinced him. Stay quietly in the berth, he said, and the door banged.

I took a lungful of air. I dashed the width of the gunroom and came up the ladder into the screaming, drenching air. I reached the companionway to the maindeck and ascended, although I could not see the steps. The storm sounds died and I was engulfed by the swaying stillness. I pressed forward into the dark, a hand held out for the pillar I expected. It was where I knew it would be; I went down on my hands. I felt the timbers, the emptied pens and cut myself on sharp metal. My hanger lay where it had fallen. I estimated the distance to the last vision of Mahia and pushed forward. I crossed and recrossed where I believed the place was. There was no body; she had been sacrificed to superstition and put over the side. I found mounds of straw from our time as an agricultural ark; I pushed about here and found the proof that had to exist. A pool of tackiness, still warm I imagined, was lying on the timber. I could see nothing for I had no light. But I knew it was from Mahia and I licked at it to be certain and the strong salty taste was unmistakably blood. A boom came from above my head; a shuddering, splitting noise as though the upper deck were being rent back to open the ship to the sea. I shivered in fright for the horror that would follow, but the darkness did not change. My position was near the foremast; the noise had to be it splitting along its length under the pressure of the storm. And then as if in a happy dream the jolts went and were replaced with a grace that was too extraordinary to be real. Oil was being spilled into the sea and fate was deferred. I hurried back to the sickbay, my head throbbing, to David's questions and admonishings, and slowly I sank away from the noise and the wetness of the surgeon washing Mahia's blood from my face.

The self-same visage was there in the candlelight when I opened my eyes. 'You're awake then, our John?'

'God, my head.'

'You've been asleep a good twenty-four hours. I hope you're feeling better.'

'Don't talk about it.' The ship's motion seemed much easier.

'The weather?'

'I am very pleased to say that Dame Fortune has smiled upon us. The storm has gone. But so has the foremast. Well, it's split.'

'Don't say we're. . . .'

'I'm afraid there's no choice. We're returning to Kealakekua Bay. Not that a soul on board does not abhor the notion, but there's nowhere else to go.'

I repeated 'there's nowhere else to go' and felt numbness in the statement. Without a foremast, we would never make Nootka Sound of West America and there was no other anchorage for us between or in the archipelago than that ill-fated bay.

'And there's nought for you but lie here and get better.'

'There's a pressing matter. You'll be my second of course.'

'What are you talking about?'

'You'll present my challenge now and I'll meet him in the waist one hour before dawn, when few are about.'

'You'll do no such thing. Are you mad? You are at least badly concussed. Possibly your skull is fractured. As your doctor and your friend I'll not permit it.'

I expected Phillips to choose pistols. He was not to know I would have been a poor swordsman with the crushing in my skull. James acted as my second and David was the impartial medic. We faced each other near the wheel and the helmsman pretended to be looking elsewhere. Our masts were full above us, but a strange light filled the foredeck for none of the usual sails protected it. The mast was stripped ready to be taken out and replaced.

Powder was emptied in to the .67 barrels, the seconds thrust down ball wrapped in wadding and poured fine powder into the pan. They were cocked. I recognised the pair as Mr Gore's possessions which I had long admired. They were made in 1749 and marked Hawkins and R. Wilson, two prominent London gunsmiths. A pistol was handed, butts first, to each of us. Mine was beautifully balanced.

Mr. Gore said, 'You will step off ten paces each and then turn. You will fire in your own time.'

I did not feel nervous but then I could not say I felt anything. This was *utu* for Mahia yet it was no revenge at all for she would not come back; how would a ball exploding the brain of this fool ever pay for the pain and destruction of an intelligent, beautiful woman? But I stepped out and I could hear plainly his own feet, heavy, fearful. Eight, nine, ten. I turned, side-on, as in a conversation of the blades, and brought the pistol up. But I was late, as I suppose I knew I would be. The ungainly being swung towards me and was holding the pistol in an ungentlemanly fashion, two-handed, to be sure of his aim. His whole silhouette was carelessly outlined. His hands jumped with nerves as he held that sinister beauty and then flames spouted from the barrel and pan and the crack arrived. I felt a burning against my forehead and a high-pitched whistling. I was scorched by the wadding but the ball was wide. I thought him a slasher, too, in his approach to the pistols.

I aimed and his whine reminded me of a dismounted war horse. I kept the pistol trained on him with one hand behind me in the custom. A moan came again as he waited for the wings of death; his flintlock was still pointing at me, that complete, large, unco-ordinated frame exposed. I thought about not killing him. I could play with him like a cat and mouse. All I risk losing is something that I no longer care about. I squeezed the fine trigger.

The cock sprung, the flint scraped into a pretty shower of sparks against the frizzen which pushed back the all-weather pan cover. The priming powder was exposed and nothing could stop the destruction now. The sparks set it alight and instantaneously the powder behind the ball roared. The heat burned my hand, the flash blinded me for a second and later the noise arrived. I had aimed for an upper shroud.

We stood together. Powder, ball in wadding. The walnut butt was so warm and feminine; I imagined I could feel the silver inlay of the contesting lion and a spoiling brutish unicorn with its bloodied horn. This time he nearly dropped the pistol. He coughed nervously and James stepped optimistically forward.

'You have something to say, Lieutenant Phillips?'

The marine leader stood still, dumb, his hand panicking, juggling and dropping words that might save him.

'Are you going to apologise?' Mr Gore's colonial accent came next in the dark of the waist.

The large head was staring at me. I returned the look with indifference. He wanted to ask, will Williamson accept an apology as satisfaction enough?

'I, I. . . .' he began.

'Are you apologising?' Mr Gore repeated, but Phillips was caught between pride and cowardice and could not form any words.

The steps came again. Eight, nine, ten. I turned. Phillips was well ahead this time. I caught the movement of his spin. The pistol came whipping up, too swiftly for the bulk of the man. Both hands again, and he hesitated a second. Then the flash and the noise of the gun and my cheek and chin were on fire. My right eye closed and tears spilled and mingled with a stream of blood from my head.

I kept absolutely still. My brain somehow inspected me; I had been burned about the face by the wadding; a piece was stinging my eye. The ball had nicked my chin as it went passed. I breathed out slowly. Phillips shouted and an object hit my chest; he had thrown the beautiful pistol in his fear. I raised the weapon.

Now, Lieutenant Rapist Murderer bloody Phillips. My turn. I had to bring my head over from the usual position to allow my left eye to sight along it. Thankfully it did not copy the tears of its twin. Aurora was here and now I had a perfect view of the man; I could not miss. I aimed for the unicorn weapon. It was a moment before he realised and the noise of a whimpering dog reached me. Sweet mother of Jesus . . . I heard. His hands remained extended from throwing the pistol; he could not lower them to offer any protection. I held my aim just so for a moment longer and then brought it up to linger at his stomach, his heart, his throat. The barrel passed over the pronounced chin, the slack lips, the broken nose and hovered at the bridge, between those terrified eyes.

The pistol was steady, waiting, and Voltaire's rallying cry surfaced triumphantly after years of patient storage. *'Ecrasez l'infame!'* And then in case he might go to the grave misunderstanding I interpreted, 'Crush the evil thing.' I part filled my lungs and added, 'For Mahia.'

'Holy mother of Mary,' he wailed and the voice went off into sobs. I walked the paces back towards him, the aim held true and with each step his knees gave until he knelt like disgraced Admiral John Byng before a firing party. I was ten paces, five, and the witnesses stood as still as Mahia would be forever more. The ball would destroy the brain and tear open the other side of the brute's skull. The face was wider with every step and became the more uncomprehending the closer I came. It was in its predicament because of some gentleman's game; it did not associate the punishment with the shocking crime this body had committed. I thought revenge is a waste of time.

I stood before him. I laughed; it was the last time I did so. I placed the Hawkins-Wilson in those outstretched hands and brown dull eyes moved from viewing death in the barrel to the incredible sight of the butt safely in his own hand. I turned my back and walked away. The captain was standing in the doorway of the aft-cabin in his shirt and I wondered had the shots roused him; had he been there all along to see if Phillips's ball would find me? Then came the call of land-ho. Figures poured onto the deck and in the thunder of rushing feet the dawn gave way to the morning and we were standing into Kealakekua Bay.

The water was acquiring the early-day colour we knew so well. The mountains were crisply pronounced and the villages stood as neat as before. But not a canoe was to be seen; truculent stares came from the green of the palms and we experienced the emotion Phillips had felt only a short time before.

21

Captain Cook was dead. He turned his back on the natives and they killed him. We watched him fall. Scores forced his head beneath the water and we could do nothing but stare and disbelieve our terrified eyes. We retreated to the ships and flew our flags at half-hoist. Then Captain Clerke moved into the aft-cabin, Mr Gore took command of *Discovery* and it seemed the nightmare must be so.

The natives carried the body of the captain away and a few came down to the beach to taunt us and to let us know we would be part of their menu soon. Gradually we accepted the truth of our loss and hung our heads in despair and shame; hysteria took the sailors who screamed at the shore, called him father and pulled at their hair. The foremast, our ticket to freedom, lay abandoned on the island and on the first night berserk sailors were seen rowing into the darkness. In the morning natives lay mutilated in the surf.

A deputation called on Captain Clerke demanding the right to take their revenge on the population. Had they made any *demands* upon our late captain, their punishment would have been swift, but the new commander was a different man. He was filling a new role and trying to find his way with sensitivity. Furthermore, Captain Clerke was consumptive and could not live long. Weakness of course was perfectly forgivable in his command, but the first to recognise it on a Navy sloop of war are those who it need most be kept from – the people themselves.

'Men, this is not the way,' he said, his uniformed arms resting where the late captain worked on the journals. 'However, you've troubled yourselves to come here, so I will give the matter serious consideration. I will let you have my answer promptly.

'When?'

'Sir, you dog, sir!' Bligh shouted at the large-boned deputation leader.

'Mr Bligh, these fellows are understandably upset; please be so good as to wait outside. Now, men, I will let you know tonight.'

They shambled from the room. That afternoon two launches were commandeered; sailors began firing at natives from the low surf and soon smoke rose from houses. Natives answered with stones but they were no alternative to muskets and more bodies were put into the sea. At the bow of the returning boats stakes displayed impaled native heads. Blood flowed down the cutwaters and sharks busy at the strand's edge broke away to join the grim parade.

The petitioners returned to the aft-cabin and William Bligh was sensibly reinstated beside the door.

'Men, the late captain was my friend and he was your commander. Which of us has the greater right to revenge? I'm sure you'd agree friendship comes first. But I like you am no savage; I was brought up to believe in the law, as you was, and therefore I am compelled to put down the broadsword that my arm would have me swing in retribution.'

'So you're saying we don't do the natives? Sir.'

'I will hold an enquiry into the death, a proper legal hearing, if you people will abide by humane English practices.'

The deputation leader, James Millett, kept closed the square mouth in his wide square body.

'I take it by your silence you agree and I am pleased to see that such matters can be happily resolved no matter how upset we are by the tremendous loss. The hearing will begin in the morning, Millett, and I would prefer it if there were no repetitions of recent events.' Captain Clerke's grey eyebrows were raised, but the deputation added no comment. 'Excellent, all agreed then.' The deputation turned for the door. 'Oh, Millett, if you hadn't assented I would have sought out the murderers from this afternoon and hanged them. Naturally I will have recourse to that action should our agreement be breached. Thank you, men.'

We were quiet in the great cabin. I had been chosen for secretary because of a reputation for journal-keeping. I had on my knee a pad and rather precariously balanced a sanding box and ink container. The captain was opposite me at the table and in the silhouette I imagined him already dead. Mr Gore sat to his right; now Captain Gore, *Discovery*, I should say as my role today was of keeping a precise account of the proceedings. Lieutenant Burney, the first officer on *Discovery*, was to the captain's left. His demeanour revealed neither sadness nor accusation. If his name seems familiar to the reader, his sister, Fanny, is the well-known writer and novelist of the day.

Captain Charles Clerke stood and I noted his name at the top of the pad. He was much shorter than the old boy; I should say, the late captain, but I am still unable to really accept what I know. A noise reached us from the shore. Natives drunk with victory; we had heard it the last two mornings. The jeering and the chant of God is dead. . . .

Captain Clerke cleared his throat and the noise seemed unnaturally loud; he felt it too for he changed his mind and sat down. Over our heads came the shuffle of feet of the watch. Carpenters were working on the foredeck with the spar we had the reluctant people recover last night from the island. 'Gentlemen,' he began, and a dash of stained teeth came through the grey complexion. 'I'll remain seated if it pleases you; my health you see. . . ,' and he coughed illustratively. 'First let me say that I have posted the promotions and I hope you will all agree they are the right choices. John Gore takes over my old post – a damn fine ship,' he said, trying to ease the heat and depression in the room. 'James King will be my first lieutenant and James Burney keeps his important post on *Discovery*. And promotion for you, John Williamson, as number two here on *Resolution*.'

He smiled as if to say that ugly rumours circulating were above him. I nodded politely, gratefully.

'It is not to apportion blame; I want that understood,' Captain Clerke returned. 'Now while the occurrence is so fresh in our minds is the time to record formally what happened and if possible to suggest reasons why. But we must not forget that my lords of the admiralty are the correct people to make the proper judgement.'

He pulled a kerchief from his long jacket and coughed; his body shook and blood speckled on the cloth. He swallowed. 'I propose that we first hear evidence of the man whose responsibility is the protection of the gentlemen when we go ashore, the lieutenant of marines.'

The said officer was then invited within – and we discovered we had not provided a chair for witnesses. A few moved politely as if to offer to find one and were grateful when Captain Clerke did not pursue the suggestion. James was sitting on the berth and made room for Phillips; the marine chose to ignore it.

'My name, sir, is Molesworth Phillips. I am twenty-four years of age, coming on twenty-five. I hold the King's commission of second lieutenant and I am of the Chatham division.' He was standing to attention before the desk, his overly wide back towards me. His marine hat was carried under an arm. Phillips outlined the tragedy from his point of view and I made rough notes.

My view of Captain Gore was of the end of his knee-breeches and below. A shoe moved and I wrote his name on the paper. 'What can you say of the men who were with the captain at the end?' His New England accent was an odd contrast to Phillips's brogue and Captain Clerke's smart Kent tongue.

'The marines was good men, sir. The company will be sadly off without them.'

James King was next to question. 'Take your mind to the moment that the captain fired the second shot. I want you to recall exactly where you were standing. Are you doing that?'

This was an interesting point for many felt the marines botched the last moments on the beach; after all, they should have died before the commander, such was their role.

'Now what orders do you hear given by the late captain?'

'It's very difficult to hear anything, sir. The niggers was making so much noise and threatening.'

'How far were you from the captain?'

'As close as you to me, sir.' The marine was sweating and the smell was far from pleasing.

'Lieutenant Phillips, imagine that three minutes have passed. Where were you and your men at this time?'

Phillips was swallowing and his legs displayed a nervous twitch. 'Well, me sir, I was not far from the captain. And the men was lined up at the water's edge.'

'And then?'

'And then I walked to the water but the captain still faced the crowd.'

'How far was he from you?'

'Why, then he must have been . . . I couldn't be sure.'

'Of course not, Lieutenant Phillips. In the terrible circumstances, no one would expect you to judge everything perfectly.' Phillips rode up on his toes as if this were a parade ground. 'But you'd have an idea. Was he within musket shot, or further off?'

'Closer.'

'As close as you and Mr Williamson?'

Phillips swung on his boots and our eyes met. His had a frightened, hunted look, as if he had forgotten I was in the room. He looked down at the notebook in my lap and the goosefeather being replenished within the inkwell. Then he jerked his head back to the captain. 'It might have been thirty or forty feet.'

'Were you that distance from the commander because he was walking towards the horde?'

'How could he have walked?' he said. 'The niggers was on top of him, pressing all round.'

'Then you walked away from the late captain?'

The shaking returned to the marine's legs and he leaned towards Captain Clerke. 'Sir, they're trying to trap me; trying to blame me and by Jesus they're wrong. Didn't I rescue one of my men? And me injured at the time. Sir, by God, we know who caused the late captain's death and it weren't me.' His voice was raised. He spun about as I expected him to. 'We all know. . . .,' he was shouting.

Lieutenant Burney pulled himself noisily onto his feet and insisted angrily in the claustrophobic heat that the question was unfair, and Captain Clerke called quietly for order.

Shouts and the sound of a *haka* came through the sternlights as another group of natives arrived at the beach to goad the ships' companies. Captain Clerke shifted his chair noisily. A curse came from the foredeck; a carpenter's mate chipped with an adze. 'Lieutenant Phillips, it is not the purpose of the enquiry to lay blame.' He was speaking quietly and struggling with the pain. He had to pause while he swallowed; the whites of his large eyes were coloured. His chin spoke determination but his brow twisted with insecurity.

'Then sir, what's the point at all of the hearing? We've got to lay blame and. . . .'

'Not at all,' Captain Clerke replied quickly. 'You see, this is a Navy matter and all conclusions will be reached by my Lords.'

'But surely, sir, the enquiry is being held because the people of the ship need it. If they wasn't sure something was happening, they'd as likely be handing out some justice themselves.'

Captain Clerke didn't like that; none of us did. I looked up from my minuting and saw him press the handkerchief to his mouth. But for that pain from his lungs he might have shot Molesworth Phillips where he stood, for what dying man wants other great fears confirmed? Phillips did not know of the cocked pistols on Captain Clerke's lap, and nor was he privy to our belief that the people were on the point of mutiny.'

Burney interrupted. 'Lieutenant Phillips, please control yourself. We need your information and nobody is trying to lay any blame at your door.'

Captain Clerke said, 'It occurs to me, Mr King, that a great deal of confusion covers the ground you were opening up, but I think this area is too painful just yet. Lieutenant Phillips, I would like to add that in the matter of apportioning blame it would have been helpful had we been able to name the assassin. We know who struck the first blow. Dr Samwell and I were on the quarterdeck and witnessed that and the dreadful following events. But we saw him walk more steps before he collapsed at the water's edge. He was still alive. Afterwards, to the horror of all, many set upon his hapless form and death must have followed quickly.' Clerke tried to see round the large form of the marine. 'Do you have anything to add at this stage, Dr Samwell?'

David stood behind Phillips, fingers in his unbuttoned waistcoat. 'I would like, sir, gentlemen, to refer to the great bard's remarks in *Hamlet* when. . . .'

'I mean as to the cause of death, Dr Samwell,' Captain Clerke persisted.

He became the precise medic and spoke of the likely effect of the first blows; the natives were both shorter than the late captain and much of the force would have been lost. 'Death is most likely to have occurred by the intake of seawater to the lungs. The captain was seen struggling, while several held his head under the water. A few shots fired at this stage might have effected a rapid change of events.'

Captain Clerke looked up concerned lest that started more arguments and returned Samwell to the question. 'I think that natives stabbing his body after that had little effect. I am sure our dear captain would have passed beyond before then and would not have borne any awareness of it nor pain. However,' he added after seeking unsuccessfully for a handkerchief, 'in the absence of a body. . . .'

Samwell sat and the room paid a silent respect to our late commander. Soon my turn came to question the witness.

I put the notebook, inkwell, sand and quill on the chair, and walked beside the table, behind Burney and a little aft of Captain Clerke. I could see the butts of the pistols on his lap. Phillips wore a bayonet in his webbing and I wondered if I ought not modify my questions. But I believed Captain Clerke could level at him before the blade found me.

'Lieutenant Phillips, who is the officer charged with the training of your little band?'

Phillips started at that, but Captain Clerke beat him. 'Mr Williamson, please confine yourself to the incident.'

'Sorry, sir. Lieutenant Phillips, do you know the reloading times for the musketry of your division?'

'Pardon? Sir.'

'Is this relevant, Mr Williamson?'

'Very, sir, if you will permit me.'

The captain nodded and Phillips withdrew his head protectively towards the wings of the tunic collar and the flabbiness revealed an idle life on this voyage. 'The reloading time for your muskets, sir?'

'I can't say as I have ever timed it myself.'

'Have you not heard of others timing the reloading procedure?'

'I wouldn't know, sir.'

'Lieutenant Phillips, what ought a rifleman pride himself on the most?'

The face smirked and he took the challenge of my eyes. 'Why sir, the aim, of course.'

'Then, Lieutenant Phillips, I would have to challenge you.' The face flushed and his eyes tightened. 'Confronted by the enemy, a shot will down a man, but what of the next adversary? You know as we all do that the speed of reloading is the key. So tell us now, what is the speed of the average marine rifleman?'

Phillips lowered his eyes. 'I couldn't say, sir.'

'If I told you that in the Americas campaign, British soldiers were getting away two or three rounds a minute, how would you say?' Phillips did not reply. 'Come now, tell the captain what you would say to that? Can I tell you that Mr Bligh timed your men at the fiasco at Omai's farewell?'

Phillips coloured at that. 'I know nothing of it, sir.'

'Would you say your shooting and reloading was good on that particular occasion?'

'Not that I recall, sir.'

'Have you practised your men since?'

'We have shot together since, yes.'

'I repeat, Lieutenant Phillips. Have you practised since?'

'Then I repeat to you, sir. We have shot together since and I remember now that I instructed the men to practise their reloading.'

Captain Clerke interrupted. 'Mr Williamson, we do know that the standard of the marines has been somewhat lacking.'

Phillips seemed to imagine me surrendering to Captain Clerke and murder fixed his expression, but I moved in for the kill. 'I submit, sir, that Lieutenant Phillips and his men were entrusted by King George to protect the late captain. Faced with an overwhelming number of natives as we often were, our defence could only be a healthy barrage of shooting. I need hardly say, sir, in a small group of marines that requires several reloads. I submit that. . . .'

Burney was on his feet. 'Come, sir,' he addressed me. 'Captain Clerke has already stated we are not apportioning blame. . . .'

'I submit, sir. . . .,' I continued loudly because I knew Captain Clerke would support his former number one and that this important point would be lost. 'I submit that the space between shot and reload was a full two minutes, and in three cases almost three minutes. The rate was as poor as one round for every nine of a British soldier. They were failing in their duty then; apart from the humiliation they called upon His Majesty's ships *Resolution* and *Discovery*. But in the protection of the life of. . . .'

Burney caught my temper as he tried to defend the marine captain. 'I object, sir. You have ruled this out. . . .'

Captain Clerke was attempting to reply and at the same time quell a threatening attack from his lungs. But I would not be stopped. 'Further, sir, I charge that Lieutenant Phillips himself saw the scandalous lack of skill on the part of his riflemen and from then on was duty-bound by conscience and love of the captain . . .'

Burney turned to me shouting. 'Will you shut up, Williamson?'

'. . . was bound by his conscience, sir, to see his men could protect his captain till the last of them dropped. But there was no practice and at that terrible scene, sir. . . .' I saw the captain falling, the club crunching down, the hand clutching for air, those masculine features disappearing into the sandy water. The screaming. . . .

Captain Clerke was the texture of parchment behind Burney, fighting his lungs and trying to bring order to the disruption.

'Come . . . Mr Williamson. . . .'

'Shut up, man!' Burney demanded in his squeaky anger.

'I'll answer no more of these questions,' Phillips got out, trying to salvage a reputation I would sink forever.

'I saw them, sir. I watched them fire and I saw the pathetic attempts to reload, while they were running.'

'By Jesus, sir, my men did not run. . . .'

'While they ran from the scene.'

'I was signalling to you to fire,' he said, trying to turn the attack. 'Why didn't your men fire?'

I said, 'They ran from the scene tripping over their ram-rods, sir. And me; I was waiting to time their reloading efforts, but it wasn't necessary. They didn't bother to try.'

'I kept calling "come in with the pinnace",' Phillips shouted. Lieutenant Burney stood between us, hands shielding his ears. 'Why didn't you come in?'

The argument abruptly ended when Captain Clerke staggered onto his feet and the pistols crashed to the deck. Blood poured from his handkerchief onto the table. Gore held him tightly, trying to still that emaciated form; the captain's face was red as he forced his rotting lungs to work, but the strain showed in streaks like the rivers of lava as if much of the circulation of blood in his face was already destroyed.

James and Captain Gore lifted him onto the berth; the medics were at his side, and Captain Clerke's body heaved with the fit of coughing.

As we left the room, James said, 'What do you mean you were waiting to time the marines?'

'I was trying to emphasise the delay in their reloading.'

'Shite, John, our captain was about to die. I hope to God you were trying to help him and not trap that half-wit. Your score with him was well settled in the duel.'

'I should have killed him. I knew when they were on the beach, when they were under pressure, I'd made a big mistake.'

We were standing away from the wheel and our conversation stopped as Bligh passed. 'You've got to learn to forget; when people die, that's that.'

'I wish it was so easy.'

22

My duty this afternoon was to exercise the gun-crews with four-pounders which lined the upper deck. The men freed them from the gunwales and the boys, the powder monkeys as we say, carried the equipment onto the deck; sponge, worm, ladle and rammer. The gun-captains wore powder horns around their necks; slow-match burned in the linstock and shot garland kept the balls from rolling about.

'Bring the guns inboard; cartridge down the muzzle, ladle out,' I ordered. 'Wad in place and the ball and ram the lot home. Linstock down the touch-hole, puncture the cartridge; captains, your fine-milled powder into the touch-hole. Very good. Run up, train and fire!'

The crews hauled and the guns ran out to the ports on noisy trucks. The captains aimed along the four-pounders, using quoins to alter the elevation. They touched the priming with imaginary slowmatch and the crews shouted Bang! enthusiastically while holding fast to the breeching tackle. The risk of war with the islanders meant we could not afford to use gunpowder. The men pulled the guns back and droned, 'Sponge, worm.'

'Mr Williamson,' Collett called afterwards as I was climbing the quarterladder. 'Captain Clerke would like to see you as soon as is convenient, sir.'

He sat on the berth, looking through the sternlights which were open to a light breeze; a dazzle came from the sea and played kaleidoscopes on the low deckhead beams. It was disconcerting not to see the late captain at the desk; one should hear the scratch of the quill, the tiny snare-drumming of sand cast onto a page.

Captain Clerke looked much improved and there was actually some colour to his face. 'What the hell are we doing here, young John?'

'Palliser,' I said undiplomatically.

A smile worked quietly around pale lips. 'Captain Cook – God rest his soul – warned me about your tongue. You know, there are some odd customs in His Majesty's service; upon attaining certain rank it is quite acceptable for men like Sir Hugh to make a little additional remuneration from differences between items quoted and goods rendered.'

'The strange custom has cost us rather dearly,' I said gloomily. 'I would not dare for sanity's sake to even begin totting up the personal price to me.'

'To us all. Now tell me how was the gun practice?'

'Good, sir. I think we can be proud of the gunners, if not the marines.'

'Can you not sympathise with their lot in our service?'

'It's a wretched existence and an impossible role; I have copious notes of it in my journal, sir. I suppose my criticism is directed more at the leadership, or lack of. . . .'

'That's what I want to speak about.' Collett knocked and opened the door and Captain Clerke ordered tea. 'There's bad blood between you two, I gather. No, I don't want to know the details, but I do want to say that it is not wise.'

'Not wise. . . .'

'At the moment we depend on each other. When an enemy is rapping on the door, that's an excellent time for a family to close ranks.'

'I think you're suggesting rather a lot, sir.'

'You think he made a botch of the stand on the beach? There are those who are similarly charged. Poor Lieutenant John Rickman from my old ship is under a cloud. Someone in his launch shot the chief Kalimu just before the massacre; it may have been him or not; he's not blaming others but keeping quiet while the cloud passes over.'

'Phillips. . . .'

'When Phillips was getting into the boats, he saw one of his people under the water and he dived in right in front of the natives and hauled him out. That has to be taken into account. He must have been terrified.'

'He had a duty to the captain and. . . .'

'Quite, but I believe he did his best; you can accept what you like; but for the present we rely on each other. Our commander has gone and I'm trying to fill his shoes, but quite frankly my toes don't even reach halfway. John, I need at least our government united.'

'And the men?'

'I hope they'll be satisfied with the hearing. But they won't if we are going to fight among ourselves. I'm asking you as a brother-officer: give Phillips the benefit of the doubt at least till we're out of this mess.'

'I'll do my best, sir,' I said and hoped God considered promises made to senior officers in a different light.

'That's the most that anyone can do. Ah, here's the tea; good show, Collett.'

I collected my quills, notepaper and sanding box ready for Hearing Number Two which began in the dusk. The damaged candelabrum was alight and several lanthorns burned in the room.

'Let there be no doubt with any of you,' Captain Clerke began with improved confidence, 'a problem exists with discipline of the forecastle. Grief can rob a man of reason. It is not my intention to put the marines in to return the orderliness we need. The men will accept the hearing as being in their best interests, and the correct legal method of retribution. Work continues on the mast.' He spoke quieter now. 'It will do no harm if that is in place before the findings of the hearing are divulged. After all, if we could sail from here, calm may settle again also upon the native population.'

James King uncrossed his arms and the movement interrupted Captain Clerke. James's hands found the berth and pushed down as if to raise his body. 'And the remains, sir, of the late captain. Could we possibly leave them here?'

It was a question that proved no matter which way we looked, there was no escaping fate.

'We know the answer to that well enough,' Captain Clerke said after a pause and we accepted that there was no answer.

'Now, let us turn to the evidence of the surgeon, Dr Samwell.' Captain Clerke rested both elbows on the table, put his hands together and pressed his lips against finger tips. In the yellow light of the candles, I could see him lying in a coffin, cocked hat across his waist, hands set into a prayer. I compared his eyes in the flamelight to Captain Cook's at this same table, at that awful dinner. His eyes were dull, even glazed, yet the commander needed a nation of savages to stamp out his life; Captain Clerke was succumbing to an enemy so small we could not even see the bacteria. Yet this dying man's eyes were alive and glowing.

'It came to pass,' David Samwell was saying, 'that my superior, the surgeon appointed by His Gracious Majesty King George the Third, one Dr William Anderson, a brilliant accessory to any voyage as we would all agree, a fully paid-up member of the esteemed Surgeons' Company, who studied under the great John Hunter. . . .'

And I thought of poor old Dr Bill, plotting the course of his disease, discovering the nguru, repairing the venereals, improving the dental health of the men while he sank lower. Our last binge together. The voyage claimed him, and two marines who went over the taff-rail and Watman who by cutting his painter at quite the wrong time possibly confirmed to the high priest that we were no gods. Then death swept down on the marines on the beach and snatched at our beloved commander who had cocked a snook so often at that insatiable spectre. And now it was back, waiting impatiently for Captain Clerke and perhaps all of us.

David's evidence continued. As was to be expected, the Great Bard was well represented in quotations both well-known and obscure. I kept a tally at the side of my notes to tease him with later but soon our pride got in the way; our friendship would be strained before we left this room. He was relaxed yet formal in his oration and it was difficult to imagine him tending his fair muses, his thorough work as pink bare officiator of the ceremony of purification. His hair was thick and assertive; he looked a little like an amateur thespian out-Garricking Garrick. Poor David; a self-critic pulled too severely the lever between relaxed Samwell and studious Samwell; between roué and righteous; amorous human and aseptic doctor. The end of the long rhetoric arrived and we knew no more: despite the assaults, the doctor said, the most likely cause of death was drowning.

They cried on the beach God is dead, long live God. Surely Lono could not die of something so ordinary.

James King was questioning David and I was studying him, the long nose Dame Nature neglected to bridge so that it fell straight from a forehead that was determinedly reclaiming his scalp. I liked and respected James; it was he I would most like to have near in a tense battle.

I wrote next to his name, 'Was there any feature to the late captain's health which concerned you, Dr Samwell?' And even as David answered, cogs – if one may so describe the brain's mechanisms – turned and whirred and I almost exclaimed, by God, I see it all. Suddenly everything fell into place.

'Our late captain was struck by recurring headaches. They troubled him.' (Yes, yes, I urged: go on.)

'What form did they take?'

'They appeared to be seated at the very front of the brain. This is the area in which we believe certain sensations are. . . .' (Going off-course; bring him back, James.)

'We all saw that he was in pain at times,' Captain Clerke said. 'Was the condition improving or deteriorating?'

'I tried with *hirudo medicinalis*, several to each temple. Perhaps we earned temporary respite, but not of a lasting nature.'

'Hiri-udo?' Gore looked puzzled.

'Leeches,' Captain Clerke said.

'Were they getting worse?' James asked. 'The headaches.' (Go on, James, keep at him.)

'As to that, sir, I can only report he said not.' (Damn, David's attention is drifting.)

Then James was finished and it was all I could do not to leap up and half-strangle the good doctor to force the answer from those slim lips. Perhaps Captain Clerke sensed my excitement for he invited me to interview David. I took a large draught of tropical air into my lungs and began at what I instinctively felt was the catalyst for one death, if not for the whole tragedy. But I approached on tip-toe; I was loathe to frighten off this valuable quarry. 'Did these headaches you mention, Dr Samwell, affect the late captain's appetite?'

'No, Mr Williamson. The captain ate like a horse, no matter what. His stomach was surely made of cast iron.' Laughter came from about the cabin.

'Could he sleep during an attack of the pain?'

'The late captain was not a great sleeper. *A heavy summons lies like lead upon me, and yet I would not sleep*. Macbeth, of course. No, there are people to whom sleep is not vital and our late captain was of that type.'

'So the headaches would not affect his rest?'

'They did not happen at those times.'

'Do you mean they occurred regularly at specific moments?' (Why must you now become a reluctant witness?)

'When he was thinking too much.'

'Pardon?'

'A captain is constantly called upon to make decisions, sometimes large important ones, and to make them quickly, and it is this pressure that I mean by "thinking too much".'

'And good decisions need a clear head. Would the pain clutter his mind, Dr Samwell?'

Captain Clerke interrupted. 'I don't know, Mr Williamson . . . I wonder if we are going a little wide of the mark.'

'Sir, I've put it badly,' I tried. Meaning that the blame is all Samwell's. 'I meant, in the experience of the surgeon, knowing the captain as he does and naval matters, if this might be the case.'

Samwell smiled, patronisingly, and it was close to the last straw for me what with Clerke steering me from discovering a truth, and now David switching to Relaxed Samwell at the wrong moment. I held down the colour threatening to rise. 'What do we know of the inside of another man's mind? Cluttered? Many could not recognise clutter, so little are they familiar with their own normal thoughts.' He waited till the laughs stopped. 'Some think on many levels, some scarcely on one. You could not expect me to know what is in an officer's mind any more than say, well, a sweet native nymph.'

Samwell had the gallery and the response was forked; for his humour and my humiliation, but worst of all it would lose this most significant point of the reason for the unavoidable fate.

'Dr Samwell,' I tried without diplomatics, determined now to bring out the answers I required. 'Was there much pain in the headache?'

'I believe so.'

'Enough to drive him to madness?'

'Certainly not.'

'Certainly not? Can you be so definite as to the contents of a mind when they seem so enigmatic to modern medicine?'

'I *believe* not.'

'Would it affect clear-headed thinking then?'

'It might.'

'He has a malady which leaves him pain-stricken, but you think it only *might* affect his thinking?'

'It would only be a temporary state.'

'Would it produce impatience?'

'The captain was . . . yes.'

'Did he explain to you how long it took the headaches to build into a climax?'

'It was instantaneous, all or nothing.'

'I remind you that this is a matter for this room.' Captain Clerke watched me closely. 'Is this malady not a terrible affliction for a Navy man?'

'Mr Williamson, it is a regrettable malady for any man, but the Royal Navy has an answer for this. In times of action, demanding important decisions, more than one officer is always on duty. If the late captain were momentarily affected, he could look to an experienced intelligent brother-officer to stand in until it passed.'

I had won the first of three important points in the questioning. 'Might this malady make him suicidal?'

'The late captain was not given to that compulsion.'

'What about the malady itself? Could it not take over the man and change his normal behaviour?'

Captain Clerke cleared his throat. 'Sorry, Mr Williamson. Could you explain your meaning?'

'The hearing is to reconstruct the tragedy, sir; I speak to contributing causes and it seems to me that the malady which we cannot see but know well enough about may have a great bearing on the matter.'

'We are talking theoretically, Mr Williamson, are we not?' Samwell asked.

Excellent, I thought, and ticked off point number two. Samwell was meandering on from my question. This would be taken as his accepting that the malady itself could change the victim's behaviour, and therefore we in that room took it as proved.

'Theoretically?' I asked quietly, but the volume soon increased. 'Thousands of natives are pressing down on him. News arrives of the murder of chief Kalimu by some sailor's hand, and the crowd goes berserk. A priest is standing beside him shrieking and the lieutenant of marines shouts that a native is about to spear him. The captain does nothing. Absolutely nothing, Dr Samwell.' Each in that room held to my words, for few were as close to the tragedy as I had been. 'Now the marines themselves tackle the man. A native jumps up beside our late commander and is about to throw a missile. Not a pebble, doctor, but a large stone and he is as close as me to you.' The drama was carrying me along and I spoke more loudly and aggressively. 'The captain has a double-barrel musket. He levels on the man. We know now that he loaded one barrel with ball and one with shot and the native is wearing a protective garment which shot cannot penetrate. The captain fires. But which barrel?'

A hush fell as if we all waited for the savage to fall, or to stagger and attack again, and we were examining the final moments of the man who had filled this aft-cabin for two long voyages of discovery: who had dominated our minds and our lives for God knows how many months and years. A supercilious smirk grew on Samwell's face; it hinted of lads pretending at men's games, but which was the errant boy?

'Oh, yes, it is most likely the malady would have manifested itself,' Samwell said, and breathed before adding the pronounced 'but' which the sentence led to. I chopped it off unspoken.

'Manifested itself,' I shouted, '*and* took over the brain *and* turned him mad or suicidal at the most critical moment.'

Samwell fell back from my insistence and replied with the frustration of a leading actor whose punchlines are continually capped. 'But his first officer would stand in at that instance had such a delay in a decision occurred; it happens all the time. Is that not so, Captain Clerke?'

The captain replied slowly, 'You see, Dr Samwell, there was no officer with him.'

'The nearest help was Phillips,' I said. 'But he was not a Navy officer. The late captain was entirely on his own in this and was forced to make a decision and act upon it. Was he struck by blinding pain when his life depended on his immediate clear-headed response?'

Nobody spoke; we were back watching the tragedy unfold on the beach for the hundredth time.

Our reverie was broken by the eerie squeak of the cabin door. It had been unlatched and allowed to swing wide and now it creaked with the gentle motion of the anchorage. We stared almost as if the ghost of ... as if some unseen hand of another world might have reached out. As we looked into the waist of the ship, the brightness of our lights reflected in the standing rigging of the mainmast. I swallowed nervously and stepped forward to close it. In the blackness through the shrouds Pollux flashed and I was thinking of this star credited with magic that protected mariners when a body blocked my vision. A head stooped and Phillips pushed into the room. I fell back from the spirits on his reeking breath.

'You focking bastards,' he shouted slurred. I was caught aback from the shock. 'You cringing weak-livered sons of nancies.'

He stood in the room, almost on the spot where he gave his evidence at the first hearing; he swayed with the unballasting of liquor and his eyes blinked in the room's brightness. We were shocked into quiet as he gazed at each of us, or at least attempted to. His shirt was filthy and open to the waist, revealing a pale body; sweaty ginger hair winked back from his chest at the candelabrum. 'You're fockin' talking of namby-pamby things that no man would talk of. I heard you, mind, I heard you,' he shouted, answering unasked questions. 'I was relieving my man for a ten-minuter and by the sweet God I heard talk from this room like you was on the focking stage. You're talking shite; the lot of you spilling it out of the wrong parts of your snivelling, mutton-mongering bodies.'

He stopped while he swept about again with that maddened bull-stare. The look that was supposed to assist an intoxicated voice found the candles and rested hypnotised.

We officers knew well enough to let alone a man with this turn of rum-soaked temper, but David was being the concerned medic. 'Lieutenant Phillips, for the life of me. . . .'

A fist like a club came through the air and connected with David's earnest face. The doctor staggered back and fell onto James who was pushed off balance onto the berth. David crashed to the deck, blood bubbling at his nostrils.

'The captain, the only man among you officers, is dead. That's the point of this gathering of gold-farmers.' He stood at the table and steadied himself with the assaulting fist. The knuckles transferred blood onto the dark wood.

James recovered his dignity. 'Come now, lieutenant,' he began, but the drunken fellow turned towards him. Phillips had just sufficient cunning left to know that striking an officer was unpardonable, but the menace of his whole being won the silence he sought. Any one of us, of course, could have drawn our sword and cut him down; but the cause of the fury was the same grief only in different form that took us all.

'If you, Captain bloody Clerke or Clark or whatever you call yourself, don't come up with something better than this, I'm personally going to. . . .' He pulled himself back again from suicide. Mutiny was not a subject that a man with a taste for life would allude to before officers, let alone his captain. '. . . going to think of other things.'

But for all that, it was a threat and the closest challenge our new commander had received in his short occupancy of the aft-cabin. He pulled himself up from the desk and stared at Phillips and somehow he did not fluster nor let the anger get the better of him. 'Get out,' he said slowly and quietly. 'You will see me again when you are sober.'

'I'll go. . . .' Phillips began.

The cabin suddenly burst into an uproar. Burney, his friend, cleverly averted further trouble by drawing his sword and swinging it before the drunken face; he ordered him back. Samwell for some unaccountable reason began to insist that there was sense in the remarks of the marine. Captain Gore shouted to the doctor to shut his Welsh trap or have it gagged and although Phillips was retreating quickly, his conversation had not improved. He shouted further accusations and went back through the door with Burney holding the blade towards his throat. The huge fellow filled the gap and then seemed to squeeze through. As he did so, Captain Clerke standing beside me, said, 'Good God.'

The waist was filled with the crew, and when they gathered and how much they witnessed neither Captain Clerke nor we officers could know. Phillips pushed through them, not realising the trouble that faced us in those silent, anxious expressions.

Bligh arrived. Too late for our major problems, I thought at that moment. We officers had followed in Phillips's and Burney's wake into the waist, as if drawn out by a vacuum in the sudden withdrawal of passion. Burney quickly sheathed his sword in the futile hope that the extreme measure had not been noticed. Bligh stood between the men and the officers, where a band of marines should have been. But their leader was mutinous, drunk and gone. Even had there been time, who knew where were the remainder of our police.

'Get back, you dogs,' Bligh shouted. The men closest to him stood a full head and shoulders above the fat squat youth; I thought of a fox terrier snapping at wolfhounds. 'You have no right on the waist; only the duty watch should be here. Now clear off and give the officers room.'

First there was my anger in the hearing. That had spread to the drunken marine lieutenant and now the temper took Bligh and to our horror it was working its way through the ranks of jack-tars. Behind me Captain Gore said in a whisper, 'Captain Clerke, we'd better retire to the cabin.'

'No, John; we have to face this.'

And I thought my God you're right. If we retreat now the mob would beat down the door before they questioned why; but what in God's name the captain could say to quieten these men, I did not know.

Then they moved towards us. Perhaps an inch at first, or it may have been that the man in front stepped forward and the others followed. But they were closing the gap and I admit a terror raced at my heart. The natives wanted the visitors, the crew wanted the blood of the natives and the only people keeping them apart were the officers. Now the crew would remove that impediment. Only heavenly intervention could save us and the strutting shouting Bligh would not be that for once the men started to rush he would be the first to be crushed.

Then the miracle arrived, if it could be called that. A flash erupted on the beach. First one and then others and the men tore themselves from the murderous self-hypnosis and stared over the land-rail. Several bands of natives were busy with torches on the beach.

'Jesus, they're coming for us,' a sailor shouted and more joined in with these words of doom. They rushed at the bulwarks.

'James, down the stairs with you,' Captain Clerke whispered. 'Pistols and grenades as fast as you dare.'

The men peeled back from the side as if one of Phillips's massive fists had been laid among them. They shouted 'Man the guns!' and the cry was repeated. Hands were at the four-pounders, wrenching them free of the bowsings.

'Get the others over this side too.'

'Where's the powder monkeys?'

'Come on, boys, let's give it to them.'

We had not a doubt that once begun the men would not stop pounding the shore till the last islander was dead. But of this we did not worry, for the realisation fell on them soon enough. Working guns in the pitch of night on this vessel was not possible. No crewman had an inch of experience of it and only teams thoroughly trained in night work could hope to cope without blasting the ship from the water. They argued among themselves, gun-captains were punched to the ground, but optimism and bullying could not alter facts. The gentlemen returned to the aft-cabin, but I stood at the door waiting for James. My sword was out and keen, but I held it behind my back.

'You could go out in the boats and attack them,' I taunted. The crew turned to stare at me. 'Go on, if you're suddenly so brave, get the boats over and go in for them. But these are not old men and women. . . .'

One of the sailors shouted, 'You could help us, Mr Williamson. Help us get the guns going.' But he knew the answer without my saying it.

James arrived with the weapons and pushed into the room; I closed the door on the confusion.

'Gentlemen, I fear I am going to have to arm the men,' Captain Clerke said. 'We'll be safe enough when the Indians attack for nothing like an enemy close by unites an army. But till then, I believe the minimum number of officers should be on the deck and perhaps we should call for volunteers.' He was loading a pistol and looking about him. I thought he and I were the coolest people in the room; even Bligh displayed sickness as he realised how near had stood death.

Captain Clerke's eyes reached mine. 'Why are you looking so unworried?'

'I am very worried sir, but we know that Polynesians never attack at night because of their beliefs. Fortunately the crew don't realise it, so they'll be too worried to endanger us. The marines seemingly are too drunk to care about anyone, so at least for tonight we officers are safe.'

23

The night passed in great nervousness. Despite my reassurances of native customs, Captain Clerke insisted that each of the younger officers maintain an hour's watch with a brace of .58 Tower pistols cocked, while about us a gentleman's orchestra acquainted the heavens of their discomfort with complaining noses as discordant instruments.

The natives did not rush the ship. They planted a row of flags of cowardice in the light of their torches, then went to bed. The crew waited and, in the manner of children, the passing of time lessened their fear until they wearied of the game of sentinels and, being very tired, went off to their hammocks.

The flame of the lanthorn vied with a brightening from the windows and failed, and dawn pushed impatiently in and our weary bodies prepared for what the day might bring. I climbed through a sternlight and sidestepped along the ledging until I could see into the body of the ship. All was still and I climbed over the rail at the spot of another unhappy adventure; the decks were clear for not one of our crew remained on guard.

A repentant Molesworth Phillips surfaced and was given the aft-cabin with Captain Clerke for a good half-hour. Fortunately he had the great British excuse of being drunk at the time, sir, and he came out a soberer man and the marines returned to their duties of protecting the officers.

'The position is quite simply this,' Captain Clerke said when we were called to the cabin after breakfast. 'The men will not be happy till they've battled the Indians.'

'Genocide,' James King said.

'And the Indians are determined to goad the ship's company into attacking them.'

'Suicide.'

'Please, James. One can understand the men's attitudes, but the Indians' surprises me. They've killed their god for whatever reason; why should they be so interested in the rest of the people?'

'Revenge, sir,' I said.

'Revenge?' James repeated irritably. 'What have we done that requires revenge?'

'We have not avenged the death of the god. In their strict code, in the way of all Polynesia, revenge is a way of life. We must take retribution for the death of Lono, or we are not worthy of the mantle of man. They despise us just as Mr Kahura and his lot did.'

'Please don't raise that topic,' Captain Clerke said.

'It does have a direct bearing, sir.'

'John, let's not get into philosophy or we'll have Samwell in here next spouting the Shakespearean maxims for exterminating aboriginals. Let's accept what you say about revenge, but I'm looking for the cure, not the cause.'

'I don't like to say it,' Gore came in, 'but there is only one way to treat savages; the mailed fist.'

'Alternatively not the light touch,' I added. 'Sir, they are as children and they expect to be punished. Spare the rod. . . .'

'The rod produces an effect which terminates in itself,' James began. 'A child is afraid of being whipped and gets his task and there's an end on't.'

'I don't want Dr bloody Johnson either,' Captain Clerke snapped.

'Sorry, sir, but by whoever's quotation, the answer is the same. We are in the position of having to punish them.'

'Sure thing,' Gore said. 'Not only will we give the natives what they deserve and want, but we'll be slaking the thirst of our complements too.'

'We can only hope to win from it,' James said.

'No, gentlemen, no, not for a moment. The natives throw stones at us, they try to intimidate us with their *hakas* and grotesque expressions. Are we going to put them to the cannon because of that?'

'No, Charles,' Gore said hotly, 'because they murdered our commander.'

'I'm sorry, John, gentlemen. We will not take our revenge. We have the late captain's opinion on the matter, and you know mine. When an army of intellect faces a duller adversary, the former must show humanity and exercise restraint in the name of conscience and our intelligence, as I've said before.'

'I doubt that our men are any more intelligent than the natives,' James said.

'But the men do not make decisions,' I replied.

'The officers do and we cannot deny those humanitarian guiding lines.'

John Gore said, 'Well, all right, but how are we to be spared our mutinous seadogs?'

'The hearing,' I offered.

'Don't mention that,' Captain Clerke said. 'The hearing, John Williamson, can get us nowhere, because certain officers I will not bother naming cannot leave well enough alone. I said at the outset – did I not, gentlemen? – that we would enquire into the circumstances. It is no use seeking blame for we are all of us charged in some way by rumour and in another way we are completely guilty because we are in this expedition together. Our first duty as officers is to protect our captain and we failed him horribly.'

After a thought-filled silence, I said, 'Sir, the men will not like it if the enquiry is to stop. It meant that at least we were doing something for our late leader. And now. . . .'

'And now, we'll go on the defensive. Mark my words, John Williamson, as long as the men are kept busy, they will be happy. I am hardly going to announce that the enquiry is closed, finished. We have to protect the ships.'

'And recover the captain's body,' Gore said quietly.

'Of course, and we will only do that by negotiation. Come now, it's not all that bad. The men will see us having parleys with the Indians.'

Fifty men took to the sea and our boats cruised the width of the bay. Marines were poised in the bow of each launch, ready to fire, but no canoes challenged us; for the moment the flags conveyed their opinions of the hearts of oak. For us commanding the boats, it was becoming increasingly difficult to discourage the men from shooting at the strand, particularly as after only half an hour our patrol line had moved rapidly inshore; now we rowed towards the sun and away, just a hundred yards off the beach.

I waved for James's boat to come alongside. 'I'm thinking of taking down those silly white flags.'

'I don't think that's part of the captain's strategy.'

'There are not many natives about. I'm sure with a few musket shots over their heads. . . .'

'Well. . . .' He liked the idea but of course was not happy to take the responsibility.

'Come on, we owe it to the men. Cover me and if you like I'll say you knew nothing about it.'

'Get going; don't make a mess of it and we won't have to explain anything.'

I turned to the rowers. 'To the beach, lads,' and there was a noisy cheer. 'You marines will fire over the heads of any natives appearing so they'll run off. Meanwhile you rowers will keep your muskets ready. I'll collect the flags and bring them back to the boat. The captain will be most unhappy if we kill anybody, so aim high.'

James was a few boat lengths off. I turned for the place where the captain fell and we ran onto the beach beside the rocks. Marines fired and some natives about a hundred yards off ran smartly for the trees. One fell with a bloody tear in his back, but I was wading ashore and had no time to remonstrate with the marines.

The village habitations looked empty but from the sound of voices I guessed many people were gathered behind the nearest house. Hopefully they would remain there.

The urge to proceed quickly with the plan was strong. There were eight of these flags and I wanted them all. I also had a strong desire to show that we English are not easily intimidated and so, quite against better judgement I admit, I ambled about the beach. The first flag came out by its pole and I walked towards the next, but taking my time; I made a show of inspecting the stake before pulling it free. The pinnace was a little distance off and the further I went the less brave I felt.

I had four flags and continued for the next. As my path lay from the boats, so too did it from the village, but the noise of the inhabitants was growing and from some of the words that reached me I could tell this act was considered an affront. Excellent. This made me feel quite jaunty and removed some of my fear. Musketshot from the boats, even at this distance, would surely be sufficient to halt any advance; this was a sort of revenge and it felt good.

I was slowly withdrawing the fifth stake when I saw my challenger. He was a fellow of perhaps my own age and if I showed bravado, how much more did he. He approached me slowly despite musketfire from the boats; he was pulling flags as he came. I continued with my exaggerated interest in this fifth flag and eventually took it into my arms. The native came closer. He was of middle height and about a trim torso wore a brief maro. On his head was a shallow wickerwork cap from which profuse false hair hung down his back. This head-dress established him as a modern, much like our young rakes. It gave him a very droll appearance despite the tension on the seafront. The shots from the boats were greatly increased and many were the sounds of ball passing on either side.

'Good day,' I said in as fearless a tone as I could manage. The rounds whistled about him but he took not the slightest notice.

'I thank you, *e hoa*,' he said and, standing before me, took the flags and their sticks from out of my arms.

The gesture took me quite by surprise and there was no alternative but to give up the bundle. I could have struggled or carved him down in a trice with my hanger for he carried no weapon. But that would take from our English display of cool nerve. He walked on towards the boats and the musketfire ceased. I stopped watching him walk away and the noise of the villagers rose to my left. The palms were very green and that hot sunshine scorched my uniform. The native stopped and planted a stake. He walked a little further and erected another. These flags were much closer together than before and I followed along in a bemused way which hopefully hid the growing thunder in my chest. The boats remained silent. The native was stopped with the last flag and we faced each other, quite near where the captain fell. He was perhaps seven yards away. I looked towards the village, but the natives remained out of sight; I could only see pale undersides of the dead native's feet. They resembled cobbler's lasts.

Suddenly my adversary began a *haka*, using the flag as if it were a warspear. I had seen this particular dance performed by the fiord Maoris; the tongue protruded, the grimaces were fierce and sweat grew on the youth's body; muscles stood out with vitality. The boats remained silent; they must have been as much in the dark of the fellow's next move. The pace increased and he grunted and jumped and threatened and lunged at the air with the stake. I knew this to be self-hypnosis for whatever were his intentions. Then I realised he meant to impale me with it. Instinct was to draw my sword and attack immediately; there was no more certain way of winning. But I admired his courage; in the face of a good thirty muskets he was acting with extraordinary bravery.

I stood still, my arms crossed, and he came slowly towards me. I watched that face and wondered if he could kill in cold blood if I did not move to the defensive. Then the guns of the boats opened up. A bullet hit his shoulder and almost pushed him over. He quickly recovered his balance and returned to the dance. Another hit close to the wound, but this time he was braced. The skin splattered with a horrible noise, crimson mixed with the red tresses, but the *haka* continued. A ball found the fleshy part of his forearm and pulled open a muscle. A bullet pounded into his waist; then a second. The men had his measure and his dancing legs smacked as rounds found him. They whistled all about and close to me yet he showed no sign of pain nor of stopping from his intentions. It was true that he was considerably slowed: his left leg would hardly move and he hopped on his good foot and could only wave his makeshift spear with his right hand. Then it too was hit; more splatting noises came that made me want to throw up. Blood poured from his ears. He now stood before me almost paralysed. He pulled the stake back to lunge and the white cloth torn from a dead sailor's shirt moved lightly in the wind over his shoulder, but there was no strength. I was absolutely still; the cool fighting side of the brain calculated the risks, gave advice, but the other side was in near panic at the risk to my person and the horror of the youth's plight. The stake dropped and he fell stiffly forward. His forehead collapsed against my forehead. 'Cowards!' he said, right into my face, and the blood that came with his words poured hot and sticky on my arms. The cap and wig fell off and dropped to the sand. His head with its thick, rooster-styled hair slumped and traced a line down to my arms, and because of that projection he was unbalanced and fell backwards.

I looked down at that face and for a brief moment in the corners of that dead mouth, I saw the beginning of Mahia's smile; the hint of a warmth that I loved though never understood. Then it was gone and the men shouted from the boats. Stones rained on the strand and a mob advanced from the houses. I knew exactly their intentions; they had shown the white foreheads courage and now they would show us death. I looked at the boat; my pinnace in the shallows, James's three waves off the beach. I estimated the distance to the crowd. The sailors yelled

'Run', but I was the teacher here; it had been my initiative and I turned my back on the boy and the boats and retraced my steps in as leisurely a way as I dared. I had three flags in my arms, five. The stones were flying around me, but so far I was unharmed. Seven flags. A boulder caught my shoulder, but I hardly noticed it. At the eighth flag, I hauled the stake from the sand and turned about. The crowd was at the tree line and shouting. The boats were pulling along the shallows towards me; muskets were firing at the natives, but to little effect. I held the sticks in my arms as before and retraced my track. The horde screamed; a stone hit my chest, I ducked a rock aiming for my face and kept walking. One hit my forehead. I felt the wetness of blood, but it did not hurt. Now I was level with the pinnace which was coming in swiftly for me. I turned my back on the natives and walked into the water. The noise of musket was very loud.

'Look out, sir.'

I threw the stakes to the boat. One fell into the sea and I stooped for it. A club swung above my head and I knew that an assassin ran for me the moment I turned my back just as he had with the captain. I put both hands round the shaft and brought it up rapidly behind me. The noise of a man's scream was terrible in my ear. The wood touched for a moment at the developed muscles of his stomach. But the momentum was too great and the stake could not stop for his intestines, diaphragm, lungs, until it rested against the roof of his mouth. He went down into the water and his hands clung hopelessly to the white flag. I pushed over the gunw'le and the pinnace was rapidly pulling from the shore as my legs came inboard. Our muskets were still firing.

A civility often adopted in eighteenth-century soldiering is that when it's time to eat, it is time to halt the fighting. We might as well be soldiers, for until the foremast was completed, *Resolution* was little more than a barracks. Accordingly, we returned to the ships for lunch and the grog which it just so happens is served at about that time. However, the gunroom table had hardly been cleared when the natives launched the next move. At least at first we took it as just such an ungentlemanly, unsporting gesture. Muskets began firing at the bow. There were shouts and the sound of running feet on the decks. I rushed out of the companionway and saw a crowd growing about the bowsprit. More muskets fired and this time youthful screams of fear were returned. James grabbed the jacket of a marine and shook him. 'What's going on?'

'Natives, sir, trying to cut our cable.'

This was serious; if we were cast ashore, our lot would be most unenviable. 'How the hell did they paddle here in the middle of the day?'

The sentinel said, 'Begging your pardon, sir; it weren't my station.'

'I can't believe natives could get out here without being observed,' James said.

'Haven't you seen the people during a meal hour? Their ears are strained towards the mess; they salivate like a dog and growl for fear mates are getting more food than them.'

A guard of marines brought two native youths to the aft-cabin for questioning. A sentry apiece remained and the boys looked frightened until the door closed and they were isolated from the sailors who wanted to hang them; they seemed to forget instantly their danger. They were like the camp followers. Some of the island girls moved onto the ship without a thought for the peril they might be in as enemies. (In a storm, of course, all that changed.) And so with these two prisoners. Now they laughed and tried to touch the ship's journal, the pen and inkstand, but one kept a firm hold of a parcel he carried.

'Tell them to be still, Mr Williamson,' Captain Clerke said. He kept the desk between him and the youths. 'Tell them they are in grave danger and I myself will cut them down if they do not pay proper respect.'

I spoke threateningly and their good humour drained; they shivered in fear as if the temperature of the cabin might have suddenly plunged.

'Ask them as to their business.' They reminded me of a cannibal Kahura just before he left this room so long ago; there was no other term than they cowered.

'I could give 'em one in the breadbasket and soften their tongues,' a marine said in a Devon accent. I was looking at an ear of the boy closest to me; it was small and delicate and I could see Mahia's profile, and the shock was as if the marine's indelicate offering had been aimed my way.

'Avast with that talk,' James shouted. 'The last thing we want is you dogs taking a hand. One more word and you'll be on a charge.'

The boys did not offer a defence. 'It seems most likely they were here to cut the cable,' Captain Clerke said. 'I need hardly suggest what we could contemplate were we cast upon their shore.'

'But why in the daylight?' James asked.

'And how in heaven's name did they get across the bay without being noticed?' David said.

'It'd only take a couple of minutes if they were quick; the people are not such good sentries at anchor.'

'By God,' Captain Clerke said, staring incredulously about him, 'I'll have the names of the sentinels and teach them a pretty lesson.'

'Sir, I doubt they were after the cable.'

'How so?' he asked, anger trying to influence cheeks of parchment.

'Were they going to bite it through?'

The captain ordered the boys searched, but concealing a knife would have been almost impossible. They wore only the modest maro, which the marines now tore off. One punched in the groin the boy with small ears. The lad fell forward and his parcel that we had somehow overlooked spun under the table. The guard hauled the boy back onto his feet. Angry shouts came through the door, reminding us of the danger to our prisoners should the crew have their way. Bligh bellowed, Phillips called to his duty watch to fix bayonets and the noise of the sailors subdued.

There was no disguising the strange smell that came from the package and shocked realisation crept over us. Captain Clerke asked his first officer to examine it, and James instructed me to pick it up, such is delegation in our service. I bit my teeth. The wrapped object was spongy, heavy, and cylindrical. David Samwell began unwrapping it and the smell quickly increased. It was sweet and sickly and forced one to swallow against the strongest desire for the opposite. The material fell open and we were looking at skin, muscles and cooked flesh, not unlike an anaemic Sunday roast.

David cleared his throat. 'From a thigh, sir,' he said. He looked up from the table.

'I regret to inform you, sir, that there is no question. This is human flesh; it has been baked, probably in an earth oven.' Tears affected the ducts in his nose and the Glamorgan accent came in sniffs. 'The size of the muscles show it is unlikely to have been one of the natives. I fear, sir, we know whose body this must have been taken from.'

The marines were sick together. In this room, curiosity gave way to fear, to horror and to hate; the heat, the smell of the muscles, the stench of the vomit made me giddy and I heard a familiar pinging and my hanger was before me and I could see the sign of the wolf. I shouted to cover the feeling of the blade penetrating; I saw Mahia's ear and nose and long lashes and a hand firmly on my wrist and others fought to hold me back. Scuffling seemed a long way off; Captain Clerke was shouting and James was at his shoulder and a grip bruised my sword arm and the spell ended. The officers and David Samwell were holding me from Mahia, from the youths. Order gradually returned.

'For God's sakes, John, gentlemen,' the captain said. He was shaking from the sudden energy and trying to hold down an attack of his distemper. 'If we are to survive at all, we'll only do it through civilised behaviour; by our greater intelligence.' He shook with fatigue and grabbed at the table to stop falling. 'Once blood flows, it will not end and we cannot hope to win. Eventually superior numbers will tell.'

Someone hammered at the door and Bligh appeared. 'A canoe's been brought down to the water, sir. Maybe it's the start of what we fear.'

'An invasion, shite,' said James.

Captain Clerke said, 'Call the men to quarters and I'll have all guns run out, if you please, Mr Bligh. But wait for my orders; not a shot till I say so.'

Bligh shouted as he ran from the cabin. 'Clear for action. Drummer, sound for quarters. Drummer! Where is that lad?'

Hatches were opened to the hold. Crews came into the cabin and furniture and partitions were taken away and lowered on yard tackles to the bottom of the ship. In an engagement most casualties come from splintered wood so everything not to do with the battle is sent below. This enemy did not have guns, but Navy commands did not allow for half-measures and when Bligh announced 'cleared for action' we were ready for almost anything.

24

*E*vents fell over themselves in the panic of the moment; James rushed down the quarterladder and stopped at the doorway, but even as he opened his mouth, strippers took away the cabin wall, so really he was at the waist, aft and to larboard of the wheel. He announced that so far only a single canoe stood on the strand surrounded by savages, and I led the native boys and their guard to the gunroom for further questioning while about us the ship echoed to orders and the deafening thunder of guntrucks on timber as we prepared for battle. All other officers and gentlemen, heavily encouraged with hangers and a brace of Sea Service pistols each, kept an anxious eye to the shore from the quarterdeck. In the dusk below decks I turned to our captives and asked where were the rest of our late commander's remains.

'All about the island.'

'What do you mean?'

'He was taken apart and distributed among different influential families.'

'What were you doing with the part of Lono you carried?'

'We were taking him to another family.'

'So they could eat him?'

'They would not eat a god.'

While I pressed this line of questioning, I studied the delicate lips providing the answers. It seemed impossible that these teeth could chew the flesh of a hand, wiping human lard from their chins as they might the fat of a baked hen. They denied they were cannibals, but often said they would not eat the flesh of a god which seemed guilt by an admittance of implication.

After the massacre, they said, the bodies were taken from the beach to the hilltop overlooking the villages. Here the corpses were stripped and prepared. I did not have the stomach to seek amplification. Yesterday the bodies of the marines were incinerated and nothing remained, they said. Lono was partially cooked and preserved. The boys reported that there were funerals for the thirty natives who died in the incident. Five were chiefs. As I expected, the boys did not know of a planned assault (it was unlikely they would be so calm if they expected a horde to set upon *Resolution* at any moment), but they said the people were trying to trick sailors into going ashore so that more could be slaughtered.

'Why?'

'Just a madness, *e Hone*, of the people.'

'What does that mean?'

'A madness of the people.'

The madness, I thought, was most likely in the form of Kao's encouragement. I left them with the marine sentinels and hurried to report to the captain. At the top of the quarterdeck ladder, the broad back of Phillips blocked the last step.

He was reporting in an excited, almost incoherent whine that four men had absconded from their posts in fear of an attack and had been discovered drinking in the orlop.

'By God,' Captain Clerke exploded, 'put them in irons, lieutenant, and tell them from me they'll regret this.'

'I don't think at the present they'll understand.'

'They will in the fullness of time, I promise you.' Then he looked round Phillips and said, 'Right, Mr Williamson, what have you for me?'

Phillips spun about. He pulled away from the ladder as if a pail of water had been dashed at him, and when I stepped onto the deck, he lunged for the steps and as quickly disappeared.

'Cowardice, sir?' I asked, a serious charge in the Navy.

'The men seemingly preferred grog to battle; let's say no more to it at the present,' he said and pushed his anger into a compartment.

I spoke to the matter of the native boys and the captain called Bligh and ordered them put into their canoe and set free, and I asked James leaning on the landrail, 'What's happening on shore?'

'Same canoe, same group of people. You know, I'm sure that's Kao with them.'

I looked through the glass and offered my telescope to Captain Clerke. 'Do you think so, sir?'

But he was obviously thinking again of the absconders. 'I'll say this, gentlemen. It shows how delicate is our present position.'

'Then may I venture that we resume the hearing?'

'Not that again,' James said.

The men packed the foredeck and waist. The aft-cabin door resting on the caprail to larboard was filling a new role. On it lay a canvas packet over which Collett draped an ensign. We officers stood at the rail with our blue jackets over white shirts, gold braid to signify authority, a dark cocked hat beneath our arms. A light southerly breathed warmly through the rigging. The bay was still; the boys had almost reached the shore where the small party was busy with the single canoe. There was no surf and the only sound reaching us came from a tide pushing the ship back on the cable.

'Goodbye to a dear commander,' the captain began in an emotional voice. 'He leaves us with the most demanding of tasks, to try to continue his work and follow his wishes.'

A whisper of amens rose from the upper deck and came down from the tops. 'His wish is for us to do our duty like civilised men. Duty often goes against a sailorman's desires, so he needs to exercise his British strength for as long as he can.' He held the rail as Captain Cook had done so often. 'He meant so much to each of us that while the first officer reads the Lord's Prayer we will build our own epitaph in the privacy of our quiet.'

James opened the prayer book, pressed the page down several times and coughed, but the nervous preparation belied the reading he had to offer. The words came to life in that educated, crisp and passionate voice and it seemed the message was written especially for us, and tears of those tough jack-tars fell on the iron of the great guns. I wondered where these lusting mutinous people hid their hearts during the voyage. I looked at their broken noses and wounds of their continual scrapping; I thought of their intellect saturated with hate, their abhorrent treatment of Mahia and innocents like her, and I was repelled and fascinated by our most complicated machinery.

Around us sounded amen, amen to that dear God, and cries of Father, Father. Then these brutes were silent in their tears and I heard David Samwell clear his throat. He was below me beside the wheel and he began to sing in his beautiful Welsh voice. It was the twenty-third psalm and I realised we had to trust in our heavenly shepherd as we had trusted in our late commander. Samwell sang in his clear familiar falsetto. The men joined in an octave lower and now came the soprano voices of the boys, from urchins out of the bowels of *Resolution* to our immature ABs learning their ropes, midshipmen learning to command. I looked at beautiful Shuttleworth with his angelic features, his concentration on the words.

Bligh stood to larboard of the wheel and that narrow mouth offered his monotone. He sang from a bland expression; dark hair was pulled tightly into a fat pigtail, a clean shirt was tucked firmly into white breeches and the accompaniment sounded like the hurt drone of a bagpipe. The chorus brought two native girls from below decks and they put their considerable voices to work, adding a sweet earthy harmony (for these people are the most gifted of musicians), and my back moved strangely; and then the music returned as in an echo; the *Discovery* people were singing too and that tragic, peaceful bay was filled with the cry of a mourning Navy.

The remains were committed to the deep with the plop! of a diving tropic-bird as down they settled to the dark, unfathom'd ocean caves.

Over my shoulder I could see figures busy with the canoe on the beach and I fancied that, were the enemy to swarm on board at this tender moment, we would die as martyrs rather than break from this expression of regret: could fatal blows be worse than the agony of our loss?

'Three men in the canoe,' James said a little later, studying the shore through his telescope. A single-hulled dug-out came quickly towards us.

The captain called to Bligh who ran up the ladder to us. 'Note clearly my instructions.'

'Aye aye, sir.'

'When you have resumed the waist, I want the guns primed and ready to fire and the marines to support them. I want your best look-outs and with their eyes skinned.'

'Aye aye, sir.'

'But Mr Bligh, at the present there is *Discovery* and us threatened by three men in a canoe. If we open fire, we will appear fools.' He looked about him to make sure none of the hands at the mizzen could hear, and then said quietly, 'One shot is all that's necessary to start every jack here firing. You must be strong with them, Mr Bligh. Fiercely so.'

'Don't worry, sir.'

'I am very worried. I wish you to be seen to put two pistols in your belt, and they must see you prime them. Tell them you will shoot the first man who fires and by God you'd better be quick about it if one does. In this way you just might stop them. Have the mates similarly armed. Good luck, master; I'm relying on you.'

'Sir,' James snapped his telescope closed. 'They've stopped now. Fifty yards off.'

'Little more than a pistol shot,' I said, and thought how typical it was of Polynesia; we had sufficient fire to bring the islands crumbling, to destroy a third of the population perhaps. We were restrained only by as nebulous a hindrance as conscience and here three men paddled out in a boxwood contraption making themselves an easy target.

'Is *Discovery* standing to?' Captain Clerke asked over his shoulder.
'Yes, sir,' I said. 'They were piping for quarters a little while back.'
'Will you send the signal to hold fire until my word.'
'Aye aye, sir.'

Silence enveloped our sloops of war; the visitors too were quiet. They had shipped paddles and sat returning our stares.

'Why don't we gun the bastards down?' This sudden jarring to our nerves came in a cockney dialect from the waist.

'Who said that?' Bligh shouted, strutting about like a bad tempered lap dog. 'I'll have discipline from you rabble. Mr Mate, take his name.'

Fishing terns crossed the bay chasing a shoal and the southerly smoothed the ripples and relaxed disregarding the tension about our ship like a vapour and so thick that one would need a cutlass to move. The natives must see it, I thought, and realise the danger it spelled for them on this breathing blue.

The palms before the village sighed in the heat and I fancied I could hear one of the multitude hiding there spitting. I thought of them waiting beyond the haze of the sand, armed with slingshots, spears, rocks and the unassailable courage of those not afraid to die. Perhaps a thousand canoes.

An hysterical giggle rose from a young powder monkey, then came the sharp crack of a slap and the boy stopped. A small wave hit under the bow of *Discovery* and the sound was amplified along the quiet decks.

'By Jesus, there's only three of them sods.' A noisy exclamation from a starboard crewman who stood to stare across the ship at the canoe. The Ulster voice moaned as the knotted-rope of a midshipman half his age struck his face.

'Get that man's name, sir,' Bligh said, sharp and cruel; then pulled a

Tower pistol from his belt as he ran for'ard to silence a murmur from the forecastle swivel-gun crew. It was obvious that the ship would burst into activity at any moment and we would see the three foolish men blasted to their heaven before the gunners turned the cannon to the palms on shore.

I imagined I could hear Kao's prompt from the orchestra pit of our unhappy theatre and a laugh sounded from the canoe, then another. A man stood and urinated towards us over the side and another joined him, waving his urination mockingly.

'Lieutenant Phillips.'

'Yes, sir.' Phillips's frightened face appeared at the quarter deck steps.

'Line ten of your men up at the quarter-rail.'

'Not to larboard?'

'You heard me. At the double.' Boots thumped on the ladder and the scarlet coats were quickly formed facing down on the crew. 'Have your men cock their muskets.' Flintlocks were pulled back.

'Men of the *Resolution*,' Captain Clerke spoke at the rail and eyes darted between him and the figures in the canoe. 'The man who opens fire before my word will be shot by these marines, and most likely some of your mates will drop with you. You are Royal Navy sailors, the world's best. Show your discipline.'

The natives shook their organs, pulling at prepuces as if they were elasticised, but the ships remained quiet. One native sat down and another turned his backside at us and waved it from side to side, smacking fat cheeks contemptuously. A second nigger stood and together they danced these pitch posteriors at us and our men remained still. I felt proud that our common people, who would flatten the nose of a friend for less than a sneer, could now face bravely the insults of these savages without retaliating. The natives had lost and must leave, knowing their pathetic show had been for nothing. It no more than increased our contempt for them: let them drag their hindquarters back in shame, I thought, like cowering hounds. Our ensign and jack hung limply in the calm, but our hearts of oak were strong and proud and I looked at Captain Clerke to signal we've won, when a groan came from the waist and was repeated from *Discovery* lying off our stern.

The natives produced their trump card and moved to win in their taunting game. One held over his head a cocked hat and we recognised it at once. He threw it into the air like a juggler and the man next to him caught it. He put it on his own foul head and pulled it down till the brim was at his eyes and made the grotesque *haka* faces that these dogs will. Against my will, my hand was at the hanger-sword and my knuckles were white, and I felt I would give the rest of my life to still that bastard's heart. The groan came from the ship louder now; men stood beside their guns and were crying in the hopeless manner of the palsied unable to co-ordinate limb and brain.

'My God, sir,' I whispered hoarsely, 'we cannot permit this. These men will be fit only for bedlam.'

'It is but grief, sir,' James encouraged, but his face was in a rage and his hand too held firmly to his sword. The scene over his shoulder in the waist of the ship was horrible; the energy for fighting brimmed over in these men; instinct demanded a fight to the death, yet eyes saw the muskets of marines and master and mates who would stop their action.

'Lieutenant Phillips. Your men to the larboard rail. At the double.' The men clattered to the landward bulwark and lined up to Phillips's command.

'Mr Bligh, hold the guns. Gun-crews stand at your stations but do not fire. Your turn will come and by the heavens you will fight hard then. Lieutenant Phillips, have your men open fire on the canoe.'

'Shoot to kill, sir?'

'Fire and do your damnedest.'

Phillips shouted, 'Your target, the nignogs in the canoe. Range fifty yards. In your own time, fire!' A cheer climbed from the ship as the muskets cracked and balls struck the sea around the canoe.

'Have them elevate their sights, Lieutenant Phillips.'

The men shouted for quicker reloading. The marines were doing their best; a measure of powder poured by excited fingers, ball into a square of lint and shoved into the muzzle; ram the bugger home with the rod; tight, tight. Powder for the pan, cocked. Lift the weighty girl back up to the shoulder. Sight her, and brown bess spits death and ears hurt. Reload. The firing became spasmodic and ineffectual and the natives were satisfied for they had elicited a response and now paddled smartly for the shore. Muskets fired again and the smell of gunpowder was strong in our nostrils. The men shouted encouragement like patrons at a cockfight and shots chased the wake of the dug-out. We willed musketballs at brown backs and cheered and the sailors chose to accept victory; in the face of English might, the niggers had taken fright and run.

However, on the quarterdeck we realised that poor shooting once again confirmed how crippled was the strength of the natives' visitors. They killed our god and without him we were as hamstrung as if war-axes had scythed our ankles. They would have us. Every white head would cover the sharpened end of a stake at the marae and they would not question the cause of the bloodshed until the end, our end, when King George's representatives would be no more and the huge ships ashes along the tidemarks.

The crews cheered and David Samwell addressed the captain passionately. 'I cannot understand these natives. This intolerable insult has added fresh fuel to our passions already in a flame.'

'Aye, Dr Samwell,' the captain said, his eyes following closely the native canoe.

David was as animated as the legendary David Garrick as anxiety filled the quarterdeck. 'This circumstance of the hat being shown to our people is like, like. . . .' Captain Clerke's eyes came back from the shore to the raised melodramatic arm of the well-meaning doctor. 'Is like the mantle of Caesar shown to the Romans. It inflames our people to madness and nothing is heard among us but a cry for revenge!'

We all looked at David now, his face red from the intensity of the announcement.

'The great bard, surgeon?' Captain Clerke asked. After a moment's silence, some officers found they could laugh again and David joined in. His theatrical pose eased the tension; we had not won this round, but we had gained a respite.

The drone of Gore's voice came through the deckhead, I heard the crisp steps of someone on the poop, but it was quiet in my cabin; I said, to amuse myself, the roaches are wearing slippers. Sleep took some time arriving after this energetic day and I went into a trance where natives rose out of the sea and clubbed huge men whose brains hung in springing curls, dancing spaghetti of thoughts. I held the late captain's double-barrel musket and fired ball into the repulsive face of a rapist whose nose became a monstrous phallus ripping Mahia and yet his jowl-testes were a midshipman's; hypnotic, furry and responding as a kitten: I was stiff with desire.

A snore must have broken from my lips and I was awake for a moment before faces rushed forward, tongues protruded *haka*-like from vulva, spears throbbed erotically, and Mahia kissed with passion her molesters who I try to recognise; my sword plunged into the dark breast of Kao which will neither bleed nor release the blade. My pistols fire and burst a native girl's forehead and it is a cabin door opening.

Muffled sounds followed and sweat poured from my brow as an unsleeping part fought to rouse the conscious; my heart hammered to repeat the warning. A hand hit my chin, smothered my lips; fingers gagged my mouth, bruising and a stench of shite and sweat filled my nose.

My heart has gone mad; I try to shout and I stare in the pitch. Sssh! a voice warns and the steel beak of a dagger pierces the gown and pecks my chest. I am looking into the face of a giant bird and its fetid claws over my mouth force me to retch. The nightcap is pulled down blinding me and I cry, save me, Mahia, and swallow.

25

I fought against the taste and stench of those filthy claws; I was retching but the sick could not escape for a gag was forced into my mouth and tightly tied.

'Onto the old belly-button, m'lad,' said a voice from the West Country, and they heaved me about as if I were a sack of Irish tubers for the galley. My hands were bound and a leather belt locked my ankles. I was being carried and my feet received the first bruise at the doorway and it seemed I was struck in all parts as these rogues construed to get me onto deck. I could hear whispers but not discern words for my blood raced at such a speed that Drummer Portsmouth might be practising at my head.

We were on deck, I realised, for although a scarf kept out all light, the free air was fresh upon my legs and wrists and its coolness contrasted with the body heat of those bearers.

Had they mutinied at last, was I to be hanged? I dared not guess my fate for my heart was already on the point of expiring. What reassurance might be found, I searched for; I accepted that this handling was not of the roughness a condemned man might expect. Whispers came from the deck, not the drunken cries to be anticipated in a ship fallen to the scum.

My heart stopped; I was over the gunwale, being lowered feet first, and I twisted anticipating the warmth of the Pacific, but hands took my feet and I fell heavily into arms below; I was with men in a boat for the water sounded here against *Resolution*'s hull.

'Easy does it,' said another voice in the darkness; I wanted to put a face to it, but only the dreadful birdhead came to my mind.

Muffled oars were rowing. I tried to estimate the number in this launch, but what difference were there, thirty-three or only one? I was trussed up like a pig and since the trouble my .58 ship's-issue pistols were beneath the mattress and my Simon Harvey sword sat in the rack outside my new cabin beside the brass telescope. Would I ever see them again? A thump came with whispers from above and I knew we must be at *Discovery*.

Fingers pushed under my arms, lifting; I was suddenly rising and as quickly standing on the deck of a ship, the wood rougher here than on *Resolution*. The leather cutting at my ankles loosened and was freed and I stretched, taking up the balance with great relief.

'Now, sir,' said a Glaswegian patois. 'There's a wee dirk in my hand here as would be happy embedded in your flesh. Do as you are bid and the sharpness will stay frustrated.' I was hardly able to argue. He directed me forward with a hand firmly gripping my arm. 'The companionway, steps at your feet now. There, no there. Aye, you can go down.'

The timber was warmer. He led me forward, or aft. I cannot say, although I tried to keep my wits about me by listening for the hull, but at a quiet anchorage, the thickness of our sloops o'war is too great to permit the passage of sound and soon I was totally lost. I was blindfolded, but I knew the moment we came among others. The warmth of their bodies around or perhaps some personal electrification.

'Sit down.'

Calves found the edge of a bench and I sat. The guard was beside me and I could feel the heat of his thighs through my gown. He was obviously big; the hams that pressed against me were well-rounded.

'Let him see.'

The order came from a little before me; hands were busy at my blindfold and gag and knuckles hit my head clumsily; the scarf came off. The nightcap was pulled up suddenly. I expected to be blinded by light, but this was a darkened place and strange shapes swam through my vision as pressure was replaced by my living blood. My jaw hurt. There were candles, a great number of forms, of beings, and pain forced my eyes shut again. These beings were huge birds. I relived instantly the dreadful vision when the people attacked, when the *creatures* attacked, and now I was in a room, a hall, full of them.

'What is your name?'

A cockney voice, yet when I opened my eyes again, it was the most frightening apparition one could imagine. At that terrifying moment, in the bewilderment of being kidnapped in the dead of night, I believed it to be an inhabitant from Venus or Mars. It surely could not be an avenging Polynesian god.

'What is your name?' it snapped again and I could not resist an urge to stand, so great was my danger, so eager was I not to offend. When I ask questions of persons, I look at them, yet this creature looked at *all* before it.

'Williamson,' I said meekly.

'Your full name?'

I describe this and it seems my mind has become unhinged, as if I were arriving straight from Bedlam, yet this account is as it happened.

'John Williamson.'

'What is your rank?'

'I am a lieutenant. Second officer of His Majesty's sloop *Resolution*. I received my commission on February 23, 1776.'

He spoke, it spoke, but the mouth stayed permanently open. Teeth were thickly collected in the jaw and they resembled those of the shark. One could assume these beings were flesh-eaters, a thought I did not find comforting. The nose was similar to the Polynesians', only it began beneath the brow. That is difficult to define; the lighting was poor and my eyes still hurt most terribly from their ill-treatment. There was a brow, eyes and then the start of the nose. Or was it a beak? However, it was as if he were an ancient being and a long life of worry produced creases of the brow that succumbed to our gravity and sagged like eyebags onto the beginnings of the beak-nose.

'What is your age?'

'My naval age is twenty-one.' My voice was still weak, my lips bruised; how I longed for some sound of authority to return, so I could represent the Royal Navy with some dignity.

'And your real age?'

I wondered whether to lie, but it was unlikely my commission would be revoked. 'I am nineteen.'

This place was set out like a classroom; at the front was a wooden table as you would see in any smaller ship in the Navy. It was a dark wood varnished. This, this thing sat between two of the birds. I was treated mainly to their profiles; occasionally their beaks and tiny evil eyes turned towards me. The expressions were lifeless, like David's three buttons' worth. Before me were several rows of benches where creatures squatted looking forward. The heads were shining smooth and there were no ears. Their bodies were wrapped in blankets; all of them were so, including the being at the desk, the inquisitor. And I now saw he had hands, not claws, which sat before him on the desk-top, with blunt working man's fingers. I was thinking how disconcerting when he demanded, 'Where was you born?'

I wanted to shout of this world, of human beings, and yet despite all the attacks upon my senses, my voice would not rebel. I was tired and prematurely aged; I could not fight, and worse, I could not be bothered fighting. 'In the county of Wiltshire; my father was an older man, a retired naval officer,' I said, and once begun could not stop my *curriculum vitae*. 'He bought the end of a leasehold of a farm; that's where I was born. It was his dream to have land; wide open spaces after the oceans, I suppose. But with the enclosures and all, when it came up for renewal the price was so much more. I had grown by now and he had contacts in the Navy. I was given the preferential treatment of being written into the muster-books to gain sea time. I was at school, a good school, and I did well among my peers. Then he got me into the conflict with the Americas as a midshipman. He died of a broken heart, as they say, when his farm was taken. He was not a strong man; he was cut down by privateers boarding his ship in the Seven Years War and only just escaped with his life. It's his Simon Harvey sword I have; he had me thoroughly trained in blade and bullet so that I would never fall in a similar fight. Well, the bailiffs came onto the farm and took away his life. Quite literally as it happened. And then there was my mother. He beat her up sometimes; I hated that. Perhaps it was her fault because she would keep blaming him.'

I stopped for breath, but my biography would not be halted. Somehow these alien creatures must understand. 'You see she was an actress in a little provincial theatre and she gave up her ambitions for my father. At least, that's how she saw it, I'm sure. She was an attorney's daughter, but she did not inherit his brain, nor anything in the end. Anyway, I came along and later age and his war wound took much of my old man's interest from her. She became very bitter and believed he was the only impediment to her appearing in Drury Lane. After his death, she tried to return to the theatre; everything had changed of course and instead of lauding her they laughed in her now matronly face. She was desperate for pride and money; she worked in a gin bar, she became a customer. A dénouement is hardly necessary; she died a hedge-whore soon after. This happened while I was fighting for King and country.'

My voice seemed not my own. It panicked and raced as though it feared being stopped before the end. It must have been me talking but the strange thing is I *never* speak of my parents. Neither were what they ought to have been; he put everything into the farm, she bitched night and day and I was happiest at my studies. Of course they did not love me. The greatest day in my life was going on a ship in my uniform for the first time. My father's stories were exaggerated. The gunroom was disgusting, my fellows stank, and the captain was a sot. But at least I had made a start in what was ordained of me.

Crazy thoughts for a grown man; but such were these moments, dragged from my bed, the bird-creatures, seeing the late captain falling under the natives' clubs.

'You are the secretary at the enquiry into the death of the captain?'

'Yes, I can read and I can spell. I am the taker of the notes.'

'What is the result of the hearing; what have you decided?'

'Nothing is decided. The captain is dead, that is all we know.' The bird-heads murmured at that. I added, 'The hearing is over. There could be no result, no finding. We were merely recording events for the lords of the admiralty.'

This sent a shock through the creatures. The inquisitor's eyes formed of an external pupil stretching from ears to nose did not blink, narrow or widen, yet somehow they signified great concern. The beakheads conferred with it.

'Is there proof that this is so?'

'The proof is in the minutes of the proceedings.'

'Where are they?'

'In the cupboard of my cabin.'

'We will get them.' He waved those rough fingers at someone, *something*, behind me.

'Will you be able to read them?' I asked in a moment of inspiration. I did not want these creatures seeing my notes, my letters to Mahia, looking at my recorded life.

'You could read them to us.'

'I do not need to read them to know what is there. My memory has it all imprinted.'

A lull again; I suppose the creature behind me returned to his post; I could have looked round but my position was hopeless. Hands bound behind my back; there would be no protecting myself should I cause offence. And standing there in my bed attire made me feel exceedingly vulnerable.

'It's the way we most feared,' he was saying, 'the people of the ships was not told. There has to be a proper enquiry, Mr Williamson. Now, before we leave these blessed islands. And those responsible for the occurrence, whether they be military shall we say, or of the ships, will pay the proper price.'

He was silent. I just managed to stay that way too; lighting remained poor, but I could see all. My imagination had the better of me: disguises; I was a fool!

'We . . .' then he corrected himself. 'Your help is needed. The men can ask for the hearing, can petition, can plead, but mere tars can't press a request. They could, er, take the law into their own hands, but the penalty for that – for men who want only to see justice – puts it out of the question.' He wound muscular fingers one upon the other. 'You are an officer and therefore you can put the argument. For you it has been chosen to show the power of the people of the ships, if they've a mind to use it. You are here on another vessel and not one other officer is even aware of it.' He stopped; I said nothing. 'Look, Mr Williamson. There's another matter. Blame is cast in many different directions. Should Captain Clerke have winched his ship in close and frightened off the crowd? Why fire only three cannon? Should the marine lieutenant have made sure he had sufficient men ashore? And you, Mr Williamson; what was your part in it? If justice is conducted here at the site of the tragedy, then justice is what will have been done and all is ship-shape and Bristol-fashion. But if we leave matters to London, sir, who knows what conclusions might be reached? There are plenty in your pinnace, as you know, who would not side with you.'

'Watch your tongue,' I shouted, unable to hold back. It was crazy to let my emotions go; I had to persuade them; I could not hope to gain anything by bullying, yet I had been gravely humiliated and the accusation was too insensitive. What hope for me with the tongues of mutinous dogs wagging, newspapers encouraging them, jealousy that fills Royal Navy gunrooms stirring them on? 'By God, man, you go too far. I have no time for the games of rabble. Untie me. . . .'

An imaginary hand grabbed my voice and silenced it before my outburst became the length of a lynching rope. I pulled in my horns and pushed down the conflicting emotions of the heart. 'I don't follow,' I tried again, 'exactly what it is you want me to do.'

'We want you . . . that is, you is wanted to appeal to Captain Clerke to hold a proper enquiry. That is all. He will listen to you.'

'Don't you realise he's desperately ill?'

'That we do, sir. And after he goes, Mr Gore will be in charge but he won't have the guts to conduct a hearing.'

'The foremast will be ready at any moment and then we'll be off very smartish. I doubt there will be time for a hearing.'

'The mast, sir, will be ready when the time is right.'

'Cleveley's in this, too? You mean the people are actually holding back on the repairs . . . do you have any idea of the risks to us all?'

'Threats will not work. Will you help us?'

'I could tell Captain Clerke about this, this meeting.'

'He'd never believe you.'

'I can't go along with you. I am a Royal Navy officer.'

'You've no choice.'

'I'll trade with you. Give me the men who took Mahia and I'll do what you want.'

'Divide and conquer, eh, Mr Williamson? But it won't work. Remember you're here to see where the power really lies in a ship. You see, you're in no position to bargain.'

'And if I say no?'

'Your friends, if you have any, will assume you went over the taff-rail. Unable to take the accusations, *et cetera*.'

'You don't think for a moment they'd accept that, do you?'

The creature laughed, the birds laughed and the mirth was cold and threatening. I felt the tip of the guard's dagger through my nightgown and I knew they would believe it all right. And blame for the whole affair would settle on my ghost.

I had hardly returned to sleep than Collett was knocking on the cabin door. All officers to report to the captain for a disciplinary hearing, he chanted, and I dragged myself out and made the aft-cabin as Bligh marched in four offenders. We officers sat at the chart-table which had been brought out from the stern. The scientist Bayley was present from *Discovery* to record the proceedings in his copperplate.

I leaned across to James. 'What news of the natives?'

'Nothing since our foray ashore,' he whispered. 'Why's your mouth bruised?' A look from Captain Clerke ended our conversation.

Bligh snapped, 'Mathew Pall, Richard Lee, William Bradley and William Passmore; all charged with desertion, sir, while the ship was at quarters.'

'How do you say as to your guilt or otherwise?' Captain Clerke asked quietly, in a queer contrast to the sergeant-major tones of the master.

The men, perhaps more boys really, looked at their feet and shifted about, but none spoke. 'All guilty, sir,' Bligh chanted.

I smiled inwardly at the incongruities of our life: natives determined to destroy us, the complements closer than ever to mutiny, the officers desperate to sail, the sailors refusing to hurry, Bligh's head-splitting efficiency, Clerke's gentlemanly voice, and us rushing through this legal quadruple murder so we could be in time for breakfast. I looked at the heads soon to be swollen and grotesque in death. 'Can't they speak for themselves?'

A fair boy, Passmore, turned a disproving eye on me and then turned away. For every moment I spoke, by such a time would their lives be extended, yet one would swear they were impatient to get on. 'I presume, sir, these people realise there is only one penalty if they are guilty?'

'*If* they are guilty?' Bligh repeated sarcastically.

Captain Clerke silenced him and said to the defendants, 'What do you say, men?'

They looked about them for an answer. Passmore said, 'Say about what, sir?'

Bligh shouted, 'Was you like newts, the lot of you, when the ship was at quarters?'

'Well. . . .'

'Guilty as hell, sir,' Bligh cut in.

'Let's have the evidence then, master.'

'The marine lieutenant heard noises from below, sir, after the call to quarters. He made a prompt and thorough search and caught these lads skulking in the orlop and very drunk.' He delivered this damning oratory at great speed and in one impatient breath. If the prosecution and defence were in such a hurry, I thought, it would not be long before they missed their last breakfast.

'Where is the marine lieutenant?' the captain asked.

'Seeking volunteers for a musket party, sir.'

'A what?' James asked.

The captain said, 'I asked the lieutenant to see if he could get sufficient people for a firing squad. I'm not at all happy about hanging these people within sight of the Indians.'

James looked incredulous. 'You mean, we would shoot these lads?'

Captain Clerke was impatient. 'For heaven's sake, Mr King, only if I can get a sufficiency of reliable shots. I mean, what is it going to look like to natives if they see bodies struggling in the rigging.'

Fortunately for the sensitivities of our young offenders, Phillips came into the cabin and changed the direction of the conversation. He offered his evidence. The sailors, he said, were almost paralytic and on the captain's orders they were put into irons. It was, he said with almost a touch of pride, several hours before they regained consciousness.

'How did they get so drunk?' The question came from James who was standing now, perhaps hoping some logic might reach his ears in this elevated position.

'Stole grog, sir.'

James King looked hard at Phillips and at Captain Clerke, as if he might wake and find this an impossible dream. 'Are they . . . are they charged with theft?'

'Don't see no purpose, sir. They're going to hang anyway.'

Captain Clerke said, 'What about your men, Lieutenant. Did you muster a squad?'

'I've not been successful in that attempt, sorry, sir. Pall here is the fiddler and Passmore has more than a melodious singing voice so nobody wants to shoot them.'

'Well, I'm damned unhappy about hanging them on the anchorage,' Captain Clerke said.

James King said angrily, 'Marine friends of the condemned men will not be available, yet who but their shipmates will be hauling them up the yards?'

'Well, sir, I see your meaning. . . .'

'It's of no matter,' James said impatiently, but his look did not support that dismissal. 'What was it Dr Johnson said, "It matters not how a man dies, but how he lives. The act of dying is not of importance, it lasts so short a time."'

Amen to that, I thought, as Johnson's brief moments can sometimes last an age in the rigging.

The captain said, 'Are you finished then, Mr King? Breakfast will be served any moment and we must push along. Have you men anything to say before we consider the evidence?'

If four lives were not at risk here, I would have taken Captain Clerke's choice of word as amusing. 'Can I ask something, sir?' I said.

'Well, ask it, Mr Williamson?'

'What evidence?'

'The evidence,' Bligh said a little incautiously, 'that has just been given.'

'I've heard from the charging officer, but not a word in defence.'

'What defence is there, sir?' Bligh sneered.

'That will do, Mr Bligh,' the captain said. 'If you want to say something on their behalf, please do so, Mr Williamson. But be quick about it.'

I turned to the boys. 'Why did you drink the grog?'

They looked up with supercilious grins and I was on the point of abandoning them, but fortunately Bligh guffawed in his foul pre-breakfast mood and that was challenge enough for me to side with the boys. I leaped from my chair. 'Did you say something, master?' His surly expression dropped. 'Very well, then,' and I turned back to the antagonists I would save, if they'd let me. I walked to the front of the table, till I was close to the poorly shaven face of the blond boy. 'So you're a coward, Passmore?' I shouted aggressively.

'No, sir.'

'You are a bloody coward, Passmore; you sneaked away with your mates and got drunk while the ship was at quarters.'

'We didn't hear the call. Sir.'

'Liar!' Bligh bellowed. 'Who could not hear Portsmouth's drumming?'

'I must agree,' Captain Clerke said. 'It may not be the finest percussion, but there could be no doubting the volume of it nor the message. Mr Williamson, we must press on.'

'But, sir, Portsmouth does not always signal and I'm damned if I remember him giving the order on this occasion. What do you say to that, Mr Bligh?'

'I'm not sure,' the master conceded, but it seemed Passmore would execute himself, given enough rope, as it were.

'Anyways,' he was saying in his Monmouthshire accent, 'drums or no, we was pretty far gone by then. I don't think we would've heard it.'

'From the horse's mouth,' Bligh said. 'Sir, I've got to say this; the people know the court-martial's to do with cowardice and discipline and I think it unwise to delay a prompt execution of the penalty. We are in a very difficult position with the crew. . . .'

'I'll thank you, Mr Bligh,' the captain returned, holding down his anger with difficulty. 'No one is more aware of how pressing the matter is. If you're satisfied, Mr Williamson?'

I looked across at James King, but no assistance was to be had there; he was staring at the table top; I think he was despairing of the inhuman King's Regs. at that moment.

'One further question, sir.'

'Very well.'

'Passmore, repeat what you have just said.'

'Really, Mr Williamson, we all heard. . . .'

'Exactly, sir. The boy tells us that they were drunk when he presumes the call to quarters came. So the rider to that question, Passmore, is how long had you been imbibing when you were discovered?'

'Sorry, sir?'

'Drinking, dammit.'

'About an hour or two.'

'Sir, how could they have become so drunk in the short time since quarters was called and Lieutenant Phillips came to us to report the incident?'

I turned back to the men who expected to choke to death before this hour was up. 'If you were already drinking while you were out of discipline, before the quarters sounded, and you had partaken of so much that you did not hear the order, you can hardly be guilty of desertion. Is that not so, Captain Clerke?'

Bligh ordered the defendants out of the cabin; they were free men.

26

We were at breakfast; pig and potatoes again in this dingy gunroom. Same diet, I thought, same faces, same torn cloth with a design I never recognised now greasily disguised by our poor table manners. Sitting here with my messmates and none of us getting any younger. The sea and its attendant hardships is no prolonger of youth.

'Who punched you in the mouth?' James asked. The court-martial stopped him from shaving and the new growth emphasised white premature bags beneath his eyes.

'Oh, knocked it on the handbowl this morning.'

My place was opposite James and to my left, at the top of the table, grumbled Gore in an unhappy state. Too much drink last night, I thought, and he looked in need of a saltwater wash. He had spent the night as guest of the aft-cabin and someone, perhaps James, had invited him to breakfast with us. The midshipmen were in high spirits next down the table. The master and his mates and David Samwell had the far corner. Dr Bill's seat was in the mother position of the table. It had remained empty since he went.

These were the men I had to convince to exhume the hearing, particularly brother-officers. I could forget Bligh because he would not side with me and his mates carried no weight. David would be a useful ally.

I stabbed the boiled pork, cut off a piece with the blunt knife and thought the crew would have their revenge for the late captain, whatever we of this gunroom desired. And they would have it before we set off into the unknown, and perhaps to our deaths with hungover Captain Gore in charge when Captain Clerke succumbed.

'What's the matter with you?' James asked across the table.

'I was thinking.'

'About getting Passmore and his people off?'

'About revenge, *utu*. It's not the preserve of the Polynesians at all; everyone's chasing it. It's the great suicidal weakness of man.'

'Bit profound for breakfast, isn't it?' Captain Gore said.

I shrugged.

'Look, you might as well know, John,' James said suddenly after a pause. 'I've asked Captain Gore and he agrees. We must force the carpenters on with the foremast and get out of here.'

'How can you force them on?'

'Threaten them to go faster.'

'Threaten an artisan? That's a laugh. Anyway, you'll not see the mast in place till they are good and ready.'

'They?'

'The carpenter and his mates.'

'We have to get the ship rigged properly.'

'You're not telling me anything. But can we leave without the captain's body?'

'I'm not happy about that,' Gore said.

'We aren't going to get it back,' James said. 'They've eaten him, haven't they, John?'

'I wish you wouldn't say that,' Gore moaned and pushed his plate away.

'I think we owe it to him to get the rest of. . . .'

'Yes, I agree,' Gore said quietly.

'And to do something about the hearing.'

'God, not the hearing,' James said. 'We don't want that cropping up again.'

'We have to hold the hearing properly and get the whole thing settled before we leave. Don't you think so, Captain Gore?'

'Could be a tall order.'

'The truth ought to be sorted out here in the bay rather than by the admiralty years after the event.'

'Don't you fear what accusations might be raised about you?' Gore asked.

'On the contrary. It would clear my name once and for all.' I called through the noise, 'Don't you agree, David. We should have a proper enquiry into the massacre?'

'What?' asked Bligh, who had been staring into his plate, chewing determinedly at the last of the meat.

'The hearing,' prompted Samwell. 'We should get it under way again.'

'Couldn't agree more,' the master said. 'And a proper full enquiry while we're at it.' His look came along the table towards me, like a barracuda on the prowl. 'Into all aspects concerned,' he added, predator eyes upon me now.

Then Collett came into the gunroom. 'Quick, Mr Williamson,' he said, 'Kao is signalling for a parley. The captain wants you to take the pinnace at once.'

I ordered the men to ship oars a good hundred yards from the white horses at the shore. The clear water dripped back into the sea from the polished blades with distinct sounds, so silent was the bay this morning. The double-hulled canoe came quickly for us, seeming to glide upon the surface; our wooden pinnace was functional but their craft was swift, beautiful and quiet as a mako shark, and emphasised just how impossible would be a conventional engagement with a flotilla comprising similar native vessels. Six rowers were in either hull and I wondered about the ceremonial masks they wore; surely Kao could not know of last night's rebellion. The old man crouched on a construction like a stage between the hulls and the canoe turned and a shadow from the sail passed over the old devil and his half-tattooed features and exposed the lie of his genial smile; black eyes were colder than Gemini in a winter sky.

'It is fine to see you, the one-they-call-Hone; I was hoping you would respond to my invitation to converse.'

'Good day, Mr Kao.'

'Fighting is for children and frustrated wives, hardly for grown men.' The canoe was alongside and the natives rested their paddles at the horizontal, as disciplined and neat as a sloop's guns. 'I propose, Hone, we settle our differences here and now.'

'I am pleased to hear you say it.'

As we spoke, I searched as well as I could for weapons. The rowers wore nothing but the unnerving bird-like masks and maro about their thighs; I did not doubt they would have concealed some daggers made from traded iron, but as to other weapons: there were no stones for throwing and no spears.

'I have presents for your table to show my good intentions,' the priest said and sat back on his ankles. He prodded a piglet which lay tied before him and it screamed like a child.

'You know what I want from you, *e koro*.'

'Peace if you have any sense.'

'Our great guns can ensure that: I want Lono.'

'He's dead; he's of no use to you.'

'Do I need to be reminded of your murder of him?'

'How amusing. Lono died generations ago; perhaps he will return one day. Legend has it that way.'

'You know who I mean.'

'Oh, the imposter.'

'The reincarnation of Lono.' I decided to dispense with his false smile. 'Oh, Mr Kao, you and your absurd vanity. You killed him because you could not share the worship of your people even for a moment. Do you imagine by his death they will forget him and turn back to you?'

Kao shouted, 'He must be denounced; you must tell my people he was not a god. I am the high priest – I represent the gods and I know he was not one of them.'

'You killed the reincarnation of Lono through jealousy. What do you suppose the gods will do to you now?'

'He was not a god!' Kao's nerves twitched out of control about his face. He hid this reaction quickly behind long fingers and when he took his hands down, his genial mask was back in place. 'You from across the sea have strange ideas. A man is dead, the fate for all men.'

The difficulties of the night, the heat in the pinnace and now this savage adopting an air of superiority did not make for good diplomatics. Yet I had to persuade this vile, covetous man to give up the body. We would put the late captain to rest and then rest ourselves in the knowledge that we had done all we could. I borrowed a tinderbox from one of our smokers which I kept below the gunwale and picked up a tin bailer from the sole. I held a match forward.

'This, Mr Kao, is life; energy, something magnificent, and occasionally in some men the spark is bigger and brighter. Lono was such a one.' I struck a stick on the box with great stealth and it exploded into flame. I held the tin inverted about it so that it cast a shadow which amplified the flare. 'In the man you murdered dwelt such a light and you destroyed it, in defiance of your gods.'

My words till this exhibition had remained as ennui among his rowers, but the flame which appeared from nowhere commanded wide uncomprehending eyes, and by shading and unshading it, I was able to make their attention even keener. Kao himself was mesmerised, but jealousy reasserted enmity when he saw the reaction of the canoeists; they clearly believed it to be magic.

'Oh, I regret the passing of the imposter. But I'll tell you this, young man, I was as deceived as perhaps you are still. Look, these hands pulled apart that white body; I opened his heart and looked into the skull and searched among his entrails. No god lurked there. He was a man, a big man, nothing more.'

The dreadful fingers with enlarged rheumatic knuckles shook at me and I had no difficulty imagining these talons tearing at our commander: his nails were unkempt and curled around the finger tips; they were serrated and yellow and thick. I fought down the nausea occasioned by the horrible revelation.

'You are a fool,' I said and pinched the match under the shade so that it expired. 'You did not know where to look for the spark, that is all, you disgusting animal.'

He swept those claws at me like an infuriated eagle. His rowers remained entranced by the smoking match and were unable to strike on the priest's behalf.

'An ignorant savage may not realise it, but there is more than death.' I leaned over the gunwale and pushed the tin down into the clear water and turned it over. Bubbles erupted with smoke from the match and lay on the surface more uncannily than I had anticipated. The natives moaned and I surreptitiously blew gently so that the small cloud of smoke moved towards them. They jumped in fear and began to paddle the canoe rapidly with ill-disciplined splashing. The priest shouted but his men were not listening; the pakeha produced a flame from his hand then smoke from the sea; he must be a wizard. The piglet began shrieking.

'Bring us the body,' I called.

'You tell my people he was an imposter; then I will return him.'

'You have till this afternoon, priest.' I ordered my men to the oars and turned the tiller for the ship.

I came out of my cabin a little later as Samwell was leaving his. 'David, will you support me if I ask the captain to consider getting a hearing together?'

'The path that is enlightened by the rays of truth, being so rarely trod, we should not miss the opportunity to help others in its direction.

Do you know, by the way, that William Harvey is coming back to *Resolution*?'

Harvey had been a master's mate who was disrated into *Discovery* for letting a native prisoner escape. 'Bligh will be pleased.'

'No, he's coming back as an officer. Third lieutenant.'

A shock hit and wounded me but I held firmly to my expression.

'That's nice,' I lied through my panic. We believed *Resolution* would sail with just two lieutenants. So was Harvey coming back as I was to be disrated because of the allegations?

I pushed past the marine sentinel and knocked. 'A word if I may, sir.'

'Come in.' Captain Clerke was sitting on the edge of the berth. 'Collett's getting me some hot chocolate. Care for some yourself?' He nodded to Collett then said, 'I've got Harvey coming across this afternoon. He'll have your old cabin, I suppose.'

'Sir, I'm here to ask you to charge me.'

'What's this?'

'With the murder of the late captain. Or as an accomplice or something.'

'For heaven's sake, man.'

'No, sir, charges have been laid unofficially.'

'They are forgotten about.'

'Not now, sir. Harvey's coming across on promotion. Everyone will know I am to be disrated.'

'They'll know wrong then. You're my number two and you'll stay that way.'

'It's the talk of the ships, sir. You must do something.'

'Would you have me put up a notice?'

'I'd have you reopen the enquiry.'

'The enquiry?'

'A proper enquiry, sir. Court-martial me. We can't leave till the foremast is rigged. Please, sir, I'm a Navy officer. This will be the end of me unless I can be cleared now.'

'I wish you wouldn't do this to me, John. Look, give me some time to think it over; an hour or two. Get James King to petition me one way or the other, and Captain Gore while he's over here. No, wait for the chocolate and tell me what you think about trying again for this elusive passage.'

I was writing up my journal when word came to return to the

aft-cabin. I came up into the sunlight and the deep blue beckoned me from our sorry circumstances. Oh for a sturdy ship to set all canvas, to escape from our nightmare here!

I entered the aft-cabin and was confronted by officers arguing, pleading and openly weeping. It was as if I had entered the wake of a most divided family united briefly by their grief. The noise of the door closing behind me introduced silence and Captain Clerke stepped from the berth to the chair with some difficulty, which emphasised his destruction.

'I'll be perfectly frank with you, Mr Williamson. Your request to be charged has started an avalanche. We all share some guilt. Who of us in this room has not been accused? With hindsight, what couldn't we have done to protect him?'

He sat carefully on the Chippendale. 'Yours has precipitated several petitions to charge individuals with . . . well, you know.'

He turned to address us all. 'You all say the same. Doubt is in the minds of others and a proper court-martial would end the accusations. What am I to do? Charge each of you and am I not to be included? We would have to put the prosecution in the hands of the ship's people, because that's about all who consider themselves free of the allegations.' He pulled the chair into the desk while we digested this thought. 'The hearing – enquiry, court-martial, whatever it's to be called – should be held here at the site of the tragedy. I accept that.' He studied us quietly for a moment. 'I have chosen a compromise. What else is there? I have decided to press charges against the late captain for neglect of duty so as to imperil His Britannic Majesty's ships *Resolution* and *Discovery*. Mr King will act in his defence. Mr Williamson, I would be pleased for you to brief yourself sufficiently to prosecute the case on behalf of the lords of the admiralty. I propose to begin the hearing after luncheon and the complements will be present. Captain Gore and myself will adjudicate.'

'Sir, there is so little time to present a defence,' James said.

'And very little time for Mr Williamson to prepare his prosecution.'

Our long chart-table was brought onto the waist and chairs placed at it, two for the captains and one at each end for James and myself. The table was set to larboard, to put the captain the least distance from his cabin: he sat inboard near James. Bayley the astronomer was appointed writer and began recording the proceedings in his neat hand when Collett as master at arms read the charge; sailors settled on the deck near the table and upon the great guns. Marines were on duty and lined the quarter-rail with musket and bayonet shining ominously in the afternoon sun.

Captain Clerke had decided upon this remarkable way out of our problems – some of them – and now it was about to become part of our history. What the world would make of the legal hearing conducted in this savage kingdom we would not know for a year or more, for that is the soonest we might reach civilisation again. Gentle Captain Clerke would be dead long before then . . . and how many others of us too, I wondered. James coughed and addressed the 'court' and so committed us to the extraordinary course of action.

He promised to defend the commander's honour and reputation with the greatest diligence and called for William Bligh who held a bible that baked on a corner of the table and said yes he vowed to be honest, amen.

The master began a history of our voyage and I suppose we relived parts of it as the monotone progressed. His pride intervened every so often with 'I navigated' and 'my course' and I noted it, for it might be useful to trap him at a convenient time.

I stood. 'Sir, I don't know that the business of the privateer ought to be aired. It was the captain's wish at the time that we would not mention it in our journals for reasons known among the officers.'

Captain Clerke looked nervous at this, touching as it did on the question of what the people ought to know. 'Quite so, Mr Williamson. The point, Mr Bligh,' he said with a message that was obviously for the crew, 'is that the late captain did not wish to have chronicled the events of the fight with the privateer; this is for a political and perfectly plausible reason. He was well proud of the crew's response and handling of the battle and regretted that for the good of all it could not take its part in the official history of His Majesty's ship *Resolution*.

Bligh continued; we were at the Verdes, the equator, the South Atlantic, and he was making heavy weather of the statement and I was tempted to challenge him and upset that mind so carefully turning the pages of his journal. But I might need him for his pride was the biggest challenge to the skill of the captain: he enjoyed the role of protégé which should have been mine, yet he was the witness most likely to sink a knife deep into the back of the late captain's reputation.

Leaving Cape of Good Hope, broken spars, Van Diemen's Land, the marines who got drunk and I said a quiet Rest in Peace for young

Moody, *Mindful of th' unhonoured dead*. The haul across the Tasman, the gloom of the Southern Ocean again and my own unhappy memories, the arrival in Queen Charlotte Sounds. 'Which I set course into on February 12,' he said. Masts had to be struck in bad weather, the effect of the voyage on the animals, the state of the men's health, the passenger Omai. This brought smiles as the images of the roué passed through our minds. Bligh continued with the struggle to beat out of the sounds and the contrary weather that made a mess of our route. Now, I thought, the prosecution will begin.

'Gentlemen,' Captain Clerke announced as though he guessed my intentions, 'we'll break for half an hour.' He stood and the men got to their feet and stretched. 'If the cook would not mind serving dinner a little late tonight, it would be in our interests to proceed during the daylight. The hearing may take a little while.'

He invited us to the comparative cool of the aft-cabin.

'A splendid start, gentlemen,' he said, 'and that's all we'll say on that subject.'

'Aye aye, sir.'

'Instead a little guessing game. Who can tell what will be on the menu again tonight for the fourteenth meal in succession? Beginning with the letter P.'

A light breeze came across the deck. 'I would like to ask Mr Bligh a question before he continues.' Bligh sat at the chair, running out guns of suspicion. 'As master you are charged with the navigation of the ship?'

'Yes, sir.'

'At the time of the contrary winds in the Pacific, who selected the course?'

'I did.' His pride was in the way of honesty, I could see, because the captain chose the course to the annoyance of all. I had to put the question differently or lose the point I wanted.

'Tell me how you selected the course.'

'I used my instruments on the chart and drew a line. . . .'

The men laughed, for sending up an officer was welcome comedy. I smiled good-humouredly.

'Did you draw a straight line to your next objective, to the next island we planned to visit?'

'This was a voyage of discovery, sir. We were looking for islands but not any particular island.'

'So you could not rule up a planned course?'
'No, sir.'
'Where was the wind relative to our direction?'
'Starboard bow.'
'We were beating?'
'Full and bye.'
'Our best point of sailing?'
'Our worst.'
'Then it must have been our best point for discovering new islands.' Bligh was silent even if the men were not; a score against the master was worth a laugh too.
'I'll ask you different, Mr Bligh. Did we not have a passenger to disembark?'
'Yes, sir.'
'Where exactly?'
'Tahiti.'
My point succeeded; by being difficult Bligh made it obvious he was protecting the captain's chosen course which implied it was the wrong one and those who could remember that far back would know it was wrong in their opinion too. Bligh waited for me now to draw his 'reluctant' evidence which would build his own reputation as a navigator and swell that insatiable pride. 'I have nothing further for the master, for the present.'
Bligh looked deflated but continued. Flukey winds plagued us and finding grass for the starving animals became imperative. Our course was north, he reported, then we took a board to the larboard and later eastward.
'Sorry, Mr Bligh,' I interrupted, and the crew sat up again sensing a challenge.
'Sir?'
'From your words I take it that we looped right round in the Pacific?'
'In a manner of speaking.'
'Well, Mr Bligh, in a manner of speaking I take it that a tack to the larboard from a northerly heading means we turned west.'
'Yes.'
'On our voyage of discovery, had you decided to find Van Diemen's Land a second time?'
Bligh flushed angrily. 'You know quite rightly where we was heading, sir.'

'I did, Mr Bligh, but did the navigator?'

He clenched his fists and I was thankful for naval discipline which saved me from the attack. He knew my inference was against the late captain but he feared those listening might believe it questioned his own skill.

Cries came from the strand and a hush fell on the ships; sailors jumped to their feet, eyes fixed on the shore. Natives were rushing onto the beach from the village and in a few moments a mob shouted Kao's answer in a single word. Cowards.

The charge by three men in a canoe was vastly different when the word came from the lips of more than a thousand angry cannibals only a few hundred yards off. The men were consumed with hate and with fear, with an overwhelming desire to fight and a desperate understandable need to flee.

A *haka* started and the war dance and the attendant stamping of feet sent a percussion of shocks into the air and through our very beings. It stunned us as the hounds in full cry bewilder Reynard. But a greater fear was to be experienced, for suddenly large war canoes were being hauled from the village across the beach to the water's edge. Now the fox had to bite back or perish.

'Mr Bligh,' the captain cut through the arguments among the people of the ship. 'Signal to quarters.' The crew was given a task and men ran to their stations. 'Mr Bligh, sort out your best gun-layers. Your best, mark you.'

27

Oh, the sweet pain that scratches the heart when the gauntlet is proffered! The initial panic and the desperate urgency to be some place else, then the madness coursing veins and finally that sense of peace and superiority as the challenge is accepted and the brain adjusts and is as clear and cool as January's ice on a Wiltshire pond. The excitement of the battle to come, the complete irresponsibility as all problems are heaved bodily to one side, for nothing matters except the strategy of the battle and unquestioned survival.

And so the justice of a British court was broken by the natives, and once the fear was tasted and put to work, the men bent to the task of battle with an English determination. They ascribe fighting as a Hibernian trait; it is only modesty that keeps Albion bloods from rightly claiming the crown themselves.

The hatches were open and the yard tackles lowered partitions, decks, chairs, the aft-cabin's private heads, into the safety of the hold. The end of the foremast lying on the deck was lifted over to give more room to the battle-ward of the ship. The guns were changed from seats at the court-martial to rowdy despatchers of death.

The forward magazine was opened. Blankets were damped down and hung as curtains and two gunner's mates began dispensing the flannel-covered powder cartridges to the boy-monkeys who carried them carefully in leather pouches to the upper decks. A lantern glowed in the magazine behind a thick-glassed window, for the hint of a spark in this part of the ship could blow us to the shore.

The last of *Discovery*'s men were on their way to their own ship and many were the cries about us of who would have Kao's testicles for teacakes. But to collect such questionable delicacies the provider must first be snared.

'All landward guns to load with powder only,' Captain Clerke called. We were standing in the waist among the paraphernalia of the cannons, the mounds of ball, the smell of slow-match, the aura of sweat, as men moved the great guns about.

'Ready, sir,' Bligh shouted after inspecting the crews.

'Run out and fire!' the captain shouted.

The guns roared, smoke poured up from the larboard and the stench of gunpowder was so strong you could chew it.

'Reload!' Captain Clerke's voice came again. 'Powder only. Run out and fire in your own time.'

The trucks played their magic giant rhythm; the cartridges were loaded. Muscles stood out on bare shoulders and backs. The drum-roll shuddered and then a slam! as the cannons went to their limit, the mighty muzzles raping the gunports. The boom came again and we were hidden in that thick white edible vapour.

'Come, Mr Williamson.' We dashed for the quarterladder, climbed it and were slightly above the smoke. James was studying the beach with his telescope and then there were three glasses trained on the horde and we watched the broken lines as natives screamed and ran in all directions in their confusion, like disturbed ants when a cloud blocks the sun.

Lono's temple had spoken in a voice more terrible than on the day of his destruction and in the wildness of that moment they expected to die.

'What now, sir?' James said.

'Now we wait.'

'For anything in particular?'

'In the particular hope that they decide against tangling with us. I don't know what it did to their ears on the receiving end, but we're not strangers to it and I confess to be damn nearly deafened.'

'Pardon?'

'Look at them falling over each other,' the captain said.

'Even now they think they will die. God, if only they will take the message and go home.'

Bligh called from the ladder, 'What would you have the guns do now, sir?'

'I think,' Captain Clerke said slowly, 'that we had better be prepared. Yes. Mr Bligh have two of the guns load ball. Run them out, but no firing till my word.'

'Aye aye, sir.'

Just as so often happens in a sea engagement, we now had a resting period. I have experienced battles where the opening broadside is despatched. Then the ships drift apart and you are left to consider the accuracy of the enemy's shooting and imminent death while the vessels are sailed back into action. And we waited for the natives to leave for the hills in a panic; we willed them to be gone and avoid the carnage that must otherwise overtake them.

'Sir, Kao's on the strand,' James said. 'They're carrying his canoe down to the water.'

We raised our telescopes quickly. Natives rushed and shouted in the confusion, but Kao had watched from some safe place and his canoe was coming out into the bay.

'He wants a parley, sir,' James reported. 'He's waving a cloth.'

'We're not going out there to meet him. Perhaps a taste of a four-pounder might answer his conversation.'

'I don't mind parleying, captain,' I said. 'The marines can cover me from the ship. If we could come to terms it'd save a lot of blood; and a lot of ours too if they take to the sea.'

We argued; Captain Clerke let me win and the pinnace went over the side and soon we were rowing swiftly for the priest.

'You spit death at us, *e Hone*, but we are protected. Not one of my people was hurt.' His rowers' cock combs replaced their masks. A surliness showed their belief that the gods protected them.

As before, I could not discern weapons in the vessel. However, we were not so trusting; in the sole lay two musquetoons and if these guns which we call boat muskets did not break the shoulder of the firer – or knock out the bottom of the pinnace for they are very powerful – they would blast an enormous path through that fine double-canoe.

'I will be especially kind to you of the vessels. We will return the body you seek and we will not attack you.'

'Thank you, Mr Kao. I accept.'

'But you must do something for me. This is the bargain. You must admit that he was no god. That is all and you will be free and we will be friends.'

'Nothing would encourage me to speak against Lono. He was more than a god to me. And now Mr Kao let me warn you, when the temple speaks next time, death will rain on that beach and your people will be decimated.'

293

Kao ordered his boat away from ours. 'I think a display of our naval tactics will dissuade you from your determination.'

'Kao, you're a fool.' But he was hurrying for the shore. As we reached our ship, the noise of the resuscitated mob was growing rapidly.

I reported to the captain the conversation. 'I fear, sir,' I added, 'we cannot stop their murderous intent by humane methods.'

'Then let us attempt to teach them a lesson with the minimum of suffering.'

Bligh appeared at the top of the quarterladder. 'The war-canoes are being launched, sir.'

'Mr Bligh, load me two cannon with grapeshot, if you please.'

The master hurried back to the waist and we heard the order passed on. Then he called, 'Guns one and four loaded with grape, sir.'

'Have number one gun aim for the group of canoes nearest us at the water's edge.'

'Aye, sir.'

'Mr King, I don't suppose it was a Johnsonism that all which glisters is not gold....' He stepped over to the rail. 'It is a heavy heart that pulls this trigger,' he said and I replied Amen.

'Number one gun only to fire. Number one gun, at the specified target. Fire!'

Smoke clouded our view as multiple death flew at the beach. Many natives would not hear the boom, for grape with its several edges is a decimator of men and small craft. Four large canoes leaped into the air and disintegrated. Warriors burst in a crimson cloud. A cheer came from the crew, but Bligh silenced them quickly.

Near this scene of devastation were three fighting canoes, with a length each of around seventy feet, and rowers and warriors clambered onto them. They were being encouraged by a group of haranguing soapbox orators who would not let them believe their terrified eyes.

'Which guns have the ball, master?'

'Two and three, sir.'

'Number two gunner. Two fingers to the left of the eastward canoe. Several people are on a dais. These are your main rabble-rousers. That is your target. Do you identify it?'

'Aye aye, sir. The raised dais. I 'ave it sighted.'

'Number two gun only. When you are certain of your sight, fire.'

The gun roared almost immediately and my head rang with whistles and the ship swayed at the mooring. The gun-crews muffled the sound with head scarves, but it was not done for officers to take such precautions. The aiming was accurate; a bloody path cut right through the crowd, but still the remaining war-canoes ignored the decimation.

'Number four gun only. Adjust your quoin. Your target the remaining canoes. Do you have them sighted?'

'Aye aye, capt'n.'

'Number four gun only. Fire!'

Through the echoing I heard the captain shouting, 'Number two gun. Four fingers to the left; several platforms together. That is your target. As you bring it in sight, fire.'

The boom came from the ship and death tore in a second ribbon through the packed crowd. Canoes were smoking ruins, their occupants bloody mincemeat, and *Resolution* fought at her cable like a triumphant dog. The noise in my ears was a roaring pain, a gunpowder vapour choked us and I thought these natives might re-form and come out and kill each last sailor, but they can see from this power that the white man will come back; he will be the ruler. The mob ran in panic from the beach. They fought and pushed at each other, fearing that the great guns would sound again and their bodies disintegrate, and I could not look away from the horror.

'Mr Bligh, we'll wait for an hour,' the captain said loud enough for the crew to hear, 'and then if all is quiet, we will resume the hearing.'

A voice called for huzzas. 'No men, we do not want cheers for this; it is no victory when a man with a pistol kills an unarmed one. It is our shame that we were not able to quell them without bloodshed. Let's not congratulate ourselves, but thank God for his guidance.'

I said, 'Thank you, sir, for not firing further.'

'Well, I hope they've learned that the boom of exploding gunpowder may or may not spell death. Their quilted shields saved them from shot from muskets and they questioned the bangs. Now I hope they will fear all guns.'

'Your remarks about all that glisters, sir,' I prompted.

'Yes, but it wasn't Johnson, was it?'

'Thomas Gray, sir.'

Captain Clerke said, 'The decision to fire was the unhappiest of my career.'

'I feel quite certain it was the proper one, sir,' I tried reassuringly, because he is a good man. The illness will terminate his life before long and unfairly history will always leave him a poor second to our late captain.

Within twenty minutes we knew the natives were beaten, in this round. They recovered the debris of their fallen comrades; matchwood burned beside dark patches in the sand while they trekked inland. For the government of the ships, one enemy was laid low and we could not wait a moment before confronting the other. The hearing had to be resumed promptly so the men would see justice at work. The hatches were opened again and furniture brought up. Soon the hearing was under way. Bligh stood before me, no longer the fighting sailmaster, but an overfed warrant officer defending his fat pride.

I turned back our pages to the day the late captain declared a personal war on civilians. 'You tell us that at Nomuka the captain ordered you to arrest a chief, which you did. How did you remove him from the aft-cabin?'

'I ordered him out.'

'Try to remember, Mr Bligh. This is the island in the Tongan group. Now did you order him out?'

'I'm not sure.'

'Do you have the language to order him to do anything?'

'I remember now; I escorted him from the room.'

'Hastily, angrily?'

'Peaceably.'

'But you took hold of him. His upper arm, and I don't suppose he requested that you lay your hands on him?'

'I don't remember.'

'Did you take part in a conversation in the gunroom in Charlotte Sounds when Dr Anderson warned of the grave consequences of a European touching a Polynesian chief?'

'I can't say I recall it.'

'Then let me ask you something you may remember better. What truth is there in the belief about the ship that you put that winch handle among the clothes of the chief?'

The breeze seemed to halt in the shrouds and not a sound came from the sailors. Captain Clerke looked at Gore, who turned to me. 'Do you expect an answer, Mr Williamson?'

'Not with this witness's memory.'

'Then we will stand the hearing down till tomorrow.'

I was in a dream crossing the gunroom gloom when Rickman called from my old cabin. 'You've left a couple of things behind.'

'I don't think so.'

'Your looking-glass.'

'It's all right, I bought another from the slops.'

'And an old sign. From an inn, I think.'

'You can keep them, or throw them away.'

'They're a bit worn, I'll chuck them. But I thought they may have some sentimental value for you.'

'That's why I couldn't bear to have them back.' (And why I'll never be able to live in that cabin again.)

The fare was boiled pork and sweet potatoes, much improved by a sauce Collett made. We were polite in that aft-cabin. James, Bligh, me, Captain Gore, the new third lieutenant, and Captain Clerke in his berth. Today's action had drained his energy; the smoke would have had a most unhappy effect upon his lungs.

'Good God, gentlemen, I can only sip my wine but I expect you to act in a manly way with yours. A good flogging for any fellow without a hangover in the morning. Here, a toast: Rule Britannia!'

'And here's to you, sir,' James said, 'and the unlikely find of you in bed at such an early hour – alone.' They laughed and drank the claret and tried not to think of liquid of that colour we spilled.

'The ship has a strange bedfellow with this hearing. But the morrow will experience what it will. For the present, there's now which we should enjoy and exclude talk of that unhappy side.' And we politely excluded too the topic of gunning the islanders.

Our old dining table, as I thought of it, was against the berth and Captain Clerke was served on a tray, so that with a little imagination we were together for the repast; brother-officers.

'Who has an anecdote for us?'

'Well, sir. . . .'

'Shut up, John Williamson; not another word from you. If I should go to my maker now, by the heavens, it'd be with your words ringing in me ears.'

James said, 'Actually it was Mr Bligh who did the talking. Recounting about sixty pages of his journal.'

'Is that right, William? My, that's some memory. Isn't it, John Gore? But you'll have to do something about the voice. I closed my mind to it entirely.'

Bligh laughed politely. We were silent. Collett brought in fruit and Gore cleared his throat.

'An odd thing, gentlemen; we've found a pile of those canoe bird-masks. Can't think what they were doing on *Discovery*.'

'Souvenirs, I expect,' Collett said and went for the port.

'Listen, Gore, this is for you and it's important. When my time's arriving, you're to arrange the finest muse for me. And if I can't get up, you're to help.'

'Me?'

'Absolutely, even if it's only a bit. Half an inch within is a damn sight finer than six without.'

The port went round. Gore supported the bottle while Captain Clerke poured his; he joked politely about stopping the captain taking it all, but I was moved by the gesture and the tragedy of the man's failing power. Perhaps he was thinking similarly as he often claimed the disorder began at Fleet. 'Gore, make it an Israelite beauty. There could be some poetic justice in that.'

James pushed back on the after-legs of the Chippendale. It was obvious the old boy was gone because he never permitted it. 'As I sat listening to good old Bligh today – no, it's nothing to do with the hearing – I thought how bloody drab our crews are.' He sounded as if he had been diligent with the captain's order to drink deeply. 'Bloody drab, sir, and then I thought why. Because we don't have Omai with us.'

'Omai!' Captain Clerke shouted and we waited while he fought back a cough. 'By God, you're right; what an amazing nancy and those boys of his. . . .'

'That rumour about him. And them. You don't think. . . .'

'You are so American, Gore. Really. You could be looking into the eye of one of our lad's monsters and think. . . .'

'And think it's a *nguru*, sir,' I helped.

'Exactly; not that it's an error our Omai would make.'

James said, 'Who'll ever forget him shaking every man's hand before he got off into his gigantic war-canoe? And him standing there staring at the captain and tears just pouring down his face? He kissed the old boy on the cheek and minced off the ship.'

Captain Clerke said, 'Our late commander moaned a lot at having Omai on board, but he missed him afterwards.'

'I wonder if he's alive still,' I said quietly.

The bottle changed hands. 'It was getting him home that was so typical. Omai had been begging the late captain to let him make his entrance, as it were, on horseback. So we and the horses are taken ashore. Omai is wearing the most extraordinary clothes of the voyage. Tight. My God, he must have had half a dozen fellows pushing and squeezing to get him into the breeches. Satin shirt, a huge coat designed by a colour-blind nancy for Henry the Eighth, if you ask me. We mount, as Omai insists, at the shoreline and trot like kings up to the first village. People wave and shout, "Look there! They ride giant pigs." Of course he comes off; he was no rider. We tried to get him back on his mount, but those trousers were too tight.'

Chairs shifted for the end of the evening. 'A moment before you go,' Captain Clerke said to me, and the others left in various stages of intoxication.

'Take a seat, John. You know, it is best for you to win this prosecution. It will clear us all, but the main reason is to stamp out the idolatry. We must take the stuffing out of the people so they will be disunited enough to work.'

'Sir, I asked for a court-martial and instead I am appointed prosecutor of the captain I loved. Well, I'm following orders and my evidence will show the captain guilty of making a mistake and the understandable way it came about and that he paid for it with his life. But there can be no question of, well, disgracing him.'

'Wait a minute, young man, before you lose control. Winning a strong case is necessary for the well-being of the officers, of the ship and discipline and the one certain way to stop a mutiny.'

'I cannot destroy his memory.'

'Oh, rubbish. You've got a sharp tongue; use it. You'll not be harming anyone.'

'This is what Kao wants, to tell the people ashore he was an impostor and thereby disgrace him.'

'Kao's worried about discipline too.'

'I can't do it.'

'Yes, you can; you'll do it for us; or I should say for your people because I won't be alive long enough to benefit.'

'Emotional blackmail won't work, sir.'

'And an emotive charge is no counter. Look, eventually we'll have to oblige Kao; once they've recovered from the shock of the big guns, they'll find a new way to reach us and we won't stand much of a chance if they get waterborne.'

'Sorry, sir. . . .'

'Do it for the living so they may continue to live. In the long run it may not be a triumph for posterity, but we must try to survive now. I know it's far from an easy request and it's a brave man who'll wear your shoes afterwards. John, I can order you to do it, but I'm asking you.'

'Then order me to, sir, because I'm damned if I'll do it any other way.'

'Where the hell are you going?' The parchment face on the pillow seemed to fly across the room and was beside me, his breath on my face. His hand caught the door and slammed it. He stood in his nightshirt shivering, but from rage or distemper I did not know. Blankets and sheets were littered from berth to door like a maddened baboon's spoor. 'I forbid you from leaving this cabin till I am ready.'

28

*W*e faced each other feeling as foolish as storming lovers when the calm returns; a pale hand appeared from the nightgown and accorded my shoulder a friendly shake and the temper was gone. He pointed to a coffee pot, collected bedclothes littering the deck and went back to his berth. Dark hair like a bear's was neatly symmetrical up the back of white legs. I poured the coffee and we sipped it as if it were still hot and he spoke of how the old boy tapped icebergs for water in the Southern Ocean on the previous voyage. Gradually he manoeuvred the conversation, as one-sided as it was, back to his intentions.

For my part, I was trying to bar warmth from my heart, but how could I not be overwhelmed by compassion for his impossible task? To take on the most demanding role of his life, Captain Clerke needed to be at the peak of physical and mental strength. Instead his lungs were rotting and each breath could be his last. He was a weak, self-destroying scarecrow and it took superhuman courage and determination to put the affairs of the expedition ahead of his own hapless plight. Sympathy, as it had to, returned.

'What we are in dispute about, sir, is the reputation of the dead. Your philosophy seems to be that one's standing is as useless after life as the body. I contend that reputation is the only contribution of value many can hope to leave to life; yet I am likely to see out my three score years and ten, whereas for you who holds so little to this, the days appear very limited.'

'Then trust me, John. I'm seeing death as participant; I tell you it matters not a jot. When the light is snuffed there's only darkness.' We were quiet. I tried to visualise the end; total nothingness, sleep without dreams, one's body decomposing. It was simply not conceivable. 'Two chores await us: the natives and the crew. Let's start with the most difficult; the former. How can you convince them that Lono was merely a man?'

'That's the easiest.'

'I can't accept that.'

'The natives are as children. They still have imagination. Well, they must do for their lives are filled with the mumbo-jumbo of religion, superstition, high priests and the like.'

'Not so different from our own people.'

'The opposite, I think. Our people are from a civilisation where imagination is considered not manly. Here it is fostered and the common herd need it and use it, accept the legends and beliefs. . . .'

'I see what you mean: our encouragement is via the cat; we have to frighten and bully them. . . .'

'So if we use this side of the native mind we have a chance of success.'

'By God, young John, I believe you have a plan.'

'Yes, sir; it came to me after I was entertained to a . . . well, a spectacle which completely took me in at first and I thought, if I can be duped by what reason says is impossible, then how much easier for simple people.'

'What spectacle was that?'

'Oh, just something, but out of it came this idea.' And I explained how I thought we could answer Kao without risking the late captain's reputation. Captain Clerke forced back a reminder from his lungs which threatened several times to overwhelm him and enthusiastically directed me to a bottle of wine and we drank and I was committed without even knowing when I gave in.

Collett was summoned and sent to wake the master who entered the cabin looking not a little sleepy. 'Sorry, sir, any planetary phenomena?' He repeated the question and flicked his hair as if this might be a dream. 'I'll have to check.'

Bligh produced the necessary volume and was turning the pages. No eclipses, the moon was in her last few days and therefore too thin to be effective. Venus was an evening planet.

'There's always shooting stars, of course.'

'By God, yes,' Captain Clerke said. 'No shortage of them in these latitudes.'

'Yes,' I said, imagining my plan adapted to that phenomenon. 'Yes, it just could work.'

'It's a perfect, still night and there's no cloud,' Captain Clerke said. 'I think the time is exactly right to put your plan into action.'

'Tonight, sir?' And I felt a bite of nerves; thinking out a plan can be very different from executing it.

'Now, Mr Bligh; let's put you in the picture.'

'Picture?'

'Well, spectacle is more the word. We're going to entertain the high priest and his savages. Right now.'

Collett was despatched to bring the actors for our performance. I chose Shuttleworth for stage manager; he had an eye for the theatre and successfully controlled the concert many thousands of miles back. We had three principal actors for this presentation: James Millett, Master Bligh and the marine lieutenant. 'We open with you, Mr Bligh, and I've chosen you for you have a good head for heights. Millett, you come on next. I need a big man for this role. We have to heave you round the rigging on tackles but you're an experienced topman; it'll be easy for you.'

'In the middle of the night?' he questioned in a tired cockney accent. 'Don't fancy that, sir.'

'I think you will. I know you to be a convincing actor. You'll do well. And your part, Lieutenant Phillips, is the easiest. All you are required to do is to walk onto the beach and stand there with your mouth open as if you were talking.'

'And you?' he asked in a surly manner, sleep still holding irritably to his mind.

'I'll be right behind you in the boats, talking.'

'Why can't you go on the beach instead?'

'Because, Phillips, your stature declares you for the part.'

'I'm no actor.'

'I saw your performance at a certain party. You were cutely convincing, but your voice gave you away. We'll not make that mistake again. I'll repeat the plan and then we'll get into costume and begin. Sir, I'd like Collett to call all hands now.'

The boats went over the side. Crews rowed into the darkness towards *Discovery*. Her anchors were taken in while her foremast and mizzen were struck to the stumps. She was hauled by two launches to the southward, well clear of her usual anchorage. Her smaller stream anchor was lowered quietly and *Discovery* sat to it, waiting for the curtain to rise.

'Be careful bringing that powder up; only the gunner's mate most familiar with the magazine should work there. Shuttleworth, what can you do about brooms for the marines?'

'Brooms, sir?'

'I don't want them just draped in hammocks; I want them serviced with brooms too. They'll remove all footprints from the sand.'

Bligh became a short fat Captain Cook. Millett sounded and looked like a cockney Captain Cook. Phillips with a papier mâché false nose seemed the most convincing reincarnation. We had ten minutes to go and nerves were no less strained behind our curtain than they would be for a first night at Drury Lane. The principals were taking their places; the orchestra was ready and the lights were set to be ignited.

James King's Pinchbeck watch showed two minutes to go. An overture of sorts began at the pinnace just off the shore. The small glow of a match came first and then the familiar sound of a pyrotechnic being despatched. The rocket raced with a silver wake for the heavens in a most spectacular fashion and burst into a series of white and orange descending planets. The moon's waning crescent began to rise just as our almanac predicted. We heard calls of panic from the village guards. A second rocket rushed noisily into the air and worried shouts greeted this phenomenon from the land. The heavens were on our side. A number of meteors tore blazing across the black and we made wishes. The moon cleared the mountain resembling a cheese rind. Now suddenly an illuminated form appeared in the sky. Aaeei! A god comes from the heavens. The god wore the uniform of a Royal Navy captain. More torches were lit on *Discovery* and indeed it was a god in the form of man who appeared to be suspended in mid-air.

'Shite, we can see some of the rigging,' James said.

'The natives won't expect *Discovery* to be there; with only one mast up they'd never recognise her. No, I think we can rely on a bit of audience participation; they'll see what we want them to see.'

'That's some balancing act,' Captain Clerke said. Bligh bravely sat upon the truck of the mainmast, a much more difficult accomplishment for him than the spare frame of the unhappy lad on the other side of the world.

The moon was three fingers above the mountain and the lights were extinguished. Bligh's part in the spectacle was over. He would direct the resetting of top hamper and the return of the vessel to cover us, should our performance lose any of the slickness so far displayed.

James, Captain Clerke and I climbed into the boats beside *Resolution* and set off with muffled oars for the shore. I held tightly to the brass speaking trumpet; I had it wrapped in a towel for fear it might clang against Portsmouth's drum.

'There she goes,' James whispered and I looked back to our ship. Crew in the rigging lighted their torches and the officer appeared. Millett in the borrowed uniform and cocked hat balanced fairly convincingly on the topgallant yard hauled almost to the truck.

To the natives, the god had reappeared in another part of the bay, much closer to the beach. Now the yard was slowly lowered. Look there! The god has reached the floating temple and descends so gently to the sea.

'That's pretty realistic,' James said.

'I think I'd believe the thing just stepped out of the heavens onto *Resolution*,' Captain Clerke whispered. 'I mean, if I were an Indian.'

'And particularly if you'd just been dragged from your bed in the middle of the night to be told a god was arriving.'

The noise from the shore was encouraging in one way. The natives were accepting the spectacle for they cried in adulation as the spirit was almost at deck level. But their sounds were also worrying. Far greater numbers were about than I expected; we really only needed a handful to witness the rising of Lono. Small numbers were more easily duped and would certainly be simpler to manage should anything go wrong with our review.

I hoped they would not rush onto the beach too soon for Shuttleworth's boat should be there now, soaking the sands with our theatrical footlights.

On *Resolution*, James Millett as Captain Cook was at deck level and still he descended. The men held their lights over the sides, faces blackened with burnt cork. Millett's feet touched the water and some gunpowder in a tin exploded in an impressive flash. Lono was on his way to the seabed to walk ashore. The lights were doused on *Resolution* and Millett was pulled onto the ship.

'They believe it,' James said enthusiastically.

'By Jesus, I don't believe it and I don't like it.'

'You'll be all right,' I said. 'Just nerves, that's all.'

'I know it's bloody nerves because I don't want to be here. You said there wouldn't be many niggers.'

'Full house, Phillips, the only way to go on. But remember you're miming this; let them hear your accent and we're all washed up. And not just theatrically speaking.'

'I can hardly breathe through this nose thing.'

'Sssh, we're almost there,' James said.

'Breathe through your mouth, you clod.'

Stage manager Shuttleworth put a match to the footlights. They came on in an eruption of gunpowder and burned with the distinctive odour of seal-oil. A heavy cloud of smoke gathered a few feet above the ground and added a sinister touch I had not planned. Splendid. Phillips was pushed over the side of the pinnace and he walked through the low waves to the blazing sand, the stage. Enter the principal. Flames showed several hundred natives at the tree line. This far and they were a most attentive audience. The brightness of our lighting blinded them to our boats at the water's edge.

'If Phillips doesn't get a standing ovation for this. . . .' Kao appeared at the side of the people.

'Shite!'

'What now?' Captain Clerke asked.

'The arch-critic,' I said. We just had to hope he was a gullible native at heart. 'The show must go on.'

Someone prompted the audience; perhaps it was him. But the cry Lono was taken up and began a much repeated chant. Please don't keep going for too long; we have to be away the moment the footlights go down, as they say. The orchestra was ready. Portsmouth began a drum-roll which sounded unearthly owing to its unprofessionalism. Now the marines arrived and marched before Phillips, about turn and marched back; in their wrappings of grey hammocks they looked more ghostly than in my imagination. The sounds of hugely amplified breathing then a pained squeaking in the boat beside me came to life and the most regrettable violation of the bagpipes began. The instrument droned, sighed, wailed and screamed in a sort of agony and Portsmouth kept drumming. I raised the speaking trumpet. But I could not hear myself over the surreal strains of our orchestra of the heavens. Our musicians accomplished an extraordinary task probably only made possible by fear of upsetting the audience. We prised them out of our boat and into the launch without a beat, or a squeal, being missed.

The ghouls marched out of step in front and brooms tied to the waists gave them the appearance of untidy tri-limbed Martians. Behind us, bursts of gunpowder in tins flashed so that it appeared our floating temple breathed fire for the Reincarnated One. Phillips's tall wide body was before me; I hoped he would remember to mime when I began talking. I cleared my throat and lifted the speaking trumpet again. For a moment, as I looked through the flames and smoke, I wondered where our audience had gone. But they were face down in supplication and their respectful chants mingled with the cacophony of our minstrels.

The words of the 'voice off' were not written and till this moment, I did not know quite what to say. Kao wanted Lono to admit to being no more than a man, but that was not my plan for the sake of the late captain's memory and because it might upset the natives. That was something we must avoid if we wished to see the performance out.

Liberal wine tonight added convincing depth to my voice and the distortion of the speaking trumpet helped to make my impersonation of Captain Cook near perfect. Excellent, excellent, Captain Clerke was whispering behind me.

I began my address; I was here only briefly, I said, to bring a message of great importance. They must understand that there can be only one Supreme Being, as there can be only one high priest. This one god was a being of love and despaired of their continual warring; he was shocked by their treatment of the visitors and of their destruction of me, Lono.

You must, the Supreme Being says, turn from the desire for revenge. This passion comes from evil and is as destructive as embracing a poisonous snake.

They should beware false prophets but mostly those patrons of false prophets. When the liar blew his trumpet, a man could tell whether the note rang true. But he would not dispute the tone an apparent expert applauded.

Phillips was warming to his role; his arms swung in gesticulations; his platoon of ghouls marched to and fro theatrically and our orchestra maintained the extraordinary music; *Resolution* breathed fire and the audience remained prone, except for Kao, who stood to their side, and resembled a bent, emaciated reed of wickedness.

A voice came from one of the supplication. 'You are not a god, *e Lono?*'

'I am a child of god.'

'The high priest said you were a god.'

'There is only one god.'

'Then the high priest is patron of a false prophet?'

I kept an eye to the topic of conversation who I feared was trying to see through the costumery of our mummers. But his attention quickly returned to his flock when the spotlight turned to him. He became even more agitated when I announced, 'Our god is not happy with Kao; he will be punished for this.'

The voice shouted, 'Kao must die.'

At this, the elderly priest looked fit to expire, but I had as much retribution as could be expected. 'No, god spoke of tooth for a tooth, eye for an eye, but he did not speak to me of. . . .'

Kao came closer to the flame before Phillips. 'Your god says no to revenge,' he shouted angrily. 'He would not allow me to be sacrificed.'

I held to my silence and the temptation to let the devil die here was an unexpected bonus of our drama. However, in a political sense we were dealing with Kao. Now was not the time to have a power struggle begin; better the Kao we knew. . . . 'I have to say it is true, High Priest. God says nothing of death to liars.'

Kao looked unhappy and I thought he might attack our Leading Man. But his skin had been saved and he knew he would be free of Lono soon enough.

The spokesman for the natives called again, 'What of the death of Chief Kalimu?'

'It was a mistake by the visitors; he was not meant to die.'

'And the death of five chiefs on the beach?'

'That too was a mistake; it is easy for man to make errors.'

Kao shouted, 'But these are the priests of the water temple whose mistakes killed our leaders. Do you suggest god could make errors?'

'Is man not made in the likeness of god?' Which reply caused the irreverent gentleman to return to the tree line to play the nervous political game of trying to count votes before the ballot box is opened.

The voice from the crowd rejoined, 'These priests of the water-temple; *e Lono*, they are cowards, they will not fight.'

Our footlights were getting low, signifying a prompt end to our performance. 'God tells them not to fight and they obey against the strong desire to defend themselves. They have the courage to match your bravery.'

Hardly had this statement been hastily put, than Phillips suddenly bent down to the sand as if he were a Scotsman retrieving farthings. Sweet mother of Joseph came across the water's edge. At this amateur diversion, the skeleton priest ran forward to the dying flames and stared.

'Impostors! Impostors!' he shouted in an enormous voice. The natives nearest him looked up from their supplication. Kao repeated his charges and at that moment the flames expired. The beach had been brightly lit one moment and now night closed in; the emaciated moon found the only cloud about and obligingly hid its introverted light.

'Phillips,' I called. 'Come on. No time for curtain calls.'

The lieutenant rushed for the pinnace and the marines picked up their brooms and ran for the launch. The three sturdy lads keeping the Scots instrument inflated abandoned the extract and oars pulled from the beach. The watery temple puffed its last fiery breath, giving us an object to aim for, and we sped back to the greenroom.

'What went wrong, Phillips?'

'Dropped me focking nose.'

'I wish you people'd stick to the script.'

James leaned across to the sternsheets and whispered, 'What was the *puri* liberally spread through your talk? I've never heard it before.'

'The closest I could get to ruddy in Polynesian.'

The performance had been a success. Our Kao would not get much of his critique published for the audience were opposed to his view from the noise behind us on the beach. The dramatist was assailed with congratulations and I was pleased with the way it had gone. We had made light of what could have been a dangerous task. We imparted a little wisdom, some enlightened theosophy, answered their determination on revenge and provided an entertainment.

The episode was exactly the opposite of the duty the morning promised.

29

*L*ast night's fantasy began with nervous anticipation but this day dawned with a sickening dread. I was beginning on a perilous undertaking; the pendulum began and momentum would see through the retribution which we discouraged in others.

The satisfaction for indulging in *utu* was not sought by me. The weapon had been forced into my grasp and I would be the reluctant executioner.

I reached out desperately in need and I chilled in the draught of the shoulder turning away; rebuffs delivered so cruelly would supply the strength for my tongue. A brave man would wear my shoes afterwards, so Captain Clerke said. Well, no matter; I could not let the risk of my popularity hamper my duty to expose a myth which so dazzled the reason of the crew that they challenged authority. Father, they described him when he died and the people loved him too as navigator, discoverer, warm-hearted disciplinarian. When the court-martial was done by tomorrow afternoon, they would think very differently. And so – I admit in the name of honesty – I grew deaf to conscience.

'Your name is Thomas Edgar?'

'Aye aye, sir. Master of His Britannic Majesty's ship *Discovery*.' He was in his middle years; he wore the gentle lines of a sentimental man and his reputation was for fairer treatment than our zealous young bully.

'When we arrived among the beautiful islands of Tonga the Polynesians were at their light-fingered best. I think it is true to say more items were stolen from the ships here than elsewhere.'

'Aye aye, sir.'

'As one of the disciplinarians of the expedition, you were kept busy, I imagine.'

'From the thieving you mean, sir?'

'Yes, Mr Edgar.'

Edgar had freshly shaved for the hearing. He wore clean white trousers currently selling at our Sunday slops for 2s. 11d. They were cut off at the knees in the fashion adopted by the people of both ships. He wore stockings of jade and white and mules of faded green leather. An open poplin waistcoat exposed a hairless body. This muscled, pleasant man looked attired for a quiet stroll, but for my bidding he could be dressed to kill. The evidence he was to present would damn our late commander as a demon.

'Wasn't our fault, like the fault of the ship people, sir, that we lost so much. I mean we was surrounded by a good ten thousand natives while the carpenters and sailmakers was at their repairs ashore. These natives were peaceful and nice and they made us very hospitalised, but with that number there's bound to be a few light-fingered ones.' A permanent half-grin of good humour vied with the seriousness of his green eyes. 'Crikey, picture a scene like that in old England and I fancy the mob would have moved off with both ships and everything in them.'

The crew cheered and said good old Mr Edgar, you tell 'im. It was a suitable moment for levity for it would heighten the information about to surface.

'So there were punishments?'

'Aye, sir. A rum business. What I'm saying is, it weren't no fault of the artisans or the people. There were just too many natives around. Anyway, I'm sorry to report that the captain used the lash like he had never done before. I've got some of it wrote down, if I could refer to it?'

I turned to Captain Clerke. 'Do you mind, sir?' The awnings were in place; the captain's face shone grey in the light shade. He nodded, without changing that expression of weary nervousness.

'Well, Lieutenant Phillips lost all his bedding and the sentry got a dozen lashings. That's the way it was with ship's people. Then a native was caught stealing and he was whipped; then the punishment got more severe. If the native was a man of property he got the cat and was ransomed for hogs and fruit.' It was a task I particularly loathed; the natives' backs were skinned and then I as translator would have to repeat the unwholesome messages of ransom. 'Our second lieutenant, Mr John Rickman, tells me at the time, you know, Tommy, he's being guilty of great cruelty.'

I mentioned my feelings to the role duty required of me in the punishments, but I have to say that I was equally unhappy with my present task. One might expect insinuation to be a necessary weapon to win a hastily arranged prosecution. Yet with the simple honesty of Thomas Edgar, the facts emerged far more tellingly than I anticipated. 'You should only speak of what involved you personally, Mr Edgar.'

James King was standing. 'I would like to ask this witness if he can read and write?'

''Fraid not, sir. I been in the King's Navy since I were six years of age; my learning's been about sailing ships.'

'Then what's this nonsense about reading from notes? Are you trying to mislead us into seeing you as a scholar?'

'I got numbers wrote down of the floggings. I can read numbers; I'm not entirely unlearned.' The crew approved noisily and James conceded defeat; he had unintentionally underlined that Edgar was working-class honest and one of the people.

'Perhaps you would read these figures, Mr Edgar.'

'On June 13th a Tongan thief got three dozen lashes. On the 14th one got two dozen and another three dozen; on the 17th one got four dozen. On the 24th a native stole a tumbler and two wine glasses and got five dozen lashes. On the 28th we got hold of three old offenders who had stoned the sentinels and wood cutters.'

I explained, 'Some of the natives did not care for our presence for a variety of reasons, sir, and you may recall they would throw stones at the working parties.'

'One of them got three dozen lashes, the second four dozen, and the other one six dozen lashes.'

'Six dozen lashes! You exaggerate, Mr Edgar,' I said, although I knew he was correct enough. Nobody on the ships would forget that horrendous whipping.

'No sir, I got it wrote down.'

'Mr Edgar, six dozen is seventy-two strokes which, if you multiply it by the tails of the cat is six hundred and forty-eight assaults of the man's flesh.' The native was unconscious long before the end; the rope cut into his wrists so that blood streamed down his arms and joined the river at his back. The different punishers looked to the captain to see if he would settle for a reduced penalty, but he stared at the minced back and silently counted off the strokes. Worse was to follow. 'Are you telling me, that in this century a captain would sentence a man, and a civilian to boot, to such a wicked, inhuman penalty?'

'I'm no liar, Mr Williamson. I know it's seventy-two strokes because we didn't know how many six dozen was and had to work it out before the punishment started. Then the captain had him cut.'

The ship was silent. 'Cut, Mr Edgar?'

'He had the man's arm scored below the shoulder with a common knife that he might be known hereafter as well as to deter the rest from theft or using us ill when on shore.'

I asked the question we knew the answer to well enough. 'Did it work?'

'This man bore the treatment with all the fortitude imaginable, as indeed they all did.'

'Mr Edgar, did the punishments deter the natives?'

'They continued their insults and thefts to the last.'

I thanked him; I could take many other episodes for the notes he squinted at were copious, but he had done his duty. I turned to James, who looked genuinely shocked; when a great tree falls we think only of the terrible waste and forget the countless plants that could never grow in its shadow.

'Mr Edgar, do you believe our late captain could really have been the author of such punishments? Where in heaven's name did you dig up this libel?'

'I got the numbers from the Ship's Journal, sir, to make sure the old memory wasn't letting me down.'

My next witness was of a similar ilk. This was a young man with a heart that had not been destroyed by our discipline. The rough life had made George Gilbert look tough, but it was a facade, helped by a helmet of dark hair. He kept it pulled back severely and trapped in a queue at the nape.

'While we were at Tonga, Gilbert, you came to see me one day to lodge a complaint. What was its nature?'

'I just couldn't believe what was happening, sir. I'd been ashore like, and I was impressed by the people, the Indians.'

'I noted in my journal at the time that you said the natives displayed an elevation of the mind that would do honour to a European in the most distinguished sphere in life. Is that your fanciful turn of phrase?'

'Aye, sir. I think so.'

'Yet they were artful thieves?'

'I have to admit it was very prevalent.'

'So the captain had to do something?'

Gilbert's sensitivity took over just as it did when he stood on the quarterdeck. On that day tears overwhelmed him in a blend of shock and compassion. I could not pursue his complaint, the Navy doesn't work that way. But I noted it in my journal for I was every bit as repulsed.

'Sir, the captain punished in a manner unbecoming of a European. By cutting off their ears, sir . . .'

'Cutting off their ears?'

'. . . and firing at them with small shot or ball as they were swimming or paddling to the shore.' The marksmen fortunately seldom found their man. When they did a back would change colour and moments later dark fins boiled the sea and the screaming culprit vanished; offal and blood rose to the surface as the thief's epitaph.

'Are you saying the captain had ball fired at natives in the water?'

'Aye, sir. And he ordered ship's people to row after them and beat them with the oars and stick the boat hook into them.'

It was James's turn to question, but the rapidity with which these revelations were being heaped on our late commander's grave understandably bewildered him. 'Gilbert,' he struggled. 'Gilbert, where have I heard that name before?'

'My dad, I expect, sir. He was master of *Resolution* on Captain Cook's second voyage.'

James hastily sat down. His question had again only helped the prosecution.

'I would like to say, sir, that we found a method of punishment that did discourage the thefts.' I stood before the two captains. Clerke held my eyes, but Gore stared at his fingernails. 'A sort of Sampson syndrome, sir. We took off the hair of half of the head, half the beard and one eyebrow and this brought ridicule and contempt upon the thief. In contrast, the barbarous punishments produced pity and compassion for the thieves and deep loathing for us. I may say, sir, that it was you, Captain Clerke, who was first to introduce this novel treatment.'

The said captain looked thoughtfully at me, and after a moment or two called for a break in the hearing. He went to the aft-cabin with Gore and James. I made a note on my pad and followed, but Collett stopped me at the door. 'Sorry, sir, the captain's having a quiet word with Mr King.'

My following witness was Nathaniel Portlock, an American in the service of the King. I would use more of his evidence than the others for I expected him to add to the statements of the captain's inhumanity, and prove his truculence and the devastation of his black moods. This would build the likelihood of the reason for the late commander's death and so prove my case.

'How old are you, Nathaniel?'

'Five and twenty years, sir. I was mate in a merchantman, English sail, then I joined the King's Navy as an AB and I was promoted to master's mate of *Discovery*. I'm under Mr Edgar, sir; one of the finest of seamen.'

'We sailed to Moorea in company with Omai's war-canoe. At this island of misery, you were given a mission ashore. Do you recall it?'

'Aye aye, sir. I was on cat guard at the time for the captain.'

'Cat guard?' He looked a decade and a half older than his years, but he was good-looking for all that; his bleached hair and teal eyes were accentuated by a deep sun colour.

Captain Clerke interrupted, 'It's a simple matter, Mr Williamson. The Polynesians had never seen anything like a cat before and they were highly prized. We had a great need of the cats because they were excellent ratters. I had already lost six in the previous archipelago as it was, so I appointed men to guard them. Now let's move on.'

Portlock took the hint. 'I was on patrol with you, Mr Williamson, on the instructions of Captain Cook.'

'What was the reason for this patrol?'

'The late captain was very much distressed over the loss of a goat. A party was despatched to the shore to search for it.'

'You may recall, sir,' I explained, 'that this island had been ravaged by a war fleet. The trees were bare and many houses razed. Food had been taken and the inhabitants were in a poor way. The chief here, Mahini, was treated kindly by the late captain, who gave him a large linen morning gown, the like that some people wear in their bedrooms. The chief was very taken with our goats and asked for one. The captain refused and. . . .'

'And why did the captain refuse?' James jumped to his feet and struck out in confusion like a swordsman in the dark. 'I think it is grossly unfair when only part of the facts are presented. The late captain was a great friend to the islanders, even if he was harsh on the question of thefts.'

'I am sorry,' I returned. 'The captain refused because there were not sufficient goats left.'

The lieutenant pushed his chair back noisily as he stood again. 'There were not sufficient goats remaining because there were other islands to be visited and it was part of King George's plan to have these animals spread widely across the Pacific. And, Mr Williamson, you should know that to give the chief one goat would be foolhardy. He would need a he- and she-goat to make the present worthwhile.'

Portlock was sitting on the wooden chair, a leg crossed, his head going from one speaker to the other.

'One of the animals went missing. Natives accused Mahini with the theft and the captain despatched a threatening message and the goat was given up the next day.'

James said, 'Plus the thief, as requested by the late captain. And here we can see his mercy. The native said he snatched the goat because some of the sailors stole his breadfruit and coconuts. The sailors denied it, but the captain accepted his word and released him.'

I returned Portlock to his evidence. 'That afternoon, two goats grazing ashore were sent for. One was missing.'

'You mean that the day after the original goat went missing – while the captain's threat was being transported to Mahini – he had two more goats taken ashore for grazing?'

'Yes, sir?'

'Did you not think this was rather baiting a trap?'

'All I thought, sir, was it's easier than carrying lumbering great armfuls of grass to the ship. We had only to fling the brutes over the side and they swam ashore.'

'So now another goat has gone missing.'

'The natives said Mahini was the thief again. The captain was furious because the missing goat was a she and big with kid.'

'Portlock,' Captain Clerke interrupted, 'you're a good fellow; please try not to speak so slowly.'

'Aye, sir,' Portlock said cheerfully. 'What happened now was that the captain asked Omai and some local people what he should do to retrieve the goat. Each of them said without hesitation that we should go ashore and shoot everyone we could. The captain, of course, was loath to do that and a party of thirty-five men was gathered and set off overland. In the meantime you, Mr Williamson, was in charge of the three armed boats and we went round the western part.'

'Portlock, I want you to repeat something which is very important to these proceedings. Tell me again the numbers involved.'

'In our group, sir, three armed boats.'

'And in the party that the captain himself took?'

'Thirty-five. All armed.'

'Mostly marines?'

'No, sir. Mainly sailors because he wanted a few good shots.'

When catcalls and laughter finished, Clerke stopped us for luncheon. Hungry men rushed from the waist, but I returned to the desk for a few moments to make a note of exactly where Nathaniel Portlock had got us to. It was only necessary now to bring out the evidence of wanton damage.

When I reached the gunroom table, the messmates were finishing and soon I was alone at my end. Samwell was the only other diner. For some reason I was thinking of him advising us all not to turn our faces from warring natives. I pictured handsome features turning away from the fury to wave to. . . . Samwell brought his plate along beside me.

'Cogitating?'

'On some advice you gave once, and . . . well, it's of no matter.'

'As the great bard put it. . . .'

'David, I want you to give a little evidence for me.'

'Stand up before those people? No thank you.'

'Come on, it won't hurt you and I won't keep you for long.'

'John, are you happy with what you are doing?'

'It's going very well; I'm delighted. We're winning.'

'But who's winning?'

'I'm going to call Bligh again.'

'He won't like it. He's furious about yesterday.'

'I want to ask him about the damaged foremast.'

'What exactly?'

'Cleveley repaired it at Nootka Sound.'

'So?'

'You're missing the point. The foremast was temporarily repaired ten months ago. We were here for repairs and it wasn't touched. It breaks and we are forced back to this anchorage. The most inhospitable for us in the world.'

'We knew we were not altogether popular when we sailed.'

'Don't you see? In the last few months his grip on the ship and the whole husbandry of the voyage had slipped.'

'The captain?'

'Who else?'

'I'd say the officers. Why in heaven's name would they not report to the captain the deterioration of the foremast? You know, if you bring this subject up at the court-martial you'll show how lax the officers had become and the extra burden he had to carry through them.'

A squall came across the bay and the ship was deluged. Marines patrolling the now peaceful bay in a launch returned to change their clothes. The hearing resumed with steam rising in small clouds from the sunny side of the awning.

'At about three o'clock the captain's party came down to the water to speak to us.' Portlock was continuing with his account. 'It was exceedingly hot and they were much fatigued with their march over mountains. They met with several troops of Indians who were troublesome but dispersed when a few muskets were fired over their heads. They burned twenty houses and many war-canoes but the captain was cautious not to destroy anything but what the chiefs said belonged to the people concerned in the theft.'

'These chiefs, Portlock. Were these the same advisers who recommended shooting anyone who could be found on shore to avenge the theft of one goat?'

'I believe so, sir. The next day I went with the carpenters who broke up three or four canoes on the foreshore and the captain announced we would not leave one canoe on the island if the goat were not returned. Later the captain had us march to the next harbour where we smashed canoes and set fire to some more. When we got back to the ship, some natives approached with the goat.'

'And that was the end of the matter?'

'Thankfully, sir. Our people said that the captain regretted it as much as the natives. We sailed off, the two ships and the mighty war-canoe, the *Royal George*.'

'The canoe Omai hired?'

'Aye, sir.'

I looked to James King to see if he had any questions, but he stared studiously at the desk. The ship was absolutely still as we relived that troubled visit to the beautiful island. A cough came from behind me. George Gilbert was standing among the seated crew.

'I'd like to say, sir, that he seemed to be very rigid in the performance of his order which everyone executed with the greatest reluctance except Omai, who was very officious and wanted to fire upon the natives.'

'Are you suggesting that Omai, a native passenger, had been giving the captain advice?'

'Omai had plenty of advice to give. I wouldn't know if the captain followed any of it.' He shifted on his feet as though embarrassed for passing the opinion, but he could not stop. 'It was all about such a trifle as a small goat. I can't well account for the captain's proceedings on this occasion as they were so very different from his conduct in like cases in former voyages. That's all I want to say.'

The people remained quiet. The breeze caught a corner of the awning and made it crack; men gazed ahead or at the deck unseeing. Captain Clerke stood slowly and came to the front of the table, and leaned against it. 'We must remember that it was the natives' ridiculous conduct and absurd obstinacy in keeping the goat which brought such damage, inflicted on them in retaliation and punishment as they will not recover from these many months. It was wholly their own seeking. We solicited their friendship at our arrival by every social attention and were upon the best of terms till the devil put it in their heads to fall in love with the goats. When they had taken these, every gentle method was tried to recover them and the consequences of their obstinacy very clearly and repeatedly explained to them before any destructive step was taken. Their strange perverseness in this business is, I think, equally foolish and unaccountable.' He returned to his chair and drank some of the water Collett had replaced.

'Dr Samwell, you are the senior surgeon of the voyage and a journal-keeper of note, you adhere rigidly to precise recordings of our history, is this so?'

'I thank you.'

I took from memory extracts from my journals. A statement by the late captain in the aft-cabin at Van Diemen's Land that when women were available, the native men offered them up. Did he see anything prudish in this to suggest that the captain opposed the men having access to the women?'

No, Samwell said, on the contrary. He interpreted the meaning to be that it would be foolish for men to press their attentions in the chaste atmosphere of that society.

I asked him of remarks the captain made off Zealand about men not having intercourse with the natives there. Was there anything unnecessarily censorious in the captain's remarks?

No, said the doctor. In fact he said he allowed the men to lie with native women because he could not stop it. A question of morals was not involved.

'Did the captain's attitude change towards the men's natural desire?'

'It changed at first because he was concerned – as we all were – with the pox being spread in the islands. Then gradually we discovered that the malady was present among all the people.'

'Did he try to stop the people's pleasure then?'

'He still held to his ideals that a man I named as carrying the venereals would not lie with the women.'

'And that was the end of the matter?'

'There were stipulations about getting a standard price for the women as the cost would fluctuate and there was of course a limit to the trinkets and gifts on the ships.'

'There was never a period when the captain said, "There will be no further sexual communion between our people and the natives"?'

'I fear there was. It was not effective of course and could only lead to a great deal of trouble.'

'Did you speak to the captain about it?'

'I did.'

'Would you care to relate these conversations?'

'I would not.'

'Presumably you pointed out that while there were women about it was perfectly normal and healthy that our men would want to take up with them?'

The doctor was silent.

'On again, off again, how do you explain this type of behaviour, Dr Samwell?'

'Men do not always adhere to one attitude; do women ever stick to the one course?'

'I can't help thinking that this boxing of the compass of his mind might well have been a sign of approaching madness,' I said, trying to camouflage the suggestion with the utmost gentleness in my voice.

James King swung towards me and was half standing, uncertain whether to continue upwards and protest. His mouth was open in shock; but I had a job to do, as unpleasant as it was, and there was little time for niceties; and I thought: if this bothers you, James, just wait till you see where our David is being led.

I was a little surprised that Samwell for his part showed no alarm at the question. He adopted the mantle of Samwell the Intellectual and replied in the way of One Learned. 'We know so little of madness; we find that bleeding a patient from about the temples can help and behaviour that had become untypical might return to normal. We have much to learn.'

But knowledgeable David also wore the look of a duellist who dreads but a single action. One experiences it when the steel locks (*sentiment de fer*), a distinct electrification running to the hilt with a message from the opponent. It might be second intention attacks or a feint, but he who guesses this fear can quickly end the encounter. When the loathed stroke threatens, the adversary – often as accomplished a swordsman as could be found – crumples. I recalled our last duel before Phillips staggered into the cabin drunk and I felt intuitively the subject he feared.

All I said was, 'You have spoken in the past, have you not, of a certain pain?'

The composure dropped; the pomegranate complexion flashed and his guard was lowered in perplexity. 'Damn your eyes, Williamson.' It was the first time I had seen him so rattled, although he came close on the previous encounter. 'You're going back to the headache business. I'll not speak to it.'

I continued gently, 'I am talking about a malady, Dr Samwell, which explodes in the mind and he – the victim – cannot think clearly. That to me seems a madness, even if medicine has a different interpretation.'

He took a step backwards as if my words were shaped as a hanger. 'I want to clear up the matter of the maladies but you can only think of your treatment by parasites. Do you really believe the proboscis of a leech could penetrate the skull and reach the seat of the madness?'

'You, you offend me.' It was a weak parry.

I sliced a superficial cut. 'Then don't let me, good doctor. Let's move on, if you are afraid of incriminating yourself, if you refuse to assist this court-martial.'

'Sir, there is no such wish,' his voice almost falsetto, his round red face turned hopelessly to Captain Clerke. 'Of course I will answer whatever. . . .'

He was subconsciously preparing himself for the *coup de grâce*, I thought. 'Very well,' I lunged. 'Was he just a little mad?'

'No,' he countered with eyes closed.

'You don't know.'

'I wouldn't know,' he stammered, 'but I think. . . .' He was now completely upset, so quite malleable for a telling change of direction. And I knew the swordsplay that could not lose.

I demanded, 'Did the captain consort with native women?'

'Sir!' James King acted as Samwell's assistant, standing and hammering the desk. 'I cannot hear an officer speak this way of another.'

James brought officer brotherhood out in public so the umpire had to decide against the second's interruption.

'We've heard the captain had stern views,' Captain Clerke said reluctantly. 'Let us hear if a double standard was at work.' And I knew the referee had not guessed the trickery of my Colichemarde blade.

'I repeat then, Dr Samwell, did the captain have native women?'

He sidestepped, *in quartata*. 'How would I know?'

'Did he tell you he had?'

'No.'

'Did you ask him?'

'No.'

'Did you never swap experiences?' It was another feint to clear his heart and the tension of the impending kill alerted the spectators. The ship was still but for this ringing of words that would send the captain's reputation to a searing death.

'No.' The parry showed his fight was almost gone. I planned a last cut. 'Would you swear on the Bible that he never touched a native woman?'

He was exhausted. His sword was scarcely able to deflect me. 'Yes, I think so.'

I took in the sweet air and allowed a moment of silence to pass so that the last scream may be even more shocking. I could see his ribs and I hardly need count them for the position of the panicking heart. I screamed within 'For King, for my ship, for the good of us all!' and I trust with all my energy. 'What about any of the crew?' I shot through the shirt, skin, a gap in the ribs and impaled the heart which throbbed on the blade and the tip of the sword severed the spinal cord of the deceased's reputation.

James King was hammering at the wooden desk-top and Captain Gore shouted but it was lost in the uproar. Samwell collapsed against the bulwark. Captain Clerke surveyed us with grey bewilderment; he'd got what he demanded and could not decide whether to chastise me or himself or the rioting audience. Perhaps it happened too quickly; the reputation was as ripped up and wasted as an exploding topsail in a storm, and if he was wrong about the innocence of defaming the dead, it was too late now.

The tumult continued, but the time was right for the winner to confess he only wished to injure the opponent and to offer apologies to the lamenting family. 'I object, sir, most strongly. My God, my question is entirely misconstrued. I was asking the surgeon if others about the ship might also have shown such gentlemanly chastity. How Mr King could possibly. . . .'

I had won, of course. I salvaged myself from an unpleasant fate and saved the insinuation. Every man-jack on that deck would harbour doubts about our late captain's manliness, the worst slur there could be, ironically, in a sodomy-sodden service. The common people of the ship believed that healthy fighting gentlemen left their balls on shore in their middle-class homes.

The consumption struck Captain Clerke as if an avenging hand reached for his lungs from a watery grave. He coughed a bucketful of dark, broth-like blood, and King, Samwell and Captain Gore helped him to the aft-cabin. I sat alone. I wiped specks like soup from my notebook. All that remained was the massacre on the strand. Did madness take a hold on that beach and so cause a dereliction which put us all at risk?

30

One last witness to complete the case for dereliction; one final duel in the cause of sweet revenge. I had sufficient satisfaction from Kao; let him find his way in one piece from the religious maze of our spectacle. Bligh's reputation for navigation (and his pride) suffered from my examination and that was price enough for the role he commandeered. Now my blade was honed for a conclusion for Mahia.

If the fear of my standing among the people lingered before, it was gone today. I was denied an invitation to last night's dinner at the aft-cabin and in the gunroom I was no more than a fly on the grubby timbered bulkheads. My God, as a Royal Navy officer I did my duty, that is all, yet none would address me. So now nothing will obstruct my questioning this last witness and settling once and for all the affair of Kealakekua Bay.

'My name is Molesworth Phillips. I am twenty-four years of age. I was born in County Kerry and I have the honour to serve His Majesty's Marines, Chatham division. I began my seafaring life in the Royal Navy, but Mr Banks – the good friend of the late captain's – recommended my turning to the marines. I am a bachelor, sir, and affianced to the sister of Lieutenant Burney of *Discovery*.'

Summer brightness lit our packed decks, but a darkness more dank than any English winter depressed my soul as I watched the large clumsy frame settling into the reluctant role of final, perhaps hostile witness. I was not afraid; his will could not match my determination. I stopped his evidence and turned to our judges, the captains, but neither would return my attention.

'On our recent Valentine's Day, sir, the first light of dawn showed that natives had made off with the cutter from *Discovery*,' I said. 'Our late captain had planned a stormy visit to the island for relations between ourselves and the islanders were at a very low level. He spoke of punishments and his intention was to spill blood; nobody knew how far he meant to go.'

I turned to Phillips and said impassively, 'When news of this latest and most audacious theft came to him, he lost his temper completely. I think that is a fair statement?'

'Aye, sir. He ordered me to have a band ready to go ashore. I had not heard of the theft at that stage and I was more than a crumb dumbfounded at being called out before breakfast.'

The story of our adventure finished within an hour of Phillips's wide hand holding the Bible. The rest of the voyage of *Resolution* and *Discovery* was a dénouement. Yet in this final scene, as relayed by Phillips, fate was an odd playwright. Our leading characters were unfortunately off-stage. William Bligh commanded a launch ensuring canoes did not leave the bay. James was on another part of the island guarding carpenters hewing the new mast. David Samwell was on board *Discovery* with Captain Clerke. These two had ringside seats, as it were, but the performers appeared smaller than fighting cocks; even so they saw the captain going down. Captain John Gore was on *Resolution* and oblivious of the event until too late. The last European in a position to help the captain was this witness. He would tell in his own words, reluctant or not, what happened. But first, the cause of the captain going ashore.

'Was not a watch kept on the stolen cutter?'

'She was a large boat and easier to leave in the water. An armed guard was maintained beside her, and to be certain, the boat was filled with water. Somehow natives reached the cutter in the dead of night, bailed her out and got clear away.'

'A guard was kept over the boat, but the natives were able to steal it?' I shook my head. 'Very well, now on to the landing party. What marines did you have with you?'

'Me, the sergeant and corporal and seven privates, a mate and boat's crew armed. We went in the pinnace in your command and the captain ordered a boat which lay at the point to give support.'

'Did you know the purpose of your mission?'

'The captain's famous for telling nobody nothing at all.'

'But you guessed he was taking you to arrest the King?'

'We'd arrested chiefs before, sir, and held them to ransom against stolen items.'

'And kings?'

'No, never, but I mean. . . .'

'Did you feel you had a sufficient army to take on a king?'

'I wasn't asked to recommend the number; that was the captain's choosing.'

'Ten marines to arrest a king. You heard, I'm sure, yesterday's evidence that to retrieve a pregnant goat, the captain took thirty-five men plus armed crew in boats.'

'It was early in the morning and we went straight into the pinnace. We lined up on the beach and marched after the captain. He stopped two boys and asked where the King was and only then did I guess his plan. I don't mind telling you sir, I thought, by Jesus, there's going to be some trouble now.'

The pinnace touched the sand and the landing party went ashore. The village was busy. The islanders gave the captain a cheery hello, but he was in a state of high dudgeon and would not answer them.

Phillips continued, 'I was nervous, but as we marched along natives fell on their faces, as they so often did.'

'They took him for a god?'

'Lono, god of the sea, they named him.'

'How did he come to be seen as a god?'

'I heard they took him for that on his previous visit. He learned the legend of Lono and when we returned, we sailed round the islands as the god is supposed to and then the niggers knew for sure he was Lono.'

Captain Clerke slowly stood; he was pale and had difficulty in holding himself straight. 'No, Lieutenant Phillips, I don't want to hear what sailors out of discipline told you.'

'Sorry, sir. Well, they took him for a god and walking towards the King's lodgings, I was glad of the protection it afforded.'

I said, 'You had no doubt that they accepted him as a god and yet they wanted us out of the bay and gone. It doesn't sound much like hospitality for a god.'

'It wasn't like that, sir. We'd taken every scrap of food off the island. Not that we wanted to; they forced the presents on us, on the god if you like. They knew they would starve if we delayed. . . .'

'Lieutenant Phillips.' Captain Gore pushed himself up at the desk. 'Captain Clerke asks me to interrupt. Please return to the matter of the happenings that led to the tragedy.'

'Sorry, sir. It's just that Mr. . . . .'

'Just continue please, Lieutenant Phillips.'

'We marched along to the King's house. Mr Williamson remained with the pinnace so the language was difficult. But we asked some savages to tell King Kari-ipu that we waited without. He didn't come for a little while, so the captain sent me into the house. It was not a job I appreciated. But there was the old fellow and I signalled that I'd like him to come outside. The captain had the better of his temper now. He took the King's hand and asked would he accompany us to the ship. No harm would befall him, he said, and I think the King understood. Old Kari-ipu wore an expression of friendship and tranquillity and the captain said, "These people are entirely innocent of the theft of the cutter, but we must get the King on board."'

Phillips moved as if his boots were too tight and looked at the chair for witnesses. I thought he might ease that bulk into it, but he changed his mind.

'I was greatly relieved on the first point, I can tell you. If we was to capture some of the people or burn their habitations in revenge, none of us would be here now. There was a whole lot of them around. However, on the second point, the captain meant that him and me and nine of the boys was going to kidnap the King in broad daylight.'

Phillips was reliving the experience like an old seadog regailing landlubbers and his overdeveloped chest pumped as he spoke. The crew watched silently and Bayley's quill scratched rapidly. The rattle of sand drying ink reminded me of countless times in the aft-cabin.

'The King sat down and natives encircled us. Two were very active in keeping order among the crowd which was swelling all the time. I could not make out the words, but it seemed they knew our plan right enough and naturally they were not for altogether going along with it. I know the marines was praying hard because our situation seemed hopeless but the captain looked quite uninvolved; maybe he expected more from his own prayers. However, we must have all been beseeching in the wrong direction for at that moment came news which sealed our fate. News came that a chief called Kalimu had just been killed by *Discovery*'s boat. We could not believe it. But the niggers accepted it all right. The captain remained looking calm but there was murder in the air. Some village girls were flirting with men in the launch and they ran away; they knew what was in store for us. I tried to confer with the captain as to which was the best course of action, though trying to think of any became impossible. An old priest pushed through the mob and stood by us and began to sing loud. And I mean loud, sir. It was raucous and horrible. The captain shouted at him to stop the claptrap. I slapped my hands over his evil mouth and then I saw what was his purpose; he was distracting us from the prospect of a great many being armed. Weapons were coming from nowhere; daggers and spears and clubs. Handfuls of stones were being passed around.'

He stopped to recover his breath for he was talking very quickly. 'I cried to our commander, "They're putting on the mats." These were the thick coverings they wore as armour which they believed shielded them from our bullets. "We'd best make progress to the boats," I called, but by the heavens the savages here was thicker than priests on a nun's. . . . Well, anyway, there must have been a good two thousand by now and we had thirty yards to reach the water, to our boats.'

James King stood slowly at the desk, hypnotised by our unveiling tragedy. He followed Phillips's every word, seeing the portrayal through the witness's eyes. I heard the marine's account, of course, but I saw it as I saw it that tragic day just off the beach.

'I didn't know what to do. Holy mother of Mary, I cried, but it was no use seeking any help but our own. Suddenly it struck me; I'd do what they least expected. I shouted, Platoon, atten-shun! And the boys being good fellows, God rest their souls, cried one-two. This is to count off the moves. . . .'

'We are aware of this; please continue.'

'I ordered, "Slope Arms!" and they cried "one-two-three, one-two-three, one-two-three", as is the way in the marines,' and Phillips was sloping an imaginary rifle. ' "Quick march! Left-right, left-right." And I marched those marines down to the water as if we was on parade and so help me the natives parted and let us through. "Right turn," I called and we formed up at the edge of the water by some rocks." He swung his arms in short staccato movements like a child pretending to parade.

I faced this brute with a poorly balanced Tower cutlass and later with the Hawkins-Wilson .67 pistol; on three separate occasions I held his life in my hands and I permitted him to live. I had the upper hand in words, too, yet my superiority was slipping. It had little to do with his questionable skill. I was being mesmerised; my mind kept leaping to the final moments of Captain Cook and I fought from the entrancing like a cachalot from killer whales, yet I was weakening. Perhaps I had not allowed for that idiosyncrasy they call the luck o' the Irish.

I could not hold from saying, 'I ordered the pinnace off to give you room. We backed the oars and you marched down through those surprised natives and I could hear the flintlocks cocking in the other boat.'

Phillips continued as if my intrusion had been rehearsed and we were actors merely reading a play together. 'The captain held onto the old King's hand and they walked peacefully behind us like a father and son on a common.'

Again I was compelled to add, 'I shouted to the men in the boats, "Don't fire!" If we started shooting we'd as likely hit the captain as spark off a massacre.'

James too was trapped in these hypnotic final events, as if Phillips and I were entering hand-painted slides into a magic lantern to replay the terrible scene. James stepped over from the table and stood between us; he studied Phillips's face during his remarks and then scrutinised mine.

Phillips continued, 'Two of the King's sons were with us, just nippers like, and I thought thank God because the niggers can't attack while we're surrounded by royalty. But it was an awful scene and so unreal. The captain and the King hand-in-hand and the nignogs – sweet Jesus, simply hordes of them – packed round us. Then the bloody priest started his infernal noise again, but this time I couldn't get at him.'

I could hear the unnerving shriek even now. 'It was like the voice of the devil,' I said and James's breath was cool on my cheek. 'And then one of the King's wives arrived, screaming and forcing her way through the crowd. She reached him and made him sit on a canoe at the water's edge.'

Phillips said quietly, 'She was crying and pleading with him and tears were like rivers down her sweet plump cheeks. But he, like the captain, looked happy enough though I don't know why.'

The script returned to me. 'She spoke quickly but I could interpret, even through that unearthly moan. She said we meant to kill him just as we slaughtered Kalimu. Then a fool in my boat stood up and shouted that he would shoot the priest dead if someone would pick off the woman. I knocked the sailor down and said I'd kill the first bastard who opened fire. I had them back the pinnace further off.'

'I was trying to direct things on land when I saw your boat going astern, Williamson. I thought I'll shoot that bugger if I get a chance.'

This insolence shocked James back to the court-martial. 'Get on with your evidence,' he snapped.

'The King looked unhappy now; he knew events had gone too far. Just then I recognised a face nearby, an unpleasant rogue if ever there was one; he was trying to keep hidden a dagger in his cloak, yet letting the others see it so they know what he planned. "Captain," I called, "watch out behind you; the nigger's armed." But the captain said nothing. "Shall I shoot him, sir?" I called and it took a lot not to squeeze that trigger I can tell you.'

Phillips re-enacted these moments and shouted to match the noise of the mob in our memory.

'This villain kept coming for the captain, as slowly as a snake. By Jesus, I couldn't wait for no orders. I advanced on the turd and struck him with the butt of my old brown bess.' His hands brought down an invisible musket. I could hear the skull cracking.

'There was a roar from the mob at that,' I said. 'Another fellow grabbed the barrel of your musket and you two fought for it. On my pinnace the men were going crazy; I had to keep pushing them over to stop them firing. I heard the captain call, "Don't shoot or we'll have to kill a great number." But he was still in some sort of trance.'

Phillips was wrestling with the native. 'I got my piece free of the nigger.' The butt slammed into his stomach; the youth folded over, could not recover his breath and choked to death. 'The captain turned to me and I swear he was on the point of ordering us into the boats, but at that very moment a nigger beside him threatened to throw a boulder. The captain levelled his double-barrel musket, but Jesus, he took so long I thought his brains would be dashed out. Then he fired.' Phillips threw his hands over his eyes to hide the mistake.

'It was a huge blast,' I continued. 'The noise stunned the crowd and stopped the confounded priest who scarpered. The King was hastily moved away and the native who thought he was dead stood there, eyes wide as pewter plates.'

Phillips's fists dropped. 'But it was the barrel the captain loaded with shot which could not pass through the mat-cloak. At this the nigger advanced with a spear. They were all watching and hungry for blood. They had seen for themselves what happened and believed they were safe from musketfire. As luck would have it . . .'

The marine lieutenant held his imaginary musket which with the power of hindsight was proud with bayonet, and if history allowed dramas to be played a second time would be bloodied steel.

'... as luck would have it,' he repeated, 'the captain bravely clubbed the bugger down with his musket instead of firing the second barrel. By Jesus, a courageous act of clemency, of enormous charity, to spare the nigger's life under such provocation.'

It was yet another horrible error that ensured the unavoidable end. I shouted, 'But it was seen as us accepting that the muskets were useless against these natives. That one action confirmed their hopes: a higher god was preserving them from angry demanding Lono.'

Phillips was not listening; his eyes were glazed and he stabbed another Indian in his mind's battleground. 'It was courage to sway us all,' Phillips intoned in a voice that sounded quite drunk.

'Courage? Charity?' I challenged and the witness remained on the beach till I repeated it louder with exaggerated derision.

James's face was white as he waited helplessly for the fatal blow. Then anger burned, starting at his throat and flooding quickly across his features. 'Exactly!' he shouted and flecks of hot spit stuck to my lips like shaving-cut tissue. 'Exactly his gesture; exactly the great charity he always showed to natives.'

'Charity? My God, James, a man storms ashore with a Lilliputian army to snatch a king from under the noses of thousands. This is the charitable man who expected blood to flow so he could teach them not to steal. *Not to steal*, Mr King, and this from charitable visitors whose appetite knew no ends, who would not stop demanding – or at the very least taking – their food. We fucked their wives and daughters and prostituted their mothers. We ripped open the chosen virgins. We stripped this island of food and we were still not satisfied.'

'How dare you!' King shouted. 'How dare you drag the ships and the captain down like this! His stand on the beach is the epitome of all that is English. It is not a matter for insinuation and. . . .'

'Insinuation? King, I was there and so was Phillips. Where the hell were you? Off protecting a piece of wood, a mast which is still not finished. We were at the mob's jaws. . . .'

'I demand you withdraw that,' King almost screamed and Phillips blinked like an insomniac owl at words that seemed bound to lead to a gentleman's challenge.

'Events prove that I am right.'

Three men shared each other's breath and were about to rupture jugulars over an event which was days old and dead and the crew were on their haunches, straining for the fight that had to erupt, and the natives were at peace ashore, their god-inspired retribution over.

Bligh bellowed and cut through our arguments and silenced us and we were guilty and sheepish.

Captain Clerke stood at the table, resting on white knuckles. His face resembled a corpse's and his voice too was lifeless. 'That's better, gentlemen. Kindly proceed with the evidence.'

'Well, that's it. The rest is history.'

Captain Gore said kindly, 'Come now, Lieutenant Phillips, you have given a fine account.' Perhaps Gore was young once and fought with brother-officers and had been saved just in time by mature consideration. 'Please continue; I'm sure the lieutenants will not interrupt again.'

Phillips thought on this a moment. 'Where was I?'

Captain Gore said patiently, 'The captain used his musket butt to spare the life of an assailant.'

'Well, a marine saw a native behind a canoe ready to throw a spear at the captain,' Phillips said and as if by magic our differences were calmed as radically as the centre of peace in a Caribbean tempest. 'I shouted and he aimed much quicker this time but hit the wrong nigger.'

Now the captain's musket was empty. There he was with Phillips and the handful of marines; he had a hanger-sword and a horde of two thousand or more after his throat.

'I called, "You got the wrong one." He told the sergeant who was a handy shot to right the wrong, which he did and killed the fellow.' Now the sergeant's rifle was empty. 'This quietened the niggers, but only for a moment. The war cries came much stronger and whole volleys of stones rained down. Then the people from the boats opened fire.'

'No, Lieutenant Phillips. Not from my boat. I knew we could cause far more hurt and I expressly forbade it.'

Phillips said, 'The captain was shocked by the lack of control and waved to the boats to stop firing.'

'He thought we had fired too,' I cut in, 'but we had not. I ordered the men to row further astern and thus avoid the temptation to shoot.'

'He called again for the boats to stop firing and if the niggers knew what he was shouting it might have helped. But they do not speak our language; it's to be expected they thought he ordered the opposite. However, the shooting stopped and he waved for the boats to come in and take off the. . . .'

'You liar, Phillips. He did not.'

'He waved to you, sir, to come in and rescue the people and you backed off your pinnace.'

'What are you saying, Phillips? By God, I saw no wave.'

James grabbed the lapels of my jacket. 'You didn't see him wave?'

'I saw him wave, yes, but I mean not for us to come in. He waved us to go off. I swear it.'

My emotions were giving way. I looked death down the barrel of the pistol Phillips held. Twice I let him fire first and I was not afraid. But now I needed all the resolve I could muster to take my panicking mind from the massacre, the screaming natives pressing down, the frightened marines, stones pouring like high-altitude hail from the skies and the captain turning his back on the horde to signal.

I was on the point of succumbing. I dragged a willpower to the surface and with supreme strength swapped parrying for the riposte, the only tactic that might save me.

'The muskets discharged from your people, Lieutenant Phillips. Some pointing at the natives, some just held in the air. I could not believe it. It was a contradiction; I knew he had not ordered it.'

'He ordered it,' Phillips said and fell back on defence. 'By Jesus, someone ordered it. I heard the cry, fire! and I repeated it to my men. I cannot stand there and say now for the life of me who was it that called out that certain order.'

I lunged. 'And your men threw down their muskets, turned their backs and ran into the water.'

'Are you calling my boys cowards?' Phillips's passion was ahead of military discipline and his fist crossed the short distance and took my nose. The force knocked me crashing against the bulwark and I collapsed down against the spirketting. Blood streamed from my face and spread onto my shirt, but I felt no pain. I sat up, my back against the bulwark and gradually the ship stilled.

I held down the panting. 'Phillips, it has to be one thing or the other.' There was little for self-satisfaction in this affair, but I could say that the matter-of-fact tone was well manufactured over the bruising and winding and the lumbering giant stared down disbelieving his misconduct, then across at the two captains. His brain was trying to function between my charges, his likely punishment for striking an officer and blood spilling on the rocks.

'I'm not there with you, Mr Williamson. One thing or another?'

'Either your men displayed cowardice the Royal Navy seeks to eradicate at the yardarm, or you were in an intolerable position because all orders from your commander had ceased. He had abandoned you and his duty.'

The pain arrived exploding in a violent pulsing concussion; my nostrils must be flattened. But I pushed against the side of the ship and forced myself into a standing position to face this quarry who was cornered, puzzled, trapped.

He remained silent. He looked at his boots and at the splashes of crimson soaking into holystoned timber, waiting for authority to attack.

'How many of your marines were killed?'

He said in as beaten a tone as Kahura used so long ago, 'Corporal Thomas, Theophilus Hinks, Tommy Fatchet and John Allen. James Thomas was stabbed in the water; they got him and they battered his brains out on the rocks. They did that to all the men.'

'And the late captain?'

'They held him under the water and pulverised his skull.'

And I heard them wailing in one loathsome voice: God Lono is dead; Long live Lono. And cried it with each of the fatal blows.

I let silence underscore the tragedy. 'So I'm asking you, was there a dereliction of duty on the part of the captain? Had he not led you and your band into a hopeless situation? Had not his temper run away with him and imperilled you on the beach and we in the boats and ultimately all in the ships?'

And now somebody should shout, 'Because of the malady,' and salvage whatever flotsam of the reputation remained. But it will not be me. I tried to have the good doctor speak to it, but he refused. I am doing my duty as prosecutor. It is for the defence to defend.

The sailors looked at their tar-streaked feet; Captain Gore studied the desk-top and Captain Clerke kept an ill-glowing eye upon me. Lieutenant Phillips watched the peaceful shoreline of white and greens a little too attentively; James King stood before me as shocked as if the captain's head had this moment been split open.

'The attention's been switched from you very neatly in this sorry business, Williamson. Well, let me be the one to ask you. Why didn't you go to his aid when he waved?'

'He knew he was a dead man and because such a multitude was bent on murder he waved us to go away.'

James's mouth remained tight, but his eyes were wide and questioning as though he could not accept the message arriving at his ears. Suddenly his mouth sprung open. A red tongue protruded with a sickly grey coating that went back to his throat. The teeth, like dark eroded rocks, would not survive the voyage. 'I don't believe you,' he accused.

'You have no option. You're his defence. If you say he was summoning us, you must accept that he was calling us to our doom; what chance was there for anyone on that beach? And that would be a dereliction a second separate time.'

The trial was over, but James was only just realising it. The evidence showed how the late captain went through his madness. Ransoming chiefs, torturing native civilians, and the night before his own death, announcing that he intended to massacre unsuspecting Hawaiians. The pathetic fatal attempt to kidnap a King.

The captain was guilty of neglect of duty and doubts were cast on every aspect of his being; from his masculinity to his capabilities as a navigator; his cruelty, tyranny, his sanity, a panic – or a mental block – that killed him and the marines on the beach. And there had been no defence because there could be no defence. It crept across James's features like a vicious thundercloud that his hero, our hero, was buried. The god is dead and stays dead.

'Damn your eyes, sir,' he stormed, 'but you must have loathed him.'

Now it was my turn for great turmoil, for I realised my duty had been far more cruel than I expected. I wanted to shout, the opposite is true; now his rejection is avenged, I love him truly. I needed to tell the world that I would pay any price to have him back, yet duty would not allow it. Such emotional approbation would only ease the pain it was vital for the crew to experience.

'Would you not, sir, if someone so disappointed and endangered ships' complements whose only fault was the devotion of their lives to him?'

The men walked away. The chart-table was returned to the aft-cabin and Mr Harvey and Captain Gore helped Captain Clerke to his bunk. Mr Bayley took a disorderly armful of notes and left for *Discovery*. I went below to record the event while it was fresh. The doctor was turning into his cabin and we met outside the darkwood rack which held my brass telescope and beautiful Harvey sword.

'I'm sorry, David, for the interrogation yesterday.'

'I'm sorry for you, Mr Williamson.'

'You know it really was a type of suicide. I'm sure of it.'

'I don't know. . . .'

'I watched him die, David, by his own hand. Or brain, to be precise. It hurt me.'

'I. . . .'

'I tried to get it out in your evidence but you wouldn't speak to it. Look, you're a doctor; couldn't you see the way his mind was going? All that business about his being a god and all.'

He turned away and then stopped at the door, a small, meticulous hand on the latch. 'So the god committed suicide, you think. You apparently were the only one to see him heading that way, presumably in your privileged position as officer and navigator; being so often in his company, I mean. And then you let him do it. I'm no lawyer, Mr Williamson, but doesn't that make you at least an accomplice to his murder, or deicide?'

'David. . . .' But his cabin door closed.

31

*B*ayley's handwriting was a pedantic neat italics. I glanced through the pages of that disturbing hearing, but I did not want to read it. I admired the lettering and checked some words for spelling; I could find no fault. I looked through the last leaves and it was all there, except the punch from Phillips. It had not been mentioned since.

This afternoon I remained in the aft-cabin with a parcel resting on the table that had been the centre of dinner parties and the captain's journal-writing. The woven flax waited unwrapped, for everyone was otherwise occupied. The foremast was going into place and both complements were involved in getting up the topmast, t'gallant and yards like industrious ants engineering top-heavy souvenirs to the nest. Then the sails would be bent on and the ships could go. The consumption struck Captain Clerke again and he was presently lying in the sickbay, the scene of Dr Bill's researches, the mountings of Samwell's fair muses, of so much of our history. I heard David say he will survive a while yet.

I was looking at the charts as no one wished to speak with me nor appoint me to a task. I presumed my name would appear on the duty roster when we got back to sea. A new priest brought the parcel in a canoe and promises of peace and well-being were exchanged. I overheard him say they awaited Lono's return with eagerness. They are like children. The high priest is unwell and could not come. The mob tore the tongue from his mouth; they felt this the punishment most likely to be approved by the Supreme Being of peace. (Kao, like men protected by evil, unlike good Captain Clerke, would survive.)

Samwell pushed open the door, looked about the room, and came in. He was uniformed in surgeon's heartless officiousness. 'If you will take the notes, Mr Harvey, I will describe the contents. It may be best if you were to keep your eyes averted for I fear this will be unattractive.'

I stood beside the broad, imposing sternlights, leaning against our chart-table. Samwell unwrapped the parcel. A reflection from the sea shimmered over his white shirt. For a moment he resembled a concerned green waterbug. A smell crept through the room and Harvey gagged. He moved a little further from the table and kept his eyes firmly away.

'Yes, hmm, let's see,' Samwell said. 'Yes, I don't think there's any doubt. Now, are you ready? You can say that the remains have the mark of fire upon them and also signs of an attempt at preservation. Have you got that?'

A shopping list followed. Thighs and legs joined together, but not the feet; both arms with the hands separated.

'The scalp disconnected from the skull and you will note please that the hair is cut short. Both hands complete, with the skin of the forearms. The hands have not been in the fire, but they have incisions for salt to be pushed in. The ears adhere to the scalp which has a cut in it, say, about an inch long. I would say that it was most likely made by the first blow on the beach, but I doubt it was mortal.'

'Is that all, doctor? I'd like to get some air.'

'That's it, Mr Harvey. No doubt about identification; the scar on the right hand tells its story only too well, but oh, those poor nails torn on the sea-bed.'

Collett was at the door. 'Captain Clerke's calling for you in the sickbay, Dr Samwell.'

He hurried past the servant. 'Oh, Collett,' I called, hoping for some tea, but he must be getting deaf for he pulled the door to without replying.

I went over to the desk and looked down on all that remained, but it was hard to see in the blur.

> I fruitless mourn to him, that
> cannot hear,
> And weep the more because I weep
> in vain.

I took hold of the large hand which waved that frantic, desperate message he needed me to recognise and I pressed my lips to the cold scar.

Postscript

The voyagers did not find the North-West Passage. Captain Clerke held on to life for six months and was buried ashore at foggy Kamchatka beneath an East Siberian tree. He was thirty-eight.

Captain Gore became expedition leader and James Burney became his first lieutenant on *Resolution*. James King took over *Discovery* with John Williamson as his first lieutenant.

The voyage ended at Deptford on the River Thames on October 7, 1780. It had lasted four years and three months.

And after the voyage. . . .

Gore was appointed to a post at Greenwich hospital and died ten years later. James King became a post captain in 1780. He commanded *Resistance*, a ship of the line, in 1781 on convoy duty to the West Indies, but his health collapsed and he died of consumption three years later. He was thirty-four.

David Samwell was 'sawbones' on a number of fighting ships and in 1798 was posted as surgeon to British prisoners-of-war at Versailles. He returned to London that year and died. He had earned a reputation as a poet.

William Bligh did not get the immediate promotion he expected. He was a master and then lieutenant in the war fleet and later spent four years as a captain in the merchant navy.

He commanded *Bounty* and navigated his extraordinary open boat journey to Timor after the 1789 mutiny. He led another expedition to the South Pacific in 1791–93 and returned to become a fighting captain.

In 1806 he was appointed Governor of New South Wales but was ousted two years later in another mutiny. He was promoted to vice-admiral in 1814.

John Williamson became a captain in 1782. In 1797 he commanded *Agincourt* in the Battle of Camperdown against the Dutch. Bligh was also present as captain of *Director*. Bligh won Nelson's congratulations and was awarded a gold medal.

But John Williamson, who appeared to misunderstand a signal, was court-martialled and retired from the Navy on half-pay. Lord Nelson was angry at the outcome and said that Williamson should have been shot.

Omai survived for two and a half years on the Tahitian island and then succumbed to a fever. His two companions died a little before Omai, also of natural causes.

The chaste sleepyhead natives of Van Diemen's Land, now Tasmania, were hunted down and killed by European settlers in the early 1800s. Survivors were taken to a Bass Straight island for their protection and the last original Tasmanian died in 1876.

A testimonial survives to this day to show that John Williamson had a way of upsetting crewmen. On September 9, 1780, Midshipman James Trevenen, aged twenty, wrote to his mother:

'Williamson is a wretch, feared and hated by his inferiors, detested by his equals and despised by his superiors; a very devil, to whom none of our midshipmen have spoke for about a year; with whom I would not wish to be in favour, nor would receive an obligation from was he Lord Admiral of Great Britain.'

With thanks

*R*esearch and preparation covered a long period and time is bound to have erased a few names of the friends, scholars and sailing people who helped. If you are one of them, please do accept my apologies. Those I've remembered and am most grateful to are:

In Britain: that great mate gentle Jack Huke and Chrissie, Gerry and Pat of the truly amazing Adamsons, Lilian McShane, Ron and Joan Pell, Derek Fawcett, Pete Sanders, inspiring Mrs Anne Greenfield, Bob Abrahams, Lady Francis-Chichester, Eddie Ball, Henri Strzelecki CBE, Trish Reynolds, Stanley and Mary Halpin.

Inspiration and help came too from Giovani Mastronardi, author Richard Hough, Maggie Body, Gavin Howe, Maggi Morro, Frank Pynn, Dr Bev Ewen-Smith, Peter Lambdon, Sarah Durose, the late James 'Rule Britannia' Myatt, Nigel Rowe, Rutger 'Rudi' Weber, Robin Knox-Johnston, Royal Western Yacht Club and Yvonne, author D. H. 'Nobby' Clarke, Sir Leslie and Lady Cindy Smith and Timothy and Lucie, Dick Kenny, subbing mates at the *Mirror*, ship construction experts Stephen Wallis and Barry Van Geffen, Olivia Caldwell, Barry Pickthall, Rosie Bellingham, Access (who stayed friendly), and to the following great and sadly late inspirers: Sir Francis Chichester, Alain Colas, Rob James, Angus Primrose and Mike and Lizzie McMullen.

At Good Hope: my good friend John 'Eye of the Storm' Rubython, inspiring Gordon Pringle and that gorgeous friend of British writers Maureen Hargraves. Good mates Mark Lory, Zoe and Tristan, expert sailor Ted Lawrence, Brenda and the 'musae'; racing aces Jeremy Flint and Anton Wollheim; ships modeller R. A. 'Bob' Lightley; advice and help from Chris Fieldgate and Joe Rabinowitz and immense help with research from Ms Petri la Roux at the SA Library, Evelyn Sachs at

Central Library and Sea Point's Evelyn Stein and her kind and patient helpers.

And for advice and help: Gerfried 'Mighty Muira' Nebe, Joan Fry and the RCYC and Dinkie; Ted Jupp and CASA, Ron Hindes, Phillipe Jeantot, Keith Stewart-Collins, Jenny Verster, Toby Wrigley, Norman Grimbeek, Alistair Campbell, Helen Rubython, David Elcock, Ian Cochrane, Dr Mike Pratt, David Campbell, Garles Grey, Jenny Cole Rous, Jacques Bognon, and Ian Duncan.

In New Zealand: my thanks to my marvellous folks, Moya and Eric, still working hard for their son, and family, particularly Chris at Gore. Lyndsay Peterson, Jo-Ann Cook, and my gratitude and admiration for that extraordinary Cook historian Dr J. C. Beaglehole.

Help came too from good mates Bill and Gloria Lowe, Jim and Brenda Hugo, Neville Gosson, Vickers Hoskins, David Underhill, with helpful advice from that master wordsmith Mr Morris West, all in Australia. In Bermuda, Mike Ternent; in Nelson's old harbour at Menorca, Dennis and Dereka Courthope-Boas, and Paul and Evelyn de Graaff; Pete Edney in Gibraltar; Sir Rex and Lady Mavis Hunt at Port Stanley and Dick Wagner at Fort de France.

In the US: my good friend Nick Simpson, 'cousin' Tom Rodgers and Gerry, Paul Kasperson, the Goat Island Yacht Club and Peter Hagerman and Mary Grady, Ingrid for photographing the fateful bay, Craig and Carol Middleton, Dr Larry Kneisley and Nurse Grant, Keith Taylor and *Sail* magazine, John C. Griggs II of Pepperidge Farms and gifted musician Bill Conti.

And for advice, journalists: Richard Barkley, John Fensham, Chris English, Beryl Roberts, Gertrude Cooper, Roger Williams, Eben Human, Peter Mann, Pamela Carmichael, Mary Robinson, Annie Woolridge, Brian Turner, and Richard Gibbon. And to anonymous help from the *News*, Portsmouth, *Motor Boat* and *Yachting*, *Sea Horse* magazine, *Lancashire Evening Post*, *RNSA Journal*, and the *Cape Times* for the long-term use of a typewriter.